THE LOST REVOLUTION

A NOVEL

TOM ULICNY

TOM ULICNY

Printed in the United States of America

ISBN-10: 1517456290
ISBN-13: 978-1517456290

For Joyce who remains my inspiration and the guiding light in all that I do.

ACKNOWLEDGMENTS

Consultation and general edit by Sarah Ulicny:
www.sarahulicny.com Editing assistance of previous versions by
John Paine: www.johnpaine.com
Cover design: Tom Ulicny with assistance from many including
Linda Merchant: www.lamgallery.com

And, Many thanks to Colleen, Sarah and Kate and to my extended
family and friends for your support, encouragement, suggestions
and tireless efforts in the tedious work of proofreading draft after
draft. From its original chaotic state, you've made this book a
much better story and me a better writer.

THE LOST REVOLUTION

"Great necessities call out great virtues. When a mind is raised and animated by scenes that engage the heart, then those qualities which would otherwise lay dormant, wake into life and form the character of the hero and the statesman."

Abigail Adams

CHAPTER 1

It was the forty-fourth year of the reign of Queen Victoria. It was the year of the British defeat by the Boers at Majuba Hill and of the assassination of Czar Alexander II. It was 1881, and it was late one morning at roughly the mid-point of that year that Julian North, a file clerk for the London *Times*, rode a carriage down Bristol Lane in London's north-end, beginning a journey that would change his life and leave a small but indelible mark on history.

From the rear of the carriage he shaded his eyes and watched his destination slowly pass by. The driver tugged at the reins and shouted but his team continued on, pulling past a butcher's shop before clopping to a halt in a shady spot under a large tree. The driver sighed then twisted around to face his only passenger. "They have a mind of their own, these two. Three-twenty-one Bristol Lane, just back there, sir."

"Your horses are smart to stay out of the sun on such a hot day," said Julian, paying the fare and stepping down onto the cobblestones where he could feel the heat radiating up. A few flies buzzed in the branches overhead. An elderly woman with a cane was just coming out of the butcher's shop, a small parcel in her hand. The street was otherwise deserted.

"We'll be staying here for a bit if you need me to wait," said the driver.

"Thanks, but that shouldn't be necessary." Julian didn't want to bear the extra expense. He dragged his wrist over his forehead and adjusted his bowler, then walked past the woman back to three-twenty-one where he looked up at the green sign with gold letters that spanned the building:

1

Hunter and McCall's Antiquities

The store was tightly sandwiched between the butcher's shop and a clock repair: two stories, green shutters, red trim. In its display window a cranberry upholstered, wing-backed chair stood beside a finely carved wooden desk; the chair askew as if someone had just gotten up from it. Atop the desk sat a blue and white porcelain tea service, an orange and red feathered turban and a glass inkwell with a writing quill. Julian wondered what other oddities might be inside the store then noticed the closed sign on the door. He tried the door anyway and, finding it unlocked, went inside.

A bell overhead jingled. He removed his hat and raked his sandy hair back off his ears, drying his hand on the back of his trousers. He ran a finger behind his bow-tie - the red one he wore on special occasions - and tugged his brown suit straight. It was cooler in the store, the air thick with the smells of furniture polish and tobacco. Paintings, lamps, brightly colored urns, and furniture of all types stretched in neat rows back into the dimly lit store. Here and there, bookshelves leaned heavily against the walls. Seeing no one, Julian called out: "Hello? Hello, Mr. Karmonov?"

There was no reply and Julian was about to leave when he heard a sniff and a grunt. Halfway back, a man in a vest and shirtsleeves appeared from behind a tall dresser. Julian guessed him to be in his mid-fifties as his unkempt hair was mostly gray. His bushy eyebrows were angled down.

"We are closed, come back later." His accent was unmistakably Russian.

Julian swallowed and forced himself to take a few steps closer. "I'm not a customer, Mr. Karmonov. I'm here to see you."

"Why would you want to see me? Who are you? How do you know my name?"

"I'm Julian North. I'm a friend of Harry Woodhouse...from the *Times*."

The Russian spread his feet slightly apart and put a hand in his pocket, fingering some loose coins. "And how do you know Mr. Woodhouse?"

"I work with him. He said you might have a job opening for a translator."

At this, Karmonov seemed to relax a little. "I might. Do you know French? Say something in French."

"*Je suis heureux de vous rencontrer Monsieur Karmonov.*

Comment ça va?" said Julian.

Karmonov rubbed his chin. "That sounded French, I suppose." He scanned Julian, once up, once down, still wary. He sniffed again. "All right, come with me."

Julian followed him deeper into the store where the aisle narrowed and the mounted heads of jungle animals gazed passively down from both walls. In a back office, Karmonov motioned Julian into a chair that creaked when he sat. A spring poking through the worn cushion jabbed his thigh and he shifted to one side as the Russian sat down behind the bare wooden desk in front of him. "Why do you want to work for me?"

"I need money."

"You said you work with Harry. You already have a job. Why do you need money?"

Julian stiffened at the question then winced as the spring got him again.

"Sorry, I must fix that," said Karmonov with a thin smile.

"I've been working as a file clerk for a year. I want something better."

"Something that will bring you more money."

"Yes."

"You don't like being a clerk?"

"No, I don't."

"How do you know French?"

"My mother was French. I learned it from her, growing up in America."

The brows went up. "You are American?"

"Born there. My parents died when I was young."

"Why did you come to England?"

"My uncle's with the *Times*. He arranged the clerk's position for me."

Karmonov tapped a finger over his closed mouth then pinched his lower lip. He slouched sideways in his chair and stared at the wall as if looking somewhere beyond it.

Julian uncrossed his legs. "Harry said you needed someone fluent in French. I know French and I need a position." He paused. "How much will you pay?"

The Russian consulted his watch then straightened. "Almost time to open. I expect a busy day." He slid a sheet of paper across the desk. "Write down your name and address. I will give some thought to you, Mr. North. You may hear from me in a few days or maybe never."

Probably never, thought Julian as he wrote down the

information. This had been a complete waste of time. He thanked Karmonov then left, relieved to see the carriage still waiting in the shade. Julian climbed aboard, unbuttoned his collar and an hour later trudged up three flights to his desk at Printing House Square, home office of the London *Times*. The heat was stifling and his desktop was littered with papers and folders needing to be filed. For a moment he just stared at the mess wanting to quit then and there, but he knew he had no choice. He couldn't leave the paper without having a place to go. He'd been looking for work for six months now with nothing to show for it. Hunter & McCall's was just the latest disappointment.

"So, did you get the job?" It was Harry who'd come up behind him.

"I don't think so," said Julian, turning. "Karmonov said he might let me know, or he might not. He's a strange man."

"I told you he was eccentric." Harry adjusted his black-rimmed glasses and cleared a few congealed strands of black hair from his forehead. Julian picked up some folders and began putting them in order.

"Sorry it didn't work out," said Harry. "Maybe it's for the best. I've heard he sometimes operates on the shady side of the law."

"You waited until now to tell me that?"

"I don't know if it's true. It's just what I heard, but it would explain why he pays so well. I've done work for him here and there and never had a problem."

"What kind of things did you do for him?" Harry hesitated but then turned his head abruptly and lowered his voice. "Here comes Hawthorne. Better get busy." He hurried off for the row of tall wooden file cabinets that lined the back wall.

Julian picked up more folders as the bug-eyed floor manager, approached. Hawthorne gave Julian a long stare but said nothing as he brushed by like the angel of death. Julian got busy and stayed late catching up on the work he'd missed.

It was dark by the time he returned to the townhouse a few blocks away where he lived with his Uncle Emory. As was their routine, he and his uncle had a quiet dinner, each seated at opposite ends of a long table. George, his uncle's butler and gentleman, hovered near the doorway to the kitchen, ready with each course. Uncle Emory was a round-faced man in his late forties who never dined without being properly dressed. Part way through the meal he dabbed his lips with his napkin and brushed a few crumbs off his tie and vest.

"Mr. Hawthorne tells me you took the morning off."

Julian put down his fork. His uncle was the managing editor of the London *Times*. For God's sake, didn't he have more important things to worry about? "I stayed late to make up for it."

"So where were you this morning?"

"I had a few errands to run."

"None of my business, I suppose." Uncle Emory made everything his business.

Julian decided that he might as well come out with it. "I'm looking for other work."

Uncle Emory remained still for a moment but his look darkened. He took a sip of wine. "You're damned lucky to have a job, Julian. I know you're not happy being a clerk, but that seems to be all you're qualified for right now. We've tried you as a journalist and you know it didn't work out. You might be passable at writing those made-up stories of yours but writing for a newspaper is much different. A journalist has to search out information and piece things together in a way that's understandable and makes sense. You have to work fast, keep your facts straight and you have to meet deadlines. When we first brought you on, you demonstrated a remarkable inability to do any of that. But that was a year ago. I suppose I could arrange a second trial for you."

Julian shook his head. "I appreciate your help Uncle Emory, but I don't think I'm cut out to be a newspaper man either as a clerk or as a journalist."

"Your father worked for a newspaper and I've worked for the *Times* all my life. If you won't be a newspaper man, what will you be?"

That was the frustrating question Julian had been asking himself for months. He stabbed a slice of carrot, talking as he chewed. "I don't know yet." He stabbed another.

"You really have no idea?"

"No, I really don't." Julian finished his plate and Uncle Emory leaned back in his chair with a long sigh. This wasn't the first time they'd had this conversation. In the silence, George picked up the dishes and came back with a pudding dessert and tea. "I should just go back to America," said Julian after a few spoonfuls.

"You've already tried to make a go of it there. If you ask me, a file clerk with the *Times* is a big step up from farm work."

The comment brought back memories of Julian's tough life in America with his ageing foster parents. He remembered the day he'd come in from the fields and opened the letter that had come for him from England. Uncle Emory, his only living relative, had evidently been stricken with pangs of guilt at having neglected his dead brother's son for so long. He wanted Julian to come and live with him. In truth, it had been a kind and generous offer and he'd jumped at the chance to leave LaPorte County Indiana for London. Uncle Emory was right, working at the *Times* had been a big step up, but now Julian needed to take another step – he had to get out on his own.

Uncle Emory drummed his fingers then lit a cigar and puffed it into life as he got up from the table. "Let's give things a few more months. Maybe you should go back to school – learn a profession. You need credentials to get anywhere these days, Julian. The university would give you the training you need. But schooling is expensive and if you don't even know what you want out of life..." Uncle Emory's voice trailed off and he didn't wait for a response. He loosened his belt and, in a cloud of white smoke, headed off into the great room.

Julian remained seated for a while. He glanced at George who kept his best butler face steady as if he hadn't heard a word of the dinner conversation. "Good pudding," said Julian.

George blinked. "Thank you, sir. It's an old family recipe."

The note from Karmonov came two weeks later. Beneath the Hunter & McCall letterhead a time and date, three days hence, were scrawled in pencil. The Russian wanted to see him again. Julian asked the skeptical Hawthorne for that particular afternoon off and at the appointed time entered the antiquities shop. Again, there was no one in sight. He walked to the back office, the door was closed. He knocked. "Mr. Karmonov? It's Julian North."

A moment later Karmonov opened the door, giving no indication that he was at all pleased to see him. He told Julian to take a seat then closed the door and sat down behind his desk. He put on a pair of spectacles. There was a blue folder in front of him. Karmonov picked it up and began talking as he flipped through the pages. "I checked with your friend Harry. He is a good man to know. It says here that you're the nephew of the managing editor at the *Times*. Apparently you were only hired there because of his influence – yes?"

"I've already told you that." Julian swallowed. "Did Harry give you my employment papers?"

Karmonov wet the tip of his index finger and turned another page. "Yes he did. I know all about you now: twenty-two years of age, blue eyes, height, weight, I know all of this." He glanced at

Julian as if confirming those specifics then went back to the folder. "You are a little thin but you seem fit enough. You are not sick are you?"

"No."

"You are un-married and it looks like you've been something of a problem at the paper. It says here, that you are argumentative and poorly organized. You failed at being a journalist and you are now a file clerk. It is not a good thing for a file clerk to be poorly organized." He gave Julian a look over the top of the folder. "If I hire you, are you going to be a problem for me Mr. North?"

"No."

Karmonov closed the folder and settled back in his chair. "I see nothing too much wrong with you and Harry has vouched for you. I like Harry – too bad he doesn't speak French. What I need is a dependable man who pays attention to details and who knows French. You must be able to read it, write it and speak it. Can you do that?"

"Yes, I already told you I could."

"I understand your mother died twelve years ago. You were just a child yet you remember the French she taught you?"

"Certaines choses que vous n'oublierez jamais."

"I'll assume that was a yes," said Karmonov. "I know English and Russian – no French." He rubbed his chin for a moment then slapped a hand on each of his armrests. "All right then, Mr. North, I suppose you will do." He opened a desk drawer. "I've got something to show you." He pulled out a brown leather pouch the size of a woman's small hand-bag. "This, Mr. North, is your project – perhaps the first of many." He placed it on the desk.

The pouch was scarred and well worn, obviously very old, but there was something else. Julian leaned forward and could see it clearly now. In dark relief, the leather had been branded with what appeared to be a medieval coat of arms. He made a mental note of it. Karmonov loosened the drawstrings on the pouch and reached inside. He pulled out a book and held it up for Julian to see. It was bound in brown leather and Julian thought it might be an old prayer book but on the front cover where a cross should have been, an H centered within a circle had been rudely carved. The pages were edged in tarnished gold and the book was held closed by a metal clasp. Julian stood for a better look as Karmonov undid the clasp and opened the book to the first page.

"Journal de Jacques Caesar Castlenau," Julian read aloud, admiring the flowing penmanship. Below the name was a date that Julian quickly translated: "17 *Brumaire*, 5. I think they had a

different calendar system back then based on the start of the French Republic but the book has to be almost a hundred years old - written in the times of Napoleon. Who is Castlenau?"

"I don't know, but for a man who took such great care in writing his name, he did not do so well with the rest of his book." Karmonov turned to the next page and moved it closer to Julian. The letters and words on this page were no more than tightly spaced strings of attached ink-blots. What seemed to be someone's idle doodling, formed a latticework in the narrow margins.

"It's a mess," said Julian.

"Yes, it is a mess, but is it a problem?"

"If it's French, I'll find a way to read it. But it's going to be like deciphering hieroglyphs."

Karmonov shuffled through another desk drawer and came up with a magnifying glass. He slid it over to Julian. "This should help, yes?"

Julian picked up the book. It felt a little greasy and smelled of sea-salt. He examined the writing then closed the book and, with his fingertip, traced the carving in the cover. "What do you think this means?"

Karmonov shook his head and spread his hands.

"Where did you get it?"

"A friend from St. Petersburg sent it to me. I have an important client here who may be interested in the book but he wants it translated first. It could have some..." Karmonov moved his hand in a circular motion, "...historical value."

Julian put the book down. It was time to get to the important issue. "How much will you pay?"

"You are living with your uncle right now, is that correct?"

"What does that have to do with anything?"

"I know you want to be free of him – on your own, yes?" Julian felt his blood rising. Was there anything Harry hadn't told him?

But Karmonov didn't wait for an answer. "I can give you a place to stay."

"I need money, Mr. Karmonov."

"I will give you two-hundred pounds for your work," Karmonov said evenly.

Julian tried to keep his face unresponsive but he was astounded. Why so much for a translation? He wondered who Karmonov's client might be.

"I see it is more than you thought. You will get paid when the job is done."

Julian shook his head. This was not going to work. "I need money now."

Karmonov lifted his hand as if berating a belligerent student. "No, you need a place to stay and you need food. I have those things."

"The translation could take months."

"Oh, I expect it will, Mr. North. Too bad for you, Jacques had such poor handwriting."

"I want fifty pounds now, one-hundred more when the translation's half done, the rest when it's completed. And, since you've offered it already, I want room and board."

Karmonov scowled then produced two, ten-pound notes. He laid them on the table. "Twenty now, fifty more when you are half done, the rest when you are done, and room and board. Don't test me further, Mr. North."

The deal was better than Julian had hoped and he hesitated only to give Karmonov the feeling that he had bargained well. He picked up the money. "Where will I be staying?"

Karmonov stood up. "Come, I will show you." There was a door behind his desk. The Russian opened it revealing a staircase that led to the upper level. Julian followed him up the stairs and at the top turned to see a single big room with a pitched ceiling and exposed rafters. It was empty except for a brass bed and a small desk that sat in front of a window that overlooked Bristol Lane. "Not as fancy as you may be used to," said Karmonov, "but you should be comfortable here. Yes? You think so? And when you are done with Jacques' book, if you do well, I will keep you on for other work."

Julian could see himself working here. There'd be no more need for Uncle Emory's handouts or for his judgmental stares or for the university.

"Our neighbor is Mr. Wolkowski the butcher. You will eat with his family. You like beef, lamb, sausages? They eat very well." He put both hands in front of his belly.

Julian walked to the desk and ran a hand across the top. It was clean and freshly polished; the chair looked comfortable. "When do I start?"

"I've already given you your first payment so you will start right away."

"I can work the rest of the day but I'll need to put in my notice at the paper."

"Of course, I understand." They shook hands. Karmonov's grip was firm and friendly. He handed Julian the Castlenau book and the magnifying glass. "One rule I have: You will never take this book out of this building. All your work will be done here. Do you understand?"

"Yes, I understand." Julian wondered about this but didn't see it as a problem.

"You will do well. I know this." Karmonov gave Julian's shoulder a hard thump then went back downstairs closing the door behind him.

Alone now, Julian opened the window and a gentle breeze ruffled the curtains. He spread them apart to get a better view of the street below where a few pedestrians dotted the walkways and an occasional cart rattled by. The suddenness of his decision to work for Karmonov and to live in his building bothered him. He remembered what Harry had said about the Russian operating on the edge of the law and wondered what he'd just gotten himself into, but he knew it didn't really matter. He wasn't about to go back to the files at the *Times*. Julian sat down with the journal on the desk in front of him. He found a pad and pencil in one of the drawers. Then, in a childhood habit of his that he'd never been able to break, he conjured up a newspaper headline about himself:

Famous Writer Discovers Secret of Lost Journal.

He always fancied himself being a famous writer in these headlines of his. He opened the book, careful not to strain the weak binding. The pages were yellowed and brittle. He turned to the first page of close writing and through the magnifying glass, examined the first inkblot – could be a J or a G. Julian wrote those two letters on a worksheet, one above the other then went onto the next blot and the ones after that, using context to pin down the correct chain of letters that made up each word. He then wrote them in English on a separate page that would become his translation. It took him twenty minutes to get through the first two sentences:

I am a son of my nation. For it and for my brothers I have committed great crimes.

It sounded like a confession and Julian had to admit he was curious about what great crimes his new friend Jacques might be guilty of, but as the afternoon wore on, the work grew tedious and his mind wandered. By five he had managed to complete only two pages which he felt was a pretty good start for not even half a day's work. He read the last few lines of his translation:

Tribal Government is an invention of the caves in which we so recently dwelt. Across millennia, the rules of the tribes have become the laws of nations and, knowing no better, we honor this invention and attach to it a value greater than life itself – fighting to the death for the glory and honor of the tribe. To what end?

Julian knew that the French Revolution had been fertile ground for philosophers. Was Jacques Castlenau just another one of them? He closed the book, tucked it and his translation into the desk drawer and went downstairs. It was a little jarring, opening the door and finding himself behind Karmonov who was still at his desk.

"Done for the day?" asked Karmonov, turning.

"Yes, just two pages so far, I'll get faster as I go along."

"I am sure you will." Karmonov handed Julian a key. "This opens the front door. Come in early tomorrow or whenever it is that you get free from the newspaper."

Julian went straight back to the townhouse. He waited until dinner to spring his news. "I have a new job," he said.

Uncle Emory put down his soup spoon. "Mr. Hawthorne put you into a new position? He didn't tell me anything about this."

"It's not with the paper and Hawthorne doesn't know yet. I'll tell him tomorrow."

Uncle Emory just stared for a moment. "You're leaving the paper? But what will you do?"

Julian told him about Hunter & McCall's and the work he'd be doing.

"You'll be a translator? Well, I suppose that makes sense. You're father always said you had a knack for the French language. Yes, that does make sense. Well good for you." Uncle Emory went back to his soup.

Then, with great satisfaction, Julian sprung his other news. "I'll be moving out."

"Julian, don't be silly, you don't have to leave."

"Yes I do. It's all arranged. I have a room all to myself on the second floor of the store. The work will go faster that way. Don't worry, I'll be fine. I'll stop by every now and then."

Uncle Emory gave him a skeptical look as George served the next course. "Who is it exactly that you'll be working for?"

"A Russian named Karmonov. He owns the place."

Uncle Emory thought for a moment, his finger tapping on the linen table cloth. "I know a lot of people in this town but I've never heard of Karmonov or his store. What is it you're translating?"

"He has a number of projects. Right now it's just an old handwritten journal." Julian took a swallow of wine then added: "Nothing important."

CHAPTER 2

Hawthorne didn't seem to mind losing his problematic file clerk and only required that Julian work the entire next day before leaving for good. The day after that, Julian moved his few possessions into Karmonov's loft. In the weeks that followed, driven both by the promise of more money and by curiosity, he worked hard on the translation of the journal.

After his brief philosophical treatise, Castlenau began to tell his own story starting with his involvement in Napoleon's Egyptian campaign. Like a terrible wind, the French army had crushed the warlike but poorly armed Bedouin tribesmen all along the Mediterranean coast from Alexandria to the Nile. The vicious battles and merciless slaughter had collectively been Castlenau's great crimes and the great shame of his nation. He described the execution of a prisoner by his own sword – the feel of the blade sliding in so easily as if it couldn't possibly have caused any harm, the man's look of surprise then of excruciating pain as he fell to the ground, blood pouring from his wound. But it wasn't the actual killing that haunted Castlenau so much as the fact that it, and all of their victories, served no higher purpose. He was part of an army of thieves and rapists and murderers.

Eventually, disease, thirst and incessant attacks on its rear-guard sapped the strength of the French Army. With little left to gain and few Egyptian artifacts left to steal, Napoleon gathered his men at Aboukir on the Nile ready to sail back to France. But that safe departure wasn't to be.

Admiral Nelson and his smaller British fleet had been shadowing the French for months and at that moment, Nelson struck, achieving a complete surprise. His ships stormed into the peaceful harbor. Under cover of darkness, they blazed away with fiery, booming, broadsides, blasting the still-anchored French warships to pieces. Castlenau, who viewed the battle from shore, described the destruction of the powder-stores aboard the flagship *L'Orient* as an explosion beyond belief, having a sustained flash that seemed to last for minutes, lighting the entire harbor as if at mid-day. Its terrible roar nearly blew him off his feet.

For the French Navy, it was a catastrophe.

But the undaunted Napoleon still had two undamaged ships and, only days after the battle, he set sail for France leaving Castlenau and thousands of exhausted Frenchmen and mercenaries to die in the desert.

Desperate, Castlenau managed to repair one of the French ships which had been only lightly damaged in the battle. Then, in the middle of the night, he and one-hundred others escaped the revenge-minded Bedouins and sailed north into the Aegean. This is where Castlenau's writings turned again to philosophy. This is where his inner journey began. He pondered the righteousness of the revolution, and the rights and dignity of the average human being. He began to write about the rise of the common man and the rebirth of the revolution.

As Julian worked, he ate well and enjoyed the hospitality of the Wolkowskis who ran their butcher shop next door like a family project. There were five of them in all: Henry, the tall and muscular, mustachioed patriarch of the family; Gerta, his fair-skinned wife who wore her blonde hair in a single thick braid that she draped over the front of her right shoulder; Maggie and Mary, their twin, fifteen year old daughters who took after their mother in appearance and always seemed to be sharing secrets; and five-year old Wilhelm whose golden hair bounced when he ran. And Willy, as he was called, ran everywhere.

At noon each day he shouted up to Julian from the base of the stairs: "Here's your lunch." He then raced up carrying a paper sack which contained a sandwich piled high with cheese and thinly cut ham along with an apple. "It's from my Mother," explained Willy every time, holding it out proudly. As he ate, Julian would tell wide-eyed Willy stories about his own childhood, growing up in America. "Mother says you write things," said Willy one day, sitting on the edge of Julian's bed.

"That's right, I work for Mr. Karmonov."

"I don't like him."

When Julian asked why, Willy just shrugged.

A month passed before Julian decided to take some time off and meet with Harry at Molly's, a pub near Printing House Square that they used to frequent when Julian was with the paper. They grabbed a seat at a back table and Julian glanced around the place. "Hasn't changed much," he observed after a barmaid placed a mug of beer in front of each of them.

"How's your secret project with Karmonov going?" asked Harry.

"It's not secret. I'm just translating an old book. I've got a problem with you, though."

"With me?"

"You stole my employment folder and you told Karmonov everything about me and my uncle. How could you do that?"

Harry made a face like he was stuck explaining the obvious. "I didn't steal your employment folder. It's right back in the file where it belongs. I borrowed it for a short time. Karmonov wouldn't have hired you without it. You should thank me for that and you should thank me for telling him about your uncle. You've got a place all to yourself now. It all worked out, and it was all because of me."

"It was damned unsettling, Karmonov knowing everything about me and me not knowing he knew."

"You should be grateful. How about you buy the beer tonight and we'll call it even."

Julian groused a little but eventually swung around to the idea that Harry was right, everything had worked out. Besides, Julian still had the twenty pounds from Karmonov. They ordered another round then Julian pulled a folded-over sheet of paper from his shirt pocket. It was a drawing he'd made of the coat of arms on the Castlenau pouch. He handed it to Harry. "What do you think of this?"

Harry studied it then placed it on the table careful to avoid the beer puddles. The drawing consisted of a shield sectioned into triangular quadrants by a pair of crossed spears. At the center of each quadrant was an icon. "I can see it's a coat of arms but why should I think anything of it?"

"I just thought it might look familiar to you."

Harry shoved his glasses further up the bridge of his nose. "Where'd you get the drawing?"

"I drew it from memory so it might not be completely right. It was etched on the side of an old leather bag. Maybe you have something like it in your files."

"It's the bag the old book came in, right?"

"Yes."

"Well, it's the crest of a Christian family," he said pointing to one of the icons. "These are praying hands." He shifted to another. "And this open book icon here, that's what this is right? It probably symbolizes the bible; together with the hands it signifies religious devotion. This was a popular sentiment at the time of the crusades. Of course that's obvious enough. This is unusual though." He pointed to another icon on the crest. "It's an eastern cross. The family must have had ties to the Byzantine Church. That would be in keeping with the crossed spears. If this were strictly a European coat of arms, they would have been crossed swords or crossed axes."

Harry went on to the last icon; a half-circle symbol. "I've got no idea what that is – the setting or rising sun maybe?" He handed the drawing back to Julian.

"That's it? I could have figured that much out myself."

"You didn't know about the cross, did you? Or the spears?"

"Can you match the crest to a family name in your files?"

Harry took another swallow. "All the coats of arms we have in the files are organized by family name. There are hundreds of them. If you know the surname maybe I can find it. But that probably wouldn't tell you any more than you already know." He folded his hands and squinted, using his cheeks this time to get his glasses back where they belonged. "So, what's the surname?"

"Castlenau," said Julian. He wrote the name on the sketch then gave it back to Harry.

"All right, I'll check on it." He put it in his pocket. "Any other great problems you need solved?"

Julian took a long drink from his beer. "Tell me about Karmonov. How did you meet him? What kind of work did you do for him – besides stealing my employment papers?"

"Borrowed," corrected Harry. He scooted his chair closer to the table. "All right, I'll tell you, but you can't tell anyone about me and Karmonov – especially not your uncle. You have to promise."

Julian cocked his head and held up his right hand. "I promise."

"This is serious, Julian."

"I won't tell a soul."

Harry hesitated, then began: "Karmonov just needs information from time to time and our files are an easy place for him to get it."

"Especially since he knows you."

"Right, we met a year ago, right here in Molly's. I was just leaving when he pulled me off to the side and asked me if I wanted to make some extra money."

"So he knew even then you were with the *Times*."

"Yes. And the information he wanted the first few times seemed innocent enough – stuff on some person or some business. The money was very good."

"What made you think he might be doing something illegal?"

Harry's lips tightened. "One night I gave him information about a man he'd asked about. Two days later, the poor fellow turned up in a hospital, beaten up – almost killed."

Julian folded his hands under his chin. He knew the few customers Karmonov had at the store weren't enough to cover the rent. He had to be involved in something else. "Did you ever ask him about the man?"

Harry shook his head. "I'm not crazy; no, I didn't ask, and that's all I know. Except for your file, I haven't done much for him lately. Look, just be careful and you should be all right."

"So that's it then, I'll just be careful. Good advice, Harry, thanks." Julian couldn't keep the smirkiness out of that comment and Harry didn't say much more.

Julian got back to his loft at the store, tired from the beer and a little tired of worrying about Karmonov. He closed the curtains and, in doing so, his hand brushed against his father's bible that he kept on the back corner of his desk. It caused him to think back to before his parents died, back to when his father would read from it on Sunday nights. Julian yawned and sat down, then opened the old leather-bound volume. He began reading a familiar verse, mimicking in his mind his father's voice with the same tone and cadence and the same uplifting spirit.

He wished he had known his father better. What kind of a man was he? What had he wanted for his family? What had he wanted for himself? And what would he advise Julian to do about Karmonov? He left the bible open on the desk and turned out the gas lamp.

Julian slept late the next day and got dressed then noticed the bible again. He was about to close it when he saw a note his father had penned in its margins:

Baby boy Julian, born today 29, September 1858. Praise be God.

He had seen this note before, of course, and he knew there were others about him written in the years leading up to the death of his parents, but he avoided these. Instead, he flipped through some of the preceding pages where earlier milestones of family history were recorded, some dating back before the birth of his father. Some were just a few words in length while others rambled down the side of an entire page, each one describing an important family event. Julian realized that he was the keeper of this history now – he had been since he was ten - yet he'd never written a single word. There was nothing in the bible about the death of his parents or about his foster parents or about his trip to England to stay with Uncle Emory. But he felt no obligation to be the family historian. Some things were best forgotten.

Julian closed the book, deciding it was best to block out these thoughts and get to work. He sat down and opened Castlenau's journal to the point where he'd left off and, only then did he think to examine the doodling in the margins. The thought hit him - could they have some importance, like the notes in his father's Bible? At first he was disappointed. Even with the magnifying glass, all he saw was a jumbled mess of tiny lines going in every direction. Then he looked closer, this time at one individual pen-stroke where it angled into another to make a tiny but discrete symbol. What had been a jumble of lines slowly resolved into hundreds of closely spaced figures, each one subtly different. Castlenau or maybe one of his descendants had made these marks with painstaking precision. There was nothing random about them at all. Feeling almost giddy, like an explorer setting foot on new ground, Julian singled out one of the figures and drew an enlarged version of it on a separate sheet of paper. He did the same for the next three until he came to a separation and stopped to stare at what he'd drawn:

It had to be an encoded word - one of thousands. Julian flipped ahead in the journal, checking other pages. Some were covered as much by the marginal symbols as by the inkblot text he was translating. He'd been working with the journal for a month now, how could he have missed seeing this? Then he wondered how Karmonov could have missed it. Or maybe Karmonov already knew about the marginal notes and just didn't tell him. Julian scratched the back of his neck realizing that he was dealing now with two deepening mysteries: one named Karmonov, the other, Castlenau.

CHAPTER 3

Julian sat, tapping his pencil. His situation brought to mind his father's habit of starting the week with the one of his brain-riddles that he would pose to Julian over breakfast each Sunday morning. As part of his weekly chores, Julian struggled to work out a solution which he'd bring to the table the following Sunday. "Brilliant," his father would always say after Julian presented his answer. It was only much later that Julian realized, for the more difficult riddles, his father would drop subtle hints during the week so Julian never failed to work out the correct solution. He'd get no such help for the riddles facing him now.

He spent the rest of the day working with Castlenau's stick-figure symbols, some of which were repeated every so often. There had to be an underlying pattern but it was going to take a lot of time to find it and, right now, it was time he didn't have. He needed to complete his translation. He needed to get paid.

Julian decided to keep the existence of the symbols to himself for now. Maybe he'd mention it to Karmonov later on. Maybe it could be his next project. Another week passed, the translation proceeded slowly, then Uncle Emory decided to stop by.

"Not a bad spot at all," he said standing in the middle of Julian's room, "much better than my first place. I was stuck in the attic of a boarding house. I'd simmer in the summer and freeze in the winter. There was one small window that I couldn't open. I lived there for three years before I saved enough to move out. Yes, this place is much better. You've done all right for yourself so far, Julian." He nodded his head a few times then walked toward the stairs. "I would like to meet your employer sometime - this Karmonov fellow – thought he'd be here today. His store doesn't seem like much of a business, but that's not your problem I suppose."

Julian wasn't sure why, but he sensed it would not be a good idea for the two to meet. "You don't need to get involved with him, Uncle Emory. He's a good man and he's fair. I can't ask for more than that."

"You trust him don't you?"

"Yes, of course I do. He leaves me alone to do my work and, thanks to the Wolkowskis next door, there's always plenty to eat." Julian moved closer. "I'm on my own now, Uncle Emory. You don't have to worry about me anymore."

His uncle smiled. "I suppose not." He glanced around the room again as if preparing to leave.

"How are things at the paper?" asked Julian.

"Good as always. Subscriptions are on the rise. Oh, and your replacement seems to be working out all right according to Hawthorne."

"Good, I'm sure he didn't have much trouble filling the spot."

"No, he didn't. There are a lot of people out of work these days." He paused. "Well, I'd better be off. I just stopped by to see how you're doing. I'll let you get some work done." He headed down the stairs.

Julian went down with him, out into the street where he boarded a waiting carriage. Watching it drive off, Julian found that he missed his uncle and for the first time found himself worried about him - just he and George rattling around in all that space at the townhouse. But, maybe that's the way he liked it.

Julian climbed the stairs back up to his room. He sat at his desk and for a while did nothing. He thought about his uncle's question: Did he trust Karmonov? There was a lot he didn't know about the Russian and what he did know about him from Harry, wasn't all good. But he did feel comfortable here and he wasn't about to move back to the townhouse; so why should he worry? With Karmonov and with the Wolkowski's he was becoming part of a new family. He felt he belonged here. It was a sensation he'd never experienced at his uncle's where he'd been more of a burden, more of a problem that his guilt-ridden uncle felt duty-bound to solve.

Julian happened at that moment to glance down through the window where he saw a man taking a seat on a bench that faced the front of the butcher shop. He had seen the same man earlier in the week and hadn't thought much about him, but now he took a closer look: salt and pepper hair, dressed well, carrying a walking stick. He was too young to be retired and too old, Julian thought, not to have better things to do with his time. Then Julian saw Karmonov coming up the street. On meeting, the two men talked for a few minutes after which the walking stick man left. The bell downstairs announced Karmonov's entry into the store. Julian again thought about how little he knew about his employer. He decided to go downstairs.

Karmonov was taking off his jacket, just getting settled at his desk when he saw Julian. "I'm told you had a visitor."

Julian was taken aback at the thought that Karmonov was spying on him then realized that it was to be expected that the local shopkeepers looked out for each other. One of them must have told him about Uncle Emory stopping by. Or maybe the man with the walking-stick had seen him leave. "It was just my uncle. He wanted to see where I was staying."

"The famous Emory North was here in my store? Too bad I came in late today, I would have enjoyed meeting him."

"I'll introduce you sometime."

Karmonov opened a desk drawer and began rummaging through it. "You don't have many friends do you?"

The question surprised Julian. Why would Karmonov be concerned about his friends?

"I have a few. I haven't been in England all that long. Harry's one, there are some others."

Karmonov closed the drawer apparently not finding what he'd been looking for. He leaned back in his chair. "Do you have any lady friends?"

"Why would you be interested in my lady friends?"

"I did not say I was interested – just curious. It is good to have friends."

"That man outside just now, was he your friend?"

Karmonov chuckled. "Are you spying on me Mr. North?"

"I happened to be looking out the window - just curious," said Julian. Without waiting to be asked, he sat down.

Karmonov studied Julian, his expression more serious now. "That man was a business associate. I do have friends though. The Wolkowskis are good people. I count them as friends. Maybe you will be one too." He opened a drawer, a different one on the other side of his desk. "Do you like vodka?" He pulled out a full bottle and two glasses. "This is very excellent," he said as he poured.

They drank to Julian, to the store, to the queen and to Mother

Russia and with the vodka flowing freely their conversation grew more comfortable. Karmonov talked about growing up in the streets of St. Petersburg and how he and his brother had managed a business there in the worst of neighborhoods.

"What kind of business?" asked Julian.

"We just sold whatever people wanted." Karmonov laughed to himself. "It was mostly legal."

"Are you mostly legal now?"

"Ah, you are pressing me, Mr. North. You are pressing me." He emptied his glass and let out a laugh. "The answer to that is yes – mostly."

At this slight admission of impropriety and, in part because of the alcohol, Julian dismissed the notion that Karmonov might in any way be dangerous. He pegged him as a man whose principles just happened to be a little gray at the edges.

Time passed. A few customers came in. An older lady made a purchase and, as Karmonov tended to her, she gave Julian a disapproving look through the half-opened back-office door. She must have seen the bottle in front of him.

"Don't mind her," said Karmonov after the woman left, "she was probably offended that you didn't ask her to join us."

It was growing late when Karmonov tossed the empty bottle in the trash and announced that it was time to join the Wolkowski's for diner. "They have a bigger than normal meal once a month for no particular reason. They are having it tonight. You should be hungry. Good vodka makes you hungry." He stood up. "My father told me so. It is true, you know."

"They haven't invited me before," said Julian.

"Ah, but you've been here two months. Now you are like family. You will be most welcome. You need no invitation."

There was that word: family. And yes, he was hungry. He was beginning to like this boisterous, red-faced Russian. Julian got to his feet with an effort. "Lead on, MacDuff," he said with a flourish.

"Ha, you betray yourself. The actual quote is: 'Lay on, MacDuff, and damned be him who first cries 'Hold! Enough!''" Karmonov said this in a loud theatrical way. "A good Russian knows his Shakespeare as well as any Englishman but always better than an American." Good naturedly, he leaned an arm against Julian at the shoulders and together they stumbled off to the butcher's shop.

There were two empty chairs waiting for them at a big round table noisily ringed with Wolkowskis and a few of their friends. For the occasion Gerta had made her special dish – pickled pig's feet. Helped by the vodka, some polish wine and the encouragement of his new family, Julian ate well and along with everyone else sang with gusto accompanied by Henry's accordion.

Much later that night, Julian managed to make it up to his bed and, with the room spinning around him, he fell immediately asleep. But too much food and drink caused him to wake up in the middle of the night. Against his chest he felt the medallion he always wore. Julian was sure it was just his imagination but it seemed to be a little heavier to-night and somehow a little more iridescent in the moonlight. It had belonged to his mother and remained for him a constant reminder of her and of the home he once had so long ago. Now, this place was his home.

He lay in the dark, listening. The half-opened windows rattled with the wind but all else was silent and still. Aromas wafted up from next door – onion, garlic, basil; could they be making sausages at this hour? He thought of the Wolkowskis: big Henry, a story teller to rival Karmonov; Gerta, always ready to poke fun at anything, the prattling twins, and last, little Willy. Despite the pounding in his head Julian felt contentment in the way things had worked out. This was a place that he could make home, at least for a while. He rolled over and went back to sleep.

Weeks passed. He'd gotten paid again, having made it to the half-way point of the translation. Castlenau the soldier had reverted to his philosophies and then became Castlenau the revolutionary. He spoke of an organization of like-minded, influential men highly placed within major world governments. He spoke of a fleet of warships and a mobile army of fifty thousand men; an army fighting, not for a single nation, but for the common man and the natural law. He was starting to lay out a plan for the overthrow of the most powerful nations of the world. The crafty anarchist presented a convincing argument and had Julian half-believing that he just might be able to bring about this global revolution of his. Was this the 'historical significance' that would be of interest to Karmonov's client? Then he wondered if Harry had discovered anything with the coat of arms or the Castlenau name. He reminded himself to check with him on that.

Julian had a few more spirited conversations with Karmonov, though none of them fueled again by vodka. Every now and then the Russian asked about the translation but he didn't seem especially concerned. Karmonov's hours grew more erratic. Sometimes he'd leave before five, other times he'd work well into the night. On those late nights, the occasional sounds of shuffling papers and Karmonov's soft humming rose up through the floorboards. It was always the same tune – slow, almost a lullaby but with a dark, melancholy flavor.

On one such night Julian had been working at his desk by gas-light when he was startled by the sound of the bell over the front door. Karmonov's humming stopped abruptly.

Instinctively, Julian turned out the light and looked through the window. The street was deserted. He heard Karmonov walk out into the store and call out: "Who is there?" There was no reply. Karmonov returned to his office. "I have a gun," said Karmonov, his voice steady. "Who is there?"

Julian swallowed and kept deathly still, listening, his heart thumping. There were footsteps – not Karmonov's. A commanding voice spoke in Russian.

Karmonov shouted back, also in Russian, then more footsteps. The two were in Karmonov's office now. He heard the low murmur of a heated conversation as if Karmonov knew the man then, silence.

Julian gripped the edge of his desk. Was Karmonov being robbed? He should go down and help him. He stood up and turned. His heartbeat quickened. The quiet was shattered by a shout from Karmonov and the blast of a gun.

Julian jumped, not knowing what to do. Had Karmonov shot the intruder? The building was silent. Julian's mouth went completely dry. He heard the stairway door creak open. A shaft of light illuminated the stairs from below. Then he heard slow, tentative footsteps. Someone was coming up and he knew it wasn't Karmonov.

Julian tried to think of what he could possibly use as a weapon: the chair, a heavy book? In the dim light from the stairwell, he scanned the room. The intruder was nearly to the top step. Julian could hear his breathing – short and measured.

Julian's eyes darted. He needed a place to hide, and a weapon – anything. He caught sight of the ornamental ball on the brass headboard of his bed. It looked heavy. He ran to it as quietly as he could, hoping the ball wasn't welded to the frame. He grabbed it and it came freely off the post. He ducked down behind the bed and looked toward the stairs.

At the top step the man turned. He was tall and wore a dark coat. He moved slowly and quietly. There was a gun in his hand. "I know you're here. I won't hurt you," he said in perfect English.

Julian kept quiet. His only advantage lay with the intruder not knowing where he was.

The gunman walked to Julian's desk where he turned again, scanning the room with the gun. He struck a match and lit the lamp. Light flooded the room and Julian's heart sank. He couldn't possibly remain hidden now. Should he make a run for the stairs? He felt the brass ball in his hand. It was heavy enough but a throw would have to score direct hit to do any good.

The man appeared distracted by something on the desk. Still holding the gun, he began gathering things up, stuffing them into his coat pockets. He tore through the drawers, his back still toward Julian.

Julian had to make his move now. He held his breath and stood. He crept forward around the bed, clutching the brass ball in his raised hand. The man was still bent over one of the drawers. He was only two feet away now. Julian braced himself, about to bring the ball down hard when he was shocked to see his own reflection in the window. The gunman must have seen it at the same moment. He dodged to the side just as Julian struck.

The ball missed the man's head but caught his shoulder. He fell as Julian ran for the stairs, still gripping the ball.

The gunman fired.

A bullet hit the plaster wall inches over Julian's head. He ducked as he reached the stairs and raced down through the open door into the office. Then Julian saw Karmonov.

The Russian was struggling with one knee on the floor and a hand on the back of his chair. He was trying to pull himself up. Blood streamed from a wound at the side of his face into a growing pool on the floor. In his free-hand was a gun. Rage and fear filled his eyes but there was a glint of recognition when he saw Julian. With the gun, he waved him out of the way.

From behind, Julian heard the intruder coming fast down the stairs. Julian leaped over the desk just as the gunman burst into the office. Two guns fired.

Julian waited then raised his head slowly. White smoke clouded the air. He saw Karmonov first, laying face up on the floor, his eyes wide.

The gunman sat with his back against the door-jam, panting, holding a wounded arm. He saw Julian. He looked straight at him through fierce red eyes and lifted his gun.

Without thinking, Julian cocked back his arm and threw the brass ball as hard as he could. From this close range he didn't miss. He caught the man square between his eyes just as the gun fired.

The shot went high and the man slumped.

Julian got up slowly, hardly believing what had just happened. He grabbed Karmonov by the shoulders. "I'll help you, Mr. Karmonov. You're all right now, I'll help you." Julian shook him but the eyes of the Russian remained fixed and there was no movement in his chest. Julian stared in disbelief - Karmonov was dead.

The only sounds were the hissing of the gas-lamp and the hard breathing of the still unconscious intruder but it was enough to stir Julian back into action. He grabbed the man's gun. Then he noticed the pages of his translation poking out from the man's coat pocket. What could the man have wanted with those? Julian pulled them out and with them came the journal itself.

Reflexively, Julian slipped the journal into his own pocket and gathered up the papers that had fallen. He froze when he heard the bell at the front door. He turned and stood up, papers in one hand, the gun in the other.

From the door, Henry Wolkowski stared at him then ran back out.

Julian knew how it must look. He dropped the gun and shoved the papers into his pocket. He ran through the door out into the street not caring where he was going, he just had to get away. He took a turn at the first crossroad and kept running for another three blocks. There were only a few people on the street and there was a mist in the air. Finally he leaned against a building to rest. His chest was heaving, his heart pumping. He checked the street signs and got his bearings knowing that there was only one place he could go now.

It was two in the morning when Julian finally made it to the townhouse. He used his key and was greeted by an alarmed George who breathed easier and put down his cricket bat when he saw who it was.

"Master Julian, are you all right?"

Julian couldn't speak at first. He was out of breath. His hands shook. His voice shook. "Where...where is Uncle Emory?"

"He's out for a few days on business – up in Coventry. Here, sit down. What's going on? Are you hungry? Maybe some tea to calm you, I've never seen you like this." George's solution to everything was a cup of tea.

Julian bent forward, his head in his hands. He closed his eyes but the scene kept repeating in his mind: the terror in Karmonov's eyes, the pool of his bright red blood, and the dark accusing eyes of Henry Wolkowski. He took a few deep breaths. "It's all right. I'll be fine." He straightened and pointed at the front door. "Lock it."

George locked the door. "I'll put on the tea," he said.

Though he took some comfort being in his old room that night, Julian slept fitfully and rose early. The first thing he did was to check the journal and to look over the mess of wrinkled pages from his translation. The book was in intact and most of the translation seemed to be there. But there were two things he didn't expect to see. One was a monthly schedule for ships into and out of Dover, the other was a stack of foreign currency wrapped in twine - fresh new bills of high denomination – Turkish lira. The gunman must have had the money and the ship schedule in the same pocket as the journal and Julian had grabbed it all.

Julian flipped through the Dover schedule. It covered the current three month period. He went to the page for today's date. Midway down, the name of a ship was circled, her destination – Istanbul.

Julian went downstairs and George asked him again what had happened and if he was all right. He told him he was, then explained that he'd just had a misunderstanding with his employer. "It was nothing serious. Nothing to worry about," said Julian between bites of his jam-on-bread breakfast.

"It looked pretty serious to me," said George.

"Well, it wasn't and it's nothing you need to mention to Uncle Emory. When's he due back?"

"Three days."

Julian stayed at the townhouse for the next two days, each day scouring the newspapers for a story about a killing at the antique store. Surely Wolkowski would have reported it. He would have also reported the culprit – one Julian North. But there was no such story in the papers. The police had to know about it, didn't they? Why would they keep it secret? But what if the police didn't know about the murder? The thought of the body, maybe two bodies, just lying in the store for so long, sickened Julian. But what could he do? What should he do? He hadn't done anything wrong. He had only protected himself against a robber...and unintentionally stole a stack of money. With Wolkowski as the only witness, he didn't have much doubt how a jury would see it.

On the morning of his third day at the townhouse Julian decided he had to go back to Bristol Lane. He hired a carriage and had the driver pull slowly past the antique store. There was a closed sign in the window and everything looked normal. Things at Wolkowski's looked normal too. There were customers inside.

Everything was as it should be. Julian wished he could convince himself that Karmonov's murder had never happened, but he knew better. Weighing his options, he thumbed the medallion under his shirt then got off the carriage another half-block down.

He walked slowly back, eyes searching in all directions for anything unusual as he approached the store. He unlocked the door and went inside.

There was no bad smell from Karmonov's body as he expected and he could see no one inside. Everything was perfectly orderly. He approached the back office and caught the faint whiff of lye. The door was closed. He swallowed and opened the door. There was no body. There was no sign of any disturbance. Julian got to a knee and checked the floor. He could just make out the faint outline where the pool of Karmonov's blood had been. Someone had cleaned it up. And someone had taken the body.

At that moment the bell over the front door jingled and Julian nearly jumped out of his skin. He thought about running, he thought about hiding upstairs, but even if he wanted to, there was no time. Julian stepped out of the office into the store and there, in coat and hat stood a man leaning lightly against a walking stick. It was the same man he'd seen from his window more than a month ago.

"It's about time you showed up," said the man in a codgerly voice. "What took you so long?"

"What? Who are you?"

The man took a few steps toward Julian. "Yes, I know you must be confused." He paused then continued. "My name's Parker. I'm a client of Mr. Karmonov's."

"I've seen you before," said Julian.

"I expect you have. Anatoly and I have been doing business for years. I was sorry to see him meet with such a tragic end." He walked to a chair and sat down. "I suppose we could talk in his office but it doesn't seem right somehow, does it?" He paused as if waiting for a response. "You are Julian North, are you not?"

"How do you know my name?"

"Easy enough to find out. It was in Karmonov's papers along with your address. If you hadn't shown up today I would have come for you. It's just as well we're meeting here, don't you think?"

Julian didn't answer. He had the feeling that the less he said the better.

"Tell me what happened," said Parker.

"Not until I know who you are."

"I told you, I'm Parker, that's all you need to know. Now tell me what happened here."

The stern look in Parker's face didn't leave Julian much choice. Reluctantly, he re-counted the night of the shooting.

When he'd finished, Parker rubbed his jaw. "That was a good throw, knocking the bugger out with the brass ball. It saved your life."

"It didn't kill him did it? He was alive when I left."

"No. Unfortunately it didn't kill him. He was gone when I arrived. Could be anywhere by now."

Julian wasn't about to tell him about the ship schedule or the money, at least not until he knew more about Parker. "What did you do with Karmonov's body?"

"We gave him a decent burial," said Parker, his tone more serious now. "It was all very respectful. I can see that you liked him. I did too. We notified his brother in St. Petersburg. This building will be sold and the proceeds will be sent to him – after expenses of course."

The fear of being accused of murder had so preoccupied Julian that he hadn't had time to feel any sense of grief for Karmonov – for Anatoly - until now. He had been good to Julian. He remembered his jovial laugh and he remembered the last terrified look in his eyes as he faced down his killer. "Who would want him dead? Why would anyone want him dead?"

Parker folded his hands over the ivory knob of his walking stick and used it as a chin rest. "I don't know exactly but I believe the answer's bound up in that book you're translating. We couldn't find it anywhere here so either the killer has it or you do." Parker looked Julian straight in the eye. "I think you have it. Am I right, Mr. North?"

Julian hesitated and in that hesitation he knew he had just confirmed Parker's suspicion. He might as well admit it. "Yes."

"Good," said Parker, obviously relieved. "Where is it now? Did you leave it with anyone?"

"It's at my uncle's. No one else knows about it."

Parker got up. "We need to retrieve it – right now."

Julian decided it was time to take a stand. "Not until you tell me who you are and who you're working with."

"This is not a game, Mr. North. You should know that better than anyone. The book and your translation are important. Now are you coming with me or do I have to tear your uncle's place apart looking for them?" He started for the door.

Julian followed Parker outside where a carriage waited - so much for taking a stand.

On arriving at the townhouse, Parker stayed outside while Julian went in. Thankfully, Uncle Emory still hadn't returned so he was able to get the journal and his translation without having to explain himself.

On their way back, Parker was silent as he began reading Julian's translation, a stack of more than a hundred pages. Once inside the store, Parker asked: "How long will it take you to finish?"

Julian was incredulous. "What? You want me to finish the translation? After all this?"

"How long?"

Julian thought for a moment. "I can have it done in about two weeks, maybe three. But why should I be the one to finish it? I'm not the only one around who knows French."

"No, but you're the only one who knows French and knows about this book. I'll be honest with you Mr. North, I don't know exactly why this book is so important, but it is. From what happened to poor Anatoly, just the knowledge of its existence may be a dangerous thing. I will pay you two-hundred pounds when you're done with it. After that you can go on your way and forget you ever saw the book or me for that matter."

What had seemed like a lot of money once, now seemed hardly enough. Then another worry struck Julian. "What if the gunman comes back?"

"He won't," said Parker. "I'll stay with you down here and I have a few other men to help out. I'll have food brought in, but not from the Wolkowskis."

"They think I killed him."

"Let's just say they're confused. But you won't have any need to contact the Wolkowskis and I'm quite sure that they'll stay clear of you."

Questions about Parker filled Julian's head but the man had made it clear he had no intention of answering any of them. What was also clear was that Julian would be best off just getting the translation done, and collecting his money, and walking away from this whole mess. So Julian got back to work and again immersed himself in the journal.

In the last fifty pages Castlenau revealed his idea to use what he called "a catalytic incident" to trigger a war that would involve all the major nations in the world. In eventual response to that war, Castlenau's people would mount a coordinated, worldwide rebellion. Weakened and distracted by war, the governments of the world would topple one by one, to be replaced by a new single entity.

Castlenau laid out the structure of a collective government that would be formed following the rebellion. It was to be a grand world order that would treat each nation much as a traditional government treated its states or provinces. With simple logic and keen insights into human nature he backed up the righteousness of his cause and the practicality of his plan. But as good as it all seemed, Julian knew that Castlenau's utopic world could never justify the thousands, maybe even tens of thousands, of lives that would be lost in the terrible effort to bring it about.

Julian spent every waking moment on the translation and it was on the tenth day after his first meeting with Parker that he turned to the last page of the journal and completed the translation of the final line:

The call to arms will be swift, my brothers. Be vigilant. Be ready.

So that was it, the entire journal of Jacques Caesar Castlenau. Julian closed the book and placed it beside his notes. If the date written on the first page of the journal could be believed, almost eighty years had passed since Castlenau had written those words to his followers, all of whom must be dead by now. But even if they were still alive, the journal only gave an idea for world revolution. It was too broad in scope to constitute an actual plan for revolution. So why was the book so important? Only one thing made sense - its real details, its real secrets, had to be hidden in the symbols Julian had found. They had to be some kind of code.

Julian stood up. He was done with the journal and free to go back to living with his uncle – back to his old life. And he would be two-hundred pounds richer, plus he had the gunman's foreign money – stealing from a killer was not really stealing, was it? He supposed he should be elated, but he wasn't.

Julian stared out through the window where the mid-afternoon shadows were growing. In a clearing across the street, in a little spot of sun, a gardener busied himself tending his vegetables. Julian opened the window wider and let the warm air pour in. The slow rhythm of the gardener's spade drifted up and Julian thought about the new life he'd briefly had working for Karmonov. That was gone now. He thought of Castlenau, the coat of arms and the stack of cash. He thought about Karmonov's killer, still on the loose. Would he kill again to get the journal? Could he really be part of a group of men out there who believed in

Castlenau's plan and were crazy enough to try and carry it out? Thousands could die. And how did Parker fit into all of this? Until he understood Parker's connection to the journal, he couldn't trust him. He couldn't trust anyone.

From all this, an idea slowly began to form.

Julian closed the window, and stood motionless, going over every conceivable twist in the scenario he envisioned. His heart began to thump with a dangerous excitement. He sat back down and took several blank sheets of paper, tearing them into quarters. He needed them small enough to hide. Next, he opened the journal to the first page and began copying - not the text but enlargements of the tiny stick-figure symbols in the margins. He had four days to write out as much of the code as he could.

On his last day at the store, Julian stuffed his notes on the code under his shirt. He walked downstairs carrying the journal and his translation and handed them to Parker. "It's all there. It's finished."

Parker skimmed through the translation, his expression darkening on reaching the last page. Finally, he put everything into a leather valise. "All right, Mr. North, here's your payment." He handed Julian four crisp fifty-pound notes. "I suggest you leave now. Talk to no one about the journal – no one. Do you understand me? I'll have the rest of your things delivered back to your uncle's house."

"Yes, that'll be fine," said Julian turning for the door. He was glad to be rid of Parker and didn't bother saying goodbye. He walked out of the store ready to reclaim control of his life. He hesitated then went into the butcher's shop and said goodbye to the Wolkowskis thanking them for their food and friendship. None of them would come near Julian; but at least Willy, who gave him a hug around the knees, seemed sorry to see him go. Julian was sorry too. He envied this energetic close-knit family and would miss them. The aroma of meats and spices stayed with him as he left and headed down the street. How different things would be if Karmonov were still alive. Julian would have a home; he would have a family. Now he was about to move back in with his uncle. He was glad it would only be temporary.

Julian walked further, that dangerous excitement building again. He checked the time and caught a carriage. He directed the driver to the Brass Ring Pub which he knew Uncle Emory frequented at this time of day. On the way, Julian rehearsed what he would say to him.

When he entered the pub he caught sight of his uncle sitting alone at a corner table. He was in his shirtsleeves bent over a ledger with a near-empty mug of beer, a half-eaten sandwich, and a freshly lit cigar all within reach.

Julian walked over and Uncle Emory looked up. His face broke into a broad smile. "Julian, how are you?" They shook hands. "It's good to see you. Did you decide to take the day off?"

Julian pulled up a chair and sat down. He didn't like lying to his uncle but he couldn't see any way around it. "I'm going to be leaving London for a while."

Uncle Emory picked up his cigar. "Oh? Where're you off to?"

"Istanbul."

Uncle Emory stopped in mid-puff then took a longer drag and blew it out as he talked. "You're going there for that Russian fellow? That's a long way to go for antiques."

Here was where the lie came in and Julian was thankful that the barmaid chose this moment to come by and take his order for a beer.

"Bring me another too," said his uncle who then turned back to him.

Julian took a breath. "He deals in rare books. I'm done with the translation and there are others he wants me to work on but they're in Istanbul at a store owned by his brother."

"And no one in Istanbul can do this translation for his brother? It has to be you? Julian, you're not making much sense."

"He has other translation projects there too. Mr. Karmonov knows I do good work. He trusts me."

"Is he going with you?"

"No, I'll be going alone."

"He's paid for your travel?"

"Yes, and I have extra spending money too, it's all been taken care of. I'll be gone for about six months. I'll be staying in a flat above the brother's store just as I've been doing here."

"Julian, I want to meet Karmonov. You may trust him but I don't."

"He's out of town right now," improvised Julian, sensing a tangling in the web he'd been weaving. The beer came and he took a big swallow.

Uncle Emory's palm began a steady pat-pat-pat on the table. He shook his head. "This is not a good idea."

"I've been on my own before, in America. I know what I'm doing."

"You're going to find Istanbul a lot different than America."

34

"You worry too much, Uncle Emory."

At this his uncle's eyes seemed to soften. "I suppose you're right there. After your parents died I reproached myself for worrying about you too little. But I had worries of my own then." He ran his fingers through his hair and leaned back. "When your father and I were growing up, we were competitive in everything but he always had the upper hand on me: going off to America as he did, marrying a beautiful, loving woman, having a son who showed confidence and intelligence." He put his hand on Julian's. "He was always talking about you in his letters and I was always envious. He was very proud of you."

Julian had rarely heard his uncle say anything about his father. "I was only ten when he died. There wasn't much I'd done back then for him to be proud of."

"You were old enough to show an excitement for life – you had what he called an inner spark, and he was convinced that you'd outshine us both, one day. The accident changed you, Julian, but I know that spark is still in you and it's up to you to rediscover it. I also know that you're old enough now so I can't stop you from going to Istanbul or anywhere else. There is one thing I insist on though."

"If I can do it, I will."

"The *Times* has an office in Istanbul. The fellow who runs it is a colleague and a good friend of mine and, if I'm not mistaken, I think he has an empty room where you can stay. Really, Julian, I'll feel much better you staying at the *Times* office than with a Russian you've never met."

Julian concealed his relief. He hadn't yet solved the problem of where he'd stay in Istanbul but now his uncle had solved it for him. "Yes, I can do that. I can pay rent too," said Julian.

"Good, it's settled then. I don't know that rent will be needed though, maybe you can do the odd jobs around the office, but you can work that out with Willoughby when you're there. That's his name: Cyrus Willoughby, a delightful man. He can be pretty demanding sometimes but I think you'll like him."

They finished their beers and left the pub together. Uncle Emory caught a carriage back to Printing House Square and Julian decided to walk back to the townhouse. Having set things in motion he sensed more strongly than ever that his plan, if he could call it a plan, was the right thing to do. He was nervous and excited at the same time and he couldn't keep another improbable headline from popping into his head:

Famous Writer Avenges Friend's Murder and Thwarts Deadly International Plot.

CHAPTER 4

So that was the big plan: sail to Istanbul, find the gunman and make him pay for what he'd done to Karmonov – make him pay for destroying the life that Julian was just beginning to get comfortable with. Julian knew he was being naive but what choice did he have? He wouldn't let himself go back to being a file clerk and he wouldn't live off his uncle's charity any longer.

He booked a shared cabin on the *Sussex*, a ship leaving from Dover in one week bound for Istanbul and other ports along the way. As those seven days passed, he grew more apprehensive. Just how exactly would he find the gunman? And if he did find him, what would he do? Would he turn him over to the authorities in Istanbul for a crime committed in London – a crime which the London police knew nothing about? No, to accomplish anything he would need to find out why Castlenau's book was so important. He had to solve the code. But just how was he going to do that?

With these thoughts circling in Julian's head and only five days before his departure, Uncle Emory glanced up at him over his breakfast plate of eggs.

"I'll notify Willoughby about you coming. Are you having any second-thoughts? I told you this whole thing smells fishy to me, you can back out anytime."

Julian forced a smile. "No second thoughts," he lied. When he got to Istanbul he'd just have to work things out one step at a time. What's the worst that could happen?

That afternoon and for the next three days, he began his struggle with the code. He thought at first that it might be based on some established naval signaling method. Some of the symbols were simply vertical, slanted or horizontal lines; others were zigzags or crossed lines at various angles. Some gave the appearance of a signalman's outstretched arms holding semaphore flags but others would have been impossible to form even for a double-jointed signalman.

The night before leaving for Dover Julian met with Harry to say goodbye. He also thought that he might have some ideas about the code but it was the coat of arms that he asked about first.

"I had no luck with your Castlenau name or with that crest you gave me," said Harry at their usual table at Molly's. "There's nothing at all in the files but that doesn't mean much. We only keep information about people and things that are newsworthy."

Julian was disappointed but not surprised. He pulled out his drawings of the Castlenau symbols. "Have you seen figures like these before? They're part of a code I think."

Harry shuffled through them quickly then put them to one side. "Does this have anything to do with you going off to Istanbul?"

"I was going to tell you about that. I wanted to meet with you tonight to say goodbye. I leave for Dover tomorrow."

"It's not the sort of thing you keep from a friend."

"Sorry," said Julian, knowing Harry was right, but feeling at the same time that he was being overly sensitive about it. "I should have told you sooner."

"You only stop by when you want something."

"Right, I should have told you. There's been a lot going on lately."

Harry sulked, arms folded.

"How did you find out about Istanbul?" asked Julian.

"There's a rumor going around that you're planning to stay at our office there. Why Istanbul? That crest you showed me had an eastern cross and Istanbul is the center of Byzantium. Is that why you're going?"

"I don't want to get into that now – it's complicated."

"It's got something to do with Karmonov, doesn't it?"

Julian took a sip of beer. There was no way to soften what he had to say next. "Karmonov's dead, Harry."

Harry sat up rigid, eyes wide. "What? Dead? How could he be dead?"

"There was a break-in at the store."

"My God, that's terrible," said Harry shaking his head.

"I haven't told my uncle about it, so please don't mention it to him. Don't tell anyone. I'm only telling you because you knew him and you would have found out anyway." Julian's eyes met

Harry's. "He was a good man."

"Yes, he was. I can't believe it." Harry took a gulp of beer then told a few stories of his about Karmonov before lapsing into a stretch of silence. "Have the police found the killer?" he asked finally.

"I don't know."

"So your boss gets murdered and now you're off to Istanbul and you've got this code you're working on. You told me once you were trying to be a novelist. You aren't making all this up are you?"

"It's all true, Harry, and I need your help." Julian put his drawings back in front of Harry. "I was hoping that you could make some sense of these. It could be important."

Harry sighed then picked them up. "If it's a simple code, then each of these symbols represents a letter and the only way to solve it is by the frequency method. How many different symbols are there?"

"I've been able to find sixty-three."

"That's a little strange. But still, some of them must be letters. Maybe others are complete words or numbers. The Chinese character set has thousands of different symbols, each a word or sometimes an entire idea which, in English would take…"

"What's the frequency method?"

"Well, for a block of regular text, say a thousand letters long, you'd count the number of times each letter in the alphabet appears. That would give you a certain percentage for each letter. If fifty of the one-thousand letters were N's for example, the frequency for N would be five percent. You do that for all the letters then do the same thing with your code: take a block of text made up of a thousand of these funny characters and get the frequency percentage for each character. The symbol appearing five percent of the time would most likely represent an N. It'll take you a long time but it's really the only way I know of to solve it." Harry handed the drawings back to Julian.

"What if the code is in French?"

"Makes no difference; you just have to know how frequently each letter is normally used in whatever language you're working with. If it's in French, you'll get a book written in French and take your thousand letters from it to work out the percentages."

Julian collected his notes and tucked them in his pocket, not quite convinced.

"I never said I knew everything," said Harry. He began drumming is fingers. "I should have never given you Karmonov's name. He's dead and you could have been killed too. I knew it was a bad idea."

"It wasn't a bad idea."

"Are you in trouble with the police? Is that why you're leaving?" Then he looked at Julian with a start. "They don't think you killed him, do they?"

"No, it's nothing like that, but I can't tell you more – I can't."

They finished off another round of beers then Julian slid his chair back. "I've got to be going. I still have some packing to do." They left the pub together.

On the street outside, Harry turned to face Julian. "I know you never liked working the files – not like I do. It's important you know, keeping all that information in good order. It's like being a historian but I guess it's not for everyone."

"You're good at what you do, Harry and, you're right, it's important."

Harry shrugged. "Well, if you need to know something about anything, just ask me." He paused as a carriage rattled by. "Good luck to you, Julian. Let me know if you solve the code. Remember the frequency method."

"I won't forget. Thanks for being a good friend, Harry." They shook hands and Julian walked slowly back to the townhouse.

The next day, over the rain and the rumble and hissing of the trains, Julian and his uncle said good-bye at Victoria Station.

"You put up with me at the paper for a long time," said Julian. "I'm sorry it didn't work out."

"Well, one thing always leads to another," said Uncle Emory. "It's a serious business finding your way in life. When you find the right path, you'll know it. Sometimes the right path has a way of finding you, you know."

Uncle Emory gave Julian a warm embrace then put a hand on both of his shoulders. "Safe travels to you Julian and, once you get there, for God's sake stay out of trouble. And if you do get into trouble, be sure to ask Willoughby for help. He's a good man. Can you promise me you'll do that?"

"I promise, Uncle Emory." They hugged again then Julian picked up his bag and boarded the train.

The last sight he had of his uncle was through the open window as his train pulled out. There he stood, like a great immovable boulder in his raincoat and hat. Julian knew he had been a lot of trouble for his uncle. He should be glad to be rid of his prodigal nephew, but there was sadness in the man's face and he waved his goodbye slowly. And so did Julian.

The station in Dover was nothing more than a customs building that routed passengers through in two directions – one for new arrivals off to trains and carriages heading into England, the other for departures out to the docks. Once off the train, Julian waited in line, had his American passport stamped then headed for the docks which were a short walk further.

Along a pier piled high with trunks and crates he found *Sussex* last in a long line of ships. Marred by rust and peeling paint she rolled and creaked in the wind. Her tall single stack at mid-ships belched a thick stream of black smoke that bent immediately sideways in the cold Dover wind.

Julian tasted the salty air and pulled his cap down tight then picked up his bag and got in line to board. There were several families in front of him led by men with long black beards in long black coats and wide-brimmed black hats, the women behind them fighting to maintain order among their excited children. When it came his turn, Julian handed his boarding ticket to a uniformed agent and walked up onto the rolling deck where he stumbled backward a step before getting his footing.

"You'll get the hang of it soon enough my lord," said a deck hand holding a pad of paper.

"Name, sir?"

Julian told him and the man checked him off his list. "Very good sir, you're one deck down on the port side – your left as you face the bow - cabin fifteen. Your mate's already down there so you won't be getting the pick of the accommodations but you'll do all right."

A steep set of stairs led Julian into a narrow aisle and as he moved along, his bag bumped into every door handle until he came to a door marked fifteen. He knocked then opened it and took a single step inside which was enough to bring him to the center of the available floor space. Almost at his feet a dark-haired man reading a newspaper lay in the lower birth.

The man put his paper down and stared up at Julian. "Noah Sanford."

"Not much room," observed Julian after the introduction and handshake. He closed the door behind him and hoisted his bag onto the upper birth where a brass-framed porthole gave light to the room as well as a view of the sea from two feet above the waterline. The glass was spotted with green droplets and waves could be heard lapping against the hull.

"I took the lower, but we can switch half-way if you want,"

offered Noah. He moved to the side so his back rested against the bulkhead, his knees up to his chin.

Julian figured Noah to be in his late twenties, maybe a little taller than him. He had a round chin and a full mustache and wore an open collar white shirt beneath brown leather suspenders.

"I suppose I should admit it right off, I'm with the New York *Times*."

"An American reporter?" asked Julian.

"Yes, and you?"

"I was born in America and used to be with the London *Times*."

"An American at the London *Times*? I didn't think the Brits allowed such things. What are you doing now?"

"I'm a writer, on my own," improvised Julian wondering why he didn't just say he was a translator. Then again, one lie was just as good as another.

"Good for you. I'm told they try to put compatible people in the same cabins. Still, two Americans, both writers, on the same ship bound for Istanbul – what are the odds of that?"

Julian just shrugged.

Noah put his newspaper aside. "So what takes you to Istanbul?"

He should have been prepared for this question too, but wasn't. "I'm researching a book."

"Oh? You'll have to tell me about it sometime."

Julian stepped onto the foot-rail and pulled himself up to his bunk bumping his head hard against the ceiling.

"Ouch," said Noah sympathetically.

Julian rubbed the back of his head. "Do you travel much for your paper?" he asked, steering the conversation away from his non-existent book.

"I take foreign assignments a few times each year. I just got back from Mexico a month ago, and now this."

Julian wondered if he himself would have traveled more were it not for his fear of the sea. His voyage from America had been an unsettling experience filled with worry and terrible nightmares. Each day at sea he had checked the waters for hidden dangers and the skies for oncoming storms. But the crossing had been a smooth one and he told himself now that this voyage would be uneventful too. Still, even with *Sussex* tied to the dock, the roll of the deck sent shivers through him that he forced himself to ignore. "Your work doesn't give you much chance to stay in one place then."

"I'm a bachelor so I have no real need to stay in one place," said Noah. "No time for a family, no time to set up a real home. There's a certain freedom to it that I like but there are times when I'd like to settle down. Istanbul is a long-term assignment. We have a one-man operation there now. With my arrival, we'll be starting up an office to handle all the news stories from that part of the world."

A jet of steam hissed loudly from somewhere deep within *Sussex*. Julian peered out through the porthole at the wooden pilings. The ship's horn blared. Shouts came from the docks and a rumbling sound came from the engine. There was a sloshing of the paddlewheels.

"Well, goodbye England," said Noah. "Only thirty minutes late, that's something of a record for this shipping line." He yawned.

Julian put his head down on his hard pillow and stared out through the porthole watching the shoreline disappear. He shifted his weight. Tied to his inner thigh was a thin, water-tight packet he had made. In it he had concealed his notes on the Castlenau code. He felt somewhat foolish for taking such a precaution but hadn't felt right putting them in his bag or in the trunk he'd had stowed. He hoped the trunk had made it into *Sussex*'s hold but wouldn't know for sure until they arrived in Istanbul. He repositioned the packet to a more comfortable spot then closed his eyes. From below, Noah snored, but Julian couldn't sleep.

Later, a crewman came by and lit an oil lamp. Julian sat up, listening to the throb of the ship's engine. The waves were rolling now and he held onto the frame of the cot noticing the straps he'd be using to buckle himself down when the sea turned rougher. At his feet a bucket hung from a coat hook. It clanked gently against the bed.

For three days *Sussex* battled the Atlantic around the Iberian coast. Julian's waking hours were spent at the rail bundled up against the cold, retching dryly over the side. His nights were filled with nightmares, the old familiar ones that had plagued him since he was a boy: a capsized ship, tumbling as it sank, his mother floating beside him calm and serene. In his dreams he was always able to save her, and when he awoke it was always a shock to remember that he had failed.

On the fourth day, *Sussex* passed through Gibraltar and entered the milder waters of the Mediterranean. Finding his sea-legs at last, Julian was able to eat. He spent more time on deck enjoying the warm sun and, for a while, managed to push his fear of the sea out of his mind. His bunk was the only private space he had and every night he worked there on the code, trying to come up with Harry's frequency percentages.

Noah proved himself to be a good traveling companion and worthy opponent at chess. One afternoon they sat on deck near the rail, just clear of the spray as *Sussex* rounded Italy's heel. The chessboard was open between them with only three pieces of each color still in play.

Noah shook his head. "I hate draws."

"Better than a loss. I had you five moves ago, you were lucky to get out of it." Julian sat back in his chair looking over the sparkling waves to the sunbaked Italian coast that lined the distant horizon.

"I saw what you were trying to do. Luck had nothing to do with it." Noah stowed the chessboard. A wet breeze picked up and they sat quietly for a while.

Julian put a foot up against a rail post. "So what's going on in America these days?"

"Everything's bustling. The big story is still the huge bridge over the East River in New York. It'll be the largest in the world and it's nearly done now."

"I saw it rising when I left for England." Julian remembered the massive stone-block piers towering over the water almost too big to have been built by man. "Even the papers in London are talking about it."

"Edison's electric lighting station's running at full power now. Electric cables are being strung all over New York. One day they expect people to have electric lamps in their homes. There's even talk about electric carriages." Noah pulled out a couple of cigars and handed one to Julian.

Julian rarely smoked but he accepted the cigar that took him two matches to light. The smell of the tobacco reminded him of his uncle and his father too.

"Are you sorry you left?" asked Noah. "America, I mean."

Julian folded his arms. "Sometimes I am, sometimes not. It was good to see England though, and it was good getting to know my uncle."

"What made you strike out on your own with your writing? Any journalist in the British Empire would kill to work for the London *Times*."

Julian wasn't about to admit that he'd only been a lowly file clerk. He reached over the rail and tapped his ashes, thankful for the favorable cross-wind. "I didn't work well with their deadlines. I had an idea for a book and needed time to focus on that."

"So you left and now you're off to Istanbul doing research."

"Yes."

"Sorry for saying so but you seem a little young to be doing such a thing. This will be your first book? Can you tell me anything about it?"

"It'll be my first book, yes and it's to be something historical but I'm keeping the details to myself right now. You're a writer, I'm sure you understand."

Noah hesitated for a moment as if first thinking to press the issue then changing his mind. "Of course I understand," he said. "I'd do the same in your position."

Two days later *Sussex* entered the Marmara Denizi, just east of the Dardanelles where the coastline on both sides hung close for miles then slowly separated into an open expanse of calm blue. The next morning they approached Istanbul harbor.

It was the sheer size of the city that struck Julian first. Its golden domes, tall minarets, and squat, starkly white buildings gradually became more distinct. They blanketed the hills of the city on both sides of the waterway, which was filled with vessels of both sail and steam. Ferries crowded with passengers scooted across the harbor, Europe on one side, Asia on the other.

From tall masts, colorful flags fluttered in the soft breeze as beneath a blazing sun *Sussex* maneuvered among them. Slowly she approached a dock choked with barrels and crates, busy and noisy with men of every color and description, each carrying impossible loads.

"Not your average village wharf," Julian said to Noah beside him.

Further down along the rail, laughter broke out among some of the families gathered there. One of the bearded men Julian had seen in Dover had a boy sitting on his shoulders, the boy pointing this way and that.

After tying up, the crew wasted no time routing the passengers and their luggage down the narrow gangway and off the boat. Julian grabbed his bag and, once on the dock, was glad to feel something solid under his feet. Around him workers rushed, sweat-drenched and naked to the waist. All of them were shouting in every language but English.

"I see some carriages over there," said Noah, raising his voice, pointing through the crowd. "We need a driver to take us into the city."

"How do we tell him where we want to go? You don't happen to speak Turkish, do you?"

"No, but I have a note in Turkish that gives the address of my office."

"Good," said Julian, still looking around. "I thought there might be someone here to meet me." He hoisted his bag over his shoulder and was about to follow Noah into the crowd when someone shouted from behind.

"Hold on there, stop!"

Julian and Noah both turned to see a clean-shaven man in a white shirt and hat making his way through the crowd. He caught up with them and with a handkerchief dabbed the beads of sweat spotting his sunburned forehead. "Might one of you be Mr. North?"

"I am," said Julian, relieved that he'd apparently made contact with the right person.

The man looked equally relieved. "I was looking for someone traveling alone. The fact that there were two of you had me a bit confused." He turned to Noah. "So who are you?"

"I'm Noah Sanford with the New York *Times*. Who are you?"

"Oh yes, of course, how rude of me – sorry. Thomas Baker is my name. I'm with the London *Times*. Pleased to make your acquaintance - both of you." They shook hands.

"All right then," said Baker to Julian, "you've got your things? What? Is that all?"

"I've got a trunk that'll be delivered to the office - according to the cargo master at the ship."

"Yes, of course, a good plan. It'll cost you a bloody fortune, though. You've got to watch for that kind of thing here you know. Steal you blind if you give them a chance." Baker scanned the dockhands with distaste, as if they were all thieves. "Well now, let's be off, shall we?" He pointed in the general direction of a three story brick building topped by a Turkish flag. "That's the customs office. You'll have to check in there first. Then we'll hire a carriage and be on our way."

"Mind if I join you?" asked Noah. "There doesn't seem to be anyone here from my paper."

"Why, of course you may," said Baker, heading off.

As they followed, Noah asked Julian: "I thought you said you were no longer with the London *Times*."

"I'll just be staying at their office while I'm here."

"Nice of them to put you up; you must still have connections there."

Julian nodded. "I left on good terms."

The Istanbul office of the London *Times* occupied a small frontage roughly centered in a redbrick building that stretched an entire block. A brass plaque affixed to the white wooden door bore the lion and unicorn emblem of the *Times* while gold lettering spanned the white trimmed windows on either side proclaiming this to be Ottoman Office of the London *Times*. Brass gas lamps were affixed to the brick beyond each window.

After stepping off the carriage, Julian retrieved his bag and glanced in through one of the windows. He saw more of his own reflection than the space within. He took off his cap and ran a hand through his longish hair then down over the whiskers on his face. He should have shaved. Straightening, he turned to look up the street. Red brick structures with white woodwork identical to the *Times* office lined both sides as far as he could see.

"This area of the city is generally known as the Western Quarter," explained Baker, beside him. "An appealing sense of order amid all the Oriental chaos don't you think?"

"It *is* very organized," agreed Julian. From the harbor, they had ridden through the riotous colors, noises and excitement of the city and its Great Bazaar where the smells of exotic foods and spices filled the air. The contrast of the sedate European quarter was startling and, Julian thought, a little depressing.

Baker turned to pay the driver, but Noah intervened. "It's the least I can do," he said pulling a Turkish note from his wallet. "Thanks for letting me share the ride."

"Well, that's very kind of you," said Baker. "By the looks of it, I'm just up the street. I'll be off, then."

Noah got back into the carriage and Julian walked over to shake his hand. "Good luck to you Noah. You've been a good cabin-mate, maybe you can stop by for chess sometime."

"I'll be sure to do that. Good luck on your book."

After the carriage pulled away Baker cleared his throat: "Your book?"

Julian shook his head. "It's nothing – just something we talked about. It was a long voyage, we got on pretty well."

"It's a good idea to have a friend at the New York *Times*, just don't share any secrets with him."

Julian was confused for a moment then realized that Baker was alluding to the natural competition between newspapers; each one trying to be the first to break a story. "I'm pretty good about keeping secrets, Mr. Baker," he said.

Baker sighed as if not quite convinced then stepped to the door. "So, Mr. North, here is our humble office." He held the door open for Julian as a bell jingled overhead.

Inside, the cooler air and the smell of furniture oil struck Julian and took him immediately back to Karmonov's store. But those were the only similarities between the two. On either side, walls of white stucco and dark oak trim framed the room while, before him stretched a long center aisle defined by wooden rails which ran to the back.

"This will be your desk," said Baker, indicating an oak table to the left. It had a slanted top and was flanked by a straight-backed wooden chair. Against the wall, was a library table topped by an empty letterbox.

"Oh, I won't be needing a desk," said Julian.

Baker raised a brow. "Where will you work then?"

"I was told you have a room. I'll just be staying a few months. I'm not actually with the *Times* anymore."

Baker looked befuddled at this information. "Well, you can take that up with Mr. Willoughby I suppose." He continued with his tour of the place.

On the other side of the aisle was a duplicate work area. On that desk some papers were neatly stacked beside an inkwell. The letterbox behind the desk contained several envelopes. Further down the aisle, a framed map of the world hung on the wall beside a pendulum clock.

"Everyone seems to be away," said Baker, walking to a back office, Julian following. Baker knocked on the door. "Hello, Mr. Willoughby? Mr. Willoughby?" He waited, then knocked harder.

"Just a moment, hold on," came the response through the closed door.

"He can be a cranky bugger," confided Baker, his voice low.

Julian put down his bag and straightened his shirt as the door opened.

There stood a man with a rumpled head of gray hair who looked as though he had just woken up. The whites of his half-opened eyes were tinged pink, and his shirt on the left side had escaped the best efforts of his belt to contain it. Willoughby rubbed his eyes and squinted first at Baker, then at Julian. "Mr. North, I assume?" he asked, extending his hand but not stepping out beyond the doorway.

"That's me," said Julian as they shook hands. "Good to meet you sir."

Willoughby fished a note from his shirt pocket, looked at it, then put it back. "So, Mr. North, late of the society pages and before that, God knows what, welcome to the most obscure office in the entire *Times* organization."

"Thank you, sir," said Julian wondering how he'd gotten the idea that he'd ever worked on the society pages. He sensed Uncle Emory's hand in it.

"What do you think of our place?" Willoughby asked, scanning the deserted office.

"It looks very...orderly."

"We do our best here," Willoughby remarked. His long thin face was blemished by age spots on his forehead and cheeks. A patch of skin hung down from his neck just below his chin and oscillated when he talked. "Trying circumstances at times you must understand, professional journalists amidst the wilds of the Ottomans." He turned to Baker. "Has he met Wilder yet?"

"Not as yet, sir. It seems she's out at the moment."

"Oh yes, out at the embassy – all that commotion." Julian wasn't sure he heard right.

"You have a question, Mr. North?" asked Willoughby, more introspectively.

"Wilder is a woman?" asked Julian.

"Why yes, Mr. North, Kate Wilder is indeed very much a woman. Came to us, what, almost three years ago?" Baker nodded. "Right," continued Willoughby, "made herself bloody well indispensable, I'd say, eh, Baker?"

"I should say so."

Julian swallowed. At Printing House Square there were only two women on the entire staff and they were both, like he, the lowliest of clerks. "Wilder is a journalist?"

Willoughby put his hands on his hips. "Yes, Mr. North, she is – and a very good one. From what I've seen of your work, you can learn a few things from her."

Julian wondered what work he was talking about but it was Baker who tried to set things straight.

"Mr. North says that he's not with the *Times* any longer. He says that he'll just be staying here for a few months."

"Oh? Are you on holiday, Mr. North? Are you under the impression that we run a hotel here?"

"No sir. I've got a project I'm working on and my uncle had arranged with you that I stay here..."

"Yes," said Willoughby, "as the assistant journalist that I requested from the home office nearly two years ago. Your desk is over there, *if* that's all right with you."

Julian hesitated. Somehow his uncle had connived him back into the *Times* and this old man in front of him looked ready to throw him out into the street if he said the wrong thing right now. He took a breath. "Yes sir, that'll do just fine."

"Very good then. Baker, help get Mr. North settled, then show him to his luxury accommodations upstairs." He turned back to Julian. "You can make use of yourself by getting your things where they belong. We start the business day at eight o'clock."

"Yes sir," said Julian, picking up his bag.

Willoughby took a step back into his office but then turned back to Julian. "You know, Mr. North, the question you *should* have asked about Wilder was: 'What's she doing at the embassy, and what's all the commotion about?' A good journalist is always inquisitive but only about things that matter." He then stepped back into his office and closed the door.

Julian shifted his weight and looked at Baker. "So what's going on at the embassy?"

"Actually, I haven't the slightest idea," said Baker, scratching the side of his nose.

CHAPTER 5

Julian spent the rest of the day acclimating himself to his new surroundings and waiting for his trunk from *Sussex*. When it was getting late and the trunk still hadn't arrived, he decided to take Baker up on his offer to join him for dinner at a nearby restaurant that served western food, then went to bed early. His room on the second floor of the office was furnished with a bed, dresser, desk and chair. A blanket and sheets were folded neatly at the foot of the bed. The walls and floors were bare. A cooling breeze flowed through a window that overlooked the flat roof of the attached, single story building next door.

He made the bed, took off his clothes and turned out the gas lamp. He was dead tired but found himself lying there staring up at the dark ceiling feeling the room swaying around him as if he were still aboard *Sussex*. Adding to his consternation was the poor impression he'd made with Mr. Willoughby who had it in his head that he was his new assistant journalist.

It was well past midnight when Julian finally fell into a restless sleep.

The warm sunlight streaming in through the curtains woke him. He tossed off the covers and checked the time – already half-past eight. He pulled on yesterday's rumpled clothes and stepped into his shoes and was halfway down the stairs when he saw the woman who must be Wilder. He stopped.

In a frumpy blue dress she sat at her desk leaning over her work. He could see the side of her face but not much more. She didn't look up so maybe she hadn't noticed him yet. Slower now, he continued to the base of the stairs and as he walked closer, she turned. Her eyes were brown with a touch of amber. She had a petite, feminine turn to her nose that blended with her rounded chin and cheeks. Her long black hair fell across her shoulders. Julian swallowed. Wilder was beautiful.

"You must be Mr. North," she said, holding out her hand.

Julian stood a little straighter. "Mr. North, yes, that would surely be me, all right." He smiled. "A bit late, but here just the same...Miss Wilder?" He took her hand and met a firm grip.

"Yes, that would surely be me – call me Kate." She gave his hand a single shake then released it.

He told her to call him Julian as he sat down at his desk and looked over some work Willoughby had left for him. For the time being he decided to play his role as the new assistant journalist. He positioned the stack of papers neatly in front of him just as Kate had positioned hers. Why was he suddenly so nervous?

"Tea's over there," said Kate.

"Thank you, this has not been a good day so far."

"What could have possibly gone wrong already?" she asked.

Julian poured his tea and explained that his trunk had not yet arrived from the docks and that he'd had no choice but to wear his shipboard clothes. "And I didn't sleep well," he added, "need to get my land legs back I guess."

"It was a long voyage. It's understandable that you'd need time to readjust." She sounded sympathetic but kept up with her writing.

Julian sat down at his desk and occupied himself with tapping the tip of his pencil on the desktop. He stole a look at Kate, noticing the graceful way her dark hair draped over her neck and across the fabric of her dress. He imagined her in a dress fitting more tightly about her shoulders and across her breasts. He stopped tapping his pencil when she raised her eyes.

"Something wrong, Mr. North?"

"What was that?" Julian asked, shifting his gaze, feeling a hot wave of blood rushing to his face.

Kate put her pen down. "Is something wrong?"

Julian felt his eyes widening. "No, nothing's wrong. I'll get to work then."

"That would be a good idea."

Julian's experience with women was limited. Having spent his formative years in LaPorte County Indiana, he had been confused with England's more formal gender boundaries and had relationships with only two British girls. The first and more casual of these had been with a serving girl at Molly's. The second was with a girl he'd met at a bakery who'd left him when he confessed to her that he was a clerk with the *Times*, not a journalist as he'd led her to believe. She'd taken the news angrily, blaming him for wasting her time when she needed to find a man with a more promising future.

Julian ruefully contemplated this new situation. He was attracted by Kate's beauty while, at least so far, being put off by her stiff manner. Adding to that, her position in the office made her his boss. *A woman for a boss?* Well, there was a ridiculous idea.

The work left for him by Willoughby involved transcribing a pad of notes he had taken earlier in the week about the recent opening of a new training school for young Turkish seamen. Several retired British officers were to be instructors. Julian easily deciphered Willoughby's scrawled handwriting, inserting proper spelling and grammar as he went. Flipping over a page, he glanced at Kate. Absorbed in her own work, she seemed to be taking no further notice of him. He supposed that she must have her share of admirers. Going back to Willoughby's notes, he silently read a quote:

> *It is one thing to strengthen the Turkish navy so as to oppose Russian expansion. It is quite another to hand over our strategies and tactics to a nation that cannot even be trusted with its own affairs.* - E

"Who is '*E*'?" Julian wondered aloud.

"It's Sir Edward – our ambassador," said Kate, without looking up.

"Thank you."

"You're welcome."

He had a new thought. "I was wondering, maybe you could fill me in on the goings-on at the embassy last night."

"I sent out my notes on that already, and I'm nearly finished with my follow-up story. Perhaps you'd like to proofread it?"

From her tone Julian surmised that she fully expected him to decline so he decided to rise to the challenge. "I'd be happy to. But, I wouldn't presume to proofread *your* work here on my first day."

Kate gave no reaction. "It's quite all right. I'll be sure to be proofreading *your* work – once you produce some." She held out the pages to him. "There's to be a celebration later this year to commemorate the fifth anniversary of the Turkish constitution."

Julian took the papers. "That's it? That's the big news?"

"Yes. Sir Edward announced it last night. You'll find he has a flair for the theatrical. He tries to compensate for our mundane political scene by dramatizing every little thing that happens. Each year at the embassy ball he shows up dressed as Richard III - walks around hunched over with a limp the whole time."

"Sounds like an interesting fellow," said Julian.

"Flamboyant, is the best word - a flagrant self-promoter. He actually *requires* that we interview him and do a story on him twice a year."

Julian turned his attention to Kate's pages. Her writing was competent and complete, he thought, but a little too tidy for him. He decided to add a few flourishes, conscious of her glare as he penned his changes. "A celebration of the Turkish constitution should be very exciting indeed," he concluded, handing back the pages.

Kate rifled through them. "Thank you for your suggestions."

"Glad to be of service, Kate." He was pleased with himself. He felt as if he had the upper hand, which, with his experience at the London office, was only right. For the time being he ignored the inner voice that reminded him that his experience had been as a file clerk, not a journalist.

At nine-thirty, a Turkish boy came into the office. The bell over the door announced him noisily. Maybe fifteen years old, guessed Julian - bright black eyes, a dark native complexion and a handsome smile.

"This is Steven," said Kate, explaining that he helped out in the office as a messenger, clerk, translator, and janitor. "He grew up an orphan and came to my father's mission when he was only three. We taught him English, arithmetic, geography and religion."

"Hello, I'm Julian North, a journalist from the London office." Julian just couldn't bring himself to say he was an *assistant* journalist – or a file clerk. He ignored Kate's glance as he shook Steven's hand then quipped: "Sounds like you're ready for Oxford."

Steven immediately shook his head. "I'm planning on Cambridge. I've never been to England but I've been saving for a long time. I should have enough in three years."

Julian was impressed. "Good for you. My uncle may have some connections there. I can speak to him about you when the time comes."

Steven glowed at the offer and had just finished saying how indebted he'd be for such a recommendation when the bell over the door jingled again.

A long-haired man whose muscular build was well displayed by a gray sleeveless shirt bumped through the door carrying a large black trunk. Once inside, he stood there for a moment then let it fall to the floor with a loud bang.

Kate jumped.

"Good God," yelled Willoughby from upstairs, "what the hell was that?"

"Just my trunk, Mr. Willoughby," Julian shouted back.

"You're North then?" asked the man. "Sign here if you please."

Julian did so then paid the fellow with one of his Turkish lira notes.

"I can't make change sir."

"That's all right, put the extra on my account for when I need you again," said Julian, noticing the look this drew from Kate. The man left and Steven helped Julian carry the trunk upstairs.

"You don't expect to be here long then?" asked Kate when Julian came back down and took his seat.

"Why do you think that?"

"You told the dock man you'd be needing him again."

Julian shrugged, "I'll be here a few months at least, maybe more."

Kate nodded, digesting that information but not questioning him further. "It was nice of you to offer your help to Steven – with his college I mean."

"My uncle knows a lot of people. It was his help I was offering. You said your father has a mission here?"

"He did; he died three years ago."

"I'm sorry."

"It's all right." And with that, Kate dove back into her work.

Willoughby came down at ten, dressed neatly, looking nothing like he had at Julian's first meeting. They all exchanged good-mornings then, with the toe of his shoe, Willoughby became preoccupied with smoothing over a gouge left in the floor by Julian's trunk. Once done with that, he raised his head. "So, how're we getting on?"

"Just fine, I think," said Julian, trying to catch Kate's eye.

"Perfectly," said Kate, her gaze fixed on Willoughby.

"Excellent! I'd hoped you'd hit it off. You've got enough to do, I take it?"

Even though this question had been directed at Julian it was Kate who answered crisply.

"He's got enough to fill the morning and I'll be sending more over to him this afternoon."

Julian winced at the remark that was clearly intended to put him in his place. He then felt the sting of her glance that seemed to be to be telling him: *Please try to keep up Mr. North.*

CHAPTER 6

At the outer gates to the Yildiz Palace, across the harbor from where Julian wondered what he'd gotten himself into, a covered carriage pulled up. Seated inside, a man dressed in a plain white tunic, parted the curtain. He would have had an average appearance were it not for his emerald green, almond shaped eyes which, in the dim light within the carriage, seemed to give off a light of their own. The man had long ago given up his birthname and was now known only as Pavel. He watched as the captain of the guard examined the papers that had been handed to him by his driver.

The captain glanced inside the carriage. "You are alone?"

Pavel parted the curtain further. "As you can see."

The captain looked closer then backed away and gave the papers back to the driver. He shouted an order and two of his men mounted up as the iron gates opened. "They will escort you inside," he said.

With a snap of the reins the carriage lurched forward down a long straight drive before entering into a gentle curve that skirted a landscaped central courtyard.

The Yildiz Palace was a complex of interconnected mansions and pavilions. There, Sultan Abdul Hamid II ruled a troubled Ottoman Empire that stretched from the Dardanelles to the Egyptian border. The palace and grounds were not the opulent courts of Europe but from the high bluff overlooking Istanbul they served their purpose of generating the proper amounts of respect and fear in the hearts of the citizens below.

The carriage continued around the courtyard. It passed the

main entrance to the palace itself then travelled another two-hundred yards stopping at a small, marble block building which stood alone on a low rise. Pavel opened the door and stepped down then allowed himself to be searched by the guards posted there.

"Your associate has already arrived," said one of the guards. Pavel nodded but said nothing. His associate, Yuri Chekov, was a former aristocrat turned assassin who both talents flaws. Pavel hadn't seen Yuri in months and he hoped he'd been able to keep their current crisis under control; that was his job after all.

Two guards led the way inside, down a flight of stairs and into a wide corridor lit by oil lamps that flickered as they passed. Pavel kept his features calm but his nerves were strung tight, ready for anything. Betrayal was commonplace within alliances like the one he'd crafted with the Ottomans and he knew that if he and Yuri were killed here, no one would ever know. But, risks had to be taken and for Pavel, risks had always been a way of life.

He had been born French but was raised as a Russian to have a knack, even a love, for the violence and rebellion through which mankind bettered itself with each generation. Socio-political evolution was for some a painful, tragic process. For Pavel it was natural and essential, endowed with a peculiar beauty.

The bloody streets of Paris had been his first training grounds then he'd moved on to St. Petersburg and finally to the finest courts of Western Europe, North America and Asia. He learned customs and cultures and the art of diplomacy. And he also learned that the more civilized a people thought themselves to be, the more subtle the hand of violence must be - more of an undercurrent, secretive and discrete. The more primitive societies required no such subtleties. Through it all Pavel had had a teacher, Dmitry Leonov, who'd taught him everything from swordsmanship and marksmanship, to mathematics, languages and the finer points of genteel society. His teacher was dead now, killed a year ago in St. Petersburg as a result of Yuri's carelessness. Pavel was thankful for all Dmitry had taught him but he was also thankful to be finally on his own, free to do what had to be done to achieve his destiny. As for Yuri, he must find a way to redeem himself.

And then there was the problem of the book.

The guards stopped. "In here," one said, motioning Pavel into a chamber where three men were seated. One of them, Yuri, got to his feet. He wore a western suit, was tall and dark skinned and had a scraggly beard that didn't hide the nasty scar across his left cheek. Pavel knew the two Turks still seated but gave no word of greeting to them or to Yuri as he sat and as Yuri retook his seat.

Pavel eyed General Ahmed Ali seated opposite him. The man was clean-shaven with a prominent jaw and he wore the brown with red-trim uniform of the Turkish Army. His arms were folded and his visored hat lay in front of him on the table.

To Pavel's left, with his silver-gray beard and formal black robes of governmental office, sat Ismail Kahn-Mohammad, Foreign Minister of the Ottoman Empire.

Ismail shouted to the guards: "Leave us and close the door." He waited, then folded his hands in front of him. He spoke in Turkish, which was well understood by everyone at the table. "Our mission has been authorized."

"This is good news," said Pavel in an even voice, "but what do we know of the British? It's been weeks now."

"The Prince of Wales has accepted our invitation. They have not yet made this information public but everything is in order. The English seem to be cooperating."

Pavel stiffened. "Seem to be? Either they are cooperating or they are not. We need a *firm* assurance, otherwise we cannot participate."

Ismail met Pavel's gaze squarely. "They *are* cooperating, there will be no mistakes."

"And what of Egypt?" asked General Ali, fingering his cap. "I understand they are having trouble controlling their army these days. They are said to be in outright rebellion. Can we expect them to be ready when they are needed?"

"With the prize we are offering, Egypt has already promised its support," said Ismail.

"Let's hope they have the power and the will to keep their promise," said Ali hitting his knuckle against the table. "Any ground we gain cannot be held without the Egyptians." He turned in his chair as if he were about to rise and walk out.

Pavel stared at the general, interested in this discord between the two Turks. It made little difference to him, but it was interesting just the same.

The foreign minister placed a reassuring hand on the table. "I will handle the Egyptians, they are not your worry," he said.

General Ali glared back then folded his arms again as the discussion continued, this time going over plans and preparations all of which were well known to Pavel. Still, his heart quickened as he pondered the grand scope of the operation. Yuri had known none of it and didn't say much but his eyes grew wide as the meeting wore on.

When done, Ismail slid his chair back and stood up. He looked at the general, then at Pavel. "I am trusting you to help restore the integrity and power of the Ottoman Empire. Our methods are unorthodox but our cause is just. We are only taking back what is ours."

Inwardly, Pavel sneered at this remark. The support of *The Will of the People* was on loan to the Turks for one reason only and it had nothing to do with the integrity of their empire.

When the meeting ended, Ismail left with Ali, leaving Pavel alone in the chamber with Yuri. He spoke in Russian, his voice low: "Where is the book? Do you have it?"

Yuri hesitated. "The thief sent it to his brother in London. He was going to sell it to the foreign office."

Pavel drew back, astonished. "Sell it to the British Foreign Office?" He cursed under his breath. "How did they find out about it and how could you have let this happen?"

"I did all I could, I was lucky to escape with my life."

Pavel stood, hands on the table and leaned toward Yuri like a lion about to pounce. "There is more in this book than you know. It is *sacred*," he said in a fierce whisper. He banged a fist into the table. "First, you get Dmitry killed, now as we are about to take action to restore the revolution of our fathers, you have our plans sent to the British. I swear by the bones of the one-hundred, if we fail because of your stupidity, I will kill you myself."

Yuri lowered his eyes then lowered his head. "I will die by my own hand before I let that happen. I cannot change what is already done."

Pavel waited for a moment then sat back down struggling to contain his rage. "Do you know anything else about the book?"

"Yes," said Yuri, raising his head slightly. "Our man in London was nearly able to recover it. The British don't yet realize its significance. It's being translated by an underling. By the time they discover our secrets it will be too late for them."

"Where is the book now?"

Yuri smiled thinly, his scar creasing in a way that looked painful. "Our people tell me that it's here in Istanbul. I *will* get it back."

"Here? Why is it here? This cannot be a coincidence. Who has it?"

"The underling...the translator - his name is Julian North."

Pavel rubbed his chin at this strange turn of events. He knew Yuri was not a weak man but he had failed him with Dmitry and he'd failed him again with the book. But Pavel was running out of time and had no better choice; he had to trust Yuri now. "Do whatever you have to do," he told him. "We cannot let them know our secrets – not now."

CHAPTER 7

At the end of his third day in Istanbul, after Kate had left, Julian walked to the rear of the office. He was unsure if Willoughby was in but he heard no sound coming from behind his closed door as he passed. He felt a little uneasy but told himself that he wasn't really doing anything wrong. As part of the office staff, at least in Willoughby's mind, he would of course have access to the office files that were stored in ten tall cabinets which stood behind the staircase.

He started going through the index of alphabetized file cards that sat atop one of the cabinets. Unsure of where to begin, he took a stab in the dark, looking up *Karmonov* – nothing there. *Castlenau* – nothing. He looked up *Russian* and found many different file headings and cross references: *Acts of War, Anarchists, Crimes of, Politics of* and so on. Julian tapped his finger on the edge of the card, deciding to check *anarchists* next.

"Looking for something Mr. North?"

Julian's heart skipped as he turned. "Mr. Willoughby, you surprised me."

"Yes, I can see that." Willoughby held his hat, regarding Julian from his office door. "I don't think I formally introduced you to our files. Are you finding everything all right? Are you searching for something in particular?"

"Just a personal project of mine. I thought I'd work on it after hours."

Willoughby waited, as if expecting Julian to tell him more. "We have a small office here, Mr. North and we have a habit of helping each other out from time to time. There's not much call for secrets."

Julian had decided to keep his Castlenau business to himself but found himself torn. A veteran newspaper man who'd spent years in Istanbul would have information that was more useful than anything he might find in the files. If he was going to trust anyone here it would be Willoughby. Besides, he wouldn't have to tell him everything. "Maybe I could use a little help," he said.

This elicited a slight smile. "Have you had your dinner yet? You can tell me about your project while we eat. I know a good place. We can work on the files when we get back." Willoughby put on his hat and headed for the door. "Well, come on now, I'm hungry."

The sun was nearly down, the air moderate and breezy and, as they walked, Willoughby pointed out a building two doors down. "This is Mrs. Potter's place. It's a small boarding house for the unmarried women who work in the area. Kate lives here."

"She doesn't have far to walk then."

"Yes, it's pretty handy for her."

After another block, they turned a corner and came to one of the few stand-alone buildings in the area. The sign over the front door read, *Molly's*.

"It's named after a place in London near Printing House Square. You might be familiar with it," explained Willoughby.

"I was just there a few days before leaving."

"Yes, well you'll find this place quite different."

Inside, they were met by an older man, British, in a white apron who smiled broadly at Willoughby then ushered them to a table. Patrons, mostly men in business dress, dotted the poorly lit room, their conversation providing a low buzz punctuated every now and then by a burst of laughter or a shout for a waiter.

"You're right. It's nothing like the Molly's I know," said Julian after they were seated. He ran his hand across the linen table cloth. No crumbs or beer-puddles here.

They ordered and were served quickly.

Julian knifed into a thick slice of meat charred black on the outside and just as black inside.

"I should have warned you about the beef," Willoughby explained as Julian chewed. "They cook things differently here. The wine's good though, don't you think? You won't find many places that serve it. Alcohol is legal here in the western quarter, but it's frowned upon everywhere else in the country."

Julian nodded and took a swallow. "The meat's as tough as the sole of an old shoe. It has an interesting flavor to it though. Is that curry they use?"

"Curry, paprika, sage, and the good Lord knows what else," said Willoughby, working at his fish with enthusiasm. "Because of the year-round heat they've got a spoilage problem, especially with beef."

"The spices keep the meat from spoiling?"

Willoughby laughed. "No, they just keep the meat from *tasting* spoiled. And," he added, pointing to Julian's plate with his fork, "they blacken it through like that to cover up its green tinge."

"Green?"

"Like I said, I should have warned you. But, no matter, I'm sure you'll live."

Julian gave up on the meat for the moment and took in a fork full of what looked like spinach. He picked up a slice of coarse bread.

"So," said Willoughby, "you seem to be doing well here – getting along with Wilder?"

"Well enough. She doesn't care much for me, I don't think."

"She's just testing you. It's her way of getting to know you. She's a wonderfully creative person. I've known her a long time – since her school days."

"How did she come to be working for you?"

"I knew her father, Henry Wilder; a strange man who left his wife in America to come over here to convert the Turks to Christianity. Oddest of all, he brought Kate with him. She was the eldest of his three daughters. It's funny how an intelligent man can get a notion to do a thing like that. His wife apparently had more sense and refused to go with him – insisted, rightfully so, on keeping her other daughters back in America. At any rate, Henry would come by the office now and again with article submissions or with one of his letters to the editor, and he always brought Kate with him. She made it her business to learn as much as she could about writing and drawing and about newspapers. She was an inquisitive girl, still is, and she was a real talent from the start. Her father died several years ago, the result of an infected boil - a most hideous thing, sickens me even now to think of it." Willoughby made a sound of revulsion and took a sip of wine. "Kate was nearly of age by that time and, after corresponding with her mother, she decided to stay on. She asked for a position at the paper and of course I was glad to have her. As you've seen, Kate's a strong woman and knows what she wants."

"Yes, I've noticed." Julian finished off the spinach and took another bite of bread following it with some wine. He eyed his meat again with suspicion.

"And how about you?" asked Willoughby. "I suppose with your uncle in the newspaper business, your place at the *Times* was pre-ordained. Yet you told Baker you were no longer with the paper. I take it something must have gone wrong."

"Yes, things did go wrong. I'd only been at the *Times* for a few months when my uncle decided that I wasn't going to work out as a journalist. He made me a file clerk. That's why I left."

"Emory told me you'd been with the society pages. He didn't say you worked the files. I just assumed... but no matter, you're here now and I need you to be a journalist so, as long as you stay at the office, that's what you'll be. I've seen that you're able to string words together in their proper order. The rest you can learn."

Julian pushed his plate aside and locked eyes with Willoughby. "Thanks Mr. Willoughby. I'll do my best. But that's not why I came to Istanbul."

"Kate thinks you're here spying for Emory because he's looking to close us down, and for all I know, she's right. Emory's always pestering me about our expenses being too high."

Julian smiled at the idea. "I'm not spying for anyone."

"All right, so tell me, why are you here?"

Julian folded his arms, resting them on the edge of the table. It was time to trust Willoughby with the truth – at least with some of it. "Two months ago a friend of mine was murdered in London."

Willoughby put down his wine glass and Julian continued.

"I was almost killed too, by the same man. I don't know much about him except that he was on his way to Istanbul."

"That's terrible of course but how did you know he was headed for Istanbul? And in any event, why didn't you just let the police handle things."

"The killer had a steam ship schedule. A ship bound for Istanbul was circled."

"That seems a little flimsy. What did the police think?"

Julian was having a hard time drawing the line between what he would tell Willoughby and what he wouldn't; but he'd gone this far. "The police don't know about the murder."

Willoughby sat back in his chair and spoke slowly as if he were starting to disbelieve Julian. "If a man was killed, how could they not know? Who was the victim?"

"He was my employer, a Russian, it was after I left the *Times*. He'd hired me to translate an old journal, written in French. The killer wanted it back."

"Your employer was killed for a journal?"

"It was a book about a revolution, written by a man named Castlenau."

Willoughby's eyes flickered for an instant. He lowered his voice. "Do you still have it?"

"No, it's in London. You've heard of the book then?"

"No, not the book," said Willoughby. "I have heard of Castlenau though. That's why you were looking through our files; you were looking for information on Castlenau."

"Yes. I'd only just started when you interrupted me."

Willoughby glanced at his watch. "It's getting late. I suggest we finish up here and get back."

Julian insisted on paying for the meal and peeled off a bill from his money clip leaving a generous gratuity.

"Thank you for paying," said Willoughby, standing, "but you ought to keep your cash to yourself. Places like this are frequented by unscrupulous men looking for a lucrative target."

"Right, I'll remember that next time," said Julian, glad he was only carrying a small portion of his bank roll. The rest he kept hidden in his room.

They left Molly's and walked back to the office at a brisk pace. Once inside, Willoughby hung up his hat and placed his keys on his desk. He went over to the files and pulled two stools out from beneath an adjoining table then lit a cigar and took a puff as they both sat. "Few people know the name Castlenau but many know and fear the anarchist group he's supposed to have started. They call themselves *The Will of the People*. We can start with that file over there." He pointed. "Look under '*W*.'"

Julian pulled open the file and extracted a thick folder labeled: *Will of the People*. It was the first of two folders. He handed it to Willoughby.

"It's roughly chronological," said Willoughby, spreading its contents over the table. With the notes, newspaper clippings and photographs they were slowly able to assemble the history of the anarchist group.

A bombing at a Vienna train station in 1822 was the first time anyone had heard of them. Other bombings and the occasional murder peppered the next few decades until the most recent and the most audacious incident - the assassination of Czar Alexander in St. Petersburg. Their leader was a shadowy figure named Dmitry but there was no direct information on him in the files and nothing of any consequence had been heard from *The Will of the People* since the Czar's assassination.

Julian chose one of the many clippings and skimmed through

it. "It says the Russian police tried and hanged seven people in connection with the Czar's assassination. All were members of *The Will of the People*, but the actual assassin who threw the bomb got away. How would they know that the assassin wasn't among the seven?"

Willoughby uncrossed his legs. "You won't find this in the files but there were two witnesses who each described the killer as having a prominent scar on his face. None of the seven did. And as I remember it, there were two bombs. The first one exploded under an escort carriage; the second was thrown directly at the Czar when he stopped to investigate the damage caused by the first bomb. It was the second bomb that killed him."

"How did you first hear of Castlenau?" asked Julian.

"It was by mistake really," said Willoughby through a yawn. "I overheard a conversation in a back-alley café here in Istanbul. I was young, more adventurous than now and I knew some Turkish but didn't let on that I did. All I heard was the phrase: 'Castlenau's *Will of the People*'. For some reason it stuck in my head. My only other time hearing that name was tonight when you mentioned it."

Julian's hopes fell. "So you don't actually know anything about him?"

Willoughby shook his head. "No, I do not. This Dmitry fellow could be the son of the original Castlenau but that's just a guess. There are some who believe that Dmitry was killed in the same explosion that killed Alexander. The bombing was about a year ago now so it would explain why his group's been relatively quiet since."

"Because they lost their leader."

"Yes." Willoughby rubbed his forehead. "I know that none of this is helping you finding your killer. Would you recognize the man if you saw him again?"

"Absolutely."

Willoughby began gathering the notes and clippings off the table and placing them back in the folder. He gave it back to Julian. "Pull out the other *Will of the People* folder. I think it contains some camera pictures, some quite recent."

Julian found the stack of photographs – about an inch thick, tied together with a blue band. He undid the band and sat back down, going through the photographs one by one. Each was taped to an information card.

The first few were posed front and side facial images of men he didn't recognize. Then he came to a series of photographs of bodies, grotesque in death, some with ghastly wounds.

"Most of them were taken by the Turkish police," explained Willoughby, "and each man is a confirmed member of the *Will of the People*."

Julian got to the last in the stack and shook his head. "I don't see him."

Willoughby shrugged. "I'm not surprised, but it was worth a try."

Julian fingered one of the information cards. "What's this notation here?" He pointed to the lower right hand corner where the letters PM had been written.

"That indicates the source."

"The source?

"Of the information. In this case a picture."

"So PM is a person? Whoever he is he must know a lot about *The Will of the People*. His initials are on nearly every one of these cards and on some of the others I've seen."

"His name is Peter McNaulty and I would stay clear of him if I were you. He's ruthless, unscrupulous, and greedy. The information we have from him in these files was purchased at great expense."

"How does he know so much?"

"He's the go-between; the conduit for communication between our embassy and *The Will of the People*. He actually did us some good a few years ago during the Russian crisis. Every now and then, when he needs extra money, he leaks information my way - a really distasteful chap."

Julian was intrigued. Maybe McNaulty knew Karmonov's killer. "How would I find him?"

Willoughby creased his forehead. "You won't. You'll stay away from him and we'll leave it at that." He glanced at the clock. "I'm going to bed. Sorry I wasn't more help." He got up with a grunt, went into his office for a small kerosene lamp, then headed up the stairs.

A week passed, then two, each spent by Julian going over all the information he could find on *The Will of the People* while still working on the code. He found nothing new from the files and was becoming convinced that the only way to move things forward was to find Peter McNaulty. Over this time Julian also dealt with the increasing amount of office work that Willoughby required of him to earn his keep. Most of this amounted to organizing field notes and cross-checking information for articles written by Willoughby or by Kate, but then Willoughby began assigning him small stories of his own. He took these on as a challenge to enliven a mundane story with colorful and engaging descriptions that both Kate and Willoughby seemed incapable of. But, far from being impressed, Willoughby marked up his first two-page effort, cutting it down to a half page with a note scrawled across the bottom: *You must get to the point! Heed the word-count!*

His next story suffered the same fate but, through the course of another week, he was able to earn from Willoughby the note: *Better!* When an article that was mostly his made it into print he was disappointed to see the C. Willoughby by-line beneath it.

"Everything that comes out of this office, mine or yours, is under his name," explained Kate from her desk. "That's just the way it's done. I would think you'd know that. But then you're not really a journalist are you? You're just here working on some secret project." She gave Julian a stern look. "Why do you even care about the by-line?"

"What did Willoughby tell you?"

"He didn't tell me anything. I'm not stupid, Mr. North, I know there's something going on and it has nothing to do with good journalism." At that moment, the clock struck five. She stood up and put her shawl over her shoulders and walked out, slamming the door behind her.

Throughout Julian's whole time in Istanbul Kate had remained aloof and businesslike, resisting his every effort at being friendly. He even made the tea one morning which she was quick to criticize as being too weak and not nearly hot enough. And now she'd taken to calling him Mr. North and putting her nose where it didn't belong. What was wrong with the woman?

Julian was still staring at the closed door when Willoughby stepped out of his office, hat in hand. "I couldn't help overhearing you and Wilder. I think it's time we had another chat."

They went to Molly's again and over dinner Willoughby told Julian that he was pleased to see that his writing was showing a definite improvement. That was the good news. The bad news was that Willoughby was getting damn tired of the tension between him and Kate and he told him that it was up to him to put an end to it. He had no suggestions as to how to do this but did point out over a second glass of wine that Julian seemed to be innovative enough to figure something out. It was dark by the time they returned to the office.

Willoughby tossed his keys on his desk, and lit his kerosene lamp. He sat down heavily and rubbed his eyes then regarded Julian. "She's a woman. Talk to her. You have talked to women before, haven't you? Maybe you need to trust her before she trusts you. But I'm no expert in any of that. Just fix it, damn it. Now, if you'll excuse me, I've got some work to finish before turning in."

As Julian headed up the stairs, he heard the release of a bottle cork. Must be a little unfinished brandy Willoughby's tending to, he thought, turning down the darkened hallway toward his room. Except for his own footsteps, the building was quiet but, as he reached his door, the floorboards creaked behind him. He turned abruptly, catching his breath when he saw a man standing perfectly still, no more than ten steps away.

"You are Julian North?" asked the man in a low voice, his face in darkness, his accent unmistakably eastern. He came closer.

Julian's heart sank when he saw the gun in the man's hand. How could he have gotten in? Julian forced himself to be calm. "Who are you?" he demanded. His voice shook even as he tried to keep it steady.

The man was only a step away now. Julian could hear his breathing, slow and mechanical. He could see the glint of the gun barrel where the man held it just inches from his chest. "You know what I want."

Willoughby had warned him this might happen; he'd flashed his cash in public once too often. Julian reached into his jacket pocket. "Here, take my money."

The man jabbed the gun hard into Julian's ribs. He grabbed his wrist then moved forward, shoving Julian hard against the door. Julian felt the man's hot breath on his ear then caught a whiff of cologne suggesting he might be something more than just a back-street criminal.

"Give me the book, Mr. North, or I will take your life."

Julian drew in a breath. He knew this man wasn't Karmonov's killer but he had to be somehow associated with him. And he thinks he still has the journal. Julian fixed his eyes on the gun. If he told the man he didn't have the journal, he might just pull the trigger killing him then and there. A picture of himself lying dead on the floor in a pool of blood just like one of Willoughby's photographs flashed through his mind. Julian swallowed. "Kill me and you'll never get it back," he managed, trying to sound threatening.

The man cocked his gun. He pressed Julian harder against the door but was distracted from behind by footsteps on the stairs. *Willoughby was coming up.*

The man raised the gun to the tip of Julian's nose. "Quiet," he said under his breath, backing away toward the stairs.

Julian could move now and he saw his chance. He lunged for the gun, but was too slow. The man side-stepped him deftly and slammed the pistol across the side of his face. Julian fell in a heap.

Stunned, Julian struggled to all fours. He perceived the blurry glow of Willoughby's lamp moving in time with his footsteps, coming up the stairs. In its light he saw the gunman's face and the jagged scar that ran across his cheek. "Run, Willoughby!" Julian gasped, pulling himself up.

In the same instant, the man pointed the gun down the stairs and fired. The loud report and the bright flash jarred Julian's senses. He heard a scream and a crash. The light from the staircase went out. *He had killed Willoughby.*

Julian realized he could only save himself now. He ran into his room and slammed the door shut behind him. He wedged his sea trunk against the door and hurried to the window. Five feet below lay the roof of the adjoining building. The door behind him rattled violently against the trunk.

Julian jerked the window open and climbed out then dropped onto the roof. He gained his footing on the gritty surface and ran to the edge overlooking the deserted street. There was no way down from there and it was too far to jump. From the still open window he could hear the door to his room burst open. He had only one choice now. Julian raced for the brick wall of the adjoining three-story building fifty yards distant. He glanced back. The gunman was on the roof, raising his gun.

Julian jerked to one side, hoping to throw off the man's aim, but the shot never came. He heard the man running from behind, gaining on him. Julian adjusted his direction, heading for a window in the next building just above the roof line - it was his only chance.

"Stop!" shouted the man behind him.

Julian charged for the window. He was almost to it. At the last possible moment, he raised his arms and crossed them over his face. He leaped forward and, in a hail of shattering glass and splintering wood, sailed through with a loud crash. His head slammed into something hard that fell back taking him with it.

Julian wasn't aware of having lost consciousness but at the sound of voices and a light coming closer he had a sense that some amount of time had passed. He lay face down on a wooden floor. His head throbbed.

"Who are you? Are you all right?" The man's voice was vaguely familiar.

Julian rolled over, eyes open, shards of glass tinkling off him.

"Julian!" This voice was female and there was no mistaking it.

"Kate?" he asked groggily. "What are you doing here?"

The lamp came closer, directly over his face.

"Julian, I live here. What are *you* doing here? Why would you do such a thing?"

Julian saw the shock and anger in Kate's face, then beside her, he saw Noah. *What was he doing here?* Julian rubbed the top of his head then jerked his hand away, as it was cut by a shard of glass. Sitting upright, he glanced at the shattered window. "There was a man, he had a gun."

Noah looked outside. "There's no one out there now."

Julian got slowly to his feet, more glass falling off. "He must have gone back into the office." Hoping to clear his clouded mind, he ran his hand tentatively through his hair again, then stopped. "Oh God," he said to Kate, "he shot Willoughby. We've got to get over there."

"Shot Willoughby? But...oh my God..."

Julian stumbled around Kate and ran out of the room. He passed a few women in their nightgowns as he raced down the stairs, his head splitting in pain at every step. Once out on the street, he heard Kate and Noah close behind. They made it to the office. There was a light inside. Julian tried the door. "Locked." He positioned himself to break it down.

"Wait, I've got a key," said Kate, shouldering him aside. She opened it and they rushed in toward the glow of a lamp coming from Willoughby's office. But there, on the floor, was something else.

Julian stopped short. "It's him. That's the gunman." He stared down at the body of a man lying face up just outside Willoughby's open door. He saw the scar on his cheek, a wild beard, deep-set eyes still open wide. Bits of glass were scattered around the body.

"Don't worry, he's dead," said Willoughby from his office sitting behind his desk. In front of him was a half-empty brandy bottle. Beside that lay a pistol.

"You *killed* him?" asked Kate.

"Damn right I killed him. I was coming up the stairs, going to bed, when this fellow fires his gun at me from up there." Willoughby pointed to the top of the stairs. "His bullet hit the lamp I was carrying. Damn thing exploded right in my hand cutting the hell out of it." He raised his left hand, which was wrapped in a bloodied cloth. "Somehow the flame went out - a damn good thing too. Otherwise, we'd have had a hell of a fire. He must have thought he hit me though because he went back up the stairs – to take care of you, I suppose." He pointed at Julian with the bloody towel.

"He chased me across the roof," said Julian.

"What would he want with you?" Kate asked Julian.

"Money; he was after money," said Julian, ignoring Willoughby's dubious glance.

"Did he say anything to you?" Kate persisted.

"Not a word. He just pointed his gun at me and shoved me against the wall. I'm only alive because Mr. Willoughby decided to come up the stairs. I tried to get his gun but couldn't. When he fired, I escaped out onto the roof. He came after me."

"And when he couldn't get you," continued Willoughby, "he came back down here." He smiled and patted the gun. "He wasn't ready for me – or for the slippery lamp oil that had splattered all over the stairs. Hell of a night." The old man was clearly pleased with the sequence of events then caught sight of Noah. "Who in blazes are you?"

"And how did you happen to be with Kate?" Julian asked, recalling his earlier confusion on that point.

Kate's blushing cheeks gave Julian the answer. She turned to Willoughby and made an awkward introduction.

"You're Sanford? From the New York *Times*?" asked Willoughby in an accusing tone. "I've heard about you. You're working with Ira Goldsmith, aren't you?" Then he gave a cry of frustration. "Can we *never* have a story all to ourselves, even when it occurs in our own bloody office?"

Noah raised both hands. "Oh it's quite all right. I won't publish a word –at least not until you have."

"You're damned right you won't," grumbled Willoughby.

"And you just happened to be visiting Kate?" asked Julian.

"That's right," said Noah, indignant. "We met at the embassy on the night you and I arrived."

Julian opened his mouth, but Kate, her jaw set, glared back. "I think, Mr. North, that who comes calling on me is my business – not yours." She then fired a glance at Willoughby. "And not anyone else's either."

Knowing she was right didn't make Julian feel any better. Kate, who had never given him a chance at even a civil conversation, had permitted Noah, whom she barely knew, to call on her. That was not just unfair; it was downright unsettling. What did she see in *him*?

Willoughby cleared his throat. "All right, enough of this. We have a body to take care of." He sent Kate and Noah off to notify the police and told Julian to take a seat beside his desk.

Julian did so, rubbing the bleeding welt on the side of his head. It was pounding like a steam engine.

With one elbow on an armrest, Willoughby rested his chin on his good hand. "I assume that fellow on the floor over there has something to do with this book you translated?"

Julian nodded. "He thought I still had it; that's what he wanted. Did you notice he has a scar on his face just like the Czar's assassin is said to have had?"

"Yes, I noticed. We'll have to tell Sir Edward. His people will want to take a look. If this dead man was in on the assassination he must have been high up in *The Will of the People*. Hell, he might even be their leader Dmitry."

"I tried to stop him and I tried to warn you. He knocked me down then fired at you. All I could do was run."

"You did all you could. We were both lucky." Willoughby grabbed an empty glass, poured some brandy and slid it toward Julian. Then he refilled his own. "I think it's time you told me everything about this book and about your friend who was killed."

Julian took a sip and then another. "The book I translated was Castlenau's Journal, written about eighty years ago. It describes his idea for a world revolution on behalf of the common man. Most of it seemed like philosophical ramblings. It wasn't as if it were a real plan."

"So Castlenau and his book helped spawn *The Will of the People* – it was their bible so to speak. That friend of yours in London who was killed; tell me about him."

Julian told him about Karmonov and about the mysterious Mr. Parker.

"Lots of questions then," said Willoughby, pouring out more brandy. "Interesting though that Karmonov said he obtained the book from a friend in St. Petersburg and our scar-faced friend out there on the floor may have been involved in the Czar's assassination there."

Kate and Noah came back with four, black-shirted policemen and a mustachioed inspector in a western business suit. In halting English, the inspector asked his questions. A picture was taken and the body was removed. The next day, Kate and Julian helped Steven clean up the mess in the office. After having his hand tended to, Willoughby personally notified the British embassy about the incident. When he returned, he called Julian into his office.

"They weren't interested in the least," said Willoughby. "They're too busy with other things to worry about our little break-in."

"What did they say about the man's scar?"

"According to them, half the men in Istanbul have scars on their faces. But they're going to ask the Turks for a copy of the photograph which they'll send to St. Petersburg."

"Did you tell them about the book?"

"No. The book is your affair and I'll leave it to you to tell them...or not."

When Julian returned to his desk Kate raised her head. "What was that all about?" she asked.

Julian shrugged as he sat down. "Nothing much; Mr. Willoughby wants me to find a way to reduce the tension between us. He says we aren't working well together."

"Well, flying through my window in the middle of the night didn't help, and keeping secrets from me here in the office won't help either."

Julian didn't know what to say to that, so he said nothing. He pulled out some work and began writing, but his mind was on other things. He knew now that the scar-faced intruder and the man who killed Karmonov were connected to *The Will of the People* which was connected to the assassination of the Czar. They were the fanatic followers of Castlenau and because of the journal, they were after him.

There was only one thing Julian could think to do: He had to find Peter McNaulty.

CHAPTER 8

It was Steven who told Julian how to find him.

"McNaulty runs a trading company near the docks," he said. "I met him once. I can take you there."

But Julian went alone.

It was windy by the waterfront and the weathered sign reading *Hiller & Fox Importers* creaked on its chains over Julian's head. He stood at the entrance to one of the dozen ramshackle wooden buildings that lined both sides of a gravel road. Gulls circled among the dark, racing clouds. Rain was coming.

Julian knocked and went inside where a thin, narrow-faced man with black matted hair hanging down over his collar looked up from his desk.

"Yes, what do you want?" the man asked gruffly.

"You're Peter McNaulty?"

"I am; what do you want?"

Before Julian could answer, a large fellow stood up from a chair beside an open window in the back of the room, feet spread, arms folded. Like McNaulty, he wore a tan suit, wrinkled and spotted.

"That's my partner, Mr. Wallace."

Julian shared an unpleasant stare with Wallace then said to McNaulty: "I'm here to talk to you about *The Will of the People*."

"So talk."

"I have something they want. I understand you sometimes operate as an intermediary."

"Are you with the embassy?"

"No."

There was a roll of thunder and the clatter of rain began on the roof. The wind picked up and Wallace shut the window.

"If you're not with the embassy, I can't help you," said McNaulty. "I don't know anything about those ruffians and I don't want to. I do know that if you have something they want, they'll find you."

"They killed a friend of mine and they tried to kill me a few nights ago."

McNaulty spread his hands. "There, you see, they found you. So what's the problem?"

"I want to talk with them."

"They're not much good at talking. I'm truly sorry but I can't help you."

Julian pulled out his money-clip and saw the interest in McNaulty's eyes as he peeled off three one hundred-lira notes. "Consider it advance payment for any information you might be able to come up with. My name is Julian North and I'm at the London *Times* office in the western quarter." He placed the money on McNaulty's desk.

"You work for Willoughby? It's unlike him to make such an...investment."

"In this matter, I'm working for myself," said Julian. "You'll be well paid for any information you can provide."

McNaulty picked up the money. "Thank you, Mr. North. I'll keep that in mind."

Julian left and was thoroughly drenched by the time he was able to flag down a carriage that he took back to the office. He'd been moderately encouraged by his visit to McNaulty but, in the weeks that followed, he heard nothing back from the man and wrote it off as another dead end.

Over this time, Noah began stopping by more often. He said he was just checking in to see how Julian was getting along but Julian knew he was only there to see Kate. It bothered him to see the smile she gave him whenever he appeared. Why couldn't he make her smile like that?

In May, the bi-annual interview with Sir Edward came up and it became Julian's first real assignment with Kate.

"She normally conducts these interviews by herself," Willoughby told Julian before they left the office. "The ambassador likes to impress her and because of that he's always been fairly open. So she'll be the one to ask the questions. You're just there to listen and observe."

Once at the embassy Julian, with his red bow-tie, followed Kate into the marbled main hall and, from there, they were escorted upstairs by a uniformed guard. After a fifteen minute wait, they were allowed into Sir Edward's private office. The neat and tidy black-suited ambassador rose from behind his desk to meet Kate, kissing her hand formally. She introduced Julian and they all sat. Sir Edward gave Kate a nod.

"I know you haven't much time, Sir Edward," Kate said, speaking quickly, "so I'll get right to my first question: What do you think is the biggest challenge facing the British Empire here in the east?"

"An excellent question," said the ambassador who then launched into a long-winded answer. Kate took notes furiously then went on to her next excellent question. As this was going on, Julian did exactly as he had been told: He listened and observed.

The office was of modest size, cluttered with furniture, paintings and artifacts attesting to Sir Edward's many years as a statesman at several foreign posts. Julian took it all in, in a half-interested sort of way until his eye was caught by a photograph on the wall just beyond where Kate sat. He stared at it, casually at first then more closely, hardly believing what he saw. It couldn't be, yet there it was – there *he* was.

Without a thought about Sir Edward or about Kate, Julian jumped up and went over to the wall for a closer look. There were perhaps twenty men in the photograph. They were arranged in three tiers and, except for one, all were dressed in ceremonial military uniforms. At the far left of the top tier, markedly older than the others and dressed in what looked to be the same business suit he wore now, stood a younger Sir Edward. In the same row, two men down, stood the man who had caught Julian's attention - those eyes unmistakable. It was the man who had killed Karmonov.

The more Julian looked at him, the more he was convinced of it. Then, going over the other faces in the photograph, Julian had another surprise: At the far right of the lowest tier, stood another familiar figure – Parker.

Julian was flabbergasted and it took him a moment to realize that Sir Edward had stopped talking and both he and Kate were now staring at him.

"Julian, what are you doing?" said Kate testily.

Julian collected himself, his mind racing. "Sir Edward, can you tell me who these men are?" He put a finger first on the killer then on Parker.

"Why do you care, young man? Who are they to you?"

"Please, just tell me Sir Edward, it's important."

"Julian, *sit down*," said Kate in a fierce whisper.

At that moment a knock at the door by Sir Edward's secretary signaled the end of the meeting. Sir Edward stood and gave an apologetic sigh directed at Kate who also stood. The ambassador stepped closer to the photograph. "Let's see, that was from about ten years ago I think. It's one of the graduating classes from the officer's academy here in Istanbul. I have no idea who those men are. I'm sure I knew at the time but not now, it's been too long." Only inches away from Julian, the ambassador turned to face him. "How do *you* know them?"

"One of them, this man here, killed a friend of mine and he tried to kill me."

Like a wronged schoolmaster Sir Edward's face hardened. "Young man, I'm not in the mood for jokes. These are all honorable men, highly placed now in the service of Her Majesty the Queen. You must be mistaken." He shook his head and turned to Kate. "Really Miss Wilder, tell Mr. Willoughby that he'd better start taking greater care when selecting his employees. This man is obviously a hot-head, totally unfit to take part in such a high level interview. Now I'm sorry, I must get on to other things. Good day to you both."

Kate blanched and said a quick thankyou to Sir Edward. She then gave Julian a fiery glance and headed out the door. Julian followed.

"What the hell was that all about?" she demanded once in the great hall, approaching the outer doors.

"I just asked the one question. I thought you were all done with yours," said Julian feeling a little emboldened by the incident. It was a real breakthrough. He finally had a lead on the killer. Some record of that graduating class should be easy to find in the *Times* files.

Kate kept walking. Outside, she stopped part-way down the steps. "We were there to get a perspective on what it's like to represent England at the Sultan's court, not to get Sir Edward mixed up in a murder investigation. Why didn't you tell me you were going to do this? And, while you're at it, just how many people are there running around trying to kill you? That burglar was one, this fellow in the photograph is another. Don't try to tell me they're not connected."

"I didn't know about the photograph until I saw it, and I

didn't accuse Sir Edward of anything, but yes, there is a connection between the officer in the photograph and the burglar." Julian paused for a moment, realizing that at last he had Kate's interest. He decided to make the most of it. "Are you hungry? Let's get something to eat." He started down the steps again.

"Are you going to explain yourself or not?"

Julian shrugged. "Maybe I will, but it'll have to be over lunch." He headed up the street, hoping she would follow.

She caught up then took the lead. "I know a place."

Julian smiled to himself. "I thought you might."

She took him down a side street where they entered a small, cafeteria-style café and, as she ate, Kate was all business. "We don't have nearly enough material to write the article." She shuffled through her papers. "I noticed you didn't take any notes."

"I was there to listen and observe, remember? Willoughby didn't say anything about writing things down."

"Well you're going to be a big help." She bit down on a rolled grape-leave stuffed with an aromatic mix of rice and roasted lamb.

"I plan to be helpful. Did you know that Sir Edward has won three commendations from the Sultan for his diplomacy with the Russians? Did you know he has three children and that his eldest son plays cricket in the same league as the son of the foreign minister? He's been married for more than twenty-five years. His wife is involved in local charity work and, for a Christian woman, she's very well thought of in the community. He was wounded in India and walks with a constant limp as a result. He gardens as a hobby, likes Turkish coffee and has an interest in the Muslim religion."

Kate stopped chewing.

"Sir Edward keeps a lot of personal things in his office," explained Julian.

Kate put down her notepad. Her eyes met his. "Yes, I suppose he does." She paused. "Julian, you were obviously mistaken about the photograph and now you've got Sir Edward angry at us both."

Julian knew he'd made no mistake but decided it might be best not to press the issue. "You're probably right, I'm sorry for causing trouble. Still, with all your notes and with my amazing powers of observation, I think we're in good shape to do a bang-up article about Sir Edward, don't you?"

"Amazing's not the word I would have used but yes, I suppose there's enough." She glanced at his still half-full plate. "How do you like the food?"

Julian smiled. "Do you know that's the first real effort you've made at conversation since I've been here? You don't even discuss the weather with me. Why is that?"

Kate dabbed her lips with her napkin. "I guess I have been a little guarded."

"There's nothing to be afraid of with me, Kate. We work together every day. I'd like to get to know you better."

She gave him a smile of her own and pointed to her empty plate. "Well, you know I like grape leaves."

"And I guess you know I don't." He shoved his plate toward her. "You can help me out with what's left of these."

They lingered at their table more than an hour and, over tea, shared stories about growing up, about their friends and about working for the *Times*. She told him about her early interest in the newspaper business and the help Mr. Willoughby had been after the death of her father. Julian told her about his family and life in the mid-western United States, and he talked about London and his powerful uncle.

"What brought you to Istanbul?"

"I'm trying to find the man who killed my friend."

"The man in the photograph, the one you're mistaken about, you mean."

Julian thought back to that night and decided to be more honest with Kate. "There is no mistake. He's a murderer, Kate."

"So you're here playing detective."

"I'm not playing detective – well all right, maybe I am."

"Julian, I admire you for what you're doing but you're talking about murder. There are police to handle such things."

"The police don't know about it."

"They don't know about your investigation you mean."

"They don't know about the murder, Kate. The only man who does know is the other man in Sir Edward's photograph."

Kate blinked three times in quick succession. It was something Julian noticed her doing when she was confused or unsure about something. She didn't do it often. "How could that be? When somebody gets killed, the police are always involved. There's always an investigation."

"Kate, it's complicated and that's all I'm going to say." He got up and they left the restaurant, heading back for the main street.

"This is the thing you and Mr. Willoughby were talking about after the break-in, is that right? Did it ever occur to you that, if I knew more, I might be able to help?"

"Maybe you're right. The man in the photograph in Sir Edward's office is the key to it all. The last time I saw him, he was pointing a gun at me from no farther away than you are from me right now."

"How did you escape?"

"I beaned him with a brass ball."

"You beaned him?" Kate started laughing. "You must be joking."

She had a delightful laugh that made Julian laugh too. "You don't believe me?"

"Well, you are a man of many surprises," said Kate drying her eyes. "But if you ever want Sir Edward to believe you about any of this, I suggest you leave out the part about the brass ball."

When they returned to the office they found it empty except for Steven. Kate got to work on her article and Julian headed for the files. He flipped through the documents dealing with the officer's academy and was disappointed to see that they only went back five years.

"No luck?" asked Kate as he went back to his desk.

"Our files don't go back far enough," explained Julian. "But there must be records at the academy. You don't happen to know anyone there do you?"

"Maybe I do," said Kate in a tantalizing way. "But right now you need to write a few paragraphs about Sir Edward. You'll have to do some real work if you want to be included in the by line."

"But everything's in Willoughby's name."

"He sometimes makes exceptions."

Working on the article with Kate proved to be a satisfying experience for Julian. He was able to liven up her dry text and she was able to keep him grounded in the facts.

Two days later Kate handed Julian a note. "It's an appointment for you at the Officer's Academy – two weeks from now."

"Not sooner?"

"Well you could show a little gratitude."

"Sorry, how about I thank you over dinner tonight?"

She agreed reluctantly then explained: "The academy likes everyone to think they're really busy. I tried to get you in sooner but two weeks was the best they could do. They asked what you were up to, wanting to see their files. I told them you'd let them know when you got there. You'd better have a good story. I wouldn't tell them that you think one of their graduates is a murderer."

"I'll think of something."

They went to Molly's and, remembering his first meal there,

Julian ordered the fish; Kate, the grape leaves. Their conversation went smoothly enough but Julian sensed that she wasn't quite comfortable being with him. Trying to sound casual about it, he blurted out a question that had been on his mind for some time: "Is Noah still calling on you?"

Now she really wasn't comfortable. She glanced down at the table then gathered her shawl around her shoulders. "He and I are just friends - like us."

"I want to be something more than just your friend, Kate. Has he kissed you?"

"You and I work together, Julian. It's not proper that we should be more than friendly and what Noah and I have done or have not done is none of your business."

So Noah had kissed her thought Julian, his resolve hardening. "Proper or not, Mr. Willoughby wants us to get along better. I'm just following orders."

They didn't talk much on the walk back but at her door he leaned closer.

Kate pulled away gently. "I'm not some prize in a competition, Julian. I like you but that's the extent of it. And don't ask me about Noah again."

Julian stiffened at the rejection. He didn't know what to say.

Kate let out a frustrated sigh as if she couldn't find the right words either. Finally, she turned for the door. "Good night, Julian," she said, going inside.

The following Monday, Steven burst into the office huffing and puffing, holding a sheet of paper over his head "This is just off the telegraph. It's an announcement from the embassy," he managed. "Someone's coming from England – someone important." He nearly ran into Willoughby who was standing in the aisle beside Julian.

"What the devil are you talking about, Steven? Who's coming?"

Steven handed him the sheet of paper. "It's in here, Mr. Willoughby. But who is coming is still a big secret."

Willoughby read the note and gave it to Julian.

The telegram announced that indeed there would be a British personage of great importance arriving today aboard HMS *Resolute*. It was part of the constitutional celebration which was still officially ten days away. The welcoming ceremony would be held at the docks this afternoon at three o'clock.

"Why would they wait so long to tell anyone?" asked Julian.

He handed the announcement to Kate.

"They're worried about security, that's why," said Willoughby checking the time. It was approaching one. "You've got just enough time to still get a good spot. You should be off right away." He sent Steven to flag down a carriage.

"You're coming of course," said Kate to Willoughby.

"No, sorry to say, I have an appointment here. I'm sure you and Julian will handle the job just fine without me."

Steven stuck his head back in through the door. "The New Yorkers are here. They say you can ride with them. But you need to hurry."

'The New Yorkers' could only mean Noah and his boss, Ira Goldsmith. Julian moved quickly. He had to make sure that it was he and not Noah who sat next to Kate. Julian had been stung by her rebuff but that didn't mean he had to give up on her entirely, especially if it meant giving ground to Noah.

They climbed aboard the open-air coach already occupied by Noah and Ira. Well dressed with his salt and pepper hair exposed beneath his hat, Ira greeted Kate as he helped her into the seat next to him. Julian ended up sitting next to Noah, opposite Ira. Julian introduced himself, shaking Ira's hand.

"You're the displaced American working for the Brits. Noah told me about you," said Ira as the carriage pulled away. Then Ira turned in his seat. "What? Where's Willoughby? He's not going to miss this, is he?"

"He's busy with something else but I think he just wasn't feeling up to dealing with the crowd and the heat," Kate told him. "He was also doubtful that this surprise arrival would be worth the effort."

Ira blew his nose. "He should have come. They wouldn't be making all this fuss over just anyone. It might even be Queen Victoria herself. Who do you think it'll be, Mr. North?"

Julian had been mulling over that same question. "The queen doesn't travel much, but it must be one of the Royals – maybe a couple of them - could be the Prince of Wales."

Ira nodded. "We'll find out soon enough. As you can see, Noah has his camera, so we're prepared for anything." He gestured at the shrouded wooden box that, along with its tripod and case of chemicals, lay across the floor of the carriage.

"I didn't know you could operate a camera," said Julian.

Noah made no secret of his disinclination. "With only three weeks of training, I'm no professional. Ira insisted that I learn."

"It's the only way we can keep up with Kate," Ira explained.

"As I'm sure you know, she's one of the best journalists in the city. She's also one hell of a good artist – she's gotten many sketches published. And, we have to watch out for her detective work. She'll beat you to a story and cover it in greater detail than most would ever think to." He gave her a tip of his hat. "And how *are* you, my dear?"

"I'm very good as always," said Kate, smiling. "But don't let me keep you from singing my praises. Go on, please."

"Modesty is not her strong point," said Ira. "Yet, of all her talents, there *is* one you may not know about that impresses me the most."

Noah's expression brightened. "And what might that be?"

"Now you *are* embarrassing me Ira," said Kate.

"Show them," said Ira.

"I will not." Kate folded her arms. "It would frighten the horses."

Ira laughed. "Ha, I suppose you're right." He turned to Julian and Noah as if he were confiding a great secret. "Kate has a very powerful whistle; the loudest and shrillest I've ever heard. Really, my dear, you'll have to demonstrate it to them sometime."

"I'll do no such thing."

Julian smiled at Ira's fondness for Kate. Everything he had said about her abilities, except perhaps for the whistle which he had not yet heard, was true – and he admired her for it. As the carriage rolled on, Kate continued to trade pleasantries with Ira while paying little attention to either him or to Noah. It occurred to him that she might be toying with them both.

They pulled up to the diplomatic station at the docks where a crowd was gathering. In the distance Julian spotted a row of British flags that flew over a long line of red-jacketed British marines. Towering above it all was the black iron profile of a huge British warship. The big guns of her forward turret were elevated at a threatening angle and from bow to stern, her guns were run out. As if countering this dangerous profile, brightly colored signal flags waved gently from her lines and black smoke drifted lazily from her tall stack.

"That's HMS *Resolute* out there," observed Ira, the last to step off the carriage.

"She's flying the flag of the Prince of Wales," said Kate. "Looks like you were right, Julian."

Julian squinted and saw the yellow triangular pennant fluttering high above the deck just below the Union Jack. The Prince of Wales had come to Istanbul. He pulled out his notepad.

Well, something newsworthy *was* happening here at long last.

After passing through a security checkpoint they moved into the area that had been cordoned off for the press. Noah began setting up his camera. Fifty feet in front of them, surrounded by a ring of Turkish soldiers, a large wooden platform maybe six feet high had been decorated with flags and banners. Over the rear half of the platform a sheet of white canvas shielded two rows of empty wooden chairs from the sun.

Julian heard hammering from the platform where workmen were busy nailing in the last of the planking. Every aspect of this event seemed to have been completed at the last possible moment. A mix of Turkish citizens and westerners had begun filling the large square, each of them waved a flag – the Union Jack and the red chevron with yellow crescent of the Ottoman Empire, in equal numbers. A group of schoolchildren, guided by their teachers, moved noisily forward up to the barricades positioned along the eastern edge of the square.

"Quite a mob," said Noah, raising his voice to be heard.

"It's always impressive yet totally inexplicable," said Ira, "the number of people who show up just to catch a glimpse of royalty. We rarely have ceremonies like this here. The Kaiser once made a secret visit to the sultan, but except for that, there've been no royal westerners here since your good King Richard a few centuries back. I understand that *he* drew a larger crowd."

"With good reason," said Kate pulling a sketch pad from her satchel. She quickly began composing the scene.

Julian glanced at his watch – three-fifteen. "They're running late." He started tapping his notepad against his leg.

Aboard *Resolute* a marine band was assembling at the bow, their shiny brass instruments gleaming.

"Looks like we're starting now," observed Kate with a glance to Julian. "Stop fidgeting, would you?"
Julian stopped his notebook tapping.

Noah tinkered with his flash chemicals, a delicate mix, Julian knew, of black powder and granules of magnesium.

The crowd grew quiet. A steady drumbeat came from the band. At a slow-step, a line of British regulars in sparkling white pantaloons and bright red jackets marched off the deck and onto the gangway that angled down the side of *Resolute*. Spacing themselves perfectly, they came to stiff military attention along the dock with their rifles held vertically in front of them. An order was shouted and the band raised their instruments. They struck up a majestic march – the anthem of the Ottoman Empire. The schoolchildren, and many in the crowd, sang along. When it ended, everyone cheered and waved their flags.

At the front of the wooden platform six Turkish officials had positioned themselves.

"The man on the far left is Foreign Minister Ismail," Kate told Julian. "He's the top-ranking Turkish official - answers only to the sultan."

Julian nodded, keeping his eyes on the British ship. From a distance he had seen the Prince of Wales in London several times and had heard that he detested ceremonies like this. He wanted to get a glimpse of his dour expression.

"You might want to take a few notes this time," Kate suggested.

Julian scribbled something and ripped the page off the pad. He handed it to Kate.

"Want to check my spelling?" It said: *I think you're beautiful.*

She playfully elbowed him in the ribs but Julian could see her face redden.

Several British officers moved forward, down the gangway followed by the royal entourage. Julian recognized the Duke of Sutherland and Lord Charles Beresford. A roar went up from the crowd when the Prince of Wales finally came into view.

Known amiably to the British public as Bertie, the prince wore the dark blue jacket of a naval officer with striking white trousers and a white-plumed hat with a gold visor. To Julian, his face, with its forward thrusting bearded jaw, looked more passive than dour – as if he were simply bored by the whole affair.

The line of nobles stepped in time to the drumbeat onto the dock, then up onto the platform. Kate had stopped her sketching. Noah fumbled with his focus. When everyone on the stand had taken their positions, the crowd again grew silent. A Turkish band from somewhere beyond the platform began to play *Rule Britannia* and as before, the crowd sang along. When the anthem ended, a sustained roar went up and all the men on the stand exchanged dignified bows and handshakes. They then struck a formal pose – the Turkish officials on the right, the British on the left. Where they met at the center, Ismail and Bertie stood close together, both with serious expressions until Bertie took off his hat and waved to the crowd. Everyone cheered. Noah's camera and a dozen others flashed and popped. The prince and the other dignitaries took their seats while Ismail remained at the podium.

"The foreign minister's not very charming to look at, is he?" said Ira to Kate, making reference to Ismail's stiff posture.

"Even so, I hear he's very much a ladies' man."

"Oh? I suppose he and Bertie will exchange information on *that* topic this evening," laughed Ira.

Ismail began speaking in Turkish. Though the crowd was respectfully quiet, he shouted, trying valiantly to be heard around the square. Each person in the press section had been given a translated copy of his prepared comments and most followed along. To impress Kate, Julian made a few more notes.

Up on the platform Bertie wondered why they always seemed to schedule these ceremonies during the hottest part of the day. He sat in the direct glare of the sun just beyond the poorly positioned white canopy. Or maybe it was his chair that was poorly positioned. Either way there wasn't much he could do about it. He folded his arms and tried to appear attentive to the ramblings of the foreign minister.

As the man droned on, Bertie felt his eyes getting heavy. His mind drifted. He was hoping Sir Edward had planned a good dinner for tonight. His stomach growled at the thought.

Suddenly he heard a popping sound and his eyes snapped open. Was that a gunshot? He jerked upright. He saw the foreign minister turn toward him. There was another shot, then two more. The wooden planks at Bertie's feet erupted in a hail of splinters. Without thinking, he pushed himself backward in his chair, and toppled back, falling onto the platform.

"He's been shot!" Bertie heard someone yell, amid shouts of confusion from the crowd. Had he been shot? He assayed his body for pain and only registered a sore spot on the back of his head.

"Form the guard! Form the guard!" That was Beresford's booming voice.

Bertie lay stunned, face up on the wooden platform, the sun beating down. He felt the pounding of a dozen boots move to encircle him. He could make out the shapes and faces above him where the marines stood, rifles elevated. He watched Beresford bend down over him and call out as if through a fog. "Are you hit, my lord?"

"I...I don't think so," said Bertie slowly, "I'm all right."

Beresford pillowed Bertie's head in his arms. "You there, and you, lend a hand." They stooped over Bertie and a moment later lifted him up.

"I'm all right, I can walk," Bertie insisted as he was carried down the stairs. He hated being treated like some valuable government artifact. "Put me *down*, Goddamnit." In the background he heard screams and yelling coming from the crowd.

"He's been shot," shouted Julian, on his toes, straining to see what was going on.

The crowd pressed in. A man just in front of Julian stumbled sideways and tripped over Noah's tripod. The man was able to recover his balance, but the camera fell to the cobblestones with a crash and a tinkle of broken glass.

"Damn it!" cursed Noah, pushing the man away. "Get off! Get off!"

"Can't see anything," said Ira, shading his eyes. "They've got the soldiers in front of everyone on the platform. Hold on! They're aiming their rifles out at *us*. Don't make any sudden moves, they could start firing."

Julian forced his way closer to the platform. He was only twenty feet from it when another gunshot rang out, this time from one of the marines. He saw a puff of smoke rising from the platform.

"They're aiming up there," a man cried, pointing to the rooftop of a three-story warehouse behind the crowd.

Julian felt the crowd thinning in front of him, running to get out of harm's way. He was about to press forward again when from behind he heard a piercing whistle - it could only be Kate - Ira hadn't exaggerated. Looking back, he saw her waving to him, pointing to the warehouse. Seeing what she had in mind, Julian wasted no time in running toward her.

"*Come on!*" Kate shouted, heading for the building.

As he ran, Julian glanced back. The marines were now charging off the platform in his direction. Kate was at the door to the warehouse when Julian caught up to her. She pulled it open. It was completely dark inside. "I know this building. The stairs are through there." She pointed then broke into a run, her long skirts bustling. She opened a second door and headed up, Julian hurrying from behind.

By the second flight they heard the marines behind them, their scabbards clattering against the stairs. "Stop!" one of them shouted. Kate hesitated but Julian did not. With his eyes adjusting to the dark, he took the lead and they continued their race up the stairs.

"That's the door to the roof," said Kate, nearing the last flight, breathing hard. "Damn these skirts."

When Julian got to the door, he burst through it onto the roof and into the bright sun. He headed for the side of the building that overlooked the square. Then he saw the body and, after a few steps more, he stopped cold.

There, lying face up with a rifle beside him, was the man who had killed Karmonov.

He had been shot in the neck. The bullet had mangled the flesh so horribly that the head appeared nearly severed. Its only connection to the rest of the body lay in a grizzly mass of spine and blood. With wide eyes, the man's face wore the look of profound shock.

"You there," came a shout from behind. "Stop where you are." Five marines ran toward them. They came to a halt at the body. The sergeant holstered his gun and stared at the dead man. "That was one bloody good shot," he said to his men. "He won't be doing much talking though I don't think." He then turned to Kate and Julian. "Now, who the hell are you?"

"We're with the *Times*," said Kate.

The sergeant ran a hand over his face. "You bloody press people are everywhere these days. Don't recollect having seen one that's a woman though."

"How is the prince? Was he shot? Is he all right?" asked Kate.

The sergeant laughed. "Judging from his majesty's feisty reluctance at being carried bodily off the stand, yes, I think he's just fine. There was no blood that I could see. But you can't be here. You'll have to leave."

"Yes," Kate said, "we'll be on our way."

The sergeant ordered one of his men to go back down to the square to get a stretcher for the body. "He'll escort you and..."

"Sergeant, I know this man," interrupted Julian, still staring at the body. Everyone turned to face him.

Kate stepped back giving Julian a here-we-go-again look.

"The dead man you mean? You know *him*?" asked the sergeant.

"Sir Edward may know him too. He is, or was, a British officer." Julian looked down at the body again then noticed something about the man's hand. He knelt closer, reaching down, studying the man's open palm, still warm from life. There, just at the base of the thumb, was a very small mark – a tattoo: an *H* enclosed in a circle.

Back at the customs house, in a windowless room spotted with cracks and peeling paint, Bertie sat opposite Beresford and the Duke of Sutherland around a plain wooden table. It occurred to him that, in their bright ceremonial uniforms they could have been mistaken for off-stage actors waiting for their cue. Behind Bertie a portrait of the sultan hung at a slight angle which Sutherland, easily bothered by such things, got up and straightened. Bertie drummed his fingers.

He had not been hurt at all from the shooting and now it was only security issues that were delaying their departure for the embassy. Foreign Minister Ismail had advised them that a thorough search of the entire area was underway, but that had been some time ago. The air was hot and stifling.

Finally, with a soft knock on the door, Ismail returned, flanked by a Turkish Army officer. He announced that all was ready.

"It had Goddamn well better be," exploded Bertie, standing. "You've had enough time to build us a bridge to the embassy."

Ismail only nodded. "These men will escort you to your coaches. We've arranged for each of you to travel separately and there will be several empty coaches with us."

"Decoys," said Beresford.

"Yes, decoys. In this way the chances for another attack are reduced considerably." Ismail bowed humbly to Bertie. "You have my apologies for the inconvenience, your highness, but it is safe now."

"You found no more of the blackguards then?" asked Sutherland.

"That's correct," said Ismail. "This all appears to have been the doings of a single man and, thanks to your marine guard, that man is now dead."

"Very good," said Beresford. "Let's get on with it then."

Ismail bowed again, not quite as deeply, and led them out through the door into a long, wide hallway where they were joined by the haggard Sir Edward and two, four-man columns of British marines. Behind these followed an additional guard of six Turkish soldiers making a total of fourteen rifles loaded and ready to shoot to kill at the slightest provocation.

Bertie surveyed the guard then indicated his approval. He, Beresford and Sutherland took their places between the columns.
The captain of the British guard took the lead. He was a small man for such a rank, Bertie thought as they marched briskly forward down the long hall and through a set of double-doors to finally emerge outside. A long row of identical black carriages were strung along the cordoned off street. Soldiers were everywhere.

The captain halted the column and maneuvered his way to Bertie's side. "This way, your highness," he said, ushering him quickly into one of the carriages. The captain climbed in behind Bertie, closed the door and knocked on the driver's window signaling their readiness.

Immediately, Bertie heard the slap of the reigns and they were off.

Seated stiffly at attention, the captain laid his rifle beside him and reached into his coat pocket. Bertie watched, tired but curious. "Sir Edward asked me to give you this, my lord. He knows you are very fond of the brandy of St. Remy."

"Indeed I am," said Bertie, taking off his cap and gratefully accepting the silver flask. He took a long drink that gave a delightful burn on the way down. "Thank you captain, this is most appreciated – it has been a trying day." Bertie leaned back, resting his head against the side of the carriage, only then noticing the odd green color of the captain's eyes which were now fastened on his.

CHAPTER 9

It was dark by the time Kate and Julian returned to the office. They found the gas lamps turned up and Willoughby waiting for them.

"Where have you been?" he demanded. "I've been worried sick. You're both in one piece I see, well, there's work to do. You've got to put your story together and it better be good. They've stopped the presses in London."

"You know about the assassination attempt?" asked Julian.

"Of course I know about it, everyone does except for our readership in London. Now sit down and get your pens going. I can give you two hours and that's all." He motioned to the back of the office where Steven sat snoring lightly, face down on his worktable. "When you're finished, Steven'll make a run to the telegraph office. Then, if I'm still awake, you can tell me why it took you so Goddamn long to get back here. Now get to work, both of you."

"We...well I, was being interrogated at the embassy," explained Julian. "Sir Edward wanted to know how I knew the assassin."

"Oh Christ! What is it with you, North? How could you possibly know the assassin?"

"He's the man who tried to kill me in London."

Willoughby held up his hand, stopping Julian from saying more. He turned and took a few steps back toward his office, then turned again and walked back. "So a few weeks ago a man who may have killed Czar Alexander stops by the office here and tries to kill you. Then a man, who tried to kill you in London, turns up here in Istanbul and tries to kill the Prince of Wales." He stared at

Julian.

"That's right."

"What does the Czar have to do with any of this?" asked Kate.

Willoughby held up his hand again. "We don't have time for this now. London's waiting and we need a story from you; from both of you."

"Sir Edward won't let us write anything about who the assassin was. That's all being kept quiet," said Kate.

"I'm not surprised. Just write about the assassination attempt itself. Write what you saw. And if it's any incentive to you, we'll put it under your by line: Wilder and North. I won't have time for any editing and after listening to the two of you just now, I'm not sure I want my name associated with it anyway. This is your story – make it good!" Willoughby stalked back to his office. "Two hours," he yelled back over his shoulder.

Three hours later, after Steven had taken their ten pages to the telegraph and long after Willoughby had gone to bed, Kate and Julian sat slouched over the table at the rear of the office. Cups with tea gone cold sat in front of each of them and crumpled notes littered the table and the floor.

Kate yawned as the clock struck the hour. "So the killer you'd been looking for is dead. Your friend has been avenged. Do you feel better about things now?"

Julian shrugged. "I suppose I do. My friend was avenged, but not by me."

"Did you really want to be the one who actually killed the man?"

"I just wanted him brought to justice. I wanted him to know that he couldn't get away with threatening me and killing my friend. But he's dead now, he got what he deserved." He didn't add that he also wanted to ask the man why the journal was so important.

"He was your only reason for coming to Istanbul, wasn't he?"

Julian nodded.

Kate finished off her tea. "So what's next for Julian North?"

Julian didn't answer. He couldn't answer. He shook his head and ran his fingers through his hair.

They sat in silence for a time before Kate spoke again. "The story we put together tonight, it's good. When you first arrived and I saw how little experience you had, I thought you won this post just because of your uncle. But now I can see that you're a good writer. Maybe too much the embellisher for the *Times* but I think you'd have done well for yourself even without your uncle."

Julian gave her a sleepy smile. This was the first complement he had received from Kate and he felt that it was time he set things straight, at least about some things. "I was a file clerk, Kate. When I first came over from America, my uncle tried me out as a journalist but it didn't work out. I never wrote anything in London. I came here just for a place to stay while I played detective. It was Mr. Willoughby who gave me the chance to write."

"Why did you leave America?"

"My uncle offered me a position with the paper. I was getting a little tired of working the farm with my foster parents so I jumped at the chance. I think Uncle Emory just felt guilty for ignoring me in the years after my parents died."

"How old were you when you lost your parents?"

"Ten."

"That must have been hard for you."

"It was." Julian had always kept a lock on these memories but now the door had opened a crack. He suppressed a tremor that ran through his body. He took a deep breath, hoping Kate hadn't seen. "It was a long time ago."

"Julian, what's the matter?"

"Nothing." He hesitated. "You need to go. I'll walk you home." He started to get up, but she placed her hand on his.

"Julian, what happened to your parents?" She asked this in a whisper.

"I can't talk about that." Julian reached for his hat.

"You have too many secrets Julian. I'm here. I'll listen."

Kate gripped Julian's hand and he felt the terrible, familiar dread coming up to the surface. Maybe he could tell her. Maybe he needed to tell her. His mind cleared and, like he never had before, he wanted this woman to know everything about him – even the worst. He leaned against the back of his chair and closed his eyes. Haltingly, he told his story and in the telling relived a June day in northern Indiana twelve years ago.

A bright sun beamed in a brilliant blue sky – it was a perfect day for sailing. On an impulse, Julian's father decided to take the day off and take his family out on a touring boat that sailed Lake Michigan in daily excursions north, up the coast toward Chicago then back again. He was the last to purchase tickets on a boat already too full. Extra chairs were brought on board and, with a stiff breeze behind them, the single-deck coastal cruiser named

Whispering Jenny cast off and chugged her way out.

By mid-afternoon, following a lunch of sandwiches and lemonade, the first clouds appeared. Julian was passing the time playing a word game with his father and looking off to the distant shoreline. The sky grew dark, the air turned cold and the first drops of rain began to fall.

"Let's get under cover," said his mother. Along with all the others on the boat, they crowded beneath a canopy as the boat began to rock with the increasingly powerful waves.

Julian watched the shoreline disappear.

His father's grip on his shoulder tightened. "Don't worry, Julian, these storms come up all the time. It should be over in a few minutes." And he didn't worry. But a few minutes had long since passed when the rain began coming down in large pelting drops.

His mother leaned down and held Julian close to keep him warm. He smelled her lavender perfume and felt the comforting warmth of her body as the waters grew rougher. Waves began crashing up over the side. Julian heard shouts from the people closest to the rail but could not see what was happening. He shut his eyes and wrapped his arms around his mother just as the boat rose high on a great swell and rode the wall of water back down. His mother held him tighter. "Stay with me, Julian," she shouted. Her voice wavered.

When a sudden gust of wind tore off the canopy the huddled crowd wailed in confusion. The windblown rain swirled. Julian shook from the cold and started to cry.

"Look out!" he heard his father shout just as another wave came crashing down. Julian and his mother were swept off their feet and thrown down onto the deck with a vicious force. Wrenched from her arms he still held desperately onto his mother's hand. He stared wide-eyed at her. A tangle of bloodied hair covered her forehead. He couldn't see her eyes. Julian screamed and the deck pitched wildly. He tightened his grip on her hand and suddenly they were hurled into the sea.

The green seawater consumed Julian. He plunged deep beneath the surface, his eyes squeezed shut, still holding onto his mother's hand. He felt her weight pulling him down. The water was bitterly cold. Julian opened his eyes and looked up to see the faint brightness of the surface receding. He felt his mother's hand move in his but when he looked down all he could see was his own arm stretching down into the void. His lungs burned for air. He kicked frantically for the surface - still, it receded. His mother sank deeper, pulling him deeper. A voice inside him called out to his mother, "I'm with you. I'm with you." And, as if in response, her grip loosened. His hand slipped from hers. Suddenly he was alone. The cold and the dark closed in on him. He reached out for her and in that same unheard voice, he cried out. This time she answered, as clearly as if she were whispering into his ear. *Swim now, Julian, be a good brave boy and swim for your life.*

With all his strength, he clawed his way upward, his nose and mouth filling with water as his lungs ached to breathe in something, *anything*. Above him he saw the waves at the surface coming closer until finally he broke through. He gasped and coughed in violent spasms but kept his arms and legs moving. Rolling up and down with the waves, he was able to find a wooden plank to help him stay afloat. The wind and rain screamed around him. Ink-black clouds churned low overhead and Julian breathed in short quick breaths. In the surging waves he thought of his mother. And, what had happened to his father? He gripped the plank more tightly. He squeezed his eyes shut and cried.

Of the fifty-eight people on board *Whispering Jenny* that day, fifteen were saved – Julian among them. The bodies of Alfred and Sarah North were never found.

Julian turned away from Kate and ran a sleeve over his eyes. "So, now you know."

Tears lined Kate's cheeks and she was silent for a while. Then she spoke softly. "Your mother saved you that day, Julian. By letting go, she set you free. It was a terrible accident, but it was God's will that your mother and father be taken that day – just as it's His will that you should be alive and here with me tonight."

"I don't think God had anything to do with it," said Julian. Giving voice to his memories had colored them with a terrible vividness. He could almost feel himself being pulled from the water that night after the storm. He felt his body shake as he forced himself to stand.

"Come on Kate. I'll walk you home."

"Thank you. That would be nice." She retrieved her hat and shawl.

Julian watched her as she readied herself and, more than at any other time, he found himself wanting to be close to her, to feel her body against his.

"What's the matter?" she asked.

"Your hat's a little crooked," he said, taking a step toward her. He could smell the jasmine of her perfume as he shifted her hat slightly to one side. Then his hands moved from her hat through her hair, caressing the sides of her face. He drew her close and she didn't resist.

Then she pulled back slightly, looking into his eyes with a slight smile. "Is it straight now?"

He rested his forehead against hers. "Yes, it's perfect."

They walked slowly to her boarding house. The night was warm. At her door, Kate turned to him, her face illuminated by the gas lamp. "It must be difficult living with those terrible memories about your parents. I hope you feel better for having told me."

"I do, Kate, and I...Kate, you're not like any woman I've ever known. I love looking at you, I love being with you, I love the way you love your work. I have to be more than just your friend. I need you."

She shook her head. "Give me time, Julian. All I can tell you right now is that I'm confused. I don't know what I should do and I don't like feeling this way. I just need more time." She touched his cheek for a moment then rushed inside, glancing back as she closed the door behind her.

"Good night, Kate," said Julian, realizing that, despite her doubts about him, he *did* feel better – as if a heavy burden had been lifted from his shoulders. He stood motionless, still feeling Kate's body against his, still savoring her jasmine perfume.

CHAPTER 10

In the pre-dawn hour three days later, a man walked hurriedly along a narrow residential street near Istanbul's warehouse district. He pulled his dark cloak and hood around him tightly. There was a chill in the air. The setting half-moon and the flickering glow of the street lamps cast his shadow on the alabaster walls as he passed.

His destination was a building like all the others in the area, having only its numbered address to distinguish it from its neighbors. A wrought-iron fence guarded the entrance. Once there, he moved swiftly. He found a small metal panel built into the mortar and opened it using a key from a chain strung around his neck. From his leather belt he extracted a small envelope, tightly bound in a roll. He placed it in the cavity behind the panel and locked it shut.

Then, his work not yet complete, he hurried to a second location near the waterfront where, along a specific wall of a specific building he used a lump of chalk to make a mark that would have meaning to only two of the many men who would see it later that day.

At eight o'clock that same morning, a worried Peter McNaulty unlocked his office, hung up his hat and took his place at his desk as proprietor and owner of *Hiller & Fox Importers*. It wasn't much of a business anymore, not like the old days when it used to be mostly legitimate. Over the past year, even the income from the less seamy side of his business had dried up. McNaulty needed money. He ran his fingers through his mop of black hair then opened his copy of the eastern edition of the *Times*. It would be another long day scanning shipping schedules for perspective clients.

Brian Wallace, arrived minutes later, his flat nose and pumpkin-round face beaded with sweat. He wished McNaulty a half-hearted good morning. McNaulty grunted.

Wallace started the tea and spread open the curtains from the back window. The morning sun streamed in. "Well," he announced. "There it is."

"There what is?" asked McNaulty, looking up from the paper.

"A message from the boys - about bloody time."

McNaulty went to the window and squinted through the dirty pane. On the wall of the building next door he saw a red mark. No more than two feet long, it ran diagonally upward, left to right. From all appearances, it had been drawn in a very casual manner, but he knew that was not the case. It had been purposely drawn at that particular location, at that particular angle and in that particular color by a member of one of the many underground organizations that he and Wallace referred to collectively as *the boys*. They were ruffians, anarchists, and murderers. McNaulty had never met them and had no desire to. But it was up to him to maintain a protected line of communication between those underground elements and the British government. In payment, his business enjoyed favorable treatment on lucrative British contracts – when there were any.

Once, for his help in resolving a major crisis, he had received a direct cash payment from Sir Edward – he sensed that this message could be related to a crisis just as big.

McNaulty knew that something odd had been going on at the embassy. The Prince of Wales hadn't been seen publicly since the shooting at the docks. So where was he? The boys, specifically *The Will of the People*, could be at the bottom of that question.

"Red - we'd better pick it up right away," said Wallace.

In the code system they used, red meant urgent. The angle told the location – this one not far.

"Right." McNaulty put on his hat and left.

He returned twenty minutes later with the rolled up envelope that had been left for him to find. He cut the binding and unraveled the envelope, smoothing it over the edge of his desktop. As expected, it was addressed to Sir Edward. Carefully, he slit the envelope and read its contents. He drew in a breath.

"What is it?" asked Wallace.

He handed him the letter. As Wallace read, McNaulty fidgeted with a curl of his long hair, twirling and untwirling it from around his little finger. He recollected the visit he'd had from a young journalist a few weeks ago. North, that was his name. He had money. He did a quick calculation and formed a thin smile.

McNaulty grabbed the letter from Wallace. From it he made a few notes on a separate sheet of paper. He blew the ink dry, folded the paper twice, and put it in his vest pocket. He then put the original letter in a new envelope, sealed it and wrote Sir Edward's name on it. Thinking the envelope looked too fresh and new, he crumpled it, threw it on the floor and ground it under his shoe. Satisfied, he picked it up, straightened it flat and put it in the pocket of his trousers. He glanced at Wallace who seemed to know better than to ask what he was up to, then checked the clock on the wall. "Time to leave."

They took a coach to the embassy and approached the building on foot from behind. At an entrance known to only a few, they exchanged passwords with a guard and, ten minutes later, were met in a basement storage room by Sir Edward.

"You have something for me?" asked the ambassador, out of breath as he took a last step down the dusty staircase.

"Indeed we do, excellency." McNaulty gave him the envelope.

Sir Edward tore it opened and skimmed the letter. He cleared his throat as if composing himself. "Very well, gentlemen; come with me please."

The two followed the ambassador up the stairs, through a series of hallways, and finally into a shadowy alcove within the great hall at the front of the embassy. At this early hour it was largely deserted.

"You've done her majesty's government a great service today," said Sir Edward, shaking their hands. "We are all most appreciative of your efforts and will reward you handsomely should all go well." He motioned to the marine guards standing on the other side of the hall.

McNaulty had winced at the 'should all go well' comment but held his tongue and replied with due courtesy. "Always pleased to be of service."

The guards approached. One placed a hand firmly on the shoulder of Wallace who shook it off immediately, giving the man a menacing pumpkin glare.

"Just a precaution, gentlemen," said Sir Edward. "The stakes of this game are unusually high. You'll be released later today if we've no further need of you."

Protesting all the way, McNaulty and Wallace were herded

through a doorway and down a darkened hall.

Back at the *Times* office that same afternoon, Julian sat alone at his desk staring at his sheets of Castlenau symbols. The attempted assassination of the Prince of Wales had been at the hand of a man that Julian could link directly to the Castlenau journal. But the assassination had failed and the assassin, now known to be a man named John Hastings, was dead. If Castlenau's catalytic event was to have been the assassination of the Prince of Wales, then the world revolution had been averted, hadn't it? Julian had scratched his head over that question for the past two days, finally deciding that there was no way to be sure. He needed to play it safe and get back to the code.

By this time he knew the percentages for each letter appearing in a typical block of French language text. He also knew the percentages for the symbols contained in the first three 'words' of code. Unfortunately, when he plugged in the proper letters for each symbol all he produced was gibberish. He was missing something.

He noticed that some of the percentages for one symbol were very close to those for another. If he were off by as little as half a percent, he could have chosen the wrong letter equivalent. Starting over, he picked the first symbol on the first page of the code. Out of the over two thousand he had managed to copy, that one particular symbol occurred fifty-three times or about two and one-half percent.

The percentage was a match for a *C* but was also a close match for an M and a B. So Julian marked a *C, M* and *B* over the symbol and went on to the next. It was a method similar to the one he'd used on the Castlenau text. A rough calculation told him that at this rate it would take him more than a year to get through all the symbols. He hoped that as he went along, context would speed up the process just as it did in common word puzzles.

Julian became so caught up in this work, that he didn't hear a carriage pull up outside. It was Kate returning from a journalist's meeting at the embassy. As she came through the door, Julian scurried to conceal his notes.

"What are you up to?" she asked, leaving the door open behind her.

He was about to say something, he wasn't sure what, when Noah walked in. Julian hadn't seen him since the assassination attempt and if he hadn't been with Kate, he might have been pleased to see him.

"Hi there Julian," said Noah removing his hat. "Kate and I shared the carriage back from the embassy."

Julian tucked his notes in his desk drawer wondering where else Kate and Noah might have gone together. "Good to see you, Noah," he said, turning to Kate. "Where's Mr. Willoughby?"

"He decided to stay at the embassy for a bit longer." She took off her shawl and sat down at her desk. "Sir Edward wasn't at all himself today. Mr. Willoughby didn't think so either. He was nervous about something. At any rate, he informed us that the prince and his entourage were being kept in seclusion for the time being and that the police, and the marines, were continuing their search for possible accomplices in the assassination attempt."

"He didn't say anything about the assassin himself?"

"Not a word." Kate took some paper from her drawer. "Oh, and there was someone who asked about you."

"About me, who was that?"

"A Peter McNaulty, I think." She searched her purse. "Yes, here's his card. Do you know him?"

Julian walked over and took it from her. It was gray and worn with an H & F in scroll letters at the top. His pulse quickened. "He's a friend of Willoughby's. Does anyone else know he asked about me? What did he want?"

"He said it was a private matter. And no, I haven't told anyone else. Well, of course Noah knows. McNaulty's at the embassy now and said he'd be in the area the rest of the day. You should see what he wants. I could go with you."

"No, I'll go alone. I'll be all right."

"I know McNaulty," said Noah, with his hands in his pockets. "He's a shady character, hangs around the embassy picking up on whatever he can. He knows a lot. Ira has gotten some useful information from him in the past. Do you mind if I tag along? I promise to leave you alone when he gets into the private matter thing. If his information is something good, maybe Ira will split the cost with you. McNaulty doesn't come cheap." Noah opened the door and glanced out. "The carriage is still here, we could leave right now."

Knowing that the alternative was to leave Noah there at the office alone with Kate, Julian grabbed his hat.

On the way Julian pried his mind off McNaulty and decided to ask Noah straight out: "Are you serious about Kate?"

Noah smiled. "She's a beautiful woman and I'm always serious about beautiful women."

"I work with her every day. I know her better than you. We're getting on very well now." Julian said this in as casual a tone as he could manage.

"Good for you, but it's me she likes."

"You don't know that."

Noah waved off the comment in a way that bothered Julian – as if he weren't even in the running. "One thing's certain," Noah went on, "when the time comes, she'll be the one to decide – not either of us."

"Sorry but she's already decided on me," said Julian just to irritate Noah.

"She told you that, straight out?"

"Straight out."

"I don't believe you."

"You're wasting your time with her. I'm more her age."

"She likes older men."

"Does not."

Their conversation degenerated from there then died to a heated silence as the traffic thickened and they neared the embassy.

"That's McNaulty right there on the corner opposite the embassy." Noah pointed as the carriage came to a halt. "Don't know the fellow with him."

Julian took a look as he stepped down. "He's Wallace, McNaulty's partner."

"How do you know that?"

"I don't spend *all* my time in the office." Julian paid the driver and they walked over.

McNaulty tipped his hat. "Good to see you again Mr. North. I was expecting you to be alone." He turned to Noah. "Mr. Sanford isn't it?"

"Yes," said Noah with a nod.

Wallace stayed a step behind McNaulty.

"Well now," said McNaulty, "we have *two* journalists then, that's mighty opportune." "Why is that?" asked Noah, eyeing Wallace with suspicion.

"Oh, sorry, this is Mr. Wallace."

Wallace gave his head a tilt as McNaulty continued.

"I have something for Mr. North as I am partly in his debt from the money he gave me as an advance a few weeks ago. You may have an interest as well but I'll let Mr. North decide if he wants you involved."

Julian was immediately distrustful of the man. Maybe it was a good idea to have Noah there. "What have you got?"

McNaulty pressed a finger to his forehead, as if using it to trigger the right sequence of words. "You already know, Mr. North, that Mr. Wallace and I are in the information delivery business." He reached into his pocket and pulled out a folded sheet of paper. "I have this note here."

"A note from whom?" demanded Noah, visibly agitated. Julian wondered why.

"It's from me actually," said McNaulty. "I delivered a message to Sir Edward just this morning." He paused holding the paper between two fingers. "This is a copy. I'll tell you right now, the information is astonishing – I was surprised myself." He locked eyes with Julian. "I guarantee that no one beyond Sir Edward's innermost circle knows what I know. I'm ready to let you in on the secret – for a price."

"I won't pay you until I see what it is," said Julian.

Clearly a seasoned player at this game, McNaulty put the sheet of paper back in his pocket. "Look across the street, Mr. North. Tell me what you see."

Julian shielded his eyes. There were three carriages lined up in front and a fourth was pulling out into traffic. There was obviously more commotion than normal.

"They're heading for the docks, Mr. North, and I know why." He patted his breast pocket.

It took ten minutes to strike a deal with McNaulty who accepted the cash from Julian then handed him the note.

Julian was stunned as he read through it. He folded the note over and put it in his pocket, not sharing the information with Noah. He was about to turn and hurry back to the office when McNaulty stopped him.

"Now, Mr. North," he said, stepping between Julian and Noah, "if you're interested, I have another business proposition for you."

Julian tried to obey his instincts that told him he should leave then and there, but he could not.

It was well after dark when Julian returned to the office.

Kate looked up from her desk. "Where have *you* been all day? Mr. Willoughby's been worried about you. He went through the roof when I told him you were meeting with McNaulty."

"I didn't expect to see you here this late."

"Well, I was worried too. You look all right – no scratches or bruises that I can see." Kate yawned and stretched her arms. "So, what did the sinister Mr. McNaulty want?"

"It's about Prince Bertie."

"Prince Bertie - is that all? We know all about that."

"What are you talking about? Do you know what's happened?"

"Everyone knows," She handed him a letter embossed with the embassy letterhead. "They sent this out to the press late this afternoon. As you see, Bertie and the others are leaving to go back to London. I stayed late to write up the story." As Julian read, she got up and began collecting her things, getting ready to leave.

Julian put the letter back on Kate's desk. "This is just what Sir Edward wants everyone to believe. The Prince of Wales is not heading back to London."

They were interrupted by the sound of Willoughby, stomping out of his office. "I warned you about McNaulty, damn it," he shouted. "You had to see him anyway. I'll bet he squeezed every lira he could from that big wad of cash you've been carrying around. And, while you were at it, did you happen to wave goodbye to Prince Bertie down at the docks, or are you just now finding out about that?"

"You've got it wrong. The prince is going somewhere, all right. But it's not back to London."

"And I suppose you know where Bertie's *really* headed aboard *Resolute*?" Willoughby put his hands on his hips.

"First of all, he's not aboard *Resolute* and he's not at the embassy."

"I'm not in the mood for guessing games, Mr. North. Where else could he be?"

"I don't know where he is right now. I only know where he'll be two days from now." Julian walked over to the wall map and put a finger on a spot in the southern Black Sea. "He'll be right here – and so will I."

Willoughby's face was a puzzlement. He turned to Kate. "What the hell is he talking about?"

Julian pressed on. "The prince has been missing for three days. He never made it to the embassy. He was kidnapped. A note from the men who have him was delivered to Sir Edward today."

Kate froze. "Kidnapped? So that was the information you got from McNaulty? How could that have happened? I don't believe it. Who would have done such a thing? And what do you mean 'you'll be there too'?"

Julian told them about McNaulty and Wallace and the arrangements he and Noah had made.

Willoughby sat down, a dark expression on his face.

"McNaulty would sell his own mother for a price."

Julian had a worrisome thought. "Do you think he's lying?"

"I didn't say that; actually I don't doubt that the information is correct. If nothing else, that scoundrel is in the perfect position to know such things before anybody else. He's taking a terrible chance though, jeopardizing his relationship with the embassy and with the anarchists just to make a deal with you." Willoughby paused. "You must have given him a lot of money."

"I gave him all I had." The truth was, Julian was glad to be rid of the Hastings money.

But Willoughby persisted. "How much?"

Julian swallowed. "It was more than ten-thousand lira."

Kate's eyes widened. "You just happened to have that much spare cash?"

Julian shrugged. There was no time to explain now.

Willoughby crossed his legs. "And for that you bought the information and you chartered a boat with a captain to take you out into the Black Sea?"

Julian nodded. "That's the deal." It had been expensive but Julian would have a chance to write the definitive account on the kidnapping and rescue of the Prince of Wales. It would be a story of historical importance chronicled at the embassy, at Whitehall and at Buckingham Palace and it would always be *his* story.

"It's dangerous, Julian," said Kate, sitting down. "You could be killed."

"She's right. The kidnappers will not take kindly to you being there and neither will Lord Beresford – he's probably the one leading the rescue. You're taking a big risk."

"I think the risk is worth it. That's one reason why I decided to involve Noah. He may have his faults but I trust him. If anything goes wrong, the two of us can take care of ourselves. Besides, Noah plans on going with or without me. My deal with him is based on the London *Times* breaking the story first. If I don't go, he'll have it all to himself. You don't really want to lose the biggest story of the decade to the New York *Times,* do you?"

Willoughby grumbled.

"I didn't think so." Julian checked the time and walked toward the stairs. "A carriage is coming for me. I need to get ready."

Sweeping all uncertainty from his mind, Julian hurried up to his room to pack a bag. As part of his preparations he strapped the Castlenau notes to the inside of his thigh beneath his trousers, just as he had on the trip from Dover. He took care to re-seal the wax pouch against water, thinking as he did so of his own fears.

Tonight he would be sailing out into the open sea in a boat smaller than *Whispering Jenny*. Maybe that was his fate:

Times Journalist Lost at Sea.

Before going back down, he paused at the top of the stairs, listening to Kate and Willoughby.

"You're not really letting him go, are you?" asked Kate.

"He'll be all right. Hell, I did worse when I was young."

"That doesn't mean Julian should. He could be drowned."

Julian waited to hear the answer, but Willoughby didn't have one for her.

As noisily as he could, Julian came down the stairs, bag in hand. "I'm not planning on being drowned," he announced.

Kate's face was pale. "You don't have to do this."

"Yes I do, Kate." He was never more certain of anything in his life. This is what had been missing. Yes, Hastings was dead, yes Karmonov had been avenged, but there was much more going on here and he was in position to do something about it. He couldn't let this chance slip away.

At a clatter from outside, Willoughby parted the curtains. "Carriage is here."

Julian glanced at Kate then walked to the door and opened it.

"For God's sake be careful," said Willoughby.

Julian said he would. They shook hands. Kate was still at her desk. He gave her a thin smile. *Wasn't she even going to say goodbye?* "Well, time to go," he said. "Don't worry. I'll be back before you know it." He walked to the carriage and climbed in. He was about to signal the driver when he saw Kate hurrying toward him.

She reached through the open window, pulled him closer and kissed him, her lips soft and warm on his. "I *will* worry about you, Julian. Watch out for yourself – and Noah too."

Even though she had mentioned Noah, Julian found her touch energizing, her kiss, electric. "I will," he promised. "Goodbye, Kate." As the carriage pulled away, he found himself wanting to stay, to hold Kate in his arms. He missed her already. Still, it didn't take him long to fabricate a hopeful new thought:

Times Journalist Witnesses Historic Rescue.

CHAPTER 11

The Black Sea

There were only a few stars visible in the night sky. From the rail along the quarterdeck Pavel looked up at the stack where dark clouds of smoke flowed past a hazy half-moon. Beneath him, the ship's engine clanked away. He wondered if the linkages connecting the pistons to the long, rusted propeller shaft would hold out for another day. That was all he needed – one more day. After that, *Oracle* and her cantankerous mechanicals would be someone else's problem.

The worn-out trading vessel of Greek registry held a wide circular course in gently rolling swells thirty miles north of the Turkish port of Sinop. She chugged along, making an abundance of noise and smoke but little more than three knots. Pavel spat over the rail. On the aft deck two of his men guarded a wooden crate of coffin shape and size. One sat atop it while the other paced the opposite rail. The red glow of their cigarettes flared with each drag. Pavel shook his head. Had they known the contents of the crate they wouldn't be smoking anywhere near it. But he didn't stop them. Their lives were bound up with his and with the lives of the rest of his crew; they would all live or die with this mission.

Pavel took a final breath of cool, salty air and made his way back through the bridge and down to his cabin. He closed the door. By the light of a single candle, he readied himself for bed then sat on the edge of his cot mulling over how things had gone so far. Getting the prince onto the right carriage and out of Istanbul had been the most risky part of the entire venture but he had managed it without a hitch. The trip along the coast to Sinop had been long but uneventful and the prince was in good health after recovering from the drug-laced brandy. Their royal captive was understandably foul tempered but showed no fear - just what Pavel had expected from the eldest son of Queen Victoria. The would-be king was now locked securely in the cabin next to his.

Pavel blew out the candle, and stretched out on his cot. Around him the ship creaked and rocked and her engines throbbed like the heart of an ancient living thing. As sleep overtook him he wondered if the prince remembered their first meeting thirty years earlier – probably not.

The morning dawned cold with a calm sea and Pavel awoke, relieved to hear the engine still thumping away. He climbed up to the bridge, had a cup of tea and received the results of the first sighting. Oracle had drifted three miles during the night. Considering the fickle winds and the unpredictable currents, he was pleased to be that close to their intended position.

"Three degrees to port," he ordered in Russian. That should bring them back on station.

"Do you think the British will show up?" asked a burly, bearded seaman standing next to him. His name was Boris and the men aboard this ship were his men. But Boris was Pavel's man through and through.

Pavel had known Boris for ten years and before that, he had known and trusted his father. The son wasn't as smart as the father, but he was devoted to their cause and his crew of hardened Russian seamen would follow Boris anywhere – that was his real value.

"Of course they will come. They are desperate to have their prince back," said Pavel. He grabbed a chunk of bread off the table. It might be some time before he would eat again. He ordered the engines shut down in an attempt to generate less smoke. He wanted to see the British before they saw him. Then, with Boris, he waited and watched.

It was nearly eleven o'clock when the shout came from the forward lookout. A large ship had been spotted. This far from the shipping lanes, it could only be *Resolute*. Pavel felt his heart beating faster as he watched the British warship grow from a tiny speck on the horizon to a threatening black silhouette. She skirted a small island then tore down on them like a snarling dragon. The crew gathered against the rail for a better look.

Boris whistled in amazement. "She moves like the wind."

Pavel trained his telescope on her mast. "She's flying a flag of truce. That's appropriate under the circumstances, I suppose." He ordered the pre-arranged signal flags to be run up requesting a parlay then turned to Boris. "Bring up our guest. I'll meet you on deck."

Resolute slowed and when she pulled within a hundred yards of *Oracle*, she reversed her engines, emitting a mass of bubbling foam at her stern. With a violent hissing sound, she came to a near stop – coasting closer still. Her forward gun turret was pointed directly at Oracle. The fixed guns along her side had been run out – ready to fire. Pavel headed down the stairs and onto the deck.

"They'll blow you out of the water, by God!" muttered Bertie when Boris led him toward Pavel, now standing near the bow.

Pavel put down the telescope. "Oh, I doubt that, Albert. They'd kill us, of course, but they'd also kill you."

"There's a fair bargain," said Bertie, keeping his eyes glued on *Resolute* as if expecting a volley to be unleashed at any moment.

Pavel considered the matter. "Perhaps it would be fair, but that's not the bargain I'm planning." He paused. "Well, we must get on with things. I'm sorry Albert, but we'll need to tie your hands and feet. And we'll need to use the blindfold. We mean no disrespect, but this is quite necessary."

"Just get the bloody thing over with!" rasped Bertie, his jaw set.

As Boris handled the rope and blindfold, Pavel explained further. "You'll be taken aboard a life boat and you'll be safe as long as your friends do what we ask." He gave Bertie a pat on the back. "Well, good luck to you, we'll soon see how this all works out."

Two men came up beside Bertie and shoved him sideways, one grabbing him at his shoulders, the other at his feet.

"Gently, now, gently," said Pavel as they carried him off, banging Bertie's hip on the hatchway. "Boris, you stay with me." He shaded his eyes and turned his attention back to *Resolute* where a steam launch was being lowered. It bounded in the rolling swells and moments later approached *Oracle*.

"Cast them a line," Boris shouted.

The launch was secured and a rope ladder lowered. Two uniformed officers climbed up. Pavel recognized one of them as the ruddy, bulldog faced Lord Charles Beresford. The other man, older with gray hair spraying out from beneath his cap, he didn't know. As they stepped aboard, the sound a gun being cocked came from the ring of seamen gathered round.

Pavel raised a hand of restraint and spoke in Russian. "Hold on, these men are our guests for the moment." He then spoke in English. "You are Charles Beresford. Good to have you aboard."

Beresford assessed Pavel and gave a derisive snort. "You are in charge of this?" he asked as if he had been expecting someone more imposing.

"That's correct."

Beresford took a step closer with his eyes narrowed and his nostrils flaring. He leaned forward. "I am Lord Charles Beresford. You are holding the Prince of Wales against his will and against the will of the British Empire. You'll deliver him back to us now in good health or I swear I'll give the order here and now to blow you and this ship to pieces."

Pavel sensed it best to hold his emotions in check. "We are preparing him for you, Lord Beresford. You will see him in due time. And you will have him back – alive and well, soon after that."

"I will see him now!" roared Beresford.

Pavel moved closer to the rail and looked aft. "If you'll wait a few moments, I think we can arrange that. Yes, just a few more moments." He glanced at the older officer. "And who are you?"

"I am Captain Horatio Faulks of HMS *Resolute*."

"A pleasure, captain," said Pavel, buying himself a little time. "You have a fine ship over there. I see she's poised to kill us all."

"That's right, she is," snapped Faulks, "and I've got an ambitious first officer who'd be happy with a promotion to captain should I be lost along with you and your ship."

"What an impressive sense of duty you British have," remarked Pavel. He waited a moment longer then, on receiving a nod from Boris, he handed Beresford a telescope and pointed west toward the tiny island in the distance. It was no more than a low hill of sand spotted with a few scrubby trees. "You'll see Albert out there with two of my men."

Beresford sighted the island and held his focus then handed the telescope to Faulks. Beresford gripped the rail with both hands. "What are you up to, you bastard. Why is he out there?"

"He's quite all right, I assure you," said Pavel. "In good faith, we've simply moved him to a position of neutrality. Should all go well, we are prepared to turn him over to you. As you see, my men out there are armed and well prepared for other options."

Beresford stabbed a finger within an inch of Pavel's nose. "You kill him, you harm one hair on his head, and we'll sink you straight away!"

"Well, I suppose that is one possible outcome, but I think you might prefer another."

Beresford struggled visibly to contain his rage. He kept one fist tight around the rail; the other he clenched and unclenched at his belt.

Faulks lowered the telescope. "How do we know that's the Prince of Wales? How do we know he's even alive?"

"On his way back to your ship, Lord Beresford is welcome to take the launch near the island and see for himself." Pavel turned to Beresford. "We can't allow you to actually land there and you'll be unarmed of course but you will be able to draw close enough to call out to him. He's been well cared for. We are not rogues, Lord Beresford; I don't want to kill him."

"What is it you do want?"

"It's as simple as this," said Pavel. "We will give you back the Prince of Wales in exchange for your ship."

Faulks was stunned. "You want my ship?"

"That's right, and you and your crew would get this one, plus Albert of course."

"You think you and this rabble could run HMS *Resolute*?" said Faulks with a smirk. "You're mad!"

"Possibly, but those are my terms. If you refuse them, we will kill the prince. The choice is yours."

"We don't deal with anarchists!" hissed Faulks.

Pavel noticed that Beresford's hand, the one at his belt, had stopped clenching. Pavel spoke carefully. "Your launch will return you to *Resolute*. Captain Faulks will remain with this ship. Your crew will be ferried here in your lifeboats unarmed, and our crew will be transferred to your ship."

"Also unarmed," interrupted Beresford.

"Yes, also unarmed. Only the two of my men now with the Prince will keep their rifles – as insurance until the transfer is complete. Your men will abandon your ship from the forward deck area as we occupy the aft and the same will be done here." He paused, pleased to see that Beresford was listening closely. "You and I will be the last to cross over and as that is done, my men on the island will leave the prince to be retrieved by you."

Faulks spoke up. "You must think we're fools. As soon as you've taken *Resolute*, you'll simply sink us with a single broadside."

"You may unload all of *Resolute*'s guns and toss all your powder overboard before abandoning her."

"What will you do with a warship without guns?"

"That is our affair. You can be assured that we will leave you in peace as soon as the transfer is complete. You may try to follow, but I'm sure your engineers will find this ship a bit lacking. If you sabotage your ship or damage her guns in any way we will not hesitate to kill the prince. This is our only offer and those are our conditions."

Beresford took a step away from the rail and looked out to *Resolute* where a hundred seamen stood, lined up along the rail staring expectantly back at *Oracle*. Remaining silent, he then looked at Faulks before turning to face Pavel. "Very well, you bastard, you can have our ship. But if there's any foul play, I promise on the honor of Great Britain that you will be the first to die."

Aboard *Resolute*, first officer Nathan Briggs watched the launch as it departed the *Oracle*. He had been a navy man all his life, taking the conventional career route out of the naval school at Greenwich where he'd finished in the middle ranks of his graduating class. For five years, he had been first officer under Faulks and he had been passed over twice in his bid for promotion. At forty-five years of age his hopes for captaining his own ship one day had been fading but he hadn't given up yet. All it would take is the right opportunity to prove himself. He'd been hoping that this mission might prove to be that opportunity.

Briggs kept his eyes on the launch and grew curious when it took a sudden turn to the west, heading for a small island. Once there, it lingered for a few minutes before turning again and heading back for *Resolute*. "What was that all about?" Briggs wondered aloud, the muscles on the back of his neck tightening. When the launch drew close, he saw that that Captain Faulks was not aboard. Now he knew something was wrong.

Beresford climbed up and explained the new situation.

Briggs was dumbfounded. "You want us to do what, my lord?"

"You aren't deaf, damn it. They've got the Prince of Wales out there at gunpoint. To save him, we're abandoning this ship, trading ours for theirs and we're doing it now! Is that clear?"

"Yes sir." Brigg's stomach churned. This mission was no opportunity for promotion, this was a disaster. And the direct order had come from a man who, besides his seat in parliament, also held the rank of captain in the queen's navy. He had no choice but to obey.

Beresford explained how the transfer of crews was to take place. "Now gather some men to organize this. You and I will be busy elsewhere."

Briggs supervised the first load of confused, unarmed British sailors climbing into the lifeboats. Others unloaded the ship's guns and began tossing powder kegs overboard through the open gun ports. Then, at a time he had prearranged with Beresford, Briggs glanced around to be sure no one was watching and ducked through a hatch. Moments later Beresford joined him there and explained what he had expected - and feared.

Briggs led the way three decks down into *Resolute's* hold where they found themselves alone in the heat and darkness. The sounds of a hundred men milling about on the decks above came down as a discordant Gregorian rumble which lent a strangeness to the place Briggs thought, almost like a dark cavern beneath medieval church. He lit a lamp as Beresford followed him off the last rung of the ladder. Aft lay a planked walkway that ran along the keel with barrels and crates stacked high on either side. Thick iron beams ribbed the entire space. At the end of the walkway a metal bulkhead separated the cargo from the coalbunkers. In the other direction another bulkhead shielded the hold from the mechanism that worked the forward gun turret.

Briggs moved tentatively. Each breath he took was soaked with a salty brine.

Beresford took the lamp from him. "Where now?"

"The hatch is in the decking up ahead; this way." He moved forward ten paces before he slowed and knelt down.

Beresford stood beside him. "Come on man! Do you know where it is or not?"

Sweat dripped freely from Brigg's face. By design, *Resolute's* scuttling port was well concealed and he had to feel his way along until finally, his hand brushed against its metal panel. He felt both relief and dread. "Here! It's here."

The removal of the panel required the simultaneous action of two separate keys and the locks were positioned in such a way that one man acting alone could not release it. "I assume you have the captain's key?"

"Yes, even Faulks knew we had no choice," said Beresford as if to convince Briggs and maybe himself as well that they were doing the right thing. He dug into his pocket and produced the key which he inserted into the lock. Briggs did the same with his own key.

On Beresford's count they turned them and the locking mechanism moved smoothly. They then gripped the heavy plate and pulled up, straining with the load. As they lifted, Beresford stumbled and lost his grasp. The plate came crashing down. At the impact, the iron hull rang like a bell and both men froze, listening for the sounds of anyone coming down the ladder to investigate. But no one came. They shoved the plate fully aside and began their work.

There were three kegs of powder fused together and spliced to a longer fuse that lay coiled up at one end of the compartment. It wasn't so much the power of the blast as its placement that would cause the fatal blow to HMS *Resolute*. The kegs were laid out in a row directly along the keel. An explosion here would break her spine. She would sink in minutes.

Briggs stood and took a dozen steps back, feeding the fuse-line out as he went.

"How much time can you give us?" asked Beresford.

"This is slow-fuse, almost thirty feet at ten feet per hour – so, three hours."

Beresford wiped the sweat from his forehead. "We need more like five hours, God damn it. We can't light it now, it's too soon." He thought for a moment. "We'll be the last to abandon ship. Before leaving, I'll come back down here and light the fuse." He looked at his watch. "That will have to be good enough."

They repositioned the plate loosely over the charges but blocked up so the fuse trailed out. When Beresford returned he'd only need to touch a flame to the end of it to set it burning. They headed back up.

Once on deck, Briggs breathed in the fresher air and coughed his throat clear. He followed Beresford up onto the quarterdeck where they had a good view of the chaotic scene below.

There were numerous lifeboats in the water, shuttling men from one ship to the other. Dozens of powder kegs bobbed in the rolling waves with more being tossed overboard. Briggs shifted his gaze to the island where the Prince of Wales remained captive. From this distance and without the aid of a telescope he couldn't tell if there was anyone on the island at all. Had Beresford made the right decision? He had given HMS *Resolute* to the kidnappers yet with any other course of action the Prince of Wales would now be dead. Right or wrong, thought Briggs, there really had been no choice. He would have done the same.

"We're going to get him back," said Beresford as if reading his thoughts.

"They could kill him at any time and there's nothing we could do about it."

"They could have killed him at any time over the past week. At least now we will make them pay for what they've done." Beresford pointed to the forward gun that remained trained on *Oracle*. "We'll keep that gun loaded until the very end. If there is any treachery, we'll sink them with a single shot."

Briggs removed his cap and wiped his sleeve across his forehead seeing the problem: There were now more British seamen aboard *Oracle* than aboard *Resolute*. With that one shot, Beresford would be killing scores of his own men.

The transfer of crews proceeded smoothly and after two more hours, Beresford sneaked away. He returned a short time later giving Briggs a slight nod. The fuse had been lit. With regret, Briggs scanned the doomed ship slowly from bow to stern.

"Here comes the last of the bastards," said Beresford. His eyes were on a single boat being oared over from *Oracle* to *Resolute*. "The man seated in the middle, he's their leader, goes by the name of Pavel."

Flanked by two of his men, Pavel climbed aboard and made his way toward Beresford.

"There, that wasn't so terrible was it?" Pavel said to him. "You are now free to rescue your prince. These men behind me are the ones who've been guarding him. Albert is out there by himself now. So you see, I keep my word."

Beresford gave no reply. He ordered the last of his crew to disarm the forward gun then he and Briggs joined them in the last lifeboat. At Beresford's direction they set off for the island, directly into the setting sun. If all went well, they'd soon have the Prince of Wales safely aboard. Then their only problem would be getting back home aboard the rusty *Oracle*.

The sailors pulled at their oars while, from behind, Briggs could hear the engines of *Resolute* roar back to life. The big warship was still pointed to the east and she started moving slowly in that direction before gathering speed and turning in a wide arc to the west. As she roared past she gave two long blasts of her horn. Briggs wondered where Pavel and his band of ruffians were headed but glanced at his watch and knew it didn't really matter. In two more hours they'd all be at the bottom of the Black Sea.

Earlier that day, while Briggs and Beresford were fumbling with the plate over the scuttling charges, Julian stood at the bow of a little boat named *Maracas*. Thirty-five feet long with a twelve foot beam, she'd been designed for use as a harbor ferry, not for the open sea. A bright red canopy was stretched over most of her wooden hull and beneath it, rows of benches were fastened to the deck. On a normal day in Istanbul harbor, these would have been cluttered with passengers and luggage. Today there was only Noah lounging in the shade. At the stern a steam engine with a ten-foot high stack chugged away. Every now and then a soot-faced boy named Whiley tossed a shovel of coal into the fire-box.

The sun blazed midway down the western sky giving Julian a good view of the eastern horizon at which he'd been staring for the past hour. Then, he thought he saw something. He kept his eyes fixed on the spot and, after a time, a low mound of sand and sparse vegetation became visible. He glanced back above the canopy to the elevated helm where Massaud, the grizzled, sunbaked captain of *Maracas* nodded to let Julian know he had seen it too. The old seaman held the wheel steady, heading straight for the island which was nearly dead on McNaulty's coordinates.

Julian's greatest fear gnawed at him. If McNaulty had been lying, this trip would be a complete waste of time and money and he would be exposed for the fool he was for having believed in such a fantasy. Holding onto the rigging, he swung down beneath the canopy and joined Noah who had just spread out a map on one of the benches.

"According to this," said Noah, "that island doesn't exist."

"Maybe you should advise Captain Massaud of that."

"It's just a speck, hardly worth the ink to put it on the map."

"It would mean a lot to a drowning man."

"Never seen a drowning man consulting a map. Besides, it might not even have been there ten years ago. Sea levels change." Noah lit a cigar and took a drag. He checked his watch. "According to McNaulty, somewhere out there at this very moment, Prince Bertie is being rescued."

Julian sat down heavily. "We'll know soon enough if we've come all this way for nothing." He watched the island grow larger until it spanned the port quarter. He then worked up his enthusiasm, picked up a telescope and drew the horizon just beyond the island into focus. At first he saw nothing - only a hint of black smoke. Then, as *Maracas* rounded the southern tip of the island, he caught sight of the gray silhouettes of two large ships in the distance. He held his breath. My God, he thought, McNaulty had been right. Julian ran for the bow, his heart pounding.

He climbed up onto a bench while holding onto the rigging and tried to keep the telescope steady. "I see the British flag," he said, almost in awe. "We found them." He turned and shouted back to Massaud. "Slow down, we don't want them to see us." He handed the telescope to Noah, who had stepped up beside him.

"It's got to be *Resolute*," said Noah. "Not sure about the other ship. They're both just sitting there."

"We may not be able to get any closer," said Julian. He shouted up to Massaud: "Stay near the island."

Massaud grunted and slowed the engine.

Julian couldn't contain his excitement. He kept his eyes moving, absorbing everything so he'd be able to write it all down. They were only fifty yards off the island when his attention was distracted. There was something on the beach. He jumped up onto the rail for a better look. From there he could clearly see a black mound lying on the sand.

"What are you doing?" asked Noah.

"Something's out there." Julian grabbed the telescope. "My God," he said, disbelieving what he saw. "I think it's a body – maybe dead." He judged the distance that separated *Maracas* from the shore then turned to Noah who just stared back at him. Julian pointed and yelled up to Massaud. "Get us to the beach. Get us there now!"

CHAPTER 12

Massaud gunned the engines and turned *Maracas* into the wind. "Hold on," he shouted, steering straight for the island.

Julian, still standing on the bow rail, tightened his grip on the rigging as *Maracas* bumped and scrapped over the sandy bottom. She came to a halt still ten yards off shore. Massaud hit the throttle one last time taking them a few feet closer. That would have to do.

Julian jumped into the waist-deep water and charged for the shore. He heard Noah and Whiley splashing behind him, following. They reached the beach together and ran across the hot sand. Julian could already see that he had been right – the black mound was a body, bound and blindfolded. Once there, he stooped over it and waved off the gathering flies. The face of the man was sun-reddened with an unkempt full beard and coarse stubble on his cheeks. His hair was ragged, his lips scabbed and bloodied but Julian recognized him just the same. "My God, it's him. It's Prince Bertie," he whispered, struggling to believe it himself. Tentatively, he touched Bertie on the shoulder. There was no response but Julian saw with relief that his chest was moving, albeit in a slow, shallow rhythm. He pulled off the blindfold. Bertie's eyes were caked shut with sweat.

Noah cut the rope that bound Bertie's hands behind him. "He may have been drugged."

Julian nodded, then looked out to sea. The two ships in the distance were still maintaining their positions as if unaware that the object of their confrontation was here on the island. What was *Resolute* doing out there? They should be sending out a rescue boat, but Julian saw none. Maybe they didn't know the prince was here – *but how could that be?* "Let's get him aboard," he said.

Whiley shook his head. "He'll be very heavy. I will get the captain."

With Massaud's help they lifted Bertie and half-carried, half-dragged him across the beach. Each held an extremity, Julian his right leg, as they headed into the water. Rolling waves began splashing across Bertie's face and he began to murmur incoherently.

"Keep his head up," shouted Julian to Massaud and Whiley, who held him by his arms. "Hurry."

All four of them were exhausted by the time they reached *Maracas*. In the chest deep in the water they rested to catch their breath and rearrange their grip on Bertie. Whiley and Massaud climbed aboard so they could pull Bertie up as Julian and Noah pushed from below. In one concerted move they hoisted him up and over the side, where the first heir to the throne of England tumbled onto the deck.

"Not the most dignified way to treat the Prince of Wales," Julian commented, his chest heaving as he and Noah climbed aboard, water pouring off them.

Noah smiled. "Under the circumstances, I think the queen would approve."

Massaud wasted no time. "We go now," he said, heading for the helm. Whiley started shoveling coal and Massaud hit the throttle. The engine clanked and the wooden hull shuddered but didn't move. He tried again with the same result. They were stuck on the sand.

"You push," shouted Massaud to Julian and Noah pointing to the bow. "Get off, you push."

"Wonderful," said Noah.

They jumped back into the water and pushed up from beneath the bow as Massaud worked the throttle and Whiley continued to pour on the coal. *Maracas* didn't budge.

"Harder," growled Massaud, the engine clanking furiously.

A wave caught Julian, submerging him for a moment. He coughed up a mouthful of seawater then took a breath. "We have to...to push in time with the waves."

"Right." agreed Noah, water streaming from his face.

They waited for the next swell then gave a shove - then again and again. Finally the boat began to move; a few inches at first, then more. Suddenly *Maracas* came alive, bounding with the waves, backing out into open waters. Julian and Noah sloshed through the deepening water and pulled themselves up and over the side, falling onto the deck.

Julian was exhausted. Then he caught sight of Bertie up at the bow, lying still but breathing regularly now, and he realized what they had just done. Even in his wildest dreams he had never concocted a more outlandish headline:

Times Reporter Rescues Prince of Wales.

But it was true! Prince Bertie was right there. Kate would never believe it. Willoughby would never believe it. Julian could scarcely believe it.

Gaining distance from the island, Massaud shifted out of reverse and headed into a turn, the brave little engine clanking merrily along as Julian and Noah lay on the deck, still panting.

It seemed like only minutes passed before Julian heard a new sound; low and deep at first then growing quickly to a roar that seemed to cause the very air to vibrate - *Maybe a storm*? The sun was close to setting but there was still blue-sky overhead. It wasn't a storm. With foreboding, Julian raised himself up off the deck and turned.

There, over the port rail, framed in clouds of billowing black smoke, loomed the giant HMS *Resolute*. She was cutting through the water, steaming directly for them. She gave two deafening blasts from her horn.

Julian jumped to his feet, staring at the onrushing ship. "They're going to ram us."

Up at the helm Massaud had the wheel spinning hard to starboard trying to turn out of the warship's path. He sounded the horn frantically but *Resolute*, as if hell bent on their destruction, just kept coming.

Julian grabbed the rail wondering what act of God could possibly save them now.

"They don't see us," shouted Noah standing next to him near the stern. "We're in the glare of the sun and they don't see us."

"Goddamnit. How can they not see us? We just rescued the Prince of Wales and now they're going to sink us?"

"Hold on," yelled Massaud, his wide eyes fastened on *Resolute*'s giant bow.

Julian realized he had to protect Bertie. He ran forward and slid down onto the deck, positioning himself with one hand on the rail the other holding onto the prince by his belt. The frail wooden hull of *Maracas* shook as *Resolute* tore through the water tossing waves of white foam on either side of her bow. Her black hull towered over Julian. He could see the barnacles at her waterline and every rivet and weld that held her together. He tightened his grip on the rail and steadied Bertie's body with his feet so he was almost sitting on top of him. *Resolute* was almost on them. He took a deep breath and bent low as a torrent of white water crashed down. The warship hit *Maracas* at the stern, wheeling her around, sucking the little boat into her powerful wake, forcing her to career against her side.

The deck slipped out from beneath Julian and tilted down toward the speeding *Resolute*. Bertie's body rolled closer to the edge, where Julian braced himself with his back against the railpost and both legs on Bertie. He looked down into the foaming gap between the hulls, water shooting up the sides. Then his feet lost contact with Bertie. The prince had slipped completely under and behind Julian, their combined weight now entirely supported by the single post. If it gave way, he and Bertie would fall into the foam to be crushed between the two ships. Julian clenched his teeth. The vibration rattled his body. He was not going to die here, he told himself; he was not! And neither was Prince Bertie.

"Hang on," Noah shouted, making his way over across the slanting deck.

"Hurry." Julian felt the post bending behind him. The roar of *Resolute* and the high pitched scream of wood against iron filled his ears.

Noah reached Julian and held onto Bertie just as *Resolute*'s stern raced by. The blades of her giant propeller thrashed the waves like sabers. Three feet closer and *Maracas* would have been cut in two. In the violent wake, *Maracas* spun once around before it was all over.

"God almighty," said Julian, his whole body shaking when the rumble of *Resolute* at last began to fade into the distance. He sat on the deck with Noah beside him. Seawater poured out over the gunwale. Bertie, still unconscious through it all, lay at their feet. They were all drenched. The canopy had been torn away and half the helm had been sheared off.

"Massaud, Whiley," Julian managed to call out.

"We are back here. We are all right," said Whiley from behind the engine which, somehow, was still pounding away. Whiley helped Massaud up. The old captain was more concerned with the damage to his boat than with his close brush with death. "You pay," he demanded of Julian, his face red with rage as he climbed back up to what remained of the helm. "You pay."

Julian realized this boat was probably the old man's life's work, his only possession of any real value. "Yes, I will pay," he said, not knowing exactly how he would manage it.

But Julian had other worries now and in his mind there was not much choice about what to do next. A gust of wind came up, rustling the few strips of cloth that were left of the canopy. Julian looked around then pointed to *Resolute*. He yelled up to Massaud: "Follow her."

Maracas turned into the sun's last glow trying to keep up with the speeding warship but by the time darkness had set in, they'd lost sight of her.

Massaud stayed on the same heading and Julian stared out, over the bow. "Why haven't they lit their running lamps?" he asked Noah who sat on a bench next to him. "And why would they leave without the prince?"

Bertie lay on the deck covered with a damp blanket, his head pillowed by Julian's jacket. Every now and then his body flinched as if disturbed by a dream.

"They probably wanted to put some distance between themselves and the kidnappers before picking us up. Or maybe they don't know he's with us."

"It doesn't make sense," said Julian. "None of it does." He sat down and folded his arms against the cold wind. He started to wonder if *Maracas* could make it back to Istanbul on her own given the damage she'd sustained.

Then Julian heard the throbbing of an engine. He peered into the distance and slowly, the black form of *Resolute* appeared against the charcoal sky. Several lights on her deck were lit. She was no more than a hundred yards away, moving slower now. "She's stopping for us," he said with relief.

As *Maracas* approached the British ship, Massaud kept a safe distance from her wake. He shifted course to come up alongside from behind. Julian wondered why he didn't sound the horn then realized that it had been torn off in the collision.

Julian stared up at *Resolute*. A few men were gathered at the stern. He shouted to them through the wind and the roar of the engines, straining to be heard. But it was no use and the men seemed to have their attention fixed elsewhere. Then Julian noticed something curious about them. One was dressed in a black sea coat, another in a white tunic; another bearded man in red trousers was naked to the waist. No one was wearing a British uniform.

A revelation struck Julian with an icy chill. "Oh no, what have we done?" he breathed. He was about to order Massaud to back off, but it was too late.

With a blinding white flash, and a thunderous boom, an explosion cratered the water off the port side. The deck of *Maracas* cracked beneath Julian's feet. His hearing left him as he tumbled off the bow and plunged beneath the waves into a cold void. Like one of his lonely nightmares, Julian held out his hand, half expecting his mother to reach out to him so that, this time, he could save her.

Time slowed. As the pain in his lungs grew, his hearing returned. From above, he could make out the slow thrashing of *Resolute*'s propeller and the sounds of debris splashing into the water. He lunged upward and broke the surface in a few frantic strokes. He sucked the air in and out in short, quick breaths then, in the darkness, found a section of decking to hold onto. The scene was eerily familiar and he heard from within himself the echoing screams of a desperate boy, crying out for his mother and father. Mercifully, there was no storm this time, and he wasn't a boy. He looked up at the tall, black *Resolute*, still riding the waves without damage. Then he wondered: What had just exploded?

"What the bloody hell is going on?"

It was a shout that came from only a few yards behind Julian and, even before he turned to look, he knew who the shouter must be.

Bertie waved his hand up at the ship. "Are you blind? Can't you see me you bloody bastards? Here I am Goddamnit!"

"Are you all right, my lord?" asked Julian.

"Hell no, I'm not all right, you idiot," said Bertie holding onto a piece of floating debris, sputtering out seawater between the waves. "I'm about to drown, just like you. What the hell is going on?"

Julian's throat tightened. He might as well admit to it. "I'm sorry, your highness, but I've just got you recaptured. That's what's going on."

Julian was the last to be pulled from the water onto *Resolute*'s deck. He, Noah, Prince Bertie and Whiley had survived; Massaud had not. From his position at the helm the old seaman must have been exposed directly to the blast and killed instantly. At least that's what Julian hoped. Any other form of death for the grizzled mariner would have only been worse.

They were given blankets by a couple of bearded seamen who then, left them alone. No one spoke. Eventually, a man walked up

125

to them. He wore a British officer's uniform with the collar unbuttoned.

"Gentlemen, welcome aboard HMS *Resolute*. Well, technically, I suppose we can leave off the HMS." He gave Bertie a thin smile. "Sorry Albert. I had intended that you'd be free by now but, as you see, your rescuers here were poorly informed."

"Who are you?" asked Julian.

"This is Pavel," said Bertie. "He's the blackguard who kidnapped me."

"You'll all be released in due time," said Pavel. "I had no desire to bring you aboard but you'd have drowned otherwise."

"What was that explosion?" asked Julian.

Pavel glanced at Noah then fixed on Julian. "And who are you?"

"Julian North. I'm a journalist for the London *Times*."

Bertie turned abruptly. "You're a journalist?"

"Yes," admitted Julian, feeling Bertie's withering stare.

Pavel took a step closer to Julian. "You journalists seem to be getting more and more adventurous these days. How is it you ended up here, Mr. North? Well, never mind that, I'll just assume that you're looking out for your readership back home – trying to keep them well informed and all that. This should all make for a good story if you live to tell it." He paused, staring at Julian. "Now as to the explosion; that was for the benefit of your friends back on our old ship. We had to make them believe that this ship has been sunk. They won't be looking for us now."

"They set the scuttling charges and you diffused them," said Bertie.

"That's exactly so, Albert. The men out there now think we're all drowned. I suppose they think the same of you."

Julian couldn't believe what a terrible mistake he had made. It seemed so obvious now. "This is all my doing."

"Well, I hope you'll allow me some of the credit," said Pavel.

"What are you going to do with us?" asked Julian.

"At the moment, you four are the only outsiders who know that this ship has not been sunk. I'll simply be holding you until we complete our mission."

"And what mission is that?" asked Bertie.

"You may learn of that one day; but not today."

Pavel pointed at the larger man standing next to him. "This is Boris. He is Russian and speaks only a little English. But he understands gestures very well. He will show you to your accommodations." Pavel then pointed to Whiley and spoke to

Boris in Russian.

Before Julian knew what was happening he could only watch, horrified, as Boris picked up Whiley and, as if he were no more than a sack of garbage, threw him over the side. His receding scream was followed by a dull splash.

Noah stiffened and took a step toward Pavel. "You didn't have to do that."

Pavel raised his hand and spoke calmly. "This is serious business, gentlemen. If you want to keep your lives, you will not cause me trouble."

"You're a barbarian," raged Bertie. "That boy was no trouble at all. He caused you no harm."

"That is true, and now neither will the three of you."

CHAPTER 13

Julian's prison aboard *Resolute* measured three paces square. It contained a small table built into the bulkhead, a single chair, and a fold-out cot. These were officer's quarters, he realized, given him only because its door could be locked from the outside. He slept fitfully the first night but better the next. A bearded seaman brought food twice a day and a bucket served for a privy. A porthole above the cot was the only source of light and through its thick glass Julian could see that *Resolute* was continuing to steam west. It was sometime during the third night that Julian could feel the ship head into a turn – to the south he thought. Sometime after that, a coastline came into view. The engine slowed and eventually *Resolute* scraped up against a line of scared wooden pilings. Mooring lines stretched tight and pulled the big ship to a halt.

The thumping of *Resolute*'s engine was replaced almost immediately by the ratcheting sound of a steam crane coming from the dock somewhere above the level of Julian's porthole. Through it he could only see the tall pilings but he could hear the commotion. Orders were being shouted. Footsteps pounded the deck above and it was obvious to Julian what was happening: *Resolute* was being loaded with coal and provisions. She was being readied for something.

The loading operation continued through the night and into the next day. It was midafternoon, when the heat of the day was at its maximum that Julian lay stretched out on the cot with a wrist over his eyes. He tried to remember what wild idea had driven him to leave London in the first place. Oh yes, he was supposed to be some sort of hero, sailing to Istanbul to find a killer and save the world from the Castlenau conspiracy. Then he had embarked on a mission to be the journalist who would write the story of the decade – the rescue of the Prince of Wales. He sat up, glancing at the Castlenau notes that lay scattered on his cot. He'd been a fool to think he could figure it out. He should have stayed in London. He should have stuck to being a file clerk.

Julian stretched out his legs that were cramping from inactivity. The air was stifling. He wiped a greasy film of sweat from his forehead then heard footsteps outside his door. It was too early for his next meal, he thought as the latch turned. Hurriedly he gathered the pages of the code, covering them with his leg. The door opened and Pavel stepped into the room. Behind him, black-shirted Boris took up a position in the doorway, big arms folded.

Pavel greeted Julian like a long lost acquaintance. "Mr. North, I am sorry to have neglected you all this time. You are doing fine, I see."

"Yes, I'm doing just fine." Julian hadn't talked for two days and the words came out like a croaking sound.

"Well, that's good then, isn't it?" Pavel sat down.

"It's an oven down here. I need to go out on deck for some air."

"I suppose I could arrange that, but not before tomorrow. Tonight we sail."

"To where?"

Ignoring the question, Pavel folded his hands and tipped his chair back on two legs. "So, you are a journalist with the *Times*. What have you written?"

Julian swallowed. This man was a member of – maybe even the head of *The Will of the People*. And he was a murderer. "Did you come here just to make conversation?"

Pavel smiled. "I thought it might help pass the time. I am curious about your career at the *Times*. Tell me about it. What have you written?"

Julian decided to play along. "I haven't written much. I only started with the paper a year and a half ago and have been in Istanbul less than six months. Of course I collaborated on the story about your attempted assassination of the Prince of Wales. Your man was a lousy shot."

"If I had wanted to assassinate the prince, I would certainly have done so."

"Just as you killed Czar Alexander?" The words were out of his mouth before Julian realized it. It would not be a good idea to get this man angry.

Pavel's jaw tightened and he brought his chair back level with a thud that startled Julian. "So, after being with the paper just a short time, here you are, assigned to their Istanbul office. That's rather odd, don't you think, for someone so inexperienced?"

"They had an opening at the Istanbul office – I filled it, simple as that."

"I think it was your influential uncle that made your Istanbul assignment possible. But it wouldn't have happened unless you wanted to go there."

Julian blinked. "How do you know about my uncle?"

"I have many sources. You might be surprised by all the things I know. But there is one thing I wonder about." Pavel fingered his chin, as if puzzling out a great mystery. "Of all the many offices of The London *Times* you might have been assigned to, what made you choose Istanbul?"

Julian's mind raced, but one thought stood out as crucial: He had to make Pavel think he knew more than he actually did. It was time to be bold even if he didn't feel that way. "Just following the clues in the journal."

Pavel's lips twisted. "And what do you know about the journal?"

Julian shrugged as if he had no care in the matter. "I translated it from French into English, that's all."

"Where is it now?"

That was the big question. Julian knew he had to give Pavel a reason to keep him alive and he had to speak with confidence. He leaned toward Pavel. "I have it safely hidden. But I know its secrets are not entirely in the writings of Jacques Castlenau. I have a man working on it right now. He's not with the *Times* and he's very good with codes." Not far from the truth, Julian thought, holding his breath.

"And I suppose, in exchange for keeping you alive, you could have those efforts terminated and the book returned to me?"

Julian felt his notes beneath his leg. A bead of sweat trickled down his back between his shoulder-blades. "I could."

There was a loud thump from the deck above and Pavel shook his head as if distracted. "As you might expect, I have a few pressing matters to attend to right now, but I'll hold you to that idea." He stood up. "In the absence of a specific reason to kill you, I'll keep you alive for a few more days. If you're lying to me, Mr. North, I will toss you overboard myself. The fish are big in these waters and some are aggressively carnivorous – did you know that?"

"No, I did not." Julian thought of Whiley and his anger rose, but so did his level of fear. That would not be a good death.

"We'll continue our conversation later - out on deck where you can get some air."

"What about the others?"

"I haven't killed them yet, if that's what you're concerned about. You can see them in a few days." He walked to the door. "I'm not a barbarian, as Albert calls me, but I will do what I have to do to complete my mission. You and he have no idea that the lives and freedom of unborn generations are hanging in the balance. Our fate and theirs are being controlled by a series of events set in motion long ago."

Pavel strode out, Boris following, pulling the door closed behind him and Julian breathed a sigh of relief.

Pavel dismissed Boris and took the stairs up onto the deck. The late afternoon sun blazed. He took a breath of heated air and walked to the rail, watching his men toil with the last of the supplies. A man came up behind him, and spoke in English.

"Were you able to learn anything?"

Pavel shook his head. "He knows more than he should."

The man spat over the side. "That's unfortunate."

By twilight on that same day, the loading and fueling of *Resolute* were complete. Pavel conducted an inspection from bow to stern then returned to the bridge and gave the order to cast off. He took the wheel himself as much because of the danger of running aground in the shallows as because of the seductive feeling of power it gave him. This was *his* ship of war; *his* implement of revolution - a revolution that had been lost, but was now found. He held the wheel firmly as a tugboat pushed the big ship around, pointing her seaward, guiding her until she was centered in the channel. It was nearly dark when Pavel called for one quarter speed and the big engine began its rhythmic thump.

Resolute headed out, following the sloping hills for ten miles on her approach to the open sea. Once there, Pavel gave the wheel to Boris and signaled the engine room for all ahead full. He had eleven hours of darkness in which to make his escape through one of the busiest harbors in the world.

"Are we on schedule?" asked Boris, seeming to sense Pavel's concern.

"We should be through the worst of it by midnight and well

into Marmara by sunrise – not as good as I'd hoped, but with a little luck, we should be all right." Pavel ordered the running lamps lit. A darkened ship seen from close range near a major shipping lane would be both dangerous and suspicious and he couldn't afford problems – not now, when everything had been going so well.

True, the recapture of the prince hadn't been planned and may not turn out to be a good thing, but by a fortuitous accident he'd also gotten hold of North. Now he'd be able to find out what the bumbling journalist knew from the book and he'd be able to keep him from causing any trouble - those were both good things.

An hour passed. Pavel spotted a ship making her way east. He ran his hand across his tired eyes to make sure he wasn't imagining the yellow lights floating beneath the stars in the distance. She came no closer than five miles, after which her path diverged and the ship disappeared from view.

A while later, Pavel spotted a channel light. This is where the Black Sea narrowed. They were beginning their approach into Istanbul Harbor. He pulled the red-filtered navigation lamp from its well and, after consulting the charts, made a westerly turn into the shipping lane. He gazed through the open windows in front of him, the light breeze calming him. It took time for his night vision to return, but he could see the lights of the harbor now. He was tempted to check his charts again but decided against it. A glance at the compass confirmed that their heading was exactly as it should be. And yet – there was the shoreline, much closer than it should be. It took him five long minutes before his blood ran cold, and he realized his mistake. "Hard to starboard, turn now. Now!"

Slow to see the danger, Boris hesitated.

Pavel grabbed the wheel himself and pulled it hard over. "That's a Goddamn ship out there headed straight for us." The coastal lights Pavel had seen were actually the lamps of an oncoming ship – a ship as big as *Resolute*.

"My God, where in hell did she come from?"

Resolute had been cutting through the water at full speed, the effects of the sharply angled rudder were immediate. The ship pitched violently, her forward momentum propelling her into the turn. Boris and Pavel strained at the wheel.

The bow of the oncoming ship filled the port side windows and her blaring horn combined with the whoosh of her hull through the water to drowned out all other sounds. They were going to be rammed at the stern. "Hard to port! Hard to port, now!" shouted Pavel, working the wheel hard in the other direction.

But this time there was little response from *Resolute* as most of her forward momentum had been lost in the initial turn. "She's going to hit us," shouted Boris over the din.

Furious with himself, Pavel watched the ship close down on them. Boris held the wheel hard to port. There was nothing more they could do now. The ship was so close Pavel could see the faces of the men on her deck. He ran off the bridge and looked aft, bracing for the impact – but none came. *Resolute* had managed to swing her stern out from harm's way with a mere five yards to spare.

Pavel gripped the rail and caught his breath, watching the freighter speed by. Below her stern lights her name was spelled out in Cyrillic letters: *Saint Ivan* out of Sevastopol. Pavel knew her captain could read the name HMS *Resolute* just as easily. They had been lucky to avoid the collision but their secrecy was lost and they had yet to enter the harbor.

Pavel stomped back onto the bridge. "Ease her back to starboard and resume our course."

"I thought she would run us through."

"What happened to our forward lookout? Was he asleep?" Pavel cursed himself for not personally assigning a man to the job.

"I will find out what happened."

"I want the man locked in irons, now, and I want *you* to replace him. Send someone up here to man the helm. We cannot have any more delays."

Boris left the bridge as Pavel stepped up to the wheel and signaled the engine room to reduce speed to one-third. He'd rather lose a little time than risk a collision.

Another look at the charts, followed by a change in course, put *Resolute* squarely in the center of the inbound shipping lane, as Pavel had intended. He kept watch for the rest of the night, and by dawn they were clear of the harbor and into Mamara. It was late afternoon when she slipped through the Dardanelles, out into the open waters of the Aegean. Here, at last, Pavel could rest. He went below and slept soundly for ten hours.

With *Resolute* under way and Pavel's obvious interest in the journal, Julian forced himself back to working on the code. All his efforts with the frequency method had failed. He knew he must be missing something.

He closed his eyes, trying to remember anything he had read in the journal that might give him a clue as to the origin of the code. He had no idea how long he sat. Heat and stale air sapped his energy. His mind lost focus. He slumped, leaning back onto the cot. He dreamed of Kate and what it might be like to make love with her. Then, abruptly, he heard her telling him that he was wasting time; that he had to get back to work. In his mind he argued back but knew she was right. He sat up.

Julian rubbed his eyes. He decided to look for patterns, for repeating combinations of symbols. Before long he noticed something he hadn't seen before. There seemed to be two or sometimes three groupings, or words, made up of a wide variety of different symbols. These were each five to eight symbols in length. The third and fourth groupings on the other hand were, almost without exception, six symbols long. He decided to focus on these consistently sized groupings and saw that they were always made up of different combinations of the same ten symbols, and that those symbols were never used in the other groupings. He leaned back against the bulkhead, furious with himself that it had taken so long to figure out what now seemed obvious. "They're numbers, damn it," he said aloud. "Numbers!"

Including numbers in what he'd thought was text must have thrown all his frequency calculations off. All of his work on the code so far had been a waste of time.

The next morning, after a biscuit breakfast, Julian was allowed out on deck. The sun burned hot and glaring but the taste of the fresh air was heaven-sent. He stood, taking in all his lungs could hold letting it out slowly. Gulls cried out overhead. The wind buffeted his face and despite the heavy hand of a bearded seaman on his shoulder, Julian's spirits were lifted. The Russian guided him to where Pavel stood with his back against the rail. He still wore his British officer's uniform, the tails of his shirt hanging loose.

"Mr. North, good to see you again. You have my apologies for not bringing you out earlier but, as you may imagine, I've been preoccupied with other duties."

"Where are we?" asked Julian staring at a featureless horizon.

"This is the Aegean Sea, just west of the Dardanelles."

"That was Istanbul harbor we went through, two nights ago."

"That's right. If this fair weather continues, we should be right on time."

"On time for what?"

Pavel chuckled. "Where do you think we're going?"

Julian did not respond. The scene of young Whiley being

thrown overboard at Pavel's casual command flashed through his mind.

"Well, no matter, you'll have plenty of time to ponder our destination and our intentions." He snorted in amusement, as if certain that Julian would never guess either one. "Mr. Sanford will be joining us shortly."

"He's been confined this whole time?"

Pavel gave him a circumspect stare. "Of course, why would I treat him any differently than you? Ah, here he is."

Julian turned to see Noah, clothing disheveled, face grim, being guided toward him.

Julian gave a nod to Noah then asked Pavel, "What have you done with the prince?"

"As you might expect, Albert has certain privileges. We're old friends now. He's on the forward deck, I think." Pavel motioned in that direction. "I'll take you to him. It'll be a reunion of sorts."

They found Bertie sitting near the bow staring out to sea. He held a freshly lit cigar and, except for his growth of whiskers, his uncombed beard and his torn clothing, he gave the appearance of a tourist on a holiday voyage. Bertie turned to face Pavel, then stiffened at the sight of Julian and Noah. He looked back out to sea.

Pavel smiled slightly. "Well, I can see you've got some issues to work out. I'll just leave the three of you to yourselves." He walked further down the port side rail and took a position within sight of the bow.

For a time Bertie ignored Noah and Julian who remained silent. Finally, he tapped the ashes from his cigar. "So how are the two journalists? Have you finished your big story about how you personally sabotaged my rescue?"

Julian shifted his feet. The prince was right; this was their fault – *his* fault. "All I can say is I'm sorry, my lord. I honestly believed we were doing the right thing."

"Journalists are sewer rats bent on defiling the character and reputation of their betters. And you two are the worst of your kind." Bertie pounded a fist onto the armrest of his chair. "If we ever get out of this mess, I'm going to have you both thrown in prison for what you did. What the hell were you doing out there in the first place?"

Julian told him about McNaulty and about the note from the kidnappers.

Despite his obvious resentment, Bertie seemed to listen attentively. "So Pavel had no idea you'd be out there in the Black

Sea."

"I don't see how he could have known," said Noah.

"And why would this McNaulty fellow help you?"

Julian hesitated, anticipating what would come next. "He saw it as a chance to make some money."

Bertie's face immediately turned red. He stood up and glared at Julian. "You *paid* him?" Noah tried to help. "It was to cover the expenses; the boat and crew to get us there."

Bertie kept his eyes glued to Julian's then turned away and took a long pull from his cigar. He sat back down. "Has Pavel talked to either of you since you've been aboard?"

"He talked with me two days ago," said Noah, "He asked about my work back in New York, and if I knew anything about a book – a French book of some kind. It seemed important to him."

Julian was startled. Without knowing why, he decided to play dumb. "Why would he be interested in a book?"

"I don't know. He didn't talk to you?"

"No, he didn't," lied Julian, uncomfortable with his dishonesty but committed to carry on with it. "What else did you talk about?"

"Just small talk; he didn't stay long."

"The less you say to him, the better," said Bertie as *Resolute* entered a gentle turn to port. "I'd just like to know where in hell he's taking us and what devil's business he intends doing with this ship."

"I heard one of the crew mention Lesvos. It could be that island out there," said Noah, pointing to a distant irregularity in the horizon. "So we're heading south."

Julian shielded his eyes and looked up at the black smoke billowing from the tall stack. "Wherever it is we're going, he's in a big hurry to get us there."

They remained on deck for an hour longer until a shout came from the forward lookout. The man was pointing off the starboard quarter where the southern tip of the island was much more prominent now. Beyond the island, a ship half *Resolute*'s size had just cleared the leeward side. On a near parallel course, the ships were separated by ten miles; a safe distance, Julian thought, but well within the range of a curious man using a decent telescope.

At that moment, Pavel approached them. He shouted an order to Boris in Russian then headed for the bridge.

Boris pulled his pistol and shoved Julian and Noah back along the rail, Bertie following from behind. As they went, Julian kept his eyes on the other ship. "She's a merchantman; she must see us."

Once below deck, Boris locked Noah in the first cabin. He passed a second then pushed Julian into his cabin, the third in line. When the door slammed shut and locked behind him, Julian remained beside it listening to the footsteps of Boris and Bertie. He counted them until they stopped and another door opened then slammed shut. So Bertie's cabin was less than ten paces from his own. He hoped that information might somehow prove useful.

CHAPTER 14

HMS Inflexible: The Black Sea

In the back corner of the bridge S.M. Parker sat with arms folded, his eyes getting heavy. He had been there all morning and it was only the steady rumble of the ship's engines and the occasional gust of wind from the window beside him that kept him from nodding off completely. As a senior member of the foreign office, he had been ordered to join the three-ship squadron that had been dispatched to Istanbul after Prince Bertie's disappearance. Ostensibly he was here to represent the position of the foreign office but Parker knew the real reason for his presence aboard HMS *Inflexible* had more to do with the treason of Major John Hastings.

It didn't sit well with anyone at the F.O. that such a prominent member of the organization would first kill a man in London then attempt to kill the Prince of Wales in Istanbul. And the riddle of why Hastings did what he did and how it was bound up with the damn Castlenau book had yet to be solved.

So here Parker was, tagging along on HMS *Inflexible* out in the Black Sea searching for the now missing Lord Beresford and HMS *Resolute* and the still missing Prince of Wales. What a colossal mess. Even so, and despite his current less than alert state, he was glad to be out from behind his desk and at sea again. He shifted his weight and scratched his nose.

Three paces in front of him stood the squadron commander, Captain Jacky Fisher. Short and stocky but with an imposing demeanor, Fisher was only thirty-two and held the distinction of being the youngest captain in the fleet. He possessed influential connections but Parker knew there was more to his success than that – he had the respect of his crew and of the admiralty as a professional, no-nonsense leader who had a knack for doing the right thing at the right time.

Parker looked out to the northern horizon, empty except for the dim profile of the gunship *Condor*. He knew that the gunship *Monarch* sailed on a parallel course to the far south. If *Resolute* and the Prince of Wales were out here, Fisher and his three ships would find them.

At the moment, there was a silent tension on the bridge. They were two and a half days running into the Black Sea, intruding deep into Russian territorial waters where the Czar's navy had always shown itself to be an aggressive defender. Fisher was driving his engines hard.

The firing of a distant cannon brought Parker upright in his chair.

A shout came from the forward lookout. "Signal, from *Monarch*." Two more cannon shots followed.

"Acknowledge," said Fisher, reading the signal immediately. "We'll head for her and see what she's found. Make sure *Condor* follows."

"Aye, sir," said First Officer Griffin.

Fisher turned to the navigator. "Mr. Moon, give us a heading for *Monarch*."

Parker pinched his eyes more awake. As *Inflexible* veered sharply to the south, her bow-mounted, five-pounder fired off a single shot, letting *Monarch* know she was on her way.

That signal had no sooner been sent than a cry came down from the high mast. "Unidentified ship approaching two points off the port bow."

Parker stood up, straining his eyes in that direction, but saw nothing.

"Mr. Howard," said the captain to his gunnery officer who had just stepped onto the bridge, "as soon as you see her smoke get a fix on our visitor; Mr. Griffin, sound general quarters."

The rumble of drums sounded the order and men throughout the ship began scrambling to their stations.

"All ahead full, I want us beside *Monarch* in thirty minutes."

"Aye, sir, but with these head winds it'll be more like fifty."

"Thirty-five then."

Mr. Howard held his telescope steady. "The unidentified ship is definitely headed our way, captain."

"Mr. Griffin, what do the Russians have out here?" asked Fisher.

"In their Black Sea fleet, they have two battle ships – older ones – no match for us; also three battle cruisers and seven gunboats similar in class to *Condor*, sir."

"Any of them sighted in this area recently?"

"Not that we've been aware of, sir." Griffin wiped his brow beneath his visor. "Our intelligence is not good, though. For all we know, their entire Black Sea fleet could be out there."

"Well, I very much doubt that." Fisher narrowed his eyes. "Mr. Howard, load one of the guns in the bow turret and have it bear on our new friend out there."

"Aye, sir."

"Time to *Monarch*, Mr. Moon?"

"At least forty minutes, captain."

Fisher cursed under his breath. "Odd that we get a signal from *Monarch* just as we come across an unidentified ship, don't you think, Mr. Griffin?"

"Must be two ships out there. Could be part of a Russian battle group."

"If that's the case, *Monarch* will have her hands full with one while we're occupied with the other." Fisher resolved the matter quickly. "Fire off a signal to *Condor* and *Monarch* to rig for battle."

"Aye, sir," said Griffin.

"Mr. Moon, how far are we from Turkish waters?"

"By Russian definition, over sixty miles, sir."

Parker knew that in Turkish waters a Russian ship couldn't bother them - not legally, but he suspected that technicalities wouldn't stop them today. He could see the smoke of the oncoming ship at the horizon now.

"If it comes to a fight," said Griffin to Fisher, "*Inflexible* alone can beat any Russian ship. *Monarch* taking on a second ship will be more risky."

Fisher scratched his jaw and gave Parker a glance. "We've been cautioned by the admiralty to avoid international provocations. London needs no more incidents with the Russians." He paused then gave an order. "Helm, slow to one-third."

"One-third, aye, sir."

Fisher tugged his visor. "Let's see just who in hell these bastards are. Mr. Moon, take a good look at that ship and see if we have a match in our Russian log."

"Aye, sir." Moon steadied his extreme-distance telescope and adjusted the focus.

"Sir, they're approaching range," said Griffin.

"No sign of them turning or slowing?"

"No, sir."

"Mr. Moon, what are we up against?"

"She's fast enough sir, doing about ten knots now," said Moon. He put aside his telescope. "Looks to have twin stacks consistent with their new *Kiev* class." He pulled out a logbook of foreign ships from the chart locker and began flipping pages then settled on one. "It could be the warship *Odessa*. That would give her six, eight-inch guns with a range of...three miles sir."

"Very good." Fisher turned to Griffin. "Tell Mr. Howard to prepare to fire a single shot over her bow. Fire on my order and tell him to *please* be sure not to hit her."

"Aye, sir." Griffin relayed the order down to Mr. Howard at the bow turret.

"Gunnery speed," ordered Fisher.

"Gunnery speed, aye, sir."

Fisher turned to Parker. "It'll take a few minutes to get the range. Be sure to hold onto your britches when we fire. We'll be making a bloody loud bang."

"Thanks for the warning, Captain," said Parker coolly, "but I'll be fine I'm sure." He had been aboard a warship off Sevastopol during the Crimean war some twenty years earlier and he knew the power of big naval guns.

"We'll see just how high we can make you jump," predicted Fisher.

The gunnery alarm sounded. The big turret, already aimed, made a final adjustment a few degrees to port. The long barrel of one of the guns elevated another degree or two. Beside the turret, Mr. Howard moved into position with his hand raised. He looked up to the bridge for the command.

"Fire when ready, Mr. Griffin," said Fisher calmly.

The order was passed down and, at the low point in the ship's rocking motion Mr. Howard shouted, "Fire!"

A heartbeat of silence was just long enough for *Inflexible* to regain the crest of a rolling wave. Then, a shower of flame and smoke burst from the muzzle of the iron gun with a deafening boom that nearly knocked Parker off his feet. He grabbed a hand-hold on the bulkhead. The windows on the bridge rattled and *Inflexible* shuddered in recoil as a seventeen-hundred pound shell was sent tearing through the air toward *Odessa*.

"Still with us, Parker?" asked Fisher.

Through ringing ears Parker heard himself assure Fisher that he was. The explosion had impacted every bone in his body, leaving him limp-legged. This gun was a monster compared to the ones at Sevastopol.

Fisher trained his telescope on *Odessa*. A distant boom announced the shell's explosion but Parker with his unaided eyes could see nothing.

Fisher collapsed his telescope. "A good shot, just over their mast. Mr. Griffin, give my compliments to Mr. Howard."

"Aye, sir."

"That'll put the fear of God into them. And here we sit, a mile beyond their range. Excellent! That's the biggest gun in her majesty's navy, Mr. Parker. At eighty tons, it's the most massive implement of destruction ever conceived. Wish to God it could be aimed accurately, but what the hell, as long as it scares the bloody guts out of everyone, it may never actually have to hit anything."

"Impressive," said Parker.

"She's turning, sir," announced Griffin.

"I'd expect so," said Fisher. "All ahead full. Resume our heading for *Monarch*." "Aye, sir."

"I'm going below, Mr. Griffin. Be sure to keep your eye on the Russians. They'll likely trail us to see what we're up to. If they do nothing more than that in the next twenty minutes, secure from general quarters. Mr. Parker will stay on the bridge in your charge until I return." Fisher gave Parker a severe look. "I don't want you wandering around the ship right now."

"I'll stay right here, captain," promised Parker as Fisher left.

Inflexible gathered speed and turned southward through the now choppy waters. Coming out of the turn, she headed straight for *Monarch*. Parker retook his seat as the men on the bridge went about their work.

"Now that's interesting," said Griffin after a while, his telescope fixed on the slowly growing profile of *Monarch*.

Parker stood and looked in the same direction. "What do you see?"

"There are two ships out there."

Parker's hopes rose. Could they have found *Resolute*? He kept his excitement to himself, unsure if Griffin and the rest of the men on the bridge were aware that their true mission was to find *Resolute* and the Prince of Wales. Fisher had been ordered to give that information only to those men needing to know. A short time later, Griffin slowed the engines. Parker could see the two ships clearly now.

Just beyond *Monarch* floated a rusty freighter, dead in the water. She listed badly; a feeble stream of smoke issuing from her stack.

"She's not flying a flag," said Griffin, his telescope on her. "*Monarch*'s launch is tied alongside. They're offloading her crew. Mr. Moon, get the captain."

"Can you make out her name?" asked Parker.

"She's lost most of the paint on her stern," said Griffin. "I can just make it out. She's the – *Oracle*."

"So who the hell is *Oracle*?" asked Fisher, stepping onto the bridge.

"No idea, sir," said Griffin, "but she won't last long. She must be leaking like a sieve to be listing like that; a damn good thing for her crew that we happened onto her."

"We haven't got time for this." Fisher took off his cap and scratched his head then turned his attention to the east. "The Russians are keeping their distance, I see."

"They're staying well out of range, sir," said Griffin, "but they're trailing us just the same."

"And *Condor*?"

"On her way," said Griffin.

"Signal *Monarch* to advise when they have this situation stable. We'll then be on our way in advance to save time."

"Aye, sir," said Griffin, relaying the order.

Parker picked up the telescope and worked the focus. "Their launch with a load of survivors is leaving *Oracle* on its way back to *Monarch*."

Fisher folded his arms. "They had better be quick about it. Mr. Griffin, I want us on our way in ten minutes, no more."

"Aye, sir."

"Hold on a moment," said Parker slowly. "They're not heading for *Monarch* – they're coming *here*."

"You must be mistaken," said Fisher. "Why would they do that?" He grabbed the telescope and confirmed what Parker had seen. Five minutes later he had a better view of the men in the launch. "My God, what the hell's going on?"

The small boat rolled gently with the sea. Four men strained at the oars bringing her closer to *Inflexible* with each stroke. At the stern Beresford and Faulks sat pale and expressionless opposite Briggs. The first officer knew it was a miracle of sorts that they'd been able to keep *Oracle* afloat, but that accomplishment didn't begin to offset the utter failure of their mission. Briggs watched Beresford closely. Deep creases lined his face. His posture, which had always been tall and straight, had the hunched-over look of a much older man – a beaten man.

"Not long now," said Briggs. "It'll be good to get back onto a solid ship again."

Beresford only nodded. He hadn't talked much the whole time they had been marooned aboard *Oracle* and it was visibly clear that he dreaded the prospect of having to explain his actions to those aboard *Inflexible*.

They pulled alongside where a line was cast down. Briggs looked up to see the heads of a dozen curious seamen. He recognized Fisher among them. They climbed up and right away, Briggs took Fisher to one side. "We need some time with you alone, captain."

Fisher started to raise a question then apparently thought better of it. "Yes, of course," he said. "This way."

Tea and brandy were sent up to the captain's wardroom for the four men gathered around a table intended for a much larger group. Beresford was quick to finish his tea and pour a second cup while, uncharacteristically, leaving his brandy untouched.

"We got here as fast we could, my lord," Fisher began, facing Beresford. "We weren't looking for you to be aboard a sinking trading ship."

"The Prince of Wales is dead," said Beresford tonelessly. "I got him killed."

Fisher's face turned suddenly ashen and he sat perfectly still, as if frozen by the news.

Briggs was certain that the captain had expected the worst but hearing it plainly spoke had to be a shock just the same.

Fisher waited for Beresford to say more, then turned to Faulks and Briggs. "What happened out there?"

Briggs recounted the demands of the kidnappers and their holding of the prince at gunpoint on the island. "Our plan had been to recover Prince Bertie in exchange for *Resolute*. We set her scuttling charges. The ship would be lost but she would take the anarchists down with her. It seemed to be the only way to insure the safety of the prince. The transfer of crews took the better part of the day after which..."

Here Beresford interrupted. "...after which I went down into *Resolute*'s hold and lit the fuse. Briggs and I were the last to leave her. We immediately set off for the island to rescue Prince Bertie. When we got there he was gone. It's a small island and we searched it all until dark. We were headed back for the merchantman when the horizon flared and we heard the explosion. The charges had gone off, *Resolute* had sunk. The only place Prince Bertie could have been was aboard that ship. He's dead."

Faulks added his explanation: "From the freighter, we had our telescopes trained on the island the whole day. Prince Bertie was there the entire time while the transfer of crews was taking place. Late in the day the glare of the sun blinded our view. The anarchists must have had another boat hidden on the island. They just took him out to *Resolute* as she passed by. She wouldn't have even had to slow down to pick him up."

"But you didn't actually see any of that," said Fisher.

"No, we didn't."

Fisher thought for a moment. "What was *Resolute*'s heading when you last saw her?"

"Due west," said Briggs.

"So these anarchists were after *Resolute* all along. What do you think they intended to do with her?"

Beresford gave a futile shrug. "They were after both the Prince of Wales and *Resolute* and they succeeded until the charges went off. There's no guessing what their plan might have been."

"There were no survivors from *Resolute* after she went down?"

"The explosion was some distance from us, just over the horizon." said Beresford. "The rusted out engines of the merchantman got us to the area the next day. There were no life boats and only a small amount of debris. We recovered two bodies – that was all. These we returned to the sea. *Resolute* would have sunk in minutes – there could have been no survivors."

Fisher got up slowly.

"What are you thinking?" asked Beresford.

"From what I've heard here, there's still a chance, a small one, that Prince Bertie is still alive and even that *Resolute* is still afloat."

"Rubbish," said Beresford, snatching his brandy which he drank in two quick swallows.

Briggs saw the glimmer of hope in Fisher's reasoning; but he also saw a major flaw. "What could that explosion have been except the scuttling charges?"

"I don't know," said Fisher. "I do know that no one in this room saw Prince Bertie perish and no one saw *Resolute* go down. Regardless of the evidence, I see nothing to be gained by assuming either event actually took place." He looked around the table. "I think we've done as much as we can for right now. I have accommodations ready for each of you. Food is also ready when you want it." He walked to the door. "I'm taking us back to Istanbul."

The meeting was adjourned and, after getting something to eat, Briggs went back on deck, alone with his thoughts. It was late in the afternoon when *Inflexible* fired two shells into *Oracle* and sank the shipping hazard she had become. The squadron then sailed west and made Istanbul harbor two days later.

CHAPTER 15

Kate sat beside the files in the back of the office wilting under the full force of Istanbul's June heat. Every window and door had been opened yet the air remained thick and stagnant. She cleared a few moist strands of hair from her forehead and added another note to the pad on her lap. Around her lay old news clippings and a map of the Black Sea.

She had spent days sifting through articles, drawings and photographs, and had pieced together a decade-long patchwork history of *The Will of the People*. When she started, she had no idea what Julian and Noah had gotten themselves into. Now, she was beginning to understand just how great a danger they were facing. But something else was bothering her.

The apparent kidnapping of the Prince of Wales was something new for the anarchist group. It demanded more planning and finesse than the brute force of a murder or a bombing. Maybe it was just their new strategy directed at achieving the same goal of inflicting chaos. But maybe they had something else in mind this time; something more ambitious.

Tapping the tip of her pencil on the tabletop, she pondered the question, realizing only after a moment's pause that the pencil thing was something Julian had always done. Kate remembered that habit of his bothering her at first, but now, since he'd been gone, she found that she'd begun to value things that brought the memory of him back to her. Had he gotten to her that deeply? No, she decided, her connection with Julian wasn't like that. She was just worried about him. Still, she would be glad, no, relieved, when

147

he was finally back – Noah too. Yes, Noah too. Slowly, Kate put the map aside and started gathering up the clippings.

The bell over the front door startled her. She stood and peered beyond the stairs seeing an older man dressed in a wrinkled white suit talking to Steven. Kate put down her things and walked up the aisle toward him.

The man gave her a look as she approached and shifted his walking stick from one hand to the other. "I'm Parker," he announced.

"He says he's from the foreign office," said Steven.

"You must be Miss Wilder," said Parker. "Sir Edward told me about you." Parker reached for Kate's hand and shook it.

"What brings you here, Mr. Parker?"

"I'm looking for Mr. North. I understand he's been staying here?"

"He's out at the moment," said Willoughby stepping out of his office. "What business does the foreign office have with him?"

"You're Willoughby, correct?" Parker paused then continued. "I can explain, of course, but..."

Suddenly, Kate made the connection. "You're the man in the picture."

Parker squinted at Kate as if not seeing clearly. "Excuse me, my dear, what picture?"

Kate was certain of it just from the look of his eyes. "There's a picture of you at the embassy standing with the man who tried to kill Prince Bertie."

Parker's face darkened. "I knew that unfortunate man, yes, but how do you know anything about him? I didn't think that information had been released yet."

Wary of Parker now, Kate hesitated just as Baker rushed in, out of breath.

"Three of our warships have arrived," Baker blurted out. "They..." His voice trailed off and his eyes narrowed when he saw Parker.

"Hello, I'm Parker. I just disembarked from one of those ships. I'm from the foreign office."

Baker closed his mouth.

Parker looked from face to face. "Damn it all, must you all be so stiff? I'm from the foreign office, not the damned secret police. I'm British, for God's sake."

Baker spoke slowly. "You're here because of all the trouble with Prince Bertie."

"The queen sent the warships here because of that. The navy

was kind enough to let me tag along for the ride. I had some time, I thought I'd check in on Mr. North. He and I had a little project we were working on in London. I was surprised to learn from Sir Edward, that he was here in Istanbul working at this lovely office of yours. *That*, is why I'm here." He glanced around the room. "You're a little cramped I see, but things are neat as a pin – must be the woman's touch."

He smiled at Kate who fought to keep her eyes from rolling back. "Steven does all our cleaning Mr. Parker," she said.

"Well, he does a fine job."

But Kate was interested in hearing more about Parker and Julian's *little project*. "Julian said nothing about working with the foreign office."

"Truth be told, he didn't actually know I was with the F.O. But, you say he's not here. So where is he?"

Kate glanced at Willoughby.

"I think perhaps we can discuss this further in my office, Mr. Parker," said Willoughby.

"That is, after you show me your F.O. credentials."

"Oh, yes, of course."

Parker produced a card that Willoughby studied then handed back. "Bring a map would you, Miss Wilder? – the Black Sea. And Steven, we'll have some tea, thank you."

Once they were settled in, Willoughby closed the door and unrolled the map. "When North left, about two weeks ago now, he was headed here." He put his finger on a spot in the Black Sea.

Parker was silent. He leaned back in his chair, his thumb at his lower lip.

"What's wrong?" asked Kate.

"How much do you know about what's been happening?" asked Parker.

Willoughby spoke in a low voice. "We know...no, we believe, that Prince Bertie was kidnapped. He was to be rescued out in the Black Sea." He told him about McNaulty and about the boat Julian had chartered.

"Damn that impetuous fellow," said Parker. "I don't know how he knew to come here to Istanbul, he was a step ahead of us on that, but he was stupid to have done it. And I was stupid for underestimating him. He's been gone two weeks?"

"That's right," said Kate, growing more worried.

Parker hesitated then spoke slowly. "I just came from the Black Sea. The prince is still missing, he may be dead for all I know and there was no sign of *Resolute*. We found her captain, her crew and Lord Beresford marooned aboard a sinking freighter."

"Well that makes no sense," said Willoughby "*Resolute* passed through the harbor three nights ago – she almost rammed a Russian ship."

Parker's eyebrows rose. "How do you know that?"

"The Russian captain was pretty upset and made an entry in his log book. My contact in Sevastopol reported it to me."

"You have a man in Sevastopol?"

"When you've been in the newspaper business as long as I have, you develop connections. He thought it was unusual so he telegraphed me. We have an arrangement."

"Does anyone else know?"

Willoughby shrugged. "I didn't think it was a great secret but I didn't tell anyone about it – except for Miss Wilder of course."
Parker went back to thumbing his lip.

"We assumed," said Kate, "that Prince Bertie had been rescued and was aboard *Resolute* on his way back to England. That's why we've been expecting Julian anytime now."

"You're certain it was *Resolute*?"

"The log entry mentioned her by name," said Willoughby. He leaned back in his chair, the old leather creaking beneath him. "It did seem strange that she would have been running the harbor at night."

Kate was stunned as a thought hit her. She turned to Parker. "Are you thinking that the kidnappers might have *Resolute*?"

"That's what it looks like. The warship must have been the price for Prince Bertie's freedom."

"If that were true, the prince should have been released. He should have been with Beresford," said Willoughby.

"But he wasn't." Parker almost mumbled this, apparently preoccupied with another thought.

Kate swallowed. "So what happened to Julian and Noah?"

Parker stood up. "Get another map, would you? – of the Aegean and the eastern Med."

Kate retrieved one from the back room and spread it out on Willoughby's desk over the other map.

Parker put a finger on Istanbul. "If *Resolute* was here three days ago, heading west, she could be anywhere out here by now." His hand swept out a wide arc running half way out to Greece and down to Crete.

Willoughby rested his elbows on the map. "Lots of places to hide in that large an area."

Parker shook his head. "You and I have to get to the embassy.

There's a chance they don't know that *Resolute*'s been sighted."

"Oh come now, how could they not know?" said Willoughby.

"Maybe they do, but it never hurts to be sure. Besides, I've been looking for an excuse to see Lord Beresford. I'm itching to find out what really happened aboard *Resolute*. They don't like sharing information with the foreign office you know – always suspicious of us for one reason or another." Parker kept his eyes on Willoughby. "I'm allowing you to join me only because I expect that Lord Beresford will want to question you himself."

"I'm going with you too," said Kate.

"I assumed you would," said Willoughby, ignoring Parker's disapproving glance.

When they arrived at the embassy Parker showed his credentials and they were immediately ushered up to Sir Edward's office. Kate noticed that the picture showing Parker with Hastings had been taken down. She decided it might be best not to bring it up again.

They took their places around an oval table and formalities were dispensed with. Parker spoke first: "We have news you may not be aware of, Sir Edward: HMS *Resolute* was sighted three days ago."

The ambassador's eyes widened. "But that can't be."

Parker continued: "She was heading into Istanbul harbor, sailing from the east." He glanced at Willoughby. "We have a reliable witness."

"Hold on," said Sir Edward raising a hand, getting out of his chair. "Beresford and Faulks should be here." He strode out.

"You were right, he had no idea," said Willoughby to Parker.

"Evidently their connections aren't as good as yours." Parker drummed his fingers.

"You'll have to tell them about North's trip into the Black Sea. They're not going to like that."

"Maybe they already know," suggested Kate.

Willoughby shook his head. "They didn't even know about *Resolute*, it's not likely they know about Julian and Noah."

Parker gave a start. "You mentioned that name before, Miss Wilder. Who's this Noah fellow?"

They were interrupted by Sir Edward who quickly introduced them to Beresford and Faulks. "Tell them what you told me," he said to Willoughby.

Kate watched Beresford as he digested the news about *Resolute*. His expression turned immediately hopeful then hardened. His hand clenched to a fist. She could almost feel his mind working things through.

"She's out in the Aegean then," said Beresford, directing his attention to the map on the wall. "Faulks, we need to get Fisher on this. Thanks for your help Mister..."

"Willoughby."

"Sir Edward will caution you about keeping this quiet." Beresford rose to go.

"I'm sorry, my lord, but there's more," said Parker.

Beresford remained standing. "I've got things to do, Mr. Parker. Make it quick."

"Mr. Willoughby and Miss Wilder know about Prince Bertie being kidnapped."

Kate felt Beresford's stare. She swallowed dryly as Parker explained about the tip from McNaulty.

"Damn," said Sir Edward. "This'll be the last time I trust that man."

"Throw him in prison. He's a criminal," said Beresford. "And keep a close watch on these two until all this is over." He turned back to Kate. "Is there anyone else who knows?"

Kate swallowed. "Two weeks ago two journalists, one of ours and one from the New York *Times* chartered a boat and followed *Resolute* into the Black Sea. McNaulty had told them where the rescue of the prince was going to take place. They were just going to observe the event – nothing more. We haven't heard from them since they left."

Beresford's lower lip stiffened. He took a step back. "So there *was* another boat out there and it didn't belong to the kidnappers. If they were the ones who picked up Prince Bertie he may still be alive." Beresford paused. "It was a charter boat you said?"

"Yes, probably one of the harbor ferries I think."

Beresford nodded slowly. "I know the type." He turned to Willoughby as if getting his second wind. "It was irresponsible of you to send your man out there. I don't know what part he might have played in this whole affair but I aim to find out. Until then, both of you will stay close to your office and tell no one." He raised a finger. "*No one* is to know any of this. I want your word, the word of each of you to that effect."

"You have it, my lord. We won't say a thing," said Willoughby.

Kate nodded quickly. "Not a word, my lord. But there's one last thing if I may?" She paused. "Ira Goldsmith of the New York *Times*, he also knows about the kidnapping."

Beresford kept silent for a moment as if making sure Kate had no more surprises. He turned to Sir Edward. "Show Miss Wilder and Mr. Willoughby out. Get Fisher in here. Parker, you stay too. We need to talk this through."

A guard escorted Kate and Willoughby out of the room and out of the embassy.

"It wasn't your fault," Kate told Willoughby as they headed down the steps outside. "Julian was determined to sail out there. There was nothing we could have done to stop him – or Noah."

"That's little comfort," said Willoughby, his face drawn. "I fear they're in grave danger and there's nothing we can do to help them."

They grabbed a waiting carriage and rode back to the office in silence, Kate's mind racing with questions about where Julian and Noah might be at this moment, and about what had really happened out in the Black Sea.

Two days later, in the middle of the night, an insistent rap at the front door of Mrs. Potter's boarding house awakened Kate. She lay in bed in her second floor room, listening. The rapping stopped and she heard voices followed by the sound of someone coming up the stairs.

There was a light knock on her door. It was Mrs. Potter. "Miss Wilder, there's a Mr. Parker here for you. He says it's important."

"Parker? Yes, I'll be right there." This could not be good. Maybe they'd found Julian and Noah – their bodies. No, she wouldn't think like that. She rubbed her eyes then threw on her robe and went downstairs where she was directed by the harried Mrs. Potter, into the sitting room.

"Mr. Parker, what are you doing here? What's wrong?"

He looked a little harried himself, Kate thought. His hair was a mess and he needed a shave. At his feet was a cardboard suitcase.

"Sorry to bother you at such an hour, Miss Wilder, but there's no time to explain. You'll need to pack a bag, just the essentials. A carriage is waiting to take us to the docks. Goldsmith and Willoughby are already aboard."

"To the docks?" Kate shook her head in disbelief. "It's two in the morning."

"Sorry, my dear, but it was either this or Beresford was going to have all of you put up at the embassy. He wanted you confined there to make sure you kept things quiet while he was gone. He also seems to think you know more than you're saying."

"Why would he think that?" asked Kate. "And why are we off for the docks? Are we going somewhere?"

"We'll be boarding *Inflexible*. She sails within the hour."

"Oh, then I *do* need to pack. I'll be quick...*Inflexible*?" She headed back for the stairs then stopped. "But where is she off to?"

"I'll tell you once we're aboard. Oh, and you won't need to bring any of your outer clothing along – that's already been taken care of with this." He handed her the suitcase, his face broadening a little. "On this trip, you'll be going as Seaman Wilder."

CHAPTER 16

The Northern Sinai

Sergeant Ahmet Rashid was awakened by a kick to his feet and a voice whispering his name. The sound of a canvas flap rippling in the wind reminded him that he was lying in a military tent pitched in the open desert. In his dream he had been in a much better place. He cleared his eyes. "What...? What's wrong?"

"You are Sergeant Rashid?"

"Yes." He tried to discern the dark profile of the uniformed man standing over him. The Abyssinian wine he had consumed the night before wasn't helping his focus. He let out a belch. "Who the hell are you?"

"I am Lieutenant Shariff, General Ali's personal aide. You must come with me."

Ahmet cursed himself for having missed the lieutenant's collar insignia. "Yes, sir," he said, getting his bearings. He sat up, pulled on his boots and reached for his pack.

"Leave it. Come on, quickly now!"

Ahmet grabbed his helmet and followed the lieutenant out of the tent and into the darkness, stepping over sleeping soldiers as they went.

They were the third battalion of the western corps of the Turkish Army - a fast-moving, clandestine unit comprised of cavalry and infantry, capable of unleashing lethal force when and where needed at the sultan's personal order. Two months ago, they'd been based in the dusty wilderness just east of the Red Sea.

From there they'd been taken by boat to its eastern shore and from there they'd marched for days over rugged terrain finally arriving at this bowl-shaped depression in the sand five days ago. And here they had waited.

Early in Ahmet's mandatory ten-year enlistment he had shown an aptitude for languages and for telegraphy both of which made him an ideal candidate for the west-third. He had served his country for nine years and seven months - five months to go. When his term was over, he planned to be a real telegrapher who would actually get paid for his work. His English was very good so he could do translations too. He'd never get rich but he would have enough to afford a family. He found himself thinking more and more about this prospect as his time grew closer. One thing was certain, whatever lay ahead would be an improvement over the army. He was getting too old to be running around in the desert like this.

Ahmet followed the lieutenant across the entire camp to where six men on horseback waited. "You'll be riding with us," said Shariff, not the least out of breath as he mounted his horse and leaned over to grab the reigns of another. He handed them to Ahmet who climbed up.

The horse snorted under the load. Ahmet smoothed his mustache and straightened his helmet. He took a deep breath to compose himself. Of the other men he recognized only the man who sat tall on a white Arabian.

"Sergeant Rashid," said General Ali, "I understand you've been bored without your telegraph. If all goes well, you'll soon be busy enough setting up our communications. Are you ready to see why we're out here?"

"Yes sir," replied Ahmet. His horse snorted again as if answering for himself. Ahmet patted the animal's neck and grabbed the reins more firmly. Maybe here was a horse with a sense of humor.

They set off at a gallop, and rode hard into the cold wind. With the sky brightening they slowed to a canter and grouped more tightly. In the better light, Ahmet recognized Sergeant Ezra, a short bull of a man who now rode beside the general. Near a low ridge they came to a halt, dismounted and staked down the horses.

The rising sun cast their shadows far behind them and Ezra motioned to keep quiet. He led them up the ridge, Ahmet's boots sinking in the sugary sand. The air smelled clean, moist from dew and there was something else. He thought he smelled smoke.

At the top of the ridge they all dropped to a prone position.

Ahmet peered over the crest into the blazing sun. He squinted. From his elevated position the sand sloped down to the banks of a river a hundred feet across.

General Ali spoke in a low voice. "This is the Suez Canal."

Ahmet felt an immediate sense of dread, appreciating the significance of that statement and all that it implied. This river below him would have looked like any other had it not run as straight and as true as a well-surveyed road. He looked to the north through waves of heat already rising in the early morning air. A freighter just entering the canal ran low in the water. Beyond her, where the canal joined the deep blue of the Mediterranean, the tall gray walls of a fort stood, guarding the mouth of the canal. Above the fort a British flag waved while around it a number of outlying buildings dotted the countryside. That could only be Port Said.

"Here is the treasure of our empire," continued Ali. "It was built by the blood and sweat of Ottoman hands and it is our duty and honor to take it back for the empire."

Ahmet scanned the area, wondering how a force as small as the west-third could possibly accomplish such a task. But he knew the general must have a plan. He hoped it was a good one.

CHAPTER 17

Julian knew that something was happening. Two days earlier, *Resolute*'s guns had been fired. Between the blasts he'd heard a few shouts from the crew but nothing else. The firing continued for two hours before it stopped. Since then the guns had been silent and *Resolute* had resumed her race to the south as he sat locked in his cabin. Then during the night, the engine had slowed to nearly a dead stop. Now, an hour before dawn, they were picking up speed again.

He looked through the porthole and could make out the brighter stars and, below them, the running lamps of two other ships, stationary against the pinkening horizon. Julian's heartbeat quickened. He sensed that whatever Pavel had been planning would be happening today.

Up on the bridge Pavel spotted the outline of the fort in the hazy distance.

"They've signaled us to proceed," Boris yelled up to him.

"Steady as you go," Pavel said calmly, well-adapted by now to his role as a British naval captain. He folded his arms and bit down on his half-smoked cigar. Had fate been different, he might well have been a naval officer, he mused, though certainly not in the British navy.

The engine pounded away and a comfortable breeze flowed in through the open windows. It was the time of day Pavel most enjoyed between the chill of the night and the brutal heat of full daylight. He trusted that Boris, now standing at the bow, had everything in order: The guns of the forward turret loaded and manned, ready to fire; the side-mounted guns loaded but not yet run out, the gun ports closed preserving the element of surprise until the last possible moment.

Back in the Aegean the men had practice-fired each of the main guns. The shells that he had secured with the help of the Turks worked well, but his men had difficulty with the muzzle-loading process. At best, it took four minutes for each firing cycle – a good British crew could do it in half that time. But, in this attack, Pavel expected to fire no more than a single volley, perhaps two, and these would be at very close range. His men should be able to handle that.

Resolute continued her approach and Pavel studied the fort through his telescope. The original canal had been built by the French without fortifications and was given to Egypt in exchange for favorable fees of passage. With British ownership came the first improvement to the canal – the fort on which Pavel now focused his attention. Its stone walls rose sixty feet above the rolling waves. The dark barrels of six big guns loomed over the parapets. They probably weren't even loaded, guessed Pavel. What few hostilities the region had experienced over the past several years had been limited to a few local uprisings. The men inside this fort were trained only to enforce customs laws and collect fees. They were office boys - they would not be ready for the guns of *Resolute*.

As for the Turks, Pavel hoped that Ali and his men had taken up their position on the rise above the fort but this was very much a secondary concern. If they were absent, *Resolute* would fire on the fort, do what damage she could and escape north into the open Mediterranean. This alternative would be perfectly acceptable to Pavel, so he wasn't too worried about things going wrong today. After all, it was the Turks' plan to take the canal – not his; at least not now.

Just west of the fort, concealed behind a gently rising slope, General Ali mounted the white horse that had served him well over the past three years. He grasped the hilt of his undrawn sword and faced his men. To his right, the cavalry formed a double line that stretched along a front one hundred yards long. The horses whinnied and bobbed their heads, their hooves scratching at the hard sand. To his left, the foot soldiers stood like statues in two long columns, each four abreast. Beside Ali a horseman held the crimson and green flag of the Ottoman Army. It flapped in the light breeze. Ali glanced at the sun and tasted the air. The smells of battle were not yet present, but they soon would be.

The charge to the fort would be straight on, across a wide clearing that had been denuded by the British specifically to prevent just the type of maneuver Ali had in mind. The defenders wouldn't be expecting an attack both from sea and land. While the British were distracted on the seaward side by Pavel and his ship, he and his men would make a mad dash across the clearing. By the time the defenders became aware of his land attack, he would be on them.

Ali turned. Along the ridgeline a scout rode swiftly toward him.

"Our ship's less than a mile out," said the man when he pulled up.

Ali nodded. At the moment when the ship fired on the fort, he must begin his charge. He wheeled his horse back around to face his men. His voice boomed. "Call to the grenadiers."

Five horsemen wearing gold-colored helmets stepped out from the cavalry ranks and advanced to Ali's position. These were the men who would precede the charge. Everything depended on them. In each of their saddlebags was a bomb which, once they got to the walls of the fort, they would light then hurl at the entrance to the fort. Their combined force would blow the big double gate apart.

"Aim your bombs true," said Ali. "May Allah be with you today."

The captain of the grenadiers, a tall man with fiery eyes and a full black beard, saluted. "May he be with us all, my general."

Inside the fort, the mood was tranquil. It was just another day for the captain of the battlements who, from his position at the southwest corner, had his telescope trained on the approaching warship. Indeed, the unexpected sight of HMS *Resolute* had brought many of the fort's soldiers over to the eastern wall for a look. Colorful flags flew gaily along her lines and a trail of white on blue foamed off her bow as she slid easily through the calm waters. Off her stern waved the British flag. She continued her heading, directly toward the fort. It was at that moment the captain noticed that she had failed to make the turn that would have taken her into the mouth of the canal.

The error had the captain muttering to himself. "What is she doing?" He walked swiftly along the wall. *Resolute* drew closer still; the guns of her forward turret rose and turned.

"What in..." He eyed his men lounging along the parapet. A cold chill ran up his spine. "Back from the wall!" he shouted. "Get back..." Still unsure of what was happening, he took what cover he could while still watching *Resolute*, his eyes fixed to her forward turret.

Suddenly the guns erupted in a double stream of white smoke and bright orange flame. The roar was deafening. The heavy shells slammed into the battlements and exploded. An entire section of the stone wall burst apart in a ball of smoke and flame. Fragments of limestone and masonry tore through the men, obliterating bodies in a bloody spray. A shock wave reverberated along the wall's remaining length shaking the ground itself. The captain fell to his knees, dazed. Smoke filled the air. What the hell was *Resolute* doing? Soldiers ran to the sight of the explosion to help. Smoke billowed from the charred rubble.

The captain cleared his eyes in time to see the warship's gun ports fly open. The ship was so close he could hear the canon rumble into position. My God, she was about to fire a broadside. He had just registered this thought when smoke and flame sprayed out from the ship in a single loud boom. What remained of the wall in front of him burst apart and a hail of shrapnel and stone riddled the second gun crew. He saw a stone block spinning through the air, coming straight for him. He covered his face and dodged, too late.

At the first blast, General Ali drew his sword and raised it high above his head. His horse danced beneath him as he shouted to his men. "Today we fight for what is ours! We fight for the Empire!"

"For the Empire!" the men shouted.

General Ali signaled the mounted grenadiers who broke out of the formation and began their race to the fort. He waited long enough to give them a good head start then turned to a boy of fifteen who sat rigid with fear on the horse next to him. He spoke to him in a calm voice. "Sound the charge, bugler."

The boy took in a deep breath, faltered for a moment, then took one more. He raised his horn to his lips and blew as hard as he could. The notes rang out clear and crisp. A good omen, thought Ali leveling his sword straight at the fort, digging his spurs into the belly of his Arabian. The moment had come.

"Charge," Ali yelled, urging his horse forward. His cavalry yelled with him and the line of horses bolted from level ground up the slope. The general felt their rumble behind him as they burst over the ridge at a gallop heading straight for the fort.

At the rear-guard of the infantry Ahmet heard the command and waited for the line of men in front of him to start moving. "Port arms!" he shouted to his men. He had been up the entire night. After spotting the signal from the warship, he and the others in his small advanced group had cut the telegraph lines to the fort and then had brought word back to the general that the ship was in place. He knew he should be exhausted but he was not. He was ready. More than nine years in the army and he had somehow always managed to stay out of an actual battle – until now.

The men at the front of the column started forward. Ahmet's heart pounded through his chest. Raising his rifle high, he tried to remind himself he was a soldier now not a telegrapher. "Here we go, boys!" he shouted, trying to exude confidence. "For the Empire!"

"For the Empire!" Their shout melded into the roar of the battalion. Ahmet hoisted his rifle to the rhythm as their cheers became a screaming chant. "Empire! Empire!" He dismissed from his mind the fleeting vision of his body lying dead in the sand and waved his men forward. They moved slowly at first then broke into a wild run. Ahead, he could only see the backs of the men in the forward ranks framed against the cloud of dust raised by the cavalry.

General Ali rode as one with his horse, feeling the animal's powerful muscles flex beneath him with each lunging stride. He matched his own movements to those of his mount, staying low in the saddle, his eyes on the gates of the fort, his sword held straight. Behind him the cavalry thundered. They were only two hundred yards out and he hadn't yet seen the flash of a single rifle from the fort. They had been lucky so far. Would their luck hold? All depended now on the bombs of the grenadiers.

In the distance he could see the five men, on foot now, running along the base of the fort. Then they reached the gates. Not long now.

The blast came as a flash and a muffled boom barely audible to Ali over the pounding hooves around him. The gates were shrouded in smoke. His pulse quickened. He prayed that they had fallen but as the smoke dissipated, his heart sank. Behind a blackened crater, the gates stood as tall and stout as ever. On the wall above them Ali could see the heads of defenders poking up, rifles flashing.

There was no way into the fort - and there was no turning back. Bullets buzzed past him. A man beside Ali screamed and lurched off his saddle, falling to be trampled by the horsemen behind. The general set his jaw and kept his sword level even as the sickening truth hit him – *This will be a massacre*. He scanned the field realizing that he had only one choice. He raised his sword and guided his horse into a long turn, swerving away from the fort, hoping his men would follow.

Out beyond the seaward wall *Resolute* stormed past the fort heading directly for the rocky shoreline that jutted out ahead of her.

"Hard to port," commanded Pavel. He ran to the starboard side of the bridge, gripping the rail as he felt the ship shudder beneath him. He had no idea how deep these waters were. The big warship turned and began to roll. Pavel heard a creaking, groaning sound. *Resolute* slowed – she was scraping bottom. "All ahead full!" he shouted.

"Damn it, we are *not* going to run aground!" Pavel cursed. The ship shuddered again but continued her forward motion.

Next to Pavel, Boris staggered on the angled deck. "We're still moving," he shouted back, the sounds of the battle for the fort rising behind him. A howling screech reverberated through the hull and *Resolute* slowed nearly to a stop. But the ship kept moving then rolled back, leveling out. The screeching stopped.

Pavel exchanged a glance with Boris and blessed their good fortune. He looked back at the fort; they were beyond it now, gathering speed. He grabbed the telescope that had fallen and trained it on the smoking structure.

From this short range, the effects of *Resolute*'s guns had been devastating. The fort's seaward wall had been breached in two places. Fires rose from the openings and he could see men rushing to put them out. The guns of the fort were in no shape to return fire. "Have a look," said Pavel with satisfaction, handing the telescope to Boris.

Boris adjusted the focus but shifted the view. "Here come the Turks!" he paused. "They've got a problem though; the gates are still up."

Pavel grabbed the telescope. "What happened to their artillery?" He watched the cavalry slow, then veer away from the fort. Horses and men were going down in terrible numbers. "They'll kill them all," said Pavel. He yelled a course correction to the helmsman as he grabbed Boris by the shoulder. "Come on!"

They headed off the bridge and ran down to the main deck and along the starboard rail.

At the mid-ship turret the gunnery team was standing around thinking their job was done.

"You men," ordered Pavel, "load your gun and bear on the fort."

The men retook their positions, loaded the gun, then bent into the crank mechanism that worked the turret. It moved with agonizing slowness. *Resolute* was gaining speed; there would be time for only one shot.

"Put your backs into it, damn it," ordered Pavel climbing behind the big gun. He found the gun-mounted scope and, through the cross-hairs, the fort came into view, bobbing up and down with the roll of the ship. "Hold there," Pavel shouted to the men on the cranks. "Now lower – three degrees." Boris made the elevation adjustment.

"Stop there," shouted Pavel, his eye still fastened to the gun sight. "On my order." He raised his fist in the air then timed his command with the roll of the ship. Up, then down, then: "Fire!"

The blast from the big navel gun shook the battlefield.

General Ali turned in his saddle just in time to see the flash and the trail of smoke streaking toward the fort. Stone and timber exploded with the impact. The gates were blown back with a force that took much of the stone arch with it. *The gates were down.*

Ali was re-energized. He pulled up on his reins and wheeled his horse to face his retreating cavalry. "Turn back!" he shouted. His voice carried over the chaos. His horse reared. He raised his sword high. "Sound the charge," he yelled to the bugler.

Still unhurt, still on his horse beside Ali, the boy blew his horn, loud and strong.

It was a moment of pure exhilaration. "The gates are down! Get in there!" shouted Ali. His cavalry hesitated. Again, the bugler sounded the charge and the men turned their confused horses back toward the fort. The general shot a glance at the bugler who'd lost his helmet, but kept a firm grip on his instrument, sounding the charge, again and again.

In front of the cavalry now, the men of the infantry saw what was happening and spread apart to make way.

With his sword pointed at the breeched gates, Ali spurred his Arabian into the lead, the bugler on the horse beside him racing to keep up and the flag bearer just behind. The entire line of cavalry followed, thundering back toward the fort at a wild gallop.

Through a storm of bullets, the men yelled and rode with a fury.

Cannons roared from atop the undamaged sections of the fort and explosions tore the field behind Ali. The fort grew closer. They were nearly to its walls when their ranks closed, preparing to funnel-in through the opening in the wall where the fallen gates now lay in a smoldering ruin. The general raised his voice in a primal yell and reined his horse up over the rubble and into the fort. Behind him his men followed like an unstoppable flood and gunfire poured down from the walls.

Ali sheathed his sword and pulled drew his pistol. On his white horse, he made an inviting target, yet he rode unhurt. He fired up at the parapets as the last of his cavalry cleared the outer walls. Then the infantry began streaming in. Ali was surprised to see Sergeant Rashid and his rear-guard office boys leading the way.

"Up there - onto the walls," Ali shouted, pointing to a line of stairs built into the stonework.

The fighting was close and brutal until finally, all along the wall and around the courtyard, British soldiers began throwing down their rifles and raising their hands. By degrees, the gunfire subsided to sporadic shots and finally to nothing.

General Ali galloped from one end of the fort to the other searching for signs of organized resistance. Finally he spotted the gold epaulettes of the commander of the garrison. The man walked slowly, a bloody wound at the side of his head. He was supported on either side by two of his officers. Behind them a half-ring of Turks held rifles at their backs.

"Do you surrender?" Ali demanded in English.

The British officer gave Ali a stern look. "You will treat my men well."

"Yes. You have my word."

The commander looked around, a glaze over his eyes. He pulled his sword from its sheath and let it fall to the ground.

"You may keep your sword, but you will give up your other weapons."

The commander nodded.

It was over, thought Ali with relief. They had won the day. He looked around for his bugler and found him horseless, walking aimlessly through the center of the courtyard. His black hair was a tangled mess and a streak of red ran across his smoke-charred forehead. His arms hung limp, his instrument dangled from the gold cord around his neck.

"Bugler," shouted Ali.

The boy gave a start and looked at Ali as if seeing him for the first time.

"Sound the cease-fire."

The boy hesitated as if not understanding. Then he swallowed and lifted his horn and blew, weakly at first, then with a gathering strength.

As the notes rose clear and loud over the fort, the general guided his horse to the seaward wall. Around him, broken bodies littered the ground, many twisting in pain. Some, with bloodied hands raised up, called for help, others, with twitching and gurgling sounds, called for death to take them. Others just lay still. Ali frowned, knowing that many more lay on the field outside the fort. The breeze intermingled with smoke from isolated fires around the courtyard but still, the air ran thick with the smells of gunpowder and blood and death.

Ali dismounted and removed his helmet, patting the side of his horse. He looked up at the blackened wall that towered over him. Some sections of it remained intact, almost unaffected while others had been gouged out with deep gashes running halfway down. Through one of these he could see in the distance, the black shape of a warship riding over the sparkling waters. He was not pleased at having Russian anarchists for allies, but he knew that, without them, he and his men would all be lying dead on the battlefield outside the eastern wall.

"The British colors are down," said Pavel. He put down his telescope, his eyes stinging from the powder in the air. "Slow to one-third."

Resolute had circled around and was making a second approach to the fort – more slowly this time. Pavel stood on the bridge, Boris at his side. The men were at their stations, guns reloaded, ready to fire. Except for the engine, all was quiet. All was as it should be.

"So, we rest," said Boris. He reached into his jacket pocket and pulled out a flask. He offered it to Pavel.

Pavel smiled. He took a long swallow and felt the soothing heat of the vodka course through him.

"The men did well today," said Boris.

"Yes they did, and this ship did well. A few more salvos would have leveled the place."

They each had another go at the flask before Pavel drained it and walked to the rail just off the bridge. Within the fort, streams of smoke issued from isolated pockets. And from the blue sky high above this violent enterprise, the hot sun glared impersonally down.

Pavel felt a troubled peace. Everything had gone well yet he wondered for a moment: Why did any of it matter? He removed his officer's hat then asked the question aloud. "Why did any of it matter?" He paused, wondering where a strange thought like that would have come from. Then he shrugged – must be the vodka whispering to him.

"They're raising the Ottoman flag," noted Boris, staring out at the fort.

"That's the flag of Ottoman Egypt," corrected Pavel, noting the seven-pointed star, not five pointed, to the right of the Crescent. Strange what importance such a subtle difference could have for nations and empires.

"Same thing," observed Boris, never one for subtleties.

"All full stop, drop anchor," Pavel ordered; then to Boris, "Give the men extra portions of food and drink." It was only as an afterthought that he added: "And do the same for our guests below."

CHAPTER 18

From the first roar of *Resolute's* guns, Julian had kept his face up against the porthole.

He saw the stone walls of a fort shrouded in fire and smoke, the British flag waving over the scene. He tried to guess where they might be when the starboard guns exploded in a broadside that shook the entire ship and obscured his view with clouds of yellow-white smoke. Minutes later the ship tilted and a chilling shriek ran through the hull. *Resolute* was scraping bottom. Julian held his breath as the ship rolled further and the chair slid across the floor, but she righted herself quickly enough – level again, moving again. Through the porthole he saw only open sea now.

Eventually the fort came back into view and the British flag was no longer flying. It had been replaced by one he didn't recognize – not Turkish, but similar. He backed away and leaned against the bulkhead. Pavel's mission must have been to attack this place - and he had just succeeded. The engine stopped. He heard a splash and the rumble of the anchor-chain. He could see that they were fairly close to shore. He wondered if he could swim that far.

Hopeful, Julian grabbed the chair and removed a wooden cross-brace that he had loosened earlier. It wasn't much, but now he had a weapon.

He sat back down on the cot and listened intently for any sound coming from outside the door. Hours passed and all remained quiet until late in the day when, at last, he heard footsteps.

Julian slid off the cot and took a position beside the door, his back pressed flat against the bulkhead. The latch slowly turned. Breathless, he wrapped his fingers more tightly around his makeshift club and raised it high. The door opened and, instead of the usual guard that brought him his meals, this time it was the much bigger Boris who stepped inside. He carried a bowl of dark brown stew. In his other hand dangled a chain with a single key – it had to be a master key. A gun was tucked under his belt. He barked out something in Russian.

Then Julian struck.

He swung the club down hard onto the back of the head of the big Russian but the man only stiffened in alarm. Julian tossed the club aside and went for the gun, pulling it out from under Boris's belly. Boris jerked to one side and Julian missed his grip. The gun fell to the floor. Julian dove for it and Boris fought back with the only thing he had at his disposal – the bowl of stew. The crockery shattered against the back of Julian's head, its tepid contents splattering over the side of his face.

Julian shook off the blow. Boris easily had the size advantage, but his movements were slow and awkward.

Julian snatched up the pistol and fell backward onto the cot. He fumbled with the gun, cocking it with both hands just as Boris charged him in a screaming rage.

Julian had no time to shoot. He rolled sideways and Boris crashed into the bulkhead. The force of the impact snapped the chain holding the cot to the wall and Julian sprawled face up onto the floor. Boris rose up and tried to turn then lost his balance. His big blubberous body fell back, slamming down onto Julian like a giant felled oak.

Julian gasped. He would have doubled over breathless were he not pinned by the facedown, spread-eagled Boris. Frantic, Julian looked to his right. The gun had been knocked from his grasp and was lying just out of reach.

Julian struggled to catch his breath even as he knew that all was lost. It hadn't been much of a fight. He never had a chance against this big brute. Then he realized that Boris wasn't moving. Except for the big Russian's hot labored breathing, now uncomfortably directed into Julian's ear, he lay utterly still, knocked cold after ramming his head into the steel bulkhead.

Julian still had a chance.

He braced one hand back and away from Boris and struggled to squirm out from under him. He couldn't move. He pushed up against the massive body rocking him one way, then back again, timing his efforts to keep the body in motion. Boris groaned; with the jostling.

He was coming to.

Julian gave a desperate shove and, at the same time, brought his knees up, finally pivoting Boris off of him, rolling him onto the floor. Boris let out another groan. His hand went to his bloodied forehead.

Gasping for air, Julian got to his feet and grabbed the gun just as Boris opened his eyes. The big Russian spat out a curse and a bloody drool streamed from the corner of his mouth. He tried to stand but froze when he saw Julian with the gun.

"Don't move," said Julian, swallowing hard, holding the weapon with both hands straight out in front of him. Down its barrel he saw Boris's dark eyes glaring back at him. He motioned for Boris, now on one knee, to get back down. Like a wounded bull, the Russian snorted. His face turned a menacing red. Breathing heavily, he lowered himself to the floor.

Julian knew a shot would raise an alarm through the ship. He would fire only if he had to. Slowly, carefully, he circled around behind Boris. He moved closer then brought the pistol up and swung it down.

The butt of the pistol hit the back of the big man's skull with a sickening crack. "That's for Whiley," Julian hissed. Blood sprang from the wound and Boris collapsed.

Julian spotted the key hanging from Boris's belt, pulled it free then backed away a few steps. Had he killed him? No, Boris was still breathing. Julian steadied himself then thought to gather his Castlenau notes along with his pouch. He stuffed them into his pockets and darted out of the room locking the door behind him.

He was breathing hard, his heart racing. He had escaped from his cabin, now he had to get off the ship. But there was something else. He looked around. He stood at one end of an empty, dimly lit corridor. Cabin doors lined both sides. He rushed to Noah's but found it unlocked and empty. His throat was utterly dry, his heart still pounding. He had no time to think where Noah might be. He turned and raced down the passageway stopping at a door that should be Bertie's. He fumbled with the key and pushed the door open; the room was deserted with no sign that it had been recently occupied. Julian backed out. Boris would be waking soon and making noise. There was only enough time to check one more cabin.

He unlocked the door on the opposite side of the aisle and

shoved it open. There sat Bertie, at a small desk with his back to Julian. Ink-stained papers littered the desktop and the floor around it. "Put it down, over there," said Bertie, bent over his writing.

Julian hesitated, but this was no time for second thoughts – not now. He whispered frantically: "It's me, my lord. Come on, we've got to get out of here."

Bertie jerked his head around, staring at Julian in astonishment. "North, you're free." He stood up.

"We have to leave."

"How'd you manage to get a gun, and what's all that guak on your face? Well – no matter; nicely done." Then, as if confused, Bertie looked down at his desk. "God damn it to hell. Yes, we have to leave, right."

Julian wiped his sleeve across his cheek. The stew smelled foul but it reminded him that he hadn't eaten at all today. He forced that thought out of his head. "Follow me."

Julian headed further along the passageway until he came to a fixed metal ladder. He looked up and saw that it ran two decks up to a circular hatch. "This should be a way out," he said, hoping he was right. He shoved the pistol under his belt and eyed the rotund prince.

Bertie's jaw tightened. "Goddamnit North, I might be fat, but I'm bloody well as fit as you. Go on up, I'll be right behind you."

Julian climbed a few rungs to the next deck up. He scanned the long corridor in both directions - deserted. He hurried further up, Bertie close behind, breathing hard. When Julian reached the hatch at the top of the ladder he crooked his arm around the top rung. With his other hand he tried the wheel that locked the hatch closed. It wouldn't budge. He climbed up one more rung and leaned his back against the metal safety cage that surrounded the ladder. He gripped the wheel using both hands this time as Bertie steadied him from below.

With all his strength, he tried to turn the wheel. It still wouldn't budge.

A pounding sound came from two decks down.

"What's that?" whispered Bertie.

"Boris must have woke up. I hit him pretty hard."

"Not hard enough." Bertie took two more steps up the ladder so his feet shared the same rung as Julian's. He grabbed onto the wheel. "Come on, we'll try it together."

From an awkward position with Bertie's arm in his face, Julian regripped the wheel. At a nod from Bertie they strained against it, shifting their weight to apply as much torque as they could manage.

Julian forced every muscle he had into the job. Their escape would fail if they couldn't get past this hatch. It had to open now. He didn't let up and neither did Bertie. At last, the wheel let out a rusty groan and turned a few degrees. "Almost got it," Julian gasped, resting for just a moment.

With one more try the wheel turned a full revolution. The thumping from Boris grew louder.

"This is a precarious spot, North," Bertie whispered, his sweat-drenched face inches away from Julian's, "let's be quick about it."

Julian turned the wheel the rest of the way then, with his shoulder against the hatch, heaved upward. It opened a crack. The cool outside air filtered in. He pushed further and could see that the sky was already darkening. Men were yelling outside – there was some kind of commotion. Julian forced the hatch up all the way, holding onto it, careful not to let it slam back. He brought his head up. Gunshots rang out. Julian's heart jumped into his throat and he jerked his head back, bumping hard into Bertie.

The prince dropped a rung then recovered. "Damn it, North."

"Sorry."

"What's out there?" asked Bertie. "What did you see?"

"I couldn't see anyone. By the sound of it, the whole crew's on deck. They must have seen us."

There were more shots and more shouting.

"I don't think so," said Bertie. "Boris is still locked up, pounding away down there. It sounds like those men are celebrating. They've probably gotten into a few kegs of vodka. Listen to that - they're cheering - pretty Goddamned pleased with themselves." He pounded a fist against the rung of the ladder, venting some of his anger then slapped Julian's shoulder. "Go on up now, let's get out of here."

Julian raised his head, flinching at another shot, then climbed through the hatch. On all fours, he gave a hand to Bertie who grunted as he made his way out. They closed the hatch behind them. Julian stayed on his knees and raised himself up as much as he dared.

The sun hung low in the west. Gray clouds were rolling out from shore. He glanced over his shoulder where, only a few paces back, *Resolute*'s stack towered over them, black smoke floating out. Under different circumstances, he would have been awestruck by the massive steel structure. But there was no time for that. With the waterline far below, he found himself with the Prince of Wales, stranded on the uppermost deck of one of the largest warships in the world, crewed by men who wanted them both dead. On the plus side though, they seemed to have the top deck all to themselves.

"Look there," said Bertie, who had crawled forward to a railing. Julian came up behind him and saw the Russians massed near the bow, some waving bottles high over their heads, others waving rifles. More gunshots were punctuated by laughter and more cheering. A man standing on a crate was addressing them like a politician who had just won an election – it was Pavel.

Julian felt a wave of anger and pulled the pistol from his belt. "The bastard - I'd kill him right now if I thought I could hit him from here. I could do it with a Kentucky rifle."

"Well you're a regular American frontiersman aren't you?" said Bertie, clearly skeptical. He backed away and rose to his feet with his hands on his hips. He gazed at the open water below.

"It'll be a long jump down," said Julian joining him, guessing his thoughts.

The wind picked up and Bertie brushed his hair from his forehead. "And it'll be a long swim too, but we haven't much choice. That's about five-hundred yards I'd say."

Julian nodded, staring off to starboard at the tiny green palm trees dotting the distant beach. From the porthole the shoreline had looked much closer. He had once been a good swimmer but that was years ago. His gaze ran further east to the outline of the fort.

Bertie walked to the port rail. "This should help," he said, untying a white life ring – there was only one.

Julian joined Bertie and looked down over the rail to where the next deck jutted out below them. They couldn't jump here. They headed further aft.

Near the stern, Bertie leaned forward against the rail, looking down as if planning his trajectory. "Not a bad height. I've dove from higher than this at the Naval College in Greenwich."

"You were a swimmer?" asked Julian, his turn to be skeptical. Bertie was a head shorter than him and half again as heavy.

Bertie first took off his jacket, then his shoes, and tossed them over the side. "I admit it's been a long time. But I'm told it's something you never forget. We shall find out."

Julian took off his own shoes, then pulled out his crumpled code notes and stuffed them inside his water-tight pouch. He pressed the wax seal closed, then tied the pouch to his belt.

Bertie watched with obvious disgust. "I suppose those are your notes about your big adventure. Here we are, about to risk our lives to escape from a murdering, kidnapping anarchist and all you can think about is making yourself famous."

Julian winced at the accusation, but had no time to set things straight. "It's not what you think. I'm not like that. I'll explain when we get ashore."

"Damn right you will. If anyone publishes a word about this colossal fiasco, they'll answer to me. Do you understand?"

Julian didn't respond. He looked down at the rolling waves. The wind picked up again, more steady this time. He hoisted the life ring over the rail and let it drop, watching it glance off the side of the ship before hitting the water.

Bertie cleared his throat and climbed up and over the rail, standing now on the edge. "Remember to push away from the ship as you jump."

Julian nodded. "Good advice." He climbed over the rail causing his topaz medallion to swing free outside his shirt.

"What's that?"

"Something my mother gave me."

Bertie nodded. "A mother's love is a powerful talisman. Let's hope it brings luck to us both." The prince turned to look down at the water below. He took in a breath, then jumped.

Julian watched the splash. Holding the medallion in one hand, he sucked in a deep breath, and kicked off from the side.

Feet first, Julian hit the warm, oily water and was immediately enveloped in a torrent of bubbles. He paddled up to the surface and wiped the water from his eyes. *Resolute*'s black iron hull towered above him, caked at the waterline with a mottled growth of greens and browns. He looked up, checking for anyone who might be looking down at them. There was no one. He floated with the roll of the sea and fended off the slimy hull. Where was Bertie?

"Over here, North." Bertie had taken hold of the life ring and was maneuvering closer to the stern. "You all right?"

"Yes," said Julian, catching up at the rudder, four feet of which lay exposed above the waves. They took hold of it by the edge and rested. The sun had completely set and stars were beginning to fill the night sky. Julian looked shoreward but could see nothing over the waves. Nor could he hear the sounds of the crew at the bow. "They've stopped celebrating," he said. "They must know we've escaped. We've got to go, *now*."

"Right."

They shoved off from the rudder with Bertie in the lead pushing the life ring forward as he swam. Suddenly, the surface of the water became bathed in a light that cast an amber halo around the stern. The running lamps had been lit. Julian dove beneath the surface for cover and tried to swim toward Bertie, who was already beyond the halo's edge. He stayed under as long as he could, then came up. He heard the crack of a rifle and a bullet hit the water only inches away. They had seen him. Desperately, he dove under again, hearing the dull bang of more shots. Bullets zipped through the water, their paths marked dimly by trails of white bubbles. Julian glided deeper and swam hard until he thought his lungs would explode from the lack of air. He burst through the surface, took a breath and went down again, swimming with all his strength. There was no more gunfire.

After another long pull underwater, Julian surfaced again, gasping for breath. He looked back. He was still frighteningly close to the ship and could hear shouting from her deck. But it was dark now and he was beyond the glow of the lamps. He looked around. There was no sign of Bertie or the life ring.

"My lord?" he whispered. There was no response. Shouts came from the ship, followed by a ratcheting sound. Pavel's men were lowering a boat. They were coming after them.

Julian swam hard, this time staying on the surface to make better time; trying to keep his strokes quiet. He saw nothing of Pavel's men or of Bertie. For the time being he put thoughts of both out of his mind as he swam through the black waters in a direction away from the ship toward a shore he could not see.

His movements became sluggish, as if his hands were made of concrete. His clothing and the heavy gun under his belt were weighing him down. He tore his shirt free but kept the gun and swam until he could no longer lift his arms. He gasped and glanced back. The ship was well behind him now. He floated on his back for a while, resting, then swam on.

Eventually, Julian's sense of feeling left him and a prickly numbness spread through his body. He kept moving until at last, he heard the sound of waves rolling onto the shore. He forced his arms into stroke after stroke, his legs into each kick.

His arm struck a rock but it was already past him before he could latch onto it to rest. Then the waves carried him and he tumbled like a rag-doll. Each breath he took was filled with seawater; he could feel himself drinking it in – his lungs filling, but he couldn't prevent it. With no breath left, he was so close to salvation yet, he was drowning.

Waves picked him up and slammed him down. He was at their mercy. The razor edge of a rocky spire tore into his side and blazing pain brought Julian back to his senses.

He felt warm blood pumping out of his body. He tried to staunch the flow with his hand. Finally, his feet met the gravelly seabed. Biting his lip, he struggled to stand as the waves continued to hammer him. Gagging, coughing up seawater, he staggered out of the surf and fell onto the beach. The dry sand, still warm from the day's sun, was a comfort against his skin. But Julian knew he couldn't rest yet – not out here in the open. He had to find cover. He peered through the darkness to where he heard palms rustling in the wind. He summoned up the little energy he had left and crawled across the narrow beach and collapsed into a thicket. His chest was heaving. Exhausted, he pressed his hand harder against his bloody side and closed his eyes.

CHAPTER 19

Port Said

"Our Russian friends are coming to visit," said General Ali to Lieutenant Shariff. The two had spent the afternoon working out plans for the repair of the sections of wall that had been blasted apart by the Russians. Now it was dark and, from the parapet, they watched lights of the warship's steam launch heading for the pier.

"It will be a wonder," said Shariff, "if they dock safely considering all the vodka they must have drunk. All that shouting and gunfire, they acted as if they had just beaten Napoleon again."

"We'll see how well they bring her in," said Ali. A short time later, to his disappointment, the launch pulled straight up to the dock without incident. "Maybe vodka improves their seamanship. Go down and receive them – I'll see them in my quarters."

"I don't speak Russian."

"You won't need to," said Ali, already halfway down the steps to the courtyard, "their leader speaks Turkish. His name is Pavel."

Alone, Ali walked toward the northwest corner of the fort. All the bodies, both Turk and British, had been taken care of, laid to their rest in two large graves outside the walls, but their death-smell still lingered. He reached the residence of the former commander where two guards saluted, one of them holding the door open to him. Inside, the lamps had been lit. Rich mahogany furniture, oil paintings and ornate wall trimmings decorated the

177

office area. An adjoining dining room and a bedroom with a four-poster bed insured that Ali would live in comfort during his stay here at Port Said. This was much different from the accommodations Ali was used to and, as he settled comfortably into the heavily upholstered leather chair behind his desk, he wondered how the British commander and his family were getting along in their nearby prison barracks.

The general ordered more lamps lit then waited for the knock that came a few minutes later. "Enter," he said.

Shariff showed two Russians inside. Pavel introduced Boris who, Ali noted, had an ugly reddish-black mark bulging from the center of his forehead. Handshakes were exchanged and, with Shariff waiting at the door, the three sat down.

"Something to drink?" offered the general. "The British commander has been kind enough to leave a stock of excellent brandy."

"No, thank you," said Pavel. "We need to speak with you in private, if you please."

Ali dismissed Shariff then looked over the Russians. He had not seen Pavel since the Yildiz Palace. He seemed much older now – tired; his eyes without their former spark. He hadn't met Boris before but, from the welt, it was plain that he wasn't doing so well either.

Ali began the conversation. "You have my thanks for knocking down the gates. We would not be here were it not for your marksmanship."

"We are allies," said Pavel, "you would have done the same for me and my men."

"Of course," said Ali with a glance at Boris who responded with a shaky smile.

"He doesn't understand Turkish," said Pavel, uncrossing his legs. "Time is short general; I'll get right to the point. We had an incident aboard my ship tonight – a man escaped."

"One of your crew?"

"No, a prisoner – British."

"A soldier."

"His function is of no consequence. I need him found."

"And you want my help."

"Yes."

Ali leaned back in his chair. "As you no doubt saw, coming through the fort, we are very busy at the moment – there were many dead and many wounded. And tomorrow, according to our plan, you will be sailing south to Suez with fifty of my men to secure the southern entrance to the canal. I cannot spare anyone at the moment."

Pavel stiffened. "This prisoner is important to me, just as Suez is important to you."

Ali paused at the implied threat. "Is he armed?"

"Yes, he may be. Four of my men came ashore with us, and they are searching for him now. But he could be hiding anywhere. I need your help."

"Perhaps he drowned trying to make it to shore," suggested Ali. "That would be a long swim."

"Yes, that is possible, but it would be regrettable. I want him taken alive."

"Oh? And why is that?"

"That is not your affair."

Ali folded his arms. "I'm sorry, but everything happening here at the canal is now my affair."

Pavel hesitated, but only for a moment. "He has something of mine. I want it back."

General Ali's eyes darkened as he remembered his last meeting with Pavel. He reached back for the humidor on his credenza and chose a cigar. He offered one to both Pavel and Boris.

Pavel waved the courtesy aside. "We must begin the search now. Every minute we lose will make it more difficult."

Ali lit his cigar. "It's dark. Why don't you wait until morning?"

"The trail will grow cold quickly."

"This man you want has your book, I think," said Ali calmly.

Pavel's lips tightened. "What do you know about the book?"

Ali took a satisfying pull on his cigar. "You should be more careful with what you say in the cellars of Yildiz." He may owe this man his life but that didn't mean he had to like him.

Pavel stood up and put both hands on the desk, leaning closer to Ali. "I have an arrangement with your foreign minister. After the entrances to the canal are taken, I and my ship will head north and leave the defense of the canal to you. I have no further obligations."

"And you have other plans for the ship we helped you steal," said Ali.

"That does not concern you."

"Yet you want me to help you find this prisoner of yours," said Ali, enjoying the confrontation. "Perhaps you can help satisfy my curiosity. Why is this man and his book so important to you?"

Pavel spoke slowly. "It is our book. It contains our culture, our philosophies, and...our secrets. With it, we can be discovered. All that we are, all that we have gained could be unraveled if it falls into the wrong hands."

Ali decided to nudge Pavel just a little further. "You were foolish to write such things down."

"And you are foolish to play games with me," snapped Pavel. "We are not stupid. Our secrets are safe, concealed within the language of Napoleon himself and the man who escaped knows nothing of its meaning. But he does know of the book. I want him found. Will you help me or not?"

Ali tapped the ashes from his cigar. If this book is so important maybe he should have a look at it. "I will help you because you helped me. I will provide torches and three of my men to help in your search."

"We must begin now."

"Yes, we can begin now. My men will meet you at your launch in thirty minutes."

Pavel gave Ali a single curt nod and stalked out of the room with Boris trailing behind.

Outside in the courtyard Boris caught up to Pavel. "You did not tell him about the Prince of Wales."

"And how would you know that?"

"I think the general's reaction would have been much different if you had."

Pavel glanced at his old comrade but kept up the pace. "You can be quite perceptive at times. You are right, I didn't tell him. In truth I am glad to be rid of the prince. I gave my word to release him and I have done so. To tell General Ali about him now would have made things unnecessarily complicated."

Boris just gave an understanding grunt and as they walked on toward the launch, Pavel found himself wondering if Albert was still alive. Did he even know how to swim? For some unknown reason, he hoped he did.

"North?"

The word came to Julian as if from the far end of a long tunnel. He felt a prod to his shoulder.

"Goddamnit, North, you gave me a start." Another prod; this time rougher. "North!"

Julian opened his eyes to see a dark form against the night sky bending over him. On reflex, he shrank back.

"North, it's me. Are you all right?

"You're alive."

Bertie straightened to his full height. "I'm alive no thanks to you. What were you thinking, leaving me alone out there? I swear, if you ever again have the notion to rescue me, please don't. This is not something you're good at."

Julian swallowed weakly but he was strong enough to react. "You'd rather be Pavel's prisoner? I should have left you on the ship."

"What? And ruin a perfectly good tale about the hero-journalist? No, I don't think you'd do that."

Julian winced as a stabbing pain tore through his side.

"What's the matter?" asked Bertie, dispassionately. "You're hurt, aren't you?"

"I hit the rocks pretty hard."

Bertie shook his head, kneeling down over him. "Here, roll over."

As he did so, Julian looked down at the gash in his side. It was gaping, pulsing with dark shiny fluid.

"Damn it North, you've lost a lot of blood. It's all over the ground."

"I'll be all right."

"Not without a little mending, you won't." Bertie took the hem of his sopping shirt and tore off a strip, dabbing it in the wound. "Never done this kind of thing, but I know we have to get it clean. Stay still now, this may sting."

From somewhere out on the beach Julian heard something. "What was that? Did you hear it?"

"Someone's coming," Bertie whispered, finishing his cleaning with two quick swipes. He put the bloody cloth in Julian's hand. "Here, press hard on the wound. Maybe the bleeding will stop."

Julian struggled to sit. Pain shot through him again.

"Can you stand? We have to get out of here."

Julian nodded and, with Bertie's help, got to his feet. The pain nearly caused him to cry out. He held his side tightly. The wound was worse than he had thought – much worse. He took a breath. "I think my rib's cracked." A wave of nausea overcame him. He couldn't do this. He had to lay back down.

But Bertie held onto him. "You have to stay on your feet; we have to get out of here."

Julian felt his lower lip quiver. He leaned heavily on Bertie, overwhelmed by dizziness. "I'll just slow you down. You should leave me here."

"I'll do no such thing, North. We'll make it out of here

together. Besides, it'd certainly not go over well back at the Marlborough club, me leaving you out here like this."

Through a blur, Julian saw that they were standing at the base of a rise which ran parallel to the shore. It leveled off six feet above them at a thick stand of palms.

Bertie pointed in that direction. "This way, we'll have to climb for a bit."

Julian fought the pain. He raised his arm over Bertie's shoulder and took an awkward step up the slope. From further down the shoreline, he could hear voices.

"The gun; we need the gun," said Julian.

"I've got it, now come on."

They gained the top of the rise and kept hobbling forward to where the vegetation grew thicker and the sand became firm ground. Stones and fallen branches gouged Julian's bare feet. They approached another rise and made it to the top before stopping to rest. Julian bent over, out of breath.

"We're on level ground now," said Bertie. "It should be easier."

"Good," responded Julian after a moment. He coughed then drew a deep breath. He had lost his dizziness and could stand a little straighter now. He tested the cloth at his side and found that it stuck there. His blood was coagulating; the bleeding may have lessened.

Above him, tall palms waved in the breeze, blocking out the moonlight. The earthy scent of plant life mingled with the smells of the sea - insects buzzed and birds cried out. Julian could no longer hear the men coming after them from the beach but he felt the danger. And he felt Bertie's nervousness. They had to get moving. He let go of Bertie and tested his ability to stand on his own. He took another deep breath, but not so deep that it strained his side. "Let's go."

They forged ahead, stopping at short intervals until Julian was again forced to take a prolonged rest.

"They can't track us at night," said Bertie. "I think we've gone far enough. We must be two, maybe three miles from the canal by now. My feet can't take much more of this."

Julian slumped to his knees then carefully maneuvered into a sitting position, his back against a tree-trunk. "The Canal? My God, that's where we are – the Suez Canal."

"I must say, North, even for a newspaper man you seem slow to catch on. I recognized the place through the porthole; been here before - several times."

Julian had guessed Crete or Cyprus, but saw now that the canal was the only target that made sense. He pondered the implications. Pavel and his band of anarchists now controlled the primary commercial route from Europe to India and the Orient. What could they be planning next?

Bertie sat down, a hand on each knee. "So here we are at one of the world's busiest waterways, in the middle of a jungle with no food, water...or shoes, and no way of getting them." He felt his trouser pocket and pulled out a dripping-wet cigar. Straightening it out, he carefully tried to squeeze some of the water from it then added: "And we're being chased by a bunch of crazed anarchists."

Julian tentatively felt his wound.

"How's the pain?"

"Not, as bad as it was. I'll be all right in the morning."

"Always the optimist, eh, North?"

Julian supposed that was true. Or maybe it was just the prince's grousing that forced him to keep his spirits up. "I'd rather be out here in the open than stuck inside that prison for another night."

"A few nights here might make that prison seem like a palace." Bertie carefully laid out his cigar where it could dry. He then proceeded to pull some palm branches out by the roots, making a bed for himself. "We should try to get some sleep."

Among the palms that littered the ground, Julian flattened out a spot for himself and laid down, but his eyes remained warily open. Starry patches of night sky, visible between the swaying palms lent a dangerous beauty to this place. After a time, Bertie's snoring blended with the sounds of the jungle.

When he finally slept, Julian dreamed of Kate, her kiss, the smell of her perfume, and her last worried expression on the night he had left. He could hear her telling him to be careful, to take care of himself and Noah. Then, still in his dream she asked him where Noah was and he had to tell her the truth - he didn't know.

In the morning Julian forced his eyes open, seeing only green palms and brown vinery. The jungle around him crackled with life and he felt a stirring in his hair. Half awake, Julian ran his hand along his scalp before realizing it was crawling with insects. He jumped up but a stab of pain in his side slowed his movements. He bent over as far as he could trying to brush the bugs out of his hair. Then he straightened and flicked a few more of them off his bare chest. It was covered with welts – the insects had been feeding all night on him. He stifled his revulsion - no sense getting upset about a few bugs, he had other things to worry about.

"What the hell are you doing, North?" growled Bertie, just waking up. He lay calmly in a princely pose on his palm-branch bed.

"Just getting the bugs off."

Bertie looked down at what had once been his best formal white shirt, now rumpled and alive with black crawly things. He shrank back with an expression first of disbelief, then utter disgust. "Goddamnit, they're on me too." Frantically, he jumped to his feet and brushed them off his body and out of his hair. "Goddamn bugs, I hate bugs."

A bird fluttered through the palms and Julian looked up. It was late; the air hot and already heavy with humidity. They should be on the move, but to where? The gash in his side had turned an ugly reddish-brown. A thin stream of fresh blood trickled down at one end where a few insects had worked to exploit the tasty spot. Julian picked at them, knowing that infection was bound to follow and he had no way to prevent it. The stinging pain throbbed. He ran his tongue over his parched lips and felt the gnawing emptiness in his stomach. "We need water and food."

"You're a master of the obvious this morning aren't you?"

"All part of being a professional journalist," said Julian dryly. "The canal is that way, I think," he said, pointing. "At the fort they'll have everything we need."

Bertie looked at Julian, incredulous. "We just ran half the night to get away from there. Now you propose to head back? Maybe we should just swim back to the ship; they have everything we need too."

"I suppose we could just cook ourselves up a bunch of these bugs. What would you think about that?" Julian reminded himself too late that he was talking to the Prince of Wales for God's sake.

"Damn it, North, be serious, we've got to think of a better way."

But no bright ideas came. Julian imagined himself and the prince wandering the jungle aimlessly, weakened by thirst and hunger, falling from exhaustion, being devoured by swarms of insects:

Prince of Wales and Times Journalist found dead in the Jungle.

Bertie made a grumbling sound, maybe thinking the same thing. "If we do go back to the fort, how do you propose to get our food and water? We can't just knock on the door and hope they'll take pity on us."

"We'll have to figure a way to sneak in. There must be houses and buildings close to the fort. It's Port Said – we don't need much."

"People in this part of the world don't have much, North. It'd be like stealing from beggars."

"What choice do we have?"

Bertie folded his arms and let loose a long sigh. "So be it then, we'll head for the damn fort."

Julian then remembered something from a novel he'd once read. "I think it's best to go back the way we came for a few hundred yards, then strike off for the canal on a parallel path. We'll be more careful this time not to make our trail so obvious."

"Sounds reasonable, Captain North," said Bertie in a derisive tone, "now get out there and lead the way. I don't want to be the first of us to get shot."

Wonderful, thought Julian, the Prince of Wales already thought him to be a fool and an opportunist; now he'd managed to offend him further.

They plodded off and, after a while, veered from the path they had made the night before, this time making an effort to cover their tracks. They were careful where they stepped - careful to bend the palm blades only as far as was needed to slip by. Progress was slow and tedious.

They had been on the move along their new path for less than an hour when they heard a rustling from up ahead. Julian stopped and gave a cautionary wave back to Bertie. He strained to listen, heard the sound again and dropped to a low crouch. He parted the palms in front of him as much as he dared and eventually saw four men, moving quickly in single file, plowing their way through the vegetation. As they passed directly across from Julian, he caught a glimpse of two of them. The first man wore a Turkish army uniform and carried a rifle on his back. He moved in quick, jerky motions, taking long strides, easily brushing aside the palm branches as he went. Then, following close behind, the face of the next man became visible.

Julian flinched – it was Noah.

Julian almost called out to him. How did he get ashore? And he wasn't tied up like a prisoner. He was moving as fast as the others – and he was armed.

The truth came to him like a thunderbolt. Noah was part of the search party. He was with Pavel. All this time Noah had been working with Pavel. Julian closed his eyes. How could he have been so blind?

In an instant, the hurt of betrayal turned to burning anger within Julian. He wanted to charge out after Noah and hold him accountable for what he had done – for what he was doing. But common sense intervened. Julian waited until he could no longer hear the men. As his mind cleared, he rose slowly to his feet.

From a few yards away, Bertie whispered to Julian, "That was the American. What's he doing with those soldiers?"

"He's one of them. I was stupid to trust him."

Bertie said nothing for a moment then spoke quietly. "You should choose your friends more carefully. Come on now. We have to get out of here."

They pressed on. Julian's side ached, and his throat pleaded for water. With each labored stride, his bruised feet were pounded numb. Sweat poured down his face and chest. It was midday when the vegetation in front of them thinned to reveal the tall gray walls of the fort rising from the base of a gentle slope about five-hundred yards ahead. Beyond it, the waters of the canal gleamed.

Julian backed away from the clearing and sank to his knees, breathing heavily. He inspected his side. The wound was caked with dirt and dried blood. The flesh around it burned a bright red and, despite the heat of the day, he felt a sickening shiver run through him. Infection was setting in. He had no water to clean the wound and no way to bandage it. Fever would soon follow.

"So, we've arrived," said Bertie, oblivious to Julian's situation. He sat down and settled his back against the trunk of a palm tree wiping a sleeve across his forehead. "And now we face our dilemma: how to get ourselves some food and water from behind those walls."

"Or from those houses over there." Julian pointed to a gathering of white-plastered, grass-roofed huts that dotted a hillside off to the south. "We'll have to wait for dark or for an opportunity if one comes along."

"That's your plan?"

"Yes."

"Well, I haven't got a better one. I suppose it will have to do." Bertie stretched out his legs and crossed his ankles then looked out at the fort. "Did you notice that they're flying the Star and Crescent?"

Julian forced himself to focus on the fort noticing the crimson flag. "Doing business as usual," he said, watching the line of ships entering the canal as if everything were perfectly normal.

"You miss the point, North. That's the flag of Ottoman Egypt.

It proves that the Turks were involved in all of this, from my being kidnapped to the taking of the canal. The soldiers with your friend were Turks too, the bastards. And the captains of those trading ships out there would do business with the devil himself if it meant reaching India and China in better time...which reminds me." Bertie pulled a watch from his pocket. "Stopped - forgot to wind the damn thing. Full of water anyway." He wound it, listened to see if it was ticking, which it was, then put it back in his pocket, careful that the chain attaching it to his belt was properly draped.

Julian gauged the sunlight, filtering through the palms overhead. "We have to find a place to hide. When it gets dark we'll sneak out to steal what we need. We can't spend another night out here without food or water."

They made their way to a tall palm tree twenty yards away where a dense thicket served for cover. Julian sat down, facing away from the fort. He leaned his naked, sweat-drenched back against the tree, ignoring the insects buzzing around him and ignoring his festering wound. He just rested.

Opposite him, Bertie shifted his weight until he found a tolerably comfortable position. He stretched out his legs again. "So, I imagine there's a story behind that pendant of yours? You said your mother gave it to you?"

Surprised at Bertie's interest, Julian glanced down where it rested against his folded arms. "She didn't really give it to me. After she and my father died I took it as a remembrance. I've had it since I was ten."

Bertie nodded sympathetically. "So you raised yourself?"

"I had foster parents in America. I came to England eighteen months ago to work with the *Times*. My Uncle runs the paper. My father was a journalist too, in America."

Apparently having his fill of small-talk, Bertie was quiet for a while; then he spoke again. "Strange, the Turks would attack the canal. They must know we'll just send in the fleet and blast them to hell." He scratched his growth of whiskers.

"Pavel wants to start a war. He tried to do it with the assassination of Czar Alexander last year. Now he's trying to pit England against the Turks over the canal."

"An incredible mismatch unless..."

Julian opened his eyes. "Unless what?"

"Unless the Turks were able to ally themselves with another major power, like France or Germany - or both." Bertie scratched his nose. "How did you know about Pavel's connection to Alexander's death? I only learned of it during my captivity."

"The book Noah mentioned on the ship was found in St. Petersburg after being lost by one of the assassins. It was a journal written in French. I translated it when I was in London. The actual assassin, the one who killed the czar, broke into the *Times* office in Istanbul trying to get it back." Julian explained how the man with the scar had been killed.

A wary tone entered Bertie's voice. "You told the American you didn't know anything about the book."

"I lied."

"You must have suspected him even then. Tell me, though, why is the book so important?"

Before Julian could answer, they were startled by the distant sounds of Noah and his search party walking back toward the fort. They broke into the clearing alarmingly close to Julian and Bertie. The soldiers had rifles strapped to their backs. Machetes dangled from their belts. Noah was speaking angrily in English.

"We have to continue the search," he was saying to one of the soldiers – a sergeant by the look of his uniform. "He's got to be out there somewhere."

"This man of yours is as good as dead," said the sergeant, pointing a thumb back toward the mangroves. "No one can survive in there for long without food or water."

"We want him alive."

The Turk did not respond. Wiping his forehead, he looked up at the sun and took a drink from his canteen. "It is hot. We have other things to do. We will search again later."

The sergeant and his men headed for the fort but Noah stood there for a moment, turning to face the thick vegetation. At one point he seemed to look directly at Julian. His stare sent a chill down Julian's spine. Finally Noah turned and caught up with the others.

Julian let the tension in his body ease. He leaned against the tree again.

"They said 'him.' They're looking for one man, not two," said Bertie.

"They're looking for me - all because of the damn journal. I wish I'd never seen the thing."

Bertie shook his head. "Did it ever occur to you that you might be the inconsequential one? That they might just be looking for me because I'm the Goddamn Prince of Wales?"

"You could be right," said Julian, closing his eyes, for the moment not caring what Bertie thought.

"What are you doing? You're going to sleep?"

"Nothing much better to do right now that I can see."

Bertie brushed a mosquito from his cheek and cleared his throat. "I don't sleep during the day. Never could."

Before long, Julian fell asleep and a dream swept him away:

He was ten years old, it was after his parent's death. He was back in their family home, alone. The place was dark and quiet and still held the smell of tobacco from his father's pipe. With each step he took, the floorboards creaked.

The young Julian climbed the stairs and went into his parent's bedroom where he had often run from down the hall when a nightmare or a storm made him cry. He put a hand on the bedpost, his eyes drawn to the pillows he had shared with his parents on such nights.

He turned to his mother's dressing table where a brush lay with long strands of her brown hair still woven into its bristles. The hint of her lavender perfume hovered close. And there was her jewelry box.

Julian opened it and, like a dream within a dream, saw his mother standing there with the morning sun streaming through the window, going through the box with him as if it were filled with sweet chocolates, as if it were important that he pick out just the right one. Julian had immediately seen the green medallion. It lay there, right on top with its woven leather strap wrapped neatly in a coil around it. Julian picked it up slowly then grasped it tightly. He felt his mother's hand close around his. He could actually feel her grasp. He breathed in her perfume and his knees went weak, his eyes brimming.

"Someone's coming," whispered Bertie, shaking Julian's shoulder with his bare foot.

Julian forced his eyes open and realized that he'd been squeezing the medallion. He let go of it now and looked out toward the fort. It was the English-speaking sergeant and another soldier walking from the fort toward them. The other man was younger and carried a coil of rope over his shoulder. What would bring them back out here? Julian wondered. Both held rifles and both had packs strapped to their back. They must contain food and water.

The soldiers walked along the telegraph line that ran from the fort across the clearing and into the mangrove. They entered the dense vegetation fifty yards from where Julian and Bertie hid. Julian got to his feet with an effort. "Looks like our opportunity has arrived." Bertie hoisted himself up slowly and handed the gun to Julian.

Julian's heart started racing with the prospect of what would come next. Blood rushed to his head. His side began to throb. He hoped he could do this right. He crept silently toward the soldiers who continued to follow the telegraph line through the jungle, passing in and out of sight over another thirty yards. They stopped at one of the poles. Julian was close enough to see that the telegraph line was down, and that the rope the soldiers had with them, now on the ground, was actually a coil of wire. Speaking in Turkish to one another, they unslung their packs and rifles.

The sergeant pulled a knife from his belt and prepared the end of the new wire, showing the other man his technique. That done, he slipped his knife back in its sheath then clamped the wire in his teeth and began climbing the pole. His partner fed the wire up to him from below.

Julian took a few more steps until he was only ten feet behind the man handling the wire. He could hear his breathing. Julian adjusted his grip on the gun then looked back at Bertie who gave him a nod.

Julian held his breath, and charged forward. With both hands, he brought the pistol down on the back of the man's head. His skull caved under the blow. A blotch of red immediately formed at the point of impact, spraying down onto the man's uniform. He collapsed backward, brushing a red smear across Julian's wrist as he fell. Julian looked up to the sergeant on the pole who had seen the attack. He had dropped the wire and was struggling to pull his knife.

Julian raised his pistol.

"Don't shoot," said the Turk in English, dropping the knife.

Julian held his aim and backed away a little. He picked up the two rifles and tossed them behind him, motioning for the man to come down.

"Don't shoot," said the soldier again as his feet touched the ground, "I am Sergeant Ahmet Rashid. I am not your enemy." He raised his hands.

Julian pointed to the other soldier, who lay sprawled beneath the coil of wire. "Is he alive?"

Ahmet felt the side of the man's neck. "Yes."

"Take off his clothes and tie him up – hands and feet. Use the wire."

The sergeant did as he was told then kneeling, sat back on his haunches. "You are the man the Russians are looking for."

Julian said nothing. The gun was getting heavier – his hand was beginning to shake. He felt warm blood at his side. His wound had opened up.

"We are no friends of these Russians," continued Ahmet.

"They helped you take the canal." Julian's voice cracked with dryness, each word an effort.

"Yes, that is true. We are working together now, but only for the moment. It is important to them that they find you."

Julian said nothing.

The Turk looked past Julian. "There are two of you, yes? The Russians told us there was only you, but I saw signs on the beach."

Julian ignored the question. "Give me his clothes and your packs." He complied and tossed them at Julian's feet.

Julian glanced back and saw Bertie step tentatively into the clearing.

"And who are you?" asked the sergeant.

"You're in no position to be questioning us," said Bertie.

Julian handed the gun to Bertie and went through the packs. "This is all you have?"

"We only came out to fix the telegraph wire. We cut it before our attack."

Julian handed one of the two canteens to Bertie, then took a drink from the other. He felt the welcome flow of life back into his body.

After taking a drink of his own, Bertie took a step closer to the Turk. He cocked the pistol, his bearded chin jutting out. "You people dare make war on Great Britain?"

"Please, I am only a sergeant. It was not my idea." Ahmet hesitated then went on. "But this is our land, not yours. It was stolen from us and we decided to take it back."

"We legally purchased it from the Egyptians," countered Bertie.

"No one has the right to sell the heartland of his own country."

"Yet that is exactly what was done."

"The men who sold it are traitors to the empire."

Julian saw the rage in Bertie's eyes. Bertie placed one foot behind the other as if bracing for a recoil. Would he really kill this helpless man?

Julian stepped next to Bertie, facing the Turk. "What are your plans for the canal?"

"We are repairing the defenses now against an attack by the English."

"You can't withstand the British fleet," Bertie said with a

smirk.

Beads of sweat covered Ahmet's forehead. He turned to Julian and spoke quickly. "The Russian Pavel wants you because you know where they are going and what they will do with their warship when they leave the canal."

"I don't know these things."

"He said it is in the book."

Julian was incredulous; suddenly everyone knew about the journal. "Why would Pavel tell you about the book?"

Bertie uncocked the pistol and Ahmet breathed a little easier.

"He told this to General Ali, my commander. The general thought it best that I know why these men are after you. I just operate the telegraph and do whatever else I am told to do. And you are Mr. North? They told me your name."

"He's a journalist for the *Times*," said Bertie, as if underlining Julian's lack of importance.

"That other fellow – the American – is with a newspaper," said Ahmet, his eyes back on the gun barrel still pointed at his face. "Are you with a newspaper also?"

"Certainly not," replied Bertie. "I am Albert, Prince of Wales, first heir to the throne of the British Empire."

Ahmet flashed a nervous smile. "A good joke. Jokes are good in difficult situations."

Bertie's face reddened, he tightened his grip on the gun.

"I can help you," continued Ahmet, "You need food and water – some clothing to keep the bugs off your skin, and you need boots; I can get you these things."

"We already have them," said Julian. "We're taking yours."

"They will fit you poorly, and there's not much food."

"It'll have to do. We can't let you go back."

Julian ordered Ahmet to undress, he then tied him up.

The sergeant had been right about the clothing. Getting into the army jacket was a struggle for Julian and he had ripped the trousers at the in-seam just pulling them on. But they were enough though to shield his body from sun and from the nipping insects. The leather boots jammed his toes. He saw that Bertie's clothes fit no better.

They picked up the packs and the rifles as the younger Turk began to stir.

"Don't try to follow us," said Julian to the sergeant, trying to make his voice sound menacing. "We've got your rifles. We'll kill you if we have to."

Ahmet shrugged. "We shall see what happens. You have taken

our food and clothing but you have spared our lives. If we meet again, I will remember that."

CHAPTER 20

According to Bertie's watch, five hours passed.

Sticky sap coated Julian's hair and filled every pore of exposed skin with a tinge of green that mingled with the sweat streaming off his face. At every step, thick jumbles of bright green palms had to be swept forcefully aside. Earthy smells permeated the thick, humid air. His breathing was strained and gasping - like an old man's, he thought, like a pressman he knew back at Printing House Square who had breathed in too much printer's ink. Julian couldn't go far without resting but still, he was in better shape than before the run-in with the Turks.

The pain still cut through him as he walked but he had cleaned and bound his wound and he'd become convinced that he was going to be all right; that *they* were going to be all right. Strapped to his back were two rifles, loaded and ready.

Ten paces behind, with the pistol under his belt, Bertie stomped along, grunting and muttering to himself.

Together they forged through the mangroves away from the fort, on a path running parallel to the telegraph lines. They had eaten all the food from the packs but had enough water between them for a few days if they were careful. When they came to a clearing where the telegraph line bent sharply to the south, away from the shoreline, they stopped and sat down to rest.

Bertie wiped his sleeve across his face. "We must look a sight in these clothes. Like two desperate clowns trying to escape from the circus."

Julian smiled at the thought. "I was thinking more like Sancho and Don Quixote."

"Ha, certainly a more heroic picture. Yes, I like that better – so long as we're clear on which of us is which."

"Si, my lord," Julian bowed his head then looked out into the clearing. "We have a choice here; follow the coast or follow the telegraph lines."

"We'll stay here and decide in the morning. It'll be dark soon and these God-awful boots are squeezing my toes like a vise." He pulled them off and began rubbing his feet.

"We'll need to find some food in the morning."

"Maybe you can demonstrate some of your frontier marksmanship."

Julian unstrapped the rifles and inspected one of them. He hadn't fired one in three years. "I shot mostly raccoons and wolves back in Indiana to keep them away from the chickens. Seems like there's just scrawny birds around here." He gazed back out into the clearing.

"I'm a pretty good shot myself, you know," continued Bertie, "been on many safaris here in Africa."

But Julian's thoughts had shifted. "A while back, you said the telegraph line leads to Alexandria?"

"Yes, it's headed generally west. It could only go to Alexandria."

"Do you suppose that, right now, anyone knows the Turks have taken the canal?"

"They obviously cut the lines before their attack but since the repair of the lines was delayed because of us, they might not have gotten the word out yet." Bertie stopped rubbing his feet. "The ships going in and out of the canal would know of course but, without the telegraph, the information would get out very slowly."

"And the Ottoman allies would be very slow in coming to her aid." Julian pointed toward the nearest telegraph pole. "I'll need your help."

"Right." Bertie winced as he forced his boots back on. He followed Julian to the pole and braced himself against it, joining his fingers together to make a foot-hold.

Julian climbed up, cut the wire using the Turk's knife and slid back down. As he hit the ground awkwardly a sharp pain caused him to grimace but not so much that Bertie noticed.

"Very good," said the prince, "you may have just headed off a war."

"Thank you...my lord."

They walked back to the edge of the clearing and hunkered down in the brush to spend the night.

Julian stretched out, leaning against the trunk of a low tree. Bertie prepared his bed as he had the night before, then lay back on an elbow, shifting around until he was able to find a position that suited him. "Reminds me of a lumpy bed I used to have when I was a child – except much harder, of course." He repositioned a branch at the small of his back. "There, that's better."

Julian watched Bertie, only now starting to think of him as a mostly normal human being. He grew curious and dared to ask: "What was it like growing up in the royal family?"

Bertie laughed. "Let me see. I guess, when I was young, I had no idea that I was different from any other child in England. My mother was very protective of us, and we lived in the country for most of my youth. I must have been seven or eight when on a train trip to London we came upon quite a large crowd. I, of course, was very excited about what was so important that it had drawn them all to that spot. I hoped that perhaps the circus was in town. I had read about the circus but had never actually seen one. I was tremendously disappointed when my mother explained that all those people had gathered there just to see us. 'Why would they do that?' I asked her, to which she replied simply: 'They are our subjects.' I had no idea what that meant. It was the first time I realized that we were not an average British family."

Julian recalled that, at the same age, his greatest worry had been beating off the bullies at school. "Was that hard to get used to?"

"A lot was expected of me. My childhood was never carefree. I was drilled on how to stand, how to walk and talk, how to do everything with a regal deportment. Even now, making a good show is the greatest extent of my duties." Bertie raised a dainty finger, mimicking an early teacher. "'Regardless of the circumstance,' they would tell me, 'you must always distinguish yourself in a way that befits your royal blood.'" Bertie gave a shrug. "I must not have learned my lessons well enough – that Turk back at the canal didn't believe me when I told him I was the Prince of Wales."

"I'm not sure I would have believed you either. You weren't exactly dressed like a prince and out there in the mangrove was the last place anyone would expect to find a member of the British royal family." Julian paused. "You weren't really going to kill him, were you?"

Bertie did not seem surprised by the question; maybe he had been expecting it. He spoke slowly. "Have you ever held a gun on a man, knowing that with the slightest twitch of your finger you could end his life?"

"In the fight with Boris I did." Julian recalled that desperate moment.

"And what did you feel?"

"Boris is a big man. I was afraid of him, still intent on getting away."

"Well, I had none of those fears. I had a man kneeling helpless in front of me. It was a feeling of power that I never anticipated; a feeling I was...unprepared for." He sat up. "Would I have killed him had you not been there? I'd like to think not. But you *were* there, so I'll never know."

Julian nodded, appreciating the honesty of Bertie's answer.

After the silence that followed, Bertie decided to shift the conversation. "You've also led a life much different from most men, losing your parents as you did at such a young age. But your good connections with your uncle have served you well."

Julian shook his head. "He gave me a job as a file clerk; said that's all I was good for. No matter what I did, I could never meet his expectations. He always wanted me to do better."

"Sounds like my mother," admitted Bertie who immediately caught himself with a start as if he had revealed more than he intended. He cleared his throat, and the thoughtful expression on his face was gone in an instant. He went back to speaking in his usual, matter-of-fact voice as if the previous conversation had never taken place. "So, the Turks don't even know I'm missing. It's you they're looking for – you and that book."

It took a moment for Julian switch his thinking. He was talking to the Prince of Wales now, not Bertie. He realized that they were two very different men. "That's right, but I don't have the journal. It's still back in London. I told Pavel I had it hidden so he wouldn't kill me."

"He seems to have a powerful preoccupation with it. Tell me about it."

Julian recounted the entire story of Karmonov, of Parker and of the journal. He was about to tell him about the code when Bertie interrupted.

"Castlenau," he said, picking up his canteen. "I've heard that name before, I'm certain of it."

Julian became instantly hopeful. "He's not in the historical records."

"Which records did you check?"

"The files at the *Times* – both in London and Istanbul."

"Well, he may not have been important enough for your

records, but if I remember correctly, he was important enough to have visited us at the palace." Bertie took a drink and swished it around before swallowing. "No, it was Windsor Castle and yes, I'm sure of it; and he was Russian, not French, as you might have thought. His given name was Dmitry."

"The leader of the *Will of the People* is a man named Dmitry. But the journal was written by *Jacques* Castlenau."

"Maybe they were related. Or maybe they were one in the same."

"Did you actually meet Dmitry?" Julian asked this wondering why someone associated with the journal would be allowed anywhere near the royal family. What business could they possibly have in common?

"No, I didn't meet him," said Bertie. "I was too young at the time. But I know he and his son made a lasting impression."

"He had his son with him?" A tantalizing thought popped into Julian's head. "What was his name? How old was he?"

"Twelve maybe; I don't remember his name – don't think I ever knew it. My mother wouldn't let me and the other children near him."

"Why was that?"

Bertie looked at Julian as if he should know the answer to that question. "As I said earlier, Mr. North, my mother was and still is a very protective woman."

It was nearly dark and Julian's thoughts were diverted by a furry black spider scurrying toward the loose cuff of his pant leg. He brushed it aside thinking that he'd better keep his boots on tonight. He forced his mind back into the conversation. "You said they made a lasting impression."

"Right, and do you know why? They - the son actually - started a fire in the library. That's why I remember the name. Not much damage and nobody was hurt, but they left immediately afterwards."

"What became of them?"

"Don't know."

"Is there anyone who would know?"

"My mother might." Bertie scratched the side of his face. "And, in case you're wondering about it, the approximate date of the fire would indeed work out. That boy, the young son of Dmitry Castlenau, may indeed have grown up to become our friend Pavel."

Later, as he waited for sleep, Julian let that thought drift around in his head; Dmitry and Pavel operating in the same circles of power as British Royalty even as they grew *The Will of the People* and patiently plotted the Castlenau revolution. If their power and influence extended to such heights then, how much greater might that power and influence be now?

In the morning they decided to follow the telegraph line which led them straight into the swamps of the Nile Delta. For two brutal days they slogged through tall palms and cat tails and ankle-deep muck. It was mid-morning on the third day when Julian came to a cautious halt. Peering through parted vegetation he spotted signs of civilization ahead. He glanced behind him where Bertie continued to trudge.

Bertie stopped. "What now?" he asked sharply, adjusting his cap. He wiped his forehead, leaving a muddy smear that blended with the dirt and scratches that covered his sunburned face. His beard was a tangle of black with green blotches. His khaki army jacket, caked in mud and grime, hung open, exposing an undershirt soaked gray with sweat. Bertie's chest was heaving. His eyes were red with fatigue.

Julian knew he himself must look at least as bad. "There's a road ahead."

"Good, we have to extricate ourselves from this miserable swamp."

"We could be seen," said Julian only half-heartedly. Their plan had been to skirt the more easily traveled croplands, staying in the watery glades to avoid detection. They had spent the nights in isolated drylands.

"I don't care if we're seen or not. You can consider this a royal command if you like: We are taking that road and I don't much care where it leads." He came abreast of Julian.

Ahead of them, beyond a narrow clearing, a smooth roadway lay atop a gravel berm elevated from the surrounding lowlands by nearly ten feet. The telegraph line took a turn there and ran alongside.

"It's the road to Alexandria," Bertie judged.

"I don't see anyone."

"Good, let's go then." Bertie took the lead. He crossed the clearing, stepping over a half filled drainage ditch. Julian followed. From alongside the berm they had a clear line of sight. Stretching from horizon to horizon the road ran straight and level and it seemed completely deserted.

"Looks safe to me," said Bertie. He climbed up and walked out to the middle of the road where he promptly sat down on the dusty gravel. He took his boots off and began rubbing his feet.

Julian sat down beside him and ran the back of his wrist across his forehead. The mud and grime gave his skin a greasy, gritty feel. His face felt raw and sun baked. It bristled with a stubbly beard. His buttonless jacket hung open exposing his bare chest. Yes, he looked just as bad as the prince – maybe worse. He took his own boots off revealing bruised and bloodied toes. The thin green film between them which he had noticed the night before had grown more pronounced. Bertie was right; they had to get out of the swamp. He gave the wound in his side a brief inspection; it was healing and not as red as before. That was one good thing.

Shading his eyes he surveyed the treeless green glade bordering the road in both directions. Without the cover of the palms he felt exposed and vulnerable, but with the road they had firm, dry ground on which to walk and, more importantly, they had a direction to safety. A hot breeze came up – too hot to offer any refreshment. "How far do you figure it is to Alexandria?"

Bertie shook his head and leaned back on his elbows. "We're not close - a couple of hundred miles maybe. That's a long way but we'll make better time now." He put his soggy boots back on. "Come on, let's get started."

Julian nodded, his eyes fixed on the point where the road met the horizon. It shimmered in the heat.

"We should travel by night."

"Bunk! You're determined to make things as difficult as possible, aren't you?"

"Just being careful."

Bertie started off. He spoke when Julian caught up. "There might be signs or milestones along the way that will tell us the distance to Alexandria. You don't read Arabic, do you?"

"No," said Julian, surprised at Bertie's newfound energy.

"Some might be in French, come to think of it," Bertie continued. "Having built the canal, the French used to be well thought of around here."

"They aren't now?"

"Haven't you noticed? They hate all of us westerners, us infidels. The last I heard, they've been rioting in the streets of Alexandria protesting our presence."

"Good idea for us to go there then," said Julian, deciding he owed Bertie a few cynical comments of his own just to even the score.

Bertie rewarded him with a sour look. "It makes perfect sense.

There are always British warships at port. All we need to do is get close to the docks and we'll be saved." His stomach grumbled. "We'll also be able to get a good English meal instead of these miserable blackbirds you've been shooting for us."

They had been living off whatever vegetation they could eat, their staple being hard and bitter wild dates. Julian had managed to shoot a few desert vultures, but the time spent tearing out feathers, making a fire and roasting them was hardly worth the few mouthfuls of tough, bone-spiked meat. As for water, it was plentiful here in the Nile delta, though it came with a thick layer of green scum.

Julian adjusted the rifles more evenly on his shoulders. He would have preferred to hold onto the pistol, but Bertie wanted that and kept it under his belt. After a few hours of walking, they again rested by the side of the road.

Bertie took a swig from his canteen, careful to shake it first. "North, I think it's time you showed me those notes of yours – the article you're writing."

Julian hadn't thought much about his deciphering work since leaving *Resolute*; just staying alive had been such a constant preoccupation. He unstrung the pouch from his belt and broke open the wax seal, relieved to see that his papers had been well protected. He pulled out the pages and, as he smoothed the wrinkles, he explained that they weren't notes about his big story. He told Bertie about the code.

"Does anyone else know about this?" asked Bertie.

"No. I was just hired to translate the text of the journal. I don't think Karmonov or Parker knew about the code. These are just the symbols I was able to copy before Parker took the journal back. There's much more of it in the journal."

"And after giving the journal back to this Parker fellow, you decided to head off to Istanbul? How did you know to go there?"

Julian gave a thin smile at how many times he'd been asked that same question. He told Bertie about the Dover ship schedule and about Hastings. "He's the man who killed Karmonov and he was the man who tried to kill you in Istanbul. The royal marines killed him."

"Yes, I heard he was dead."

"He had a tattoo on his hand – an H within a circle. The journal has the same symbol on its cover. The book ties everything together."

Bertie picked up a stone and tossed it into the drainage ditch. "And because of the book and because of your friend who was killed, you decided to leave your overly critical uncle and head off to Istanbul to become a swashbuckling hero journalist. Was that the idea?"

Julian leaned back on his hands and avoided the eyes of the prince. "I suppose that's true enough," he confessed.

Bertie was silent and threw another stone.

"The real secrets of the journal are in the code," said Julian after taking a drink.

"What makes you so sure?"

"The text of the journal gives some interesting philosophical views but, beyond that, there's nothing sinister about it, nothing definite anyway. Sure, Castlenau wanted to start a war and foment a revolution in its aftermath, but without a real plan and without people to carry it out, it might as well just be idle talk. The journal has to contain more potent information than that and if it's not in the text, it can only be in the code." Julian sidled closer to Bertie and handed him a page from his notes. "It's made up of these stick-figure symbols. I don't know what they mean yet, but there's a regular pattern to them. Two or three groupings of symbols are always followed by two groups of six symbols."

Bertie studied the page with interest as Julian explained further: "Those two groups of six are always made up of different combinations of the same ten symbols. I figure they must be numbers."

"Very good, yes, that makes sense," said Bertie. "There's a method of deciphering called frequency analysis - you ever hear of it?"

"A friend of mine had - that's what I've been working on."

"You told a friend about this?"

"I just showed him a few of the symbols. I didn't tell him where they were from."

Bertie looked at him skeptically. "And have you made any progress?"

"So far, nothing seems to fit exactly."

"Thomas Phelippes," said Bertie with a raised authoritative finger, "he used frequency analysis to break Queen Mary's code in her plot against Elizabeth back in the fifteen-eighties. Did you know that?"

"No, I didn't."

"The man was a genius. Mary and her men all lost their heads over that one." Bertie handed back the page. "Your analysis may not have worked since much of this code may include names of different nationalities. That'd throw your frequency standard off."

Julian was stung by Bertie's easy revelation. "You think they're names?"

"Could be. You mentioned it a moment ago: What good is a plan without people to carry it out? That would explain why Pavel is so anxious to get the journal back. Let's get ourselves back to civilization," said Bertie, standing. "The Royal Navy has specialists in code-breaking. They're always up for a good puzzle."

They resumed their journey and traveled three more hot and dusty hours on the deserted road before coming to a halt. "About time we find some high ground off the road to spend the night," said Bertie. He pointed to a low rise in the glade. "There, that should do."

But Julian was looking straight ahead to where the road ran into the orange ball of the setting sun. Something had caught his attention but he wasn't sure what. He shielded his eyes sensing a rhythmic motion in the distance. Then he heard them.

"Riders," Julian cried, unslinging one of the rifles from his shoulder. "Get off the road. They're close and coming fast."

At the warning, Bertie turned and barreled into Julian sending them both tumbling off the edge of the road down the side of the berm. Their rolling stopped just short of the drainage ditch.

"God damn it to hell, North," cursed Bertie, collecting himself. "There're two of them."

"Probably just innocent travelers like us, but just to be safe..." Bertie drew his pistol.

The sound of the galloping horses was clear now and getting louder. "We can't stay here," said Julian, his heart pounding. He made his decision in an instant. "Come on." He made a dash over the ditch, sprinting across the clearing. A shot was fired from behind just as he entered the glade. It had to have come from the riders - so much for the innocent traveler idea. He heard a horse bellowing madly; hoof beats splashing. They were coming after him.

There was another shot and Julian felt a blazing pain in his shoulder. The cover of the vegetation wasn't effective against a hunter seated on a tall horse. Still running, Julian crouched low and changed direction. He lunged sideways and fell into the swamp, rolling onto his back, holding his rifle out in front of him. He lay still, seeing only the thick vegetation all around, feeling only the water soaking into his clothing. Then he heard a sloshing in the muck and the hard breathing of a horse. The horseman was nearly on him, about to burst through the palm blades. Julian took aim at the sound and fired. The rifle jerked back, the blast roaring in his ears. He fired again, then lay still, listening. All was quiet. Had one of his shots struck home, or was the man just waiting for Julian to show himself so he could shoot him dead?

Julian got up slowly and crept back, retracing his steps. Then he saw the man.

He wore a black military uniform and lay motionless, face up, floating in the shallow swamp with arms spread. His chest was a pool of blood. His eyes were open wide in shock, his mouth distorted. Beside the body of the soldier, his chestnut horse casually munched on a clump of grass.

Julian caught his breath and swallowed hard. Then he thought about Bertie. He looked around but there was no sign of him. He bent low and looked back to the road.

There was Bertie, standing on the road. Beside him, the other horseman, dressed in black like the dead man and still mounted, held a gun pointed directly at Bertie's head. But the man in black wasn't looking at Bertie; he was staring out into the glade looking for his partner and for Julian.

Julian bent lower and carefully unslung his other rifle. He cocked it as a desert hawk called out. The air was still. He took a deep breath. *Calmly now, calmly,* came his father's words to him from when he had taught him how to shoot. He braced the stock against his shoulder and leveled the rifle until he had the man in his sites. A bead of sweat dripped down his forehead. He curled his finger around the trigger and brought it back.

The loud boom rang out and the rifle jerked in Julian's hands. The recoil pounded his shoulder. He looked through the white smoke. Bertie was now standing beside a riderless horse. Maybe the rider just dove for cover. Julian waited.

"North?" Bertie yelled looking out from the road. "North, you killed him."

Julian let out a breath and stood up, his knees suddenly weak. Slowly, he walked back to the horse still in the glade and grabbed the reins.

Bertie yelled again. "Get up here. Hurry."

Julian led the horse across the clearing and up the berm. "Are there more of them?"

Bertie was staring at the body of the soldier beside him. "Don't think so," he said finally.

Julian's stomach, already knotted from lack of decent food, twisted at the sight of another dead man.

This man was younger than the first – about his own age.

"You killed them both," said Bertie as if not quite believing it.

"Maybe there really is something to this swashbuckling hero-journalist plan of yours."

Julian gripped his rifle tighter to keep his hand from shaking. He had just killed two men. "They probably only fired at us because we tried to get away."

"Maybe they saw our Turkish army uniforms – God knows what they thought." Then he noticed Julian's shoulder. "Blast it all, North, you're hurt again."

Julian looked down. His shirt was soaked in blood but he felt no pain. Why was he always the one getting hurt? - never Bertie. "The bullet must have just grazed me."

Bertie sighed. "I seem to have become your personal physician on this adventure of ours. Take off your shirt and we'll have a look. And while you're at it, cut a couple of strips from his shirt." He pointed to the dead man.

Julian handled that distasteful job and Bertie used the cloth to clean the wound.

"You're right, just a scratch. I thought they'd killed you out there."

"They nearly did."

Bertie used the second strip of cloth to bind the wound.

As Bertie worked, Julian was able to calm himself. He had taken two lives but he had saved his own and Prince Bertie's. He felt elation, relief and remorse all at the same time. It was not a feeling he was comfortable with.

They dragged the body off the road down into the ditch, covering it with brush so it could not be readily seen. The other man they left where he died; concealed in the swamp. Bertie took one of their wide-brimmed hats and, after seeing that it fit well on him, discarded the cap he'd taken from the Turk back at the canal. Julian took the other hat but it was wet and he didn't put it on right away.

"They must've been on patrol," said Julian after inspecting the saddlebags. "There are enough provisions here for nearly a week – bedrolls too."

"We'll have no trouble now making it to Alexandria, so long as we don't run into more soldiers."

Julian shaded his eyes, looking up the nearest telegraph pole. "Probably time we cut the line again."

"Right," agreed Bertie.

Once that was done they mounted the horses. Julian looked back. A light wind was already disturbing the brush they had placed over one of the bodies. He kicked the horse into a slow gallop.

That night they made camp on a dry bluff by the side of the road where they had a clear view of the sparkling night sky. The bedroll felt like a feather bed to Julian after the previous nights on palm branches and hard ground. The stressful day was over and he was bone tired yet he lay restless, staring at the stars. He thought of his run through the swamp, being chased by the black-shirted rider. A dog barked in the distance.

"You asleep, North?"

Julian turned his head in Bertie's direction. "Not yet," he said through a yawn. He knew the prince was only ten feet away but he couldn't make him out in the darkness.

"You saved my life today. You saved both our lives. You showed bravery and courage and I thank you for that."

"I was lucky with the first man. I couldn't even see him."

"The brave men I've known in my life, some the heroes of monumental battles, have all given luck too much credit. The important thing is that when everything was on the line, success and failure hanging in the balance, they did what had to be done. They won the day – just as you did." With a grunt, Bertie shifted his weight on his bedroll. "You can call it anything you like, but it was more than luck."

"Thank you, my lord." Julian smiled to himself, appreciating everything Bertie had said. Then his thoughts drifted and after a while the dog barked again.

"Do you have a girl back home, North?"

Julian forced himself back into the moment. Home? Where was his home? Did he even have one? Did he have a girl? Well, that question he could answer without a thought. "Yes, I do; in Istanbul."

"The love of a good woman is the best thing this world has to offer. If you have that, you are truly a lucky man. In matters of the heart it's better to pick being lucky over being skillful I suppose, if you have a choice."

"I haven't known her long – six months. She likes Noah too."

"Well, there's one good thing that will come of his treachery. She'll toss that blackguard like a rotten melon after learning the truth about him. So, it'll be up to you to take control of the situation. Do you love her?"

"I think I do."

Bertie made a disparaging sound. "You'd better decide. For me that decision was made by others. I have a marriage of state, not of love. Indeed, I know of love only from the lack of it in my life, but I do know that women like decisive men – none of this sitting on the fence poppycock. Do you love her?"

Julian cleared his throat, adjusting to the idea that, here he was, lying under the stars, somewhere in the wilds of the Nile Delta, getting advice on women from the Prince of Wales. Despite the oddness of the situation, he saw an image of Kate forming vividly in front of him and felt a conviction rising. "Yes, I do," he said.

"That's better," said Bertie, sounding tired but insistent just the same. "When we get out of this mess and you have the chance, just be sure to go after her with that same vigor. Now get some sleep."

CHAPTER 21

HMS Inflexible

Kate held onto her hat against a gust of cold wind as the drum beat to general quarters rumbled through the ship. Scores of sailors ran to take their positions. In a few short minutes the drums stopped and *Inflexible* was ready to face whatever danger lurked just over the western horizon where a thickening ribbon of black smoke betrayed the presence of a line of ships.

Three days had passed since Parker had roused her from Mrs. Potter's in the middle of the night and had taken her aboard *Inflexible* along with Willoughby and Ira. Within an hour of her setting foot on deck, they had pulled away from the docks and steamed west out of Istanbul harbor escorted by two gunships. All Kate knew was that they were off in search of *Resolute* – at least that was all Parker was telling her and the other journalists.

Kate had a cabin to herself and had promised to conceal her gender as much as possible while out on deck. She wore the shirt and trousers of an average seaman and now, after adjusting her hat, she tucked a few strands of hair back beneath it. She held onto the rail.

The wind kept up and *Inflexible* held to the southerly course she'd taken since breaking into the Aegean. Her deck rolled lightly.

"Must be a whole convoy out there, all strung out," said Willoughby squinting. He stood on one side of Kate, Parker on the other.

Parker looked up to the bridge some twenty feet overhead. "Fisher's not too worried about it – could be our Mediterranean fleet. Yes, that would make sense."

"How do you know he's not worried?" asked Kate.

Parker laughed. "He has his hat off. It's a curious habit of his that I picked up on out in the Black Sea. When things get serious, the hat goes back on and he gives the visor a tug. That's the time to worry."

"They're coming into view now," said Willoughby.

Ships began to dot the horizon; one of them flashing a signal lamp. *Inflexible's* own powerful light blinked back a reply, the shutter mechanism clicking away.

"Can you tell what they're saying?" asked Kate.

"Heaven's no," said Parker. "I've never learned to read code. They're our ships though, that much is certain. God, look at them all."

Dark, evenly spaced silhouettes moved noiselessly across the horizon on a course angling toward *Inflexible*. Kate counted eight visible now and more coming into view. "Joining the search for *Resolute*," guessed Kate.

"And for the Prince of Wales," added Willoughby. "Don't forget about him."

"I'll wager they've been involved in the search from the start," said Parker, "the fleet scouring from the west; us from the east. Maybe they've already found her...and him."

A few hours later the fleet drew close. Their thumping engines created a low background hum that sounded almost sinister to Kate. More signals flashed. A launch from one of the ships steamed alongside *Inflexible* and tied up.

"It's Seymour," said Parker, eyeing the group of officers coming up from the launch onto the deck. "He's the one in his whites. Admiral, Sir Beauchamp Seymour, commander of the entire Med fleet. He's wasting no time in transferring his flag here."

"Why would he do that?" asked Ira who had joined them. He'd spent the better part of the afternoon napping in his cabin.

"On missions of the fleet, the ranking officer always resides aboard the best ship and *Inflexible* is easily the largest and most modern in the entire navy," said Parker.

Kate watched the elderly admiral and a bevy of somber faced aides being piped aboard. Seymour gave casual salutes to *Inflexible's* lesser officers then, striding past them, he headed directly for Fisher where the two exchanged proper salutes followed by a curt handshake.

Kate knew that flag officers were expected to design and fund their own formal uniforms and that Seymour was known for his flamboyance. Standing beside the blue-jacketed Fisher, he looked in his white and gold and his distinguished gray hair, as if he were Poseidon himself, Lord of the Deep.

They talked for a short time before Seymour began tapping his foot nervously in a let's-get-on-with-it kind of way. Then they headed inside.

"I don't think they found *Resolute*," said Parker once the ceremonial passing of the flag had been completed, and the admiral's pennant was run up. "If they had, Seymour would have told Fisher about it right away and I think he would have at least looked relieved. Both men seemed tense, I thought."

"So we'll just be carrying on with the search then," said Kate.

"I suppose so," said Parker. "Can't afford to have a renegade warship on the loose."

"We've got a good many ships," said Willoughby, scanning the fleet surrounding them, "but the search area is huge, and at night, *Resolute* could easily slip by, undetected."

"She's got to make port sometime," said Kate, "and I'm sure that the government has people in every harbor on the lookout for her."

"Indeed we do, Seaman Wilder," said Briggs coming up from behind. He introduced himself and acknowledged Parker with a nod.

"So what's the news from the fleet, Mr. Briggs?" asked Parker.

"Lord Beresford and Captain Fisher have asked me to inform you that we have an idea, a good idea, of where *Resolute* might be."

"There's good news," said Willoughby. "Now we have a chance to get her back before she does something terrible."

"Unfortunately we may be a little late on that score," said Briggs. "Our telegraph lines to Port Said at the Suez Canal have been out for some time now. Whitehall thinks it may have fallen."

"What do you mean, fallen?" asked Willoughby. "The canal you mean?"

But Kate's mind was already churning with the implications. "*Resolute* attacked the canal?"

"We aren't certain but that looks like the only plausible explanation. We're making preparations to sail there immediately."

"With the entire fleet?" asked Parker.

"Yes. It will be an overwhelming force. We should be able to take the canal back without much trouble."

"Thank you for telling us," said Kate.

Briggs smiled. "In Lord Beresford's words it was either tell you straight out or put up with your badgering all the way there. Our bargain is: we'll tell you what we can and you will ask no questions." The smile disappeared as he continued. "This will be a dangerous mission, and as non-combatants in a war zone the British Navy cannot fully insure your safety. Is that understood?"

They all nodded.

"My God, the Suez Canal," said Willoughby after Briggs had left. "Why would a group of anarchists attack the Suez Canal?"

"It's the business of anarchists to create chaos," said Ira with a shrug, "and that's exactly what they're doing – simple as that."

Still, Kate pondered the question. With the taking of *Resolute*, and now the canal, *The Will of the People* had won crucial military and commercial assets. It was even possible that they continued to hold the Prince of Wales who could be a telling bargaining lever in whatever master plan they might have. That was the real question here: What were they planning next?

Four days later Kate rose from her cot and checked the time. Briggs had announced the previous day that they were close to the canal and that they should be up and alert by five the next morning. She had a quarter-hour to spare. She turned on the electric light and the magical glass bulb gave an unsteady yellow glow. She found yesterday's uniform and dressed quickly, then donned the over-sized navy sea coat she'd been issued. The sleeves hung down to her knuckles. She tied her hair in a band and put on her sailor's cap.

Kate yawned – five on the dot. Tentatively, she opened the cabin door to find the captain's aide, Mr. Samuels, standing in the corridor with Parker and Ira beside him. Like Kate, they all wore heavy sea coats.

"*Mister* Wilder," said Samuels making it clear to everyone that her disguise had not fooled him. He put a check mark on a note pad. "I show that there's one more of you," he added with a bothered expression.

"Actually there should be one less name on that list of yours," complained Parker, "I'm not a journalist. I'm here representing the foreign office. I should be up on the bridge with the captain right now."

Samuels shook his head. "Sorry sir, Captain Fisher was quite specific that you should be included in with the journalists. Now where's the last one? Where's Willoughby?"

"I'm here, Goddamnit," said Willoughby stepping out of his cabin. He stopped and looked at the others. "Just have to get my coat."

Samuels sheparded his little group down to the galley for some food, then took them out on deck. It was still dark. Kate flipped her collar up against the wet wind and looked around. They stood on the main deck, just forward of the bridge which loomed above them. Her eyes had not yet adjusted and she could see nothing out to sea. She grabbed the rail to keep her footing on the rolling deck made slippery from the spray off the bow. The sea was choppy.

The sound of the wind and sea combined with the deep hum of the engines and Samuels had to shout to be heard. He cautioned them to stay in the area that had been roped off. "You have chairs. A seaman will be by to check on you from time to time in case you need anything. Put on your floatation vests. If unexpected problems arise we may need you to go below. Now, unless you have questions, I have other matters needing my attention." Not bothering to actually wait for questions, he turned and took the stairs up to the bridge.

"He's happy to be done with us," observed Parker wrapping the life vest around his chest over his coat. The others did the same.

"I thought he was damned hospitable," said Ira. "Journalists are never allowed aboard American ships except in port - very progressive of you Brits."

"They want to keep us happy," said Willoughby. "There's no telling what mischief an unhappy newsman might get into on a ship like this."

Kate smiled thinly and made the mistake of sitting down, her thin trousers soaking up the cold sea water that had puddled on the chair. Now she was cold *and* wet but she wasn't about to get up. She gazed out to sea where the running lamps of adjacent ships floated, barely visible. Her thoughts drifted to Julian and Noah wondering where they might be at this moment. Were they out there over the horizon somewhere? Logic told her they could be, but what if they weren't? She fought off the feeling of dread lurking at the back of her mind. They weren't dead, she told herself, folding her arms as much against the wind as against that fearful thought.

"You're very quiet this morning, Kate," said Willoughby. "Are you cold? Still sleepy?"

"Oh, sorry – both I guess."

"No place for a woman – aboard a warship," observed Parker.

That comment got her going. "I'm in better shape than you, Mr. Parker," she fired back. "Leastwise I don't need a nip from that flask you carry with you."

"Oh, come now, I'll bet it would do you some good." He rummaged under his coat then produced the silver container. He held it out to the others, shaking it so they could hear that it was nearly full. "Come on, who wants some?"

Kate looked back out to sea.

"I'll have a go," said Ira, who took a single sip.

"I will as well," said Willoughby, who grabbed the flask from Ira and tested the brandy swishing it around in his mouth before swallowing. "Actually, Parker, this is of very good quality. Thank you indeed." He took another swallow and passed it back to him just as the sound of the engines rose a notch.

From the depths of the iron hull Kate could feel *Inflexible* stirring. It gave her a sense of the power that drove this sea-giant.

"Look out there," said Ira, pointing at the ship nearest them where additional running lamps were being lit as the big fleet got under way.

"With all the ships moving, there's a greater risk of collisions," Parker pointed out. "We've got a few more lit ourselves. Ours are electric you know."

"Might as well have stayed in bed another hour," said Willoughby. "Still can't see a bloody thing."

"I don't suppose that could be the effects of the brandy," suggested Kate. She turned eastward where the sky showed a dull pink through the coal-smoke haze. By Parker's count there were thirteen ships in all and, as the first rays of the sun gleamed over the horizon, the fleet was transformed from distant constellations of faint orange lamps to well defined silhouettes of black on blue.

Kate was familiar with the formation and, as if seeing it from high above, she pictured the fleet forming up in a ring, three ships wide and miles in diameter, each ship keeping a safe distance from the others. As the flag vessel, *Inflexible* occupied the last three-ship tier in the circular column.

"The canal should be out there in that direction," said Willoughby pointing, raising his voice to be heard over the engines.

"We're nearly at full speed now," said Parker.

Kate stood up. The ringed formation of the fleet was uncoiling. They were about to attack.

Aboard HMS *Condor*, at the center of the first tier of ships, Briggs checked the time and glanced at Sir Charles Beresford who had insisted on captaining the lead gunship. Beresford had also insisted that Briggs be his first officer which was fine with Briggs, anxious as he was to get back at the men who had stolen *Resolute* and made off with Prince Bertie.

At precisely seven o'clock, Beresford ordered a change in course and, with HMS *Winchester* and HMS *Reynolds* on either side, the trio of gunships peeled off from the formation and steamed south. Behind them the fleet would follow, their circular path unraveling in the classic naval strategy that was straight out of the same Whitehall textbook Briggs had studied as a cadet. He picked up his telescope and studied the featureless horizon. Thirty minutes later the first gray outline of the fort at Port Said came into view.

Briggs gave Beresford his assessment. "The guns at the fort have a three-hundred yard range advantage over us. If their gunnery is any good at all, this will be risky business for us. We'll adopt a zigzag course on the way in, I assume?"

Beresford did not hesitate. "Signal *Reynolds* and *Winchester* to take evasive action and to fire as their guns bear. They will do the zigzagging. We'll rush straight at them until they fire their first shot. We'll soon learn their intent and see how good their marksmanship is."

Briggs ordered the signals sent to the accompanying ships and concealed his concern that Beresford's judgment might be tainted by his rage against the anarchists. He knew Sir Charles wanted to pound these bastards into submission and inflict as much damage as possible by his own hand. Calmly, Briggs gave the order to the helmsman: "Steady on course, full speed ahead, Mr. Jackson."

Port Said

At the high parapet, General Ali stood with his officers beside him. The six gunnery stations along the northern wall were ready and waited only for his command. Through his telescope he tracked the three approaching ships noting the volume of smoke pouring from their stacks. They were under full steam and would be in range soon. He glanced at his men positioned along the wall. They had held the fort and the entire canal for more than a week and had worked hard at repairing its defenses. The deep gashes in the wall blasted by *Resolute* had been crudely filled in with mounds of rubble on which some of his men now stood. Ali hoped that the one damaged gun emplacement had been fixed solidly enough so its recoil would not tear it from its makeshift mount. His men passed the time by checking their weapons or having a drink from their canteens or simply looking out at the onrushing enemy. He wondered if they knew how hopeless their situation was.

The help from the Egyptian army had not arrived, and Ali cursed himself for depending on Foreign Minister Ismail to handle that critical part of the plan. It hadn't helped matters that his men had been unable to repair the telegraph lines to Alexandria. He was convinced that the man the Russians had been looking for was responsible for the lines being down. He should not have taken the search for him so lightly. Two days earlier, five Egyptian soldiers had arrived, simply to confirm that the canal was indeed in Ottoman hands. Even though they left immediately, there was no chance now that they would return in time with the promised Egyptian help. In resignation to that fact and to bolster the morale of his men, he had lowered the flag of Ottoman Egypt and ceremoniously raised Ottoman Army flag in its place.

Ali clenched his hand into a fist. As always, he would do his best for his country. He turned to Sergeant Rashid, the only enlisted man standing here among his officers. "Stay close to me, sergeant. You may have a special part to play in this fight."

"Yes, sir," the sergeant replied.

The general knew Rashid's pride had been shaken at having been surprised then left stripped by the British escapee. But that was precisely why he was the right man for the job he had in mind – should it come to that.

Ali looked back out to sea, gauging the distance. "Guns three and four, take aim at the center ship," he shouted.

The gunnery captains checked their aim and a short time later drew their sabers. They looked to General Ali.

"Fire as you bear. One shot only."

In unison the captains slashed their swords downward, shouting out the order: "Fire!" The big guns roared with smoke and flame, their iron mounts jerking back against heavy ropes.

Ali shook his head as the shells flew out over the harbor and splashed well short of their targets. They would have to do much better than that.

The range officer checked the location of the first shots in relation to the oncoming ships. Quickly he consulted his charts and shouted azimuth and elevation corrections to each gun.

"Reload!" ordered the gun captains through the smoke.

Ali made sure the men saw him timing the reloading process

– two minutes. Ali nodded and put his watch away. He turned his attention to the oncoming ships. The two outer ships were zigzagging their way in, but the one in the center had taken the lead, speeding directly at them. Ali raised his telescope to the horizon where he saw three more funnels of black smoke; three more attackers. He should have known that England would send more than three ships to retake the canal. He took a few steps back from the wall and called for Sergeant Rashid. After speaking to him in a low voice he returned to the parapet and calculated the available artillery shells. Against six ships, he would have to conserve his resources and make the most of every shot. "Stand ready," he shouted.

More ships began to dot the horizon across a wide arc; ten of them visible now. Ali heard murmuring all along the wall.

"Silence!" Ali shouted, glaring at his men. He drew his sword and held it over his head. "You are Turks! You are fighting for your homeland – for the land of your fathers now retaken by the blood of your brothers. You will fight like Turks today or I will cut you down myself." He slammed his sword into the wall kicking up a spray of sparks and stone. He ran his gaze along the line of men, seeing in each face a mix of determination and fear familiar to him from another time and another battle in the foothills above Istanbul. With an effort, he fought to keep those bitter memories buried.

The general returned his sword to its scabbard. "Guns one, two and three, aim at the center ship, the rest bear on the ship to the right." Ali had noted that ship's regular, *predictable* zigzag pattern. He stepped down from the parapet and went from gun to gun along the wall checking the aim so that, together, there was a good chance one of them would hit home. At the center gun he raised a clenched fist. "Fire!"

HMS Condor

If the enemy was capable of learning anything, Briggs knew their second shot would be much better than the first. He kept his telescope trained on the fort. He saw flashes along the wall then heard the distant boom of the guns sounding as one. The cluster of shells rocketed through the air. They made a huge arc, some heading straight for *Condor*. This would be close. Beside him Beresford stood grim and stone-faced, as if invincible.

"Take cover," Briggs shouted.

The shells whistled down then exploded, shaking *Condor* violently. Briggs fell to a knee.

A geyser of seawater erupted off the bow. He raised himself up and looked aft. "We've been hit." He yelled down to the deck. "Fire teams at your stations!"

Men were scrambling around a gaping hole in the wooden deck near the stern. Smoke and flames poured out. The shrill scream of a hand-cranked siren cut through the chaos.

Beresford remained standing, eyes still on the fort. "You take care of the fire. I'll handle the bridge," he shouted to Briggs.

"Aye, sir." Briggs began climbing down into the cloud of smoke that was beginning to engulf the aft portion of the ship. From the bridge above him he could hear the order to the helmsman: "Hold your course, Mr. Jackson!" Beresford was turning this into a suicide mission.

Briggs ran toward the fire then caught a man staring off to starboard. "Back to your job, sailor, we've got work to do."

"*Reynolds* has been hit, sir."

Briggs glanced in that direction, stunned. Where HMS *Reynolds* should have been, a pillar of fire and black smoke rose up from a smoking hulk. The fire flared, the smoke turned white and in an instant Briggs knew what that meant. The deafening roar was accompanied by a brilliant flash as the powder stores of the gunship exploded in a shower of metal, wood and seawater. The plume of smoke grew then suddenly dissipated until blackened debris and a few pockets of flame riding on the waves were all that was left of HMS *Reynolds* and her crew.

"God help them," whispered Briggs, but he had no time to waste. He headed aft where flames and black smoke issued from *Condor's* splintered deck. Two men struggled with the fire hose directing its spray into the flames. Briggs grabbed the hose ten feet back from the nozzle then took hold of the rail, steadying the process so that the man at the nozzle could direct the spray more efficiently. Others then used wet canvas to smother the fire.

"That's it, that's it," he encouraged them as the flames diminished. Beneath him he could still feel the drumming of the engine. There must be a hell of a mess down in the engine room but *Condor* was still on the move. He left the remains of the fire for his men to finish off and was headed back to the bridge when he saw a commotion at the forward gun. It was the four-inch breech loader - the biggest aboard. Several men were bent over the gun and Briggs was surprised to see that one of them was Beresford.

Briggs raced over, wondering at the same time if there was anyone on the bridge besides Jackson.

"The damned breech is jammed again," said one of the men to Briggs.

"Wouldn't have happened with an honest muzzle-loader," said another.

But Beresford was already onto a solution. "Get me that bucket, sailor," he yelled to the nearest man, pointing to a full bucket of seawater at the base of the gun. He emptied it over the jammed shell then tested the lever, straining to open it without effect. Then he picked up the empty bucket and slammed it into the lever: once, twice, and a third time. Finally, the lever sprang open, freeing the shell. "Toss it overboard, boys," Beresford ordered. "That shell won't be doing us any good today."

It took two men to lift it and roll it over the side.

"Now check the breech and load her carefully."

As this was going on, Briggs looked over the bow where the fort loomed closer, more threatening. They were still headed directly for it. "God help us," he said under his breath.

"They've got one more shot – maybe two," shouted Beresford, "then we have to be ready to give them hell." He stepped back from the gun. "How's that fire, Mr. Briggs?"

"Under control, sir, nearly out."

Briggs heard another roar of guns and flinched, but this time it came from one of the ships behind them. *Monarch*, in the second tier of ships, had let loose a blast from her twelve-inchers. The shells screamed high overhead and a cheer went up from the men of *Condor* though the salvo exploded short of its target.

"Better not be hittin' us with their next shot!" said one of the men eyeing the entire fleet bearing down from behind.

"Just get that gun loaded and be ready to fire," said Beresford. "Come on, Briggs." He crisply turned and began making his way back to the bridge. They were no more than half way there when Beresford looked again at the fort, apparently realizing they hadn't fired in a while. "Hard to port!" he shouted up to the bridge. He broke into a run. "Hard to Port, Mr. Jackson!"

Briggs hurried after him. Through the windows of the bridge he could see Jackson send the wheel spinning. Condor turned, responding to her rudder, the engine thumping away.

The guns at the fort fired just as they climbed onto the bridge joining the beleaguered helmsman.

"Get down!" shouted Briggs, ducking for cover.

Shells exploded sending white water shooting high above them, no more than twenty yards off starboard.

In a crouch, Beresford waited as seawater poured over the

ship like a pelting rain, then he stood. "Good work, Jackson!" he said calmly, clapping a hand on the shoulder of his young helmsman. "You saved us all, by God!"

Jackson swallowed hard, too shaken to say anything in response.

"Resume your heading. Take us straight at them." Beresford wiped his face with his sleeve and Briggs held his breath.

Port Said

Ali's men had cheered at their two hits on the gunships. The one had been sunk but the other one, though damaged, was still closing with the entire fleet behind her racing to catch up.

"Ready the infantry," Ali shouted down to an officer in the courtyard, where most of his men were assembled. "They'll be in rifle range soon. If we can't stop them with our big guns, perhaps we can hurt them with our small ones." He shifted his attention to the second wave of ships noting that one of them had turned to expose her full profile making for a juicy target. He knew her intent - she was about to fire off a broadside. There wasn't much time. He raced down to the closest gun. The men had just finished reloading. He extended an arm, pointing at the ship. "Aim for her; aim for her and fire. Quickly now."

The men struggled with the elevation then touched off the fuse. The great gun boomed and jerked back, sending its shell flying out over the water. At nearly the same instant, the British ship fired, her entire side erupting in a flash of flame and a huge cloud of white smoke. Ali heard the deep rumble of her broadside a heartbeat later. Her shells were in the air, somewhere crossing paths with the one Ali's men had just fired.

The general took off his helmet. Who will die with this exchange? And who will live to care? He shook his head at the obvious answer: maybe everyone, and maybe no one.

The distant chorus of whistling shells became a single overwhelming shriek. They slammed into the center of the wall where Ali stood and exploded in a blinding flash. Two of the heavy guns shifted precariously in their mounts and came crashing down. The wall gave way.

Ali felt himself swept back by the blast of heat, tumbling helplessly through a white cloud lit by bright orange flashes all around. He hung there for a moment almost as if he'd taken flight then fell, slamming heavily onto the ground below. There he lay, face up, wondering why he felt no pain. In the strange silence he could see only smoke, spotted with falling debris. He tried to cover his face as blocks and fragments of shattered stone fell on him but he found he could do nothing to protect himself – his arms would not work. He called out, unable to hear his own voice. Then, he grew calm in understanding and acceptance. *So this is what it is like to die.* Slowly, the old general felt each of his senses grow numb. The world around him darkened and faded.

HMS *Inflexible*

Kate watched the battle, transfixed and kept a tight grip on the rail. They were still five miles out, *Inflexible* speeding for the mouth of the canal, the fleet of warships strung out in front of her. Distant guns flashed and boomed and smoke rose making it difficult to distinguish between a shell's firing and its exploding impact. Men were dying out there. How could she sketch or put into words what she was seeing? Close beside her, Willoughby leaned into the rail to keep his telescope steady. She felt him flinch.

"Another ship's been hit," he said, "third row back, east end."

Parker traced his finger over the notes Samuels had given him. "That would be *Monarch*. How bad is it, can you tell?"

Kate peered through a veil of smoke and saw the dim outline of the ship. She could see nothing wrong. She nudged Willoughby thinking he hadn't heard Parker's question.

Willoughby said nothing for a while; then lowered the telescope. "She's buckled."

"She's going down?" Kate was aghast. She grabbed the telescope and drew a desperate scene into focus. The ship had broken in two, bow and stern slanting up at a horrific angle. She jerked away from the telescope. The blood drained from her face. She felt breathless, as if she had just taken a punch in the stomach. "The men can be rescued. They all have life vests on."

Willoughby gave the grim reply: "The men on deck may have a chance but with a hit like that, she'll go down quickly. Most of the crew will be trapped below."

"You should put yours back on," said Kate to Willoughby seeing his life-vest just draped, not buckled over his shoulders.

"She's right about that, Willoughby," said Ira.

"All right, all right, damn thing's tight as hell. We're miles from being in range anyway. We won't be doing any fighting today. Not like those poor devils."

Kate gazed back out at *Monarch*. There was another distant explosion.

Gently, Parker took the telescope from her, trading it

discretely for his flask. This time, she accepted and took two swallows. She put a hand of thanks on Parker's elbow as she gave it back to him then sat down. She picked up her sketchpad and began laying out a drawing. The scene she composed was not from her own distant perspective but from the view point of one of the men floating in the water watching the horror of his ship going down. Kate worked fast and when she had finished the rough composition, she closed her book feeling as if she had helped lay those many men to rest.

A loud boom shattered her thoughts. Her eyes dried in an instant. Was *Inflexible* firing her guns? No, they were still too far out, weren't they? She saw Parker turn around and the realization hit her – they were being fired on from behind. "What's going on?" Before Parker could answer, there was another blast; and another. A tower of water shot up just in front of *Inflexible* then two more rose off the port side.

Kate glanced up at the bridge. Faulks was standing behind the helmsman. Both Seymour and Fisher were looking aft where, a thousand yards out, a gray ship showed her broadside.

The mystery warship's guns flashed as she fired again.

"It's *Resolute*," shouted Parker. "How did she get back there? Get down. Get down!"

"My God, we're going to be hit." she screamed, falling onto the deck – her sketchpad beneath her, her cap flying off.

An explosion shook the ship lifting her clear of the deck then slamming her back down with a violence she hadn't thought possible. The deck rolled. On all fours, Kate scrambled, trying to get to the nearest bulkhead for something to hold onto. Fear gripped her. She thought of *Monarch* – are we going down too?

Another blast reverberated through *Inflexible*. The deck pitched and Kate was knocked flat, sliding away from the bulkhead toward the side. Her heart pounded. She shifted her leg and was able to wedge a foot against a rail support, pivoting her body but not stopping her slide. "God in heaven," she whispered in disbelief. Her foot gave way and she screamed, tumbling over the side. At the last possible moment she reached up frantically for the rail and was able to hold on.

"Help!" she yelled, her wet fingers losing their grip.

Inflexible was listing sharply, Kate dangling above the waves that raced beneath her. She was drenched with spray and she kept yelling but couldn't hear herself – she couldn't hear anything. She looked down and braced herself for the fall. Then she felt someone grab her arm. She looked up.

It was Parker. He was shouting something.

She hung onto him, drawing her breath in big wet gulps and slowly, *Inflexible* began to draw up level again. Kate swung her free hand up and was able to grab onto the rail. Then, with Parker's help, she strained to pull herself up.

Kate crawled back onto the deck. She sat there, panting for air with an exhausted Parker beside her. A coughing fit doubled her over as her lungs filled with air that had been saturated with the acidic taste of gunpowder. She spat out what she could. Just behind Parker she saw smoke pouring from the ventilation tubes. The deck was littered with debris. Men raced in every direction.

Opposite her, the port-side rail was completely missing, as was the wooden deck beneath it. Through the gaping hole Kate could see into the ship, to the gunnery deck below where the bodies of three sailors lay, not moving, their clothing bloodied. Other men scrambled to douse pockets of flame. The rest of the main deck and much of the black iron around it had been charred from the heat of the blast. Not far from her, soaked in a puddle of water, lay her sketchbook. The drawings in it were all surely ruined but the concepts should be discernible. She could recreate them.

Kate's hearing slowly returned. There was frantic shouting, and the scream of a siren, but she realized there was something missing. The engines had stopped, they were slowing down. She turned to the Union Jack rippling in the wind from the stern line. Out beyond it she could see black smoke rising from the tall stack of *Resolute* as she headed for the horizon.

"She's done firing," said Parker looking in the same direction. "She just wanted to scare the hell out of us. Look at her, turning tail now."

"Why aren't we going after her?"

Parker shook his head. "It'd take a bloody long time to get us turned around. And we've been hit. We could have some serious damage. Fisher will send some of his ships after her but it won't be us."

Kate nodded and cleared a tangle of hair from her face. She grabbed her sketchbook then, a chill shot through her spine. "What about Ira and Mr. Willoughby? Where are they?"

Parker got to his feet and scanned the deck. "I don't know." He helped Kate stand.

Her legs were limp. She felt her hands shaking and kept one of them on Parker's arm. "They might have gone below."

"Let's look out here first."

They found Ira quickly. He lay on a stretcher, a medic tending to a bloody gash in the side of his head. He immediately grabbed Kate's hand and tried to get up. His voice was strained and uneven. "He's gone, Kate."

Kate wasn't sure she'd heard him right. Ira sank back down but his grip on her hand tightened. She dropped to a knee beside him. "What is it Ira? Who's gone?"

"Willoughby."

The news hit her like a bullet. "No, you're wrong, we'll find him." She started to get up while surveying the chaos. "We'll find him."

"I saw him go over, Kate. There was nothing I could do."

"He was wearing a life vest, he..."

"He had taken it off. Too cumbersome, he said. He never gave a damn about regulations. You know him."

Kate shook her head and tore her hand free. She stumbled to the rail. Forcing tears from her eyes she looked down over the side checking the crest of every wave.

Parker came up beside her. "We've come to a stop. They're lowering the lifeboats, Kate. There are other men out there. There'll be a search."

Kate nodded, there was still some hope. She pounded the rail with the heel of her hand. "Yes, they'll find him." From the south, explosions rumbled in the distance. The battle for the canal was still going on, but Kate didn't care.

Two lifeboats appeared. In slow steady strokes, their crewmen traced the length of *Inflexible,* working their way fore and aft, moving farther out with each pass.

"If it wasn't for you, I'd be out there too," Kate said to Parker. "You saved my life."

"You're a strong woman, Kate. With or without me you would have hung on somehow."

She shook her head. She wasn't feeling so strong now. As the search progressed, Kate grew more fearful until dread overtook her. "He was a second father to me, Mr. Parker. How will I get along without him? How will I..." Nearly limp, she leaned against the rail and, through eyes brimming with tears, she continued watching the lifeboats.

Long after the canal was taken and the guns fell silent, the sun approached the western horizon and the search for the men who'd been swept overboard was called off. Five men had been rescued from the sea - Cyrus Willoughby was not one of them.

Kate returned to her cabin. Her eyes were dry, she was done with crying she told herself, but she could only sit on the edge of her cot, drained of energy from the terrible things this day had brought. Mr. Willoughby was only one of the many men who had died, but he was the only one she had known. And, without him, she knew she'd never be the same. She remembered his calm caring face as she'd first seen him when she was a little girl. Then, something made her think of Julian. How great the loss of both parents must have been for him when he was just a boy. In a strange sense she felt linked to him now by this new tragedy and she found herself wondering where at this moment he was, desperately hoping he was still alive.

Kate wasn't able to sleep that night or the next. She was remotely aware that the marines had consolidated their position at the canal but she went through her days as if in a trance. She didn't eat or talk much.

Ira was back on his feet. The ugly cut over his eye had been stitched and would no doubt leave a scar to serve as a reminder of his ordeal. It was on the third morning following Willoughby's death that Kate stood beside her cot. She rubbed her eyes, telling herself that she had to straighten up. She had to get back to work. She had to get back to normal. Mr. Willoughby was dead. It was just his time to go and that was that. It would be hard but she would carry on without him as best she could and...she would make him proud of her.

She put on her seaman's uniform, tucked her hair inside her cap and walked purposefully out of her cabin down to the galley where she found Parker and Ira. They sat at a table and looked up at her from their half-finished breakfast. Neither said a word.

"You don't have to be so careful with me," she told them. "I'm all right now."

"You *are* looking more yourself today," said Ira.

"Hungry?" asked Parker.

She ate while Parker filled her in on what she had missed.

"We lost *Monarch* and all but a dozen of her crew. *Reynolds* went down with all hands. Two of our ships have left the fleet to sail north, chasing after *Resolute*. They haven't returned yet. Fisher still doesn't know how *Resolute* managed to outflank the entire fleet. He sent two other ships through the canal to capture Suez at the southern tip of the canal. The good news is that the canal itself is now operating normally, shipping flowing as if nothing had happened."

"Who'd been holding the canal? Was it *The Will of the People*?" asked Kate.

"It was the Turks," said Ira. "They all ran off but we captured a few. They had expected help from the Egyptians to hold the canal but that help never came. It seems they couldn't get word to them that they had captured the canal."

"Why was that?" asked Kate swallowing down a mouthful of corn mush that tasted surprisingly good.

"The telegraph lines to Alexandria were down."

"Lucky for us."

"Yes it was lucky. And that brings us to the other thing, Kate," said Parker with a glance at his watch. "In an hour, we'll be leaving the canal."

Kate put down her spoon. She was relieved that they would be heading home but then she saw Parker's expression and was suddenly uncertain. "Leaving for Istanbul you mean?"

Parker shook his head. "No, not Istanbul."

CHAPTER 22

The road to Alexandria

At the familiar high-pitched scream, Julian rubbed his eyes awake. Flat on his back, he bent his knees a few times to stretch the ache from his limbs. Sleeping on the bed roll and waking up stiff as a board to the screech of circling vultures overhead had become his every-morning normal. Today was no different. He squinted. There were three of them, black against a gray sky. He imagined them looking down, disappointed that he was still alive, maybe unaware that there might soon be other scavenging opportunities for them.

Over the past few days, traffic on the road had increased. Men led skin and bone donkeys that strained to pull creaking, overloaded carts. Behind these, wives and children had trailed sullen and silent. All were headed east. Some gave Bertie and Julian looks of mild curiosity but none spoke English or French and none took the time to try to understand Julian's gestures with which he tried to ask how far it was to Alexandria.

Shacks tilted by the windblown dust and weathered gray by the heat had begun to dot the roadside in increasing numbers – a sure sign that the city couldn't be too much farther.

Julian got to his feet and retrieved their last biscuit from his saddle bag, his stomach twisting as he eyed a fuzzy greenish-black spot that had overtaken one side of it. He glanced at Bertie who had begun to stir a moment ago and was now sitting upright on his bedroll. He tossed the biscuit to him. "This is all we have left between us."

"It will have to do," said Bertie, breaking it in two, giving the half with the green mold back to Julian. "We should be in Alexandria tonight, probably aboard one of our warships, eating like kings."

Julian carefully excavated the mold with his fingernail then popped the remaining morsel into his mouth, talking as he chewed. "You said there was rioting in the city."

"Yes, that could be a problem." Bertie took a drink then stowed his canteen and began taking up his bedroll. "It's obvious we're westerners – that's going to draw attention from the greater number of travelers we're likely to run into. We were just lucky we didn't run into any more soldiers. From here, as we approach the city, things may be different." A few drops of rain began to fall.

Bertie buttoned the front of his khaki uniform and straightened his collar before putting on his hat. He smoothed the front of his jacket then saw that Julian had been watching him. He explained himself: "Whenever you're around people, it's important to carry yourself properly. You keep your backbone straight and your head held high."

"...and your clothing presentable."

"Unless you find us a laundry today, there'll be nothing we can do about our clothes. But, despite our ragged appearance, we'll still be a damn sight better dressed than some of the beggars we'll be meeting on the road today."

"I suppose you have a point there." Julian thought again of the bedraggled families they had seen on the road. He buttoned his shirt and smoothed his hair and turned to Bertie for approval.

Bertie gave his assessment: "You need a shave, your skin is burned red and blotched brown and green with dirt. There are streaks of mud in your hair and smears of dried blood on your uniform. Your eyes are shot with blood. If I didn't know better, I'd say you'd had a few too many drinks last night and had stumbled into the gutter." Bertie shook his head. "You're a sorry sight, Sergeant North."

Julian walked to his horse. "I was Captain North back at the canal."

"Serves you right - no British officer should be seen in public like that."

The rain became a steady drizzle. They saddled their horses and made their way back to the road where they continued west against a thickening current of people, mules and carts. Progress was slow and it was noon when Julian and Bertie began their climb up a broad rolling hill.

"What a Goddamn mess. Look there," said Bertie, pointing to a knot of people trying to get around the crowd by charging off the road into one of the muddy fields that bordered both sides. Men shouted and cursed, pulling at their donkeys or pushing carts from behind to free them from the muck. Children were everywhere, some crying and wandering off by themselves, others clinging to their mothers. The stench of sewage and sweat spoiled the air.

Julian spotted a boy who sat by himself crying in the mud. He was naked except for a filthy cloth wrapped about his waist. Everyone ignored his screams until one woman, struggling herself, gave him her hand. She helped him back to the road where they blended into the crowd. Julian wondered what would become of the boy. Would he live for another day; or maybe another year? And if he somehow made it to adulthood, what would he remember of this day? At ten, Julian had lost his mother and father. This boy, at three, had lost everything.

Here was fear and desperation on a huge scale. It was a scene Julian knew he would never forget. "What are they running from? What could possibly drive so many people to this?"

"The rioting in the city must have gotten worse – killing and looting; all directed against us westerners. And we're headed straight into it." Bertie paused. "On the positive side though, their flight might work in our favor. By the time we arrive, there may be no one left in the city to cause us any trouble."

"Right," said Julian. He straightened his hat, causing the accumulated rain water to pour from its brim. He urged his horse forward and by mid-afternoon they reached the crest of the hill.

And there lay Alexandria.

After traveling through so many miles of desolation, the sight below was astounding. The gigantic maze of streets and buildings stretched from the base of a long slope out into the foggy horizon. White-plastered houses and golden-domed mosques guarded by tall minarets covered the gently rolling terrain. As the wind kicked up, Julian took in a deep breath, the air fresher here but tinged with the smell of smoke. He followed Bertie who guided his horse onto a knoll that jutted out from the side of the road. They dismounted and Julian could now see thin threads of black smoke rising from the taller buildings at the center of the city.

But the prince seemed undeterred by any thoughts of danger. He assumed a commanding hands-on-hips posture. "Alexander himself might have stood at this very spot when he decided to build here," he said. "What power that man had, and what a legacy he left."

Julian wondered if the monarch-to-be was thinking about the great and valiant deeds he himself might carry out in his own reign. Could Bertie be worried that, already well into his late-middle years, his chapter in history might be short and inconsequential? That he would one day be looked upon as a ruler of little consequence, obscured by the far-reaching shadow of his powerful mother; no better than ordinary in comparison?

Bertie took a step back. He smoothed his horse's neck then spoke more quietly. "When I was young, my father and I were on a voyage when a storm came up. Riding the waves up and down, with seawater streaming off the deck and no land in sight, I was afraid. To calm my fears, or maybe just to occupy the time, he told me that on a ship there is a specific place of relative calm, where the tossing and rocking caused by the action of the wind and waves were exactly cancelled. I found out later that there's an engineering term to describe it. It's called 'the center of moments' and it sounds to me now more poetic than technical. At any rate, my father made a game out of trying to find that exact spot. We had the run of the ship and strode fore and aft. We ventured two decks down into the hold and it must have taken us the better part of an hour but, all of a sudden, we were there. And it was magical. We could feel the hull gyrating wildly as if in orbit around us while we ourselves seemed to remain stationary and undisturbed. I never forgot that."

Julian wondered at the strangeness of Bertie telling him such a story. If only there had been such a magical spot on *Whispering Jenny*. "What made you think of that now?" he asked.

Bertie waved his hand over the expanse of Alexandria. "History, Mr. North. That's what you see going on before us and all around us; these people; this city in crisis. We are all passengers on the ship of history as it's buffeted at every turn by the folly of men, the vagaries of chance and, at times, the wrath of God. And through it all, here you and I stand on this hillside, calm and serene, as if at the center of moments. We are part of everything that's going on yet somehow removed from it." He paused. "I almost hate to leave."

Julian was touched by Bertie's insight and by his sharing of such a personal story. He didn't know what to say.

Bertie gave his horse another pat and looked into the distance. "My eyesight's not so good these days, North. Can you see the harbor? Do you see any ships?"

Julian wiped the raindrops from his forehead and gazed over the rooftops leading out to the horizon where the harbor must be. "Too far, I can't make it out."

Bertie hoisted himself back up into his saddle. "No matter, our ships must be out there somewhere. Come on, let's go."

They traveled slowly down the hillside and eventually, the stream of people leaving the city became a trickle and then was gone entirely. By the time they entered Alexandria, it was night and the rain had stopped. They rode their horses at a slow walk down a main street which Julian hoped led to the waterfront. There were no lights and no sign of people. In the darkness he felt the tall, black buildings leaning over him. The air, still heavy with dampness, smelled of burned wood.

"An eerie place," said Bertie.

They continued in silence for a while, the clip-clop of their horses being the only sound. But there was a low undercurrent to the stillness. Like a bass cello's single deep note, it stirred Julian's soul. "There are people out there, and they're close," he said. Then he heard a shout followed by the crash of breaking glass. He flinched in his saddle and pulled his rifle in a move that had become a natural reflex.

Bertie grabbed his pistol and exchanged a glance with Julian. "I'll watch this side."

Julian turned to his side of the road, focusing on every shadow, looking for anything that moved. They rode on for another block, where the shouting became more distinct. Julian cocked his rifle.

They stopped at the next intersection. Noises, as if from a crowd, came from all directions now, both close and distant, echoing among the buildings. Julian's eyes darted, his nerves stretched, ready to respond at the slightest provocation. He edged his horse forward a few steps. Then, he saw them.

Around the corner and half-way down the narrow cross street, the far side of the road was lit by torches held by a dozen men. They and others were gathered around a spot where two men were swinging, then heaving, a heavy sack into a building. Glass shattered as the sack burst through a window and fell inside. Someone threw a flaming torch into the building and the crowd shouted its approval. Slowly the flames began to grow and in the firelight Julian could see another sack being tied. He saw it bulge and jerk of its own accord. Two men lifted the sack and, as they had with the one before it, they swung it forward and back in front of the fire. The mob began cheering to its rhythm. Fists were waved in the air as the men released the sack and launched it into the flaming building. A chill ran up Julian's spine - they were burning people alive!

The horror had no sooner registered with Julian than, from beside him, Bertie fired his gun.

Julian jumped. "What the hell are you doing?"

"Bloody Goddamn bastards," yelled Bertie, his jaw squarely set.

"We can't take them all on."

"I don't care."

Julian looked at the mob and saw a body lying in the street; the other men seemed not to have noticed. "You hit one of them."

"Bloody well hope so," said Bertie, his horse shifting nervously beneath him. Bertie cocked his pistol and fired again. Another man went down. This time the mob reacted and became immediately silent. One man looked toward Bertie and pointed. Yelling broke out but the Prince of Wales remained determined. "Come on, we'll put a stop to this right now."

Before Julian could object, Bertie rose in his stirrups and slapped down on the reins. His tired horse hesitated then somehow gathered herself, breaking into a gallop as if she had been saving her strength for just this moment. Bertie charged headlong down the road toward the mob, teeth clenched and his gun leveled.

"Stop, you'll be killed," Julian shouted, too late. With his own horse wheeling beneath him, he tightened his grip on his rifle and drew a deep breath, convinced that Bertie would soon be lying dead in the street or worse, tied up in one of those sacks. Julian knew he had no choice. He drove his heels hard into the belly of his horse and tore off after him.

From just ahead Bertie fired again, his flying form silhouetted black against the orange flames of the torches. The mob scattered and ran for cover. Then they started firing back. Bullets buzzed and Julian shrank lower in his saddle gripping his rifle but unable to fire while maintaining control his horse. Finally he caught up to Bertie who, for all the jostling of his horse, still held his pistol steady, firing as he rode. They were nearly to the burning storefront.

Suddenly, Bertie's horse fell, sending him rolling hard onto the street. His pistol clattered to the ground.

"Stay down," shouted Julian in a panic. He pulled up on the reins and took a position in front of Bertie who lay in the street –

not moving. Julian fired his rifle blindly into a few of the adjacent buildings where he'd seen earlier flashes of gunfire. Then he was out of bullets. This was it, he thought, he was going to die beside the Prince of Wales at the hands of a mob in Alexandria. A good journalist would have made it all sound heroic, but here and now, there was only the paralyzing fear of a violent, painful death.

But the mob stayed under cover – maybe low on bullets themselves. Except for the sounds of the fire and Julian's own hard breathing, it was quiet. In the light of the flames, he saw that Bertie was struggling to get up. His horse was still down, and five bodies lay in the street. In front of the burning building a man knelt, his hands and feet tied. His mouth was gagged and his frantic eyes were turned to Julian.

Quickly, Julian dismounted and ran to him. He pulled his knife and sliced through the ropes that bound the man. "Run," said Julian who then grabbed the reins of his horse and raced over to help Bertie. "Are you all right? Can you ride?"

Bertie looked around, dazed. "I think so, yes."

From the corner of his eye Julian saw movement in the shadows. One by one, men began to emerge from the empty storefronts, apparently realizing that Julian and Bertie were no longer a threat. One of them, a tall thin fellow with a ragged beard and black curly hair that hung down to his shoulders, raised a gun and pointed it at Julian. His eyes were brutal and wild but he didn't fire. He motioned to the others who slowly formed a ring around their new captives, intent on making two new offerings to the fire.

Suddenly, gunfire erupted. Julian ducked but saw that this time the shots came from a new direction. From behind, a horseman had burst into the street, firing into the crowd. The curly-haired man fell and the mob scattered again as the lone rider pulled his horse beside Bertie and leaned over, extending a gloved hand. "Grab on," the rider shouted. "Grab on, now."

Bertie raised his hand and the man hoisted him up. His face still in shadow, the rider turned back to Julian. "Follow me," he shouted, racing off with the prince slung over his saddle as if he were a sack of potatoes.

With a flash of hope that they just might escape their terrible fate, Julian gathered himself and mounted his horse. He urged it into a gallop around the corner, catching up with Bertie and their mysterious rescuer fifty yards later.

Together, they rode hard for three more blocks before turning into an alley where they slowed to a walk and the horseman dismounted. He helped Bertie slide down.

The prince landed hard holding his rib cage. "Damn it, I think you've broken every bone in my body."

"You should thank Allah that you are alive," said the man, tending to his horse.

Julian dismounted, staring at the stranger. He could see he wore a uniform, but could not make out his face. "Who are you?"

The man took a step closer. "You don't remember me? You left me naked at the canal. I am Sergeant Ahmet Rashid. I was your prisoner then. Now, I suppose, you are mine. A strange turn of events, don't you think?"

Julian saw Ahmet's face fully now and remembered his large eyes and hawk-like nose. "A lucky turn of events for us. How did you get here?"

"I followed you."

Julian drew back, skeptical. "We never saw you."

"Until two days ago I did not see you either. Yet, only one road heads west from the canal. I took a guess that you'd be on it."

"Why would you follow us?"

"It was General Ali's orders. You caused me much embarrassment, Mr. North, taking me by surprise, stealing my clothes, and leaving me tied up in my own telegraph wire. When I told the general you were not alone, he asked who was with you. I told him your companion called himself the Prince of Wales." Ahmet turned to Bertie. "I should have believed you."

Bertie was standing, still holding his sides. He had his eyes on Ahmet but said nothing.

Julian tied down his horse and sat down on a stump. "So, why would the general want you to follow us?"

"First he wanted me to stop you from cutting the telegraph lines. But by that time, it was too late."

"I'd like to take the credit for that," said Bertie, sitting down gingerly on a wooden crate, "but cutting the lines was this fellow's brilliant idea." He gestured toward Julian.

"It cost us the canal," said Ahmet.

"You didn't really expect to hold onto it did you?" asked Bertie.

"General Ali knew it was a desperate plan. He told me that our sultan had been lured into this crazy plot to help the Russian, Pavel, steal your ship." Ahmet shrugged. "He wanted you and your government to know the truth. So, he sent me after you."

"And what is the truth?" asked Bertie.

"The truth is, just as I said at the canal, we are not your

enemy."

"Horse shit! First you Turks kidnapped me, then you attacked our canal. You killed our soldiers, who had done nothing more than obey international law. Your country is an enemy of Great Britain, and you will pay the price for it."

"The general told me that there is a man within the Yildiz Palace who is able to twist the will of the sultan. He's a traitor to the empire and he's been working with the Russians."

"Your Foreign Minister, Ismail," said Bertie.

Ahmet nodded. "All of this was his doing."

"And Pavel's," added Julian.

"Yes," agreed Ahmet. "The general feared he might not survive the battle to retake the canal. He feared you and your government would never know what had happened. That is why he sent me to follow you."

"Why you?" asked Bertie.

"I knew what you looked like, and I speak English. The general had few options. When he sent me to find you, the first of the British ships had already appeared on the horizon at Port Said. He knew more would follow." Ahmet shifted his rifle from one hand to the other and sat down on the ground, opposite Bertie. He leaned his back against the side of a wooden staircase. "General Ali is probably dead now. He was a soldier of the empire. May he rest with Allah."

Bertie broke the reverential pause. "Thank you for rescuing us. We'd be dead right now if it weren't for you."

"You should be dead," said Ahmet. "I watched you charge into those ruffians. That was a foolish thing to do."

"Rescuing us wasn't too bright either," observed Julian.

"I suppose we were not meant to die this night."

Julian rubbed his tired eyes and for no good reason his thoughts turned to Pavel, and the journal. "Back at the canal you said that General Ali had told you about the book."

"The book of Pavel's, you mean. Yes, he just told me what Pavel had told him."

"Do you remember his exact words?"

Ahmet regarded Julian with curiosity. "He said: 'The book is important because with it they can find us.' " Then Ahmet raised a finger. "No, you are right, there was something more. Pavel had said something about the language of Napoleon."

"French, you mean," said Bertie.

"Yes, I suppose that must be. The general did not know what he meant."

"And that was all he said?" pressed Julian.

"Yes."

From some distant place a shout pierced the night. It was followed by a wailing scream that sent a shiver down Julian's spine.

Ahmet drew his rifle closer. "That was the sound of death."

They took turns through the night guarding the entrance to the alleyway. For Julian, the echoes of violence were bad enough but it was the periods of stillness that kept the fear churning inside him. It was a night he knew he'd remember forever as the longest of his life.

The sun rose sluggishly the next day and with it the smells of raw sewage and rotting food in the alley grew more pungent. Julian got to his feet and peered out beyond the entrance to the alley. The two broken windows of a blackened building on the opposite side of the street stared back. Nothing moved. All was quiet but for the cry of a few gulls high overhead.

Julian tended to his bedroll and saw that Ahmet was awake, his rifle at his side. "Our horses are in plain view, we should leave quickly," said Julian.

"Mine is the stronger," said Ahmet. "The two of you will take him."

Julian eyed the ribbed sides and the drooping head of the horse he'd been riding "That makes sense. We had little to feed her."

"Do you have any food or water for yourselves?" asked Ahmet, reaching into his saddlebag. He pulled out a lump of bread.

"We finished the last of ours yesterday morning," said Bertie, rubbing his eyes.

Ahmet tore off two portions. "Here, take this." He handed one to Bertie and one to Julian.

"Thank you, sergeant. We'll all dine better tonight," Bertie said between chews.

"Like kings," added Julian.

They each took a rifle and a pistol, loaded them and mounted up.

"I'm glad to leave this forlorn place," muttered Bertie with a glance back as they left the alley and headed down the deserted street.

Julian sat behind the prince on the horse's rump. He shifted his weight, searching in vain for a comfortable spot. Every step the animal took was a hammer-blow to the base of his spine. Julian gripped the back edge of the saddle, careful not to touch Bertie's backside.

"Let me know if you fall off, North," said Bertie.

"I'm sure the horse would be glad for the reduced baggage," said Julian.

Ahmet led the way and a moment later they heard a gunshot. Julian raised his rifle and Bertie lifted the pistol he'd brandished from the start.

"We haven't many bullets," said Ahmet, drawing his own rifle. "When you shoot, make sure you kill somebody."

Another shot rang out.

"It sounds like they're straight ahead of us," said Bertie. "We may have to fight our way through."

"You ready to make another cavalry charge?" asked Julian.

"We will have none of that today," said Ahmet. He slapped the reins and jabbed his heels and his horse broke into a slow trot.

Bertie urged his horse to match the pace and Julian struggled to hold on as they maneuvered around the wooden crates, overturned carts and splintered planking that littered the street.

"We're on a downward slope," said Bertie. "The harbor can't be far."

The ruins of three and four-story brick buildings lined the road stretching into the distance, each looking to Julian as if they might collapse at any moment. "What happened here? Did the people just go mad, burning and looting till nothing was left?"

"It began a few months back," said Bertie. "We had reports of it well before I left for Istanbul. Most of these shops are, or were, the property of honest European businessmen. The civilian population somehow became convinced that they were a bunch of cheating rouges. To add to the mess, the army revolted. It's now being led by some madman or another who has a disagreement with the way the whole country's been run. But no one's taken control and everyone's afraid. The people at our embassy here asked for some sort of military intervention to smooth things out but obviously that hasn't happened yet."

Julian tried to imagine the street as it must have been at one time; filled with people and carriages, lined with prosperous stores - almost like Istanbul or even London.

A sudden movement caught his eye. "Someone's up there." He pointed to a third-story window in a building fifty yards ahead. "A man, I think he saw us."

They all watched the spot as they passed but saw nothing more than a darkened room framed by the jagged glass of the broken window. A curtain fluttered lazily in the breeze.

"He must have left," said Bertie. "Or maybe you're just seeing things."

"He was there," said Julian. He stared back at the window and was about to turn away when he saw the barrel of a rifle poked out. "Look out, he's got a gun."

Bertie slapped the reins and the horse charged forward just as a shot was fired from the window.

Ahmet fired back, then spurred his horse into a gallop following Julian and Bertie. They rode another two blocks before slowing again. "This poor beast will not last much longer," Ahmet said to Julian as he caught up from behind. His horse was panting; streaked with lathery sweat.

"Goddamn it," said Bertie with disgust.

"What is it?" asked Ahmet.

"Damn bullet grazed my cheek," said Bertie, running a hand over the wound.

Julian saw the streak of red. "It's bleeding."

"Thank you, North, I've already discovered that." Bertie dried his hand on his trousers. "I'm all right. Let's get on with it."

As they rode, Julian sat stiff with tension. "An army could be hiding in these buildings. They could pick us off one by one if they wanted to."

"What happened to the optimistic journalist?" chided Bertie.

A volley of gunfire from up ahead rattled away then stopped.

"I don't see anyone," Julian said in frustration. "What could they be shooting at?"

"Who knows," said Bertie. "But I think it's best to get off this street."

Ahmet kept his eyes straight ahead. "We'll take the next crossroad." He quickened the pace but his horse began to falter. He waved Bertie into the lead.

Julian strapped his rifle over his shoulder and held on with both hands as they broke into a gallop. There was more gunfire and a bullet ricocheted off the pavement just behind him. "They're in there – the white building," he shouted looking ahead to a structure on the corner that seemed better preserved than the others. From the roof a puff of smoke accented the next shot.

"Come on, faster," shouted Julian, suddenly convinced that something very bad was about to happen. "We've got to get out of here, now." His heart was racing. All he could do was hold on.

Bertie worked the reins as they rounded the intersection and drew more shots from the building.

From behind Julian, Ahmet fired back, trying at the same time to gain more speed. His horse struggled to keep up but lost her footing on the uneven cobblestones. She stumbled and fell forward.

"He's down," shouted Julian to Bertie. "Stop." He looked back and saw Ahmet roll off the fallen horse and run for the corner storefront opposite the white building.

Bertie completed the turn to get them out of the line of fire then drew up on the reins. They immediately dismounted.

"He's in there," said Julian, leading the way through a door at the back entrance to the corner building. Bertie followed him inside and pulled the door closed behind them.

Julian was overwhelmed by a powerful stench, dusty and acidic. He shuddered. A body, maybe several of them, were near but neither he nor Bertie made mention of it. Julian's eyes adjusted to the darkness. They stood in a large single room littered with toppled shelves and counters. The only light came from a window that bordered the main street.

"Over here," said Ahmet from that direction.

Julian kicked aside some rubble approaching the spot where the sergeant knelt with his rifle extended, ready to fire. Glass shards spiked the window frame all around.

"They know we're in here," said Ahmet.

"How many of them, do you think?" asked Bertie.

"Three that I saw - in Egyptian army uniforms; but there are more." "On the roof of the white building," said Julian.

Ahmet nodded. "Go back and guard the door you came in," he told Julian. "We'll hold them off here."

Julian headed for the door. The rapid beating of his heart was all he could hear. The stench became stronger. He watched where he stepped and dropped to a knee when he reached the door. Carefully he opened it a crack, aiming his pistol. Out in the street he could see the fallen horse, its belly heaving with each breath. Beyond that, two men with rifles darted between the buildings across the street. Two more joined them. "God help us," Julian whispered, cocking his gun.

Then, as if from a distance, he thought he heard a *thoop* sound followed quickly by another. They seemed so irrelevant to the present danger that they hardly registered in his mind. Then he heard something else.

It started as a low whistle and quickly grew to an ear-piercing screech coming from above. Julian held his breath. What the hell is going on? He braced himself.

The blast shook the air. The building he had been staring at across the street exploded in a ball of flames. The floor under Julian rumbled and the door jerked back. He could only stare at the cloud of white smoke and wonder who or what was trying to kill him now.

HMS *Inflexible*

"They overshot the fort by at least a hundred yards," said Kate. She handed the telescope to Parker. "What possible good are we doing shelling the city like this?"

"We're not shelling the city, we're shelling the forts."

"Tell that to whoever owns that house we just blew up."

"Naval gunnery is an inexact science; that's what Fisher's always saying." Parker held the telescope steady. "*Excelsior's* firing again – a broadside this time."

Inflexible held her position beyond the breakwater, the shore three miles distant. Kate could hear the muffled roar of the guns but could only see small puffs of smoke and the occasional flash of an exploding shell on shore. There was something unsettling to her about this endeavor.

As Parker had explained it, the original mission of the fleet, even before the crisis with Prince Bertie and the canal, had been to level these rebel-held forts and to restore order to Alexandria. He'd also made mention of a possible invasion into all of Egypt but that couldn't be, could it?

Kate looked out at the nine warships lined up one behind the other, each taking turns firing at the three forts that guarded the harbor. God knows how many civilians would die simply because the British Navy couldn't shoot straight. It was more than Kate could accept.

"There's a hit," said Parker. He lowered the telescope. "Where's Ira?"

"At the stern, he thought there might be a better view from there."

"We should have been aboard *Excelsior*," complained Parker. "Can't see a thing from here, but Fisher wouldn't allow it."

"This is as close as I want to get, thank you."

"Here comes *Reliant*," said Parker. "She's entering the firing lane."

Kate squinted and shielded the sun from her eyes. A plume of yellow-gray smoke rose up near the shore followed by a low boom. More guns fired. "That must be *Excelsior* again. She's firing on the second fort," said Kate shifting her view.

"The forts are firing back," said Parker.

The entire harbor thundered and smoke began to rise up everywhere in the city. A blast just in front of the breakwater threw up a tower of water. Kate tightened her grip on the rail remembering the hit *Inflexible* had taken back at the canal.

"The rebels in the forts have got some long range guns," observed Parker.

The engines picked up their rhythm. *Inflexible* was on the move. At the bow, the huge two-gun turret began to turn, giving off a loud ratcheting sound. Slowly the guns raised.

"Be sure to cover your ears," cautioned Parker.

There was quiet for a moment then a siren sounded and Kate's heart began to pound.

"That's the signal, hands over your ears now," said Parker, "tightly."

The gunnery captain shouted: "Fire."

The guns roared and the deck shook. Flame sprayed from the long barrels as two, sixteen inch shells were shot into the air. The blast of heated air blew Kate's hat off and nearly knocked her off her feet. Smoke swirled from the muzzles and the entire ship rocked to absorb the recoil. Dazed and coughing, Kate retrieved her hat then took her place back at the rail.

Alexandria

Deafening, unnatural screams filled the air and explosions shook the building around Julian. He could see nothing but dust and smoke outside. What the hell was going on? He turned toward the window where Bertie and Ahmet had been standing guard. They had backed off and were bent over, coughing, both covering their mouths from the smoke pouring in off the street.

Julian stuffed his pistol under his belt and ran to them. More explosions came. Julian drew his breaths in shallow, nerve-wrenching gulps saturated with gunpowder. His earlier fear of getting shot had been replaced by the terror of being blown apart. Plaster dust rained down as Julian crouched on the floor next to Bertie.

"That's the British navy. They're trying to save us," said Bertie.

"They'll kill us first," said Julian.

"How do they even know you're here?" asked Ahmet.

"They have ways of finding these things out," said Bertie knowingly, between explosions. "Yet, I fear they're only here to quell the rioting. They've been planning it for weeks. Actually, they may have no idea we're here."

Julian tried to steady his nerves but found himself shaking from the inside with each explosion. What would it be like, he wondered, to be alive one moment and dead the very next? No one would even find their bodies. There'd be nothing left. He looked around and swallowed hard. This dark building would be his tomb:

Times Reporter Missing and Presumed Dead

He realized that his made-up headlines had run the gamut from impossibly glorious to depressingly grim. Maybe it was time to put an end to that habit of his.

After a while, the explosions came in clusters and with them, more loose powder and shattered plaster showered down from the ceiling. Julian looked up to see a crack open up in the beam overhead. A few explosions later he saw that the crack had widened. The building groaned. He glanced at Bertie and Ahmet who had their eyes on the same beam as it suddenly shifted.

"We've got to get out of here," Julian shouted, now on his feet. The entire building began to sway.

"It's coming down!" yelled Bertie. "Through the window – now!" He dove out.

Julian hurled himself out after him just as the building crumbled and fell. In a thick cloud of smoke and dust, he hit the ground and rolled out into the street. Then, something hard slammed into the side of his head and he felt nothing.

CHAPTER 23

HMS Inflexible

The long day dragged on and the harbor filled with smoke and shook with the rolling thunder of big guns until Kate became sickened by it all. No longer was there any attempt at aiming the guns and detecting a hit or a miss. The big ships just fired through the dirty yellow fog in the general direction of the city and the forts fired back. Kate knew there would always be evil in the world and always a need for armies and warships to protect good people but, never had war and violence seemed more pointless. Today it felt like just one kind of evil pitted against another.

At six-thirty in the afternoon, the guns fell silent.

The absence of sound felt strange. Alone at the rail Kate watched the haze lift like a veil being raised ever so slowly, allowing through its folds occasional glimpses of what lay beyond. Gradually the battered city of Alexandria became more defined until there she lay, suspended in the smoke with smoldering wounds pockmarking her hillsides. Low over it all, a ghostly pall shimmered in the orange light of the setting sun.

Inflexible maneuvered easily around the breakwater and sailed into the harbor to join the rest of the fleet. By the time she tied up at the dock it was completely dark and the long pier was lit by a line of torches. According to Parker who had come up beside her, four battalions of marines had already come ashore from other ships. An entire brigade was moving out, probably to occupy the Egyptian forts and help secure the harbor.

With fixed bayonets, *Inflexible's* marines jogged single file down the gangway onto the torch-lit dock where they gathered in columns ten deep facing the city. Crates of supplies were being hoisted onto the dock.

"We may well be watching the opening round in the invasion of all of Egypt," said Parker.

"Why would we do such a thing?"

"Falls under the heading of 'stabilizing the region,'" said Parker with a shrug. "These are the men who'll be stuck doing the dirty work." He pointed down onto the dock where Sergeant Benjamin Maddox stood in front of a line of marines. Kate had met the man earlier that day and from his broad black mustache and stern dark eyes she could almost feel his fierce confidence. She pulled out her sketchbook.

The sergeant stood with his hands on his hips addressing his men, his gruff voice carrying up to the bow.

"We've been assigned this road here." He jabbed his thumb over his shoulder. "We'll follow it to the first crossroad where we'll check in with our teams on the next roads over, to the east and to the west. Then we'll proceed to the next crossroad and do the same. You'll stay together and keep your eyes and ears open. We don't know what to expect here. There could be snipers; there could be mobs roaming around, though I doubt it. You'll have to be ready for anything." He regarded each of his men severely. "All right then, as you pass, every other man shoulder your weapon and grab a torch, the rest of you, keep your rifles at the ready." He waved them forward and led the way up the street that stretched into the darkened city.

Kate kept her eyes on the small band of men until she could no longer see the light of their torches. She roughed in her drawing and then, without bothering for dinner, she went down to her cabin to get some sleep.

Julian leaned forward against a mound of rubble. Exhausted, he peered down the road at the oncoming torches. "They're coming closer."

"They could be men from the mob from last night," cautioned Ahmet.

"Or they could be a British search party," said Bertie. "One of us needs to go out there to investigate."

Julian pressed a hand to his bloodied temple where Bertie had engineered yet another bandage for him. The pain was easing a little but the constant throbbing had put him into a fog. "I'll go," he said.

"Better you than me," said Ahmet. "If it is the British, they would probably just shoot me for being a Turk."

The torches came closer. Julian could hear footsteps now. There had to be a dozen men out there. He stood up and took a few steps out into the street. He stumbled then caught himself and blinked at the orange glare. Thoughts of the mob from last night flashed through his mind. Then the torches stopped moving. They had seen him.

Someone yelled out but he couldn't understand the words. They sounded English. Encouraged, he forced his eyes to focus. He took a few steps forward and raised his hands. "Don't shoot. I'm an American, don't shoot."

Julian had choked out the words. Sweat dripped from his forehead down into his ragged beard. His bandage was soaked with it. Ten paces separated him from a man in uniform. Julian stared through half-opened eyes then realized - this man was a British sergeant flanked by a line of marines - they were about to be rescued. His legs nearly went limp with relief.

"Tanner, take his weapons," shouted the sergeant. One of the marines put down his rifle and walked toward Julian.

"I have the Prince of Wales with me," said Julian.

Tanner stopped and looked back.

The sergeant repeated his order, more emphatically this time. "Take his weapons."

Julian gave Tanner his rifle and the knife he had tucked under his belt. The marine then backed away.

The sergeant moved closer. "The Prince of Wales, you say? And who might you be?"

Julian swallowed, his throat ashen. His eyes burned from the sulfurous air. "I'm Julian North, a journalist for The London Times."

A murmur and nervous laughter ran through the line of marines but they kept their weapons steady.

"And where exactly is Prince Bertie?" asked the sergeant.

"Lower your guns first," said Julian.

"We'll do no such thing. Tanner, take this madman back to the ship."

Tanner moved forward but stopped dead when a voice came from the shadows.

"I am here, sergeant," said Bertie, stepping forward in his ragged clothing, his back straight, his bearded jaw shoved forward.

Julian watched the line of marines stiffen with audible shock as they recognized the Prince of Wales. Even in his condition and even in the torchlight, there was no mistaking him.

"My lord," said the wide-eyed sergeant.

Without waiting for the order, the marines abruptly lowered their rifles.

"There's one more man with us," said Bertie. "He's a soldier in the Turkish Army. He saved our lives."

When Ahmet came forward unarmed, Bertie raised his voice. "This is an honorable man. You will treat him with respect."

The British sergeant cleared his throat and holstered his pistol. "Yes, my lord," he said, hurrying to Bertie's side. "I am Sergeant Maddox, my lord. You men, get a stretcher over here."

Bertie held up his hand. "Not for us you won't sergeant. We've just fought our way here all the way from Port Said. I think we can cover the last few yards without a God damn stretcher."

"It wouldn't hurt though, if you could get us some water," Julian put in.

"Yes, of course, right away," said Maddox, flustered now. Canteens were handed out and the bedraggled refugees each took a long drink.

The water was the best Julian had tasted in weeks.

Maddox ordered two of his men back to the ship to take word directly to Fisher that the Prince of Wales had been found. "'Course, I had no idea you were missing in the first place," said Maddox to Bertie, "and, begging your pardon, my lord, I can't imagine how it is that you'd be out here in the middle of a war zone. You could have been killed."

"It'd take a lot more than the Turkish Army or some riotous brigands or the entire British fleet to kill me, sergeant," said Bertie imperiously. He took another mouthful of water, swished it around and spit it out. "Damn sulfur, it's all I can taste. The air's full of it." He handed the canteen back to Maddox. "One more thing, sergeant," added Bertie shuffling through his pockets. He pulled out his cigar, now dried in a crooked shape with a greenish tinge along its length.

"North," said Bertie, catching Julian's eye with a thin smile. He broke the cigar in two and handed half to Julian. "This will be the finest smoke you've ever had."

"Thank you, my lord," said Julian, standing a little straighter, and amazingly, feeling almost energized.

Bertie passed the cigar under his nose. "There's still some good tobacco here. A light, for me and my friend if you would,

245

sergeant?"

"It'll be my pleasure, my lord," said Maddox with a broad smile. He grabbed a torch from one of his men.

Julian and Bertie walked in long strides, each puffing on their half-cigars. Ahmet followed just behind. With Maddox leading the way, his marines formed the guard marching in two lines one on either side of Julian and Bertie. After three blocks they turned a corner that opened onto the wharf. Julian shielded his eyes from the rows of torches and from a buzzing, electric-arc lamp. Hastily assembled marines and sailors were posted in front of their ship. On the deck above them a line of naval officers stood at the rail.

On seeing Maddox's marines, a burly Sergeant Major shouted the order from the base of the gangway: "Attention!"

The entire line of troops snapped into position.

Bertie acknowledged the men with a nod and a salute. "Goddamn it," he muttered to Julian. "Here I am in this ridiculous, ill-fitting uniform. I must look like a bloody fool."

Ahmet spoke up from behind: "You ought to be more careful next time, your lordship, about who you steal your clothes from."

"A good point, sergeant," said Bertie with a laugh.

They climbed up the gangway.

"Welcome aboard, my lord," said Admiral Seymour stiffly, as if Bertie had just returned from a holiday excursion. They shook hands.

"Thank you, admiral. Hell of a fireworks show today. Did any of your shells actually hit their intended targets?"

"Quite a few, my lord," said Seymour defensively. "We're moving our marines in to secure the city."

"Glad to hear it, it's a mess out there." Bertie stepped over to Beresford. "Good to see you again Charlie. Sorry about the delay in meeting you at the embassy."

Beresford struggled visibly to contain his emotions as they shook hands warmly. But his smile quickly became a frown. "It was my fault, my lord – letting all that happen. I never should have left your side."

Bertie held his grip on the hand of his old friend. "It was indeed not your fault, Sir Charles. There was nothing you could have done differently and, at any rate, you see that I'm none the worse for it all – except for these damned clothes."

Bertie then paid his respects to Captain Fisher who seemed most concerned with the prince's assessment of the bombardment. "We need more testing to work our powder measures more precisely, and we need more gunnery training for our men."

"I'll do what I can to make sure you get both, captain," said Bertie.

Boldly, Julian interjected: "Luckily, the city was already deserted except for the Egyptian army rebels, and us of course." Heads turned at this remark.

"And you are?" asked the admiral.

"I'm Julian North, sir."

Bertie explained. "Without his help, I'd still be a captive. Careful, though, he's with the *Times*."

"I know all about you," said Beresford with a cold stare. "You were the one who thwarted the rescue in the Black Sea and got the prince recaptured."

Julian swallowed. He should have kept his mouth shut. Belatedly, he did so now.

"Mr. North and I have been through all that, Sir Charles," said Bertie. "He showed his true colors when we escaped at the canal. We've been on the run for days."

In the awkward silence Beresford kept his penetrating stare fixed on Julian but said nothing.

Fisher cleared his throat. "There are two other journalists aboard. Circumstances forced us to take them with us from Istanbul. We had three but sadly lost one at the canal. I had the good sense to keep the two of them below deck tonight so as not to interfere with the prince's reception."

Julian felt a jolt. "You lost one of the journalists? You mean he's dead?"

"Swept overboard, yes, an older man named Willoughby, from the *Times*."

The news hit Julian like a kick in the stomach. "But, how...?"

"You have my sympathy. I can see that you knew him," said Fisher. "You can thank the bastard pirates aboard *Resolute* for it – they fired on us from behind. We lost a great many good men that day."

Julian felt suddenly drained. He put a hand on the rail behind him. "You said there were two other journalists; are they with the *Times*? Can I see them?"

"Yes, I believe they are and yes, you can."

Julian wondered: Could one of them be Kate?

He was ushered to the ship's infirmary, where the officer of the ward, Lieutenant Walter Merriweather, gave him food and more water. He cleaned and bandaged the wounds that pockmarked Julian's body. "You've had a rough time of it," he observed when finished. "Are you sure you're up to meeting with your friends tonight? What you need most is sleep...and a good washing."

Julian moved his arm, testing the stiff bandage on his side. "I'll be all right." Then he hesitated. "Do you know about the journalists? Is one of them a woman?"

"That's the rumor. Captain Fisher's done his best to discourage speculation but her disguise is somewhat inadequate."

Through his grief over Willoughby, Julian gave a half-hearted smile, wincing as a scab cracked open on his lip. He reached for the clean shirt beside him.

Kate checked the time – 2 a.m. An hour earlier she had been roused from her cabin and taken to the officer's mess where she now sat with Ira, and Parker amid rows of empty tables and chairs. As always, she had her hair tucked under her cap.

Ira was drumming his fingers. "They could have at least brought some tea. Waking us up in the middle of the night just so we could sit down here and do nothing – doesn't make a lot of sense."

Parker had been leaning back in his chair with arms folded and his eyes closed. He spoke without opening them. "Fisher didn't want us heading off on our own. Something's going on and we'll find out soon enough what it is."

"I don't hear any guns going off," said Ira, "it can't be too important."

Kate sensed the opposite. The man who had awakened her by pounding on her door had been insistent and harried and he had left immediately after taking her and the others to where they now sat. Whatever was going on was important and it was something unexpected. These thoughts stopped short at the sound of a door opening at the opposite end of the room.

"Here we are now," said Parker sitting up, eyes open.

A short, clean-shaven officer walked toward them. "You are the journalists from the *Times*?" he asked.

"Yes," said Kate. "I'm with the London *Times*."

"New York *Times*," said Ira raising a finger.

"And I'm with the foreign office," said Parker. "Don't ask how I happened to end up lumped in with these two."

"I'm Lieutenant Merriweather, the ship's medical officer." He pulled up a chair and sat down. "There's a man in the infirmary who you may know. He was found in Alexandria tonight, just an hour or so ago."

Kate lifted her head.

"He says he's a journalist with the *Times*," continued Merriweather, "didn't bother to ask which one, of course, but..."

"What's his name?" asked Kate, heart drumming.

"Julian North."

Kate's breath left her and she held her hand to her mouth. "Oh, thank God," she whispered. "Thank God."

"How in hell could he be here in Alexandria?" asked Parker.

"Is he all right?" asked Ira.

"Aside from a few gashes and a cracked rib, he's in relatively good condition."

"Relatively good?" asked Kate.

"He's exhausted. He was in the city during the shelling."

"There should have been another journalist with him," said Ira.

"He wasn't alone, but I don't know anything about another journalist."

"When can we see him?" asked Parker.

"That's why I came for you," said Merriweather, addressing them all but his eyes resting on Kate. "When he found out that you were aboard, he wanted to see you right away. But please, do not stay long; he's pretty weak from his ordeal."

In the infirmary's washroom, Julian ran a damp cloth over the bruises and welts covering the upper half of his body. The new bandage on his side was already stained by fresh blood. Gingerly, he put on his clean shirt, fastened the buttons and looked in the mirror hardly recognizing the bearded man who stared back: gaunt face, gouged and scratched, ruddy weather-beaten skin, clumps of dried blood matting hair that covered his ears. His eyes were red-tinged and glassy almost like those of a madman.

He tried to smooth his hair then ran his fingers over his beard. Dipping his hands into the bowl in front of him, he splashed water over his scalp and face then pressed the tips of his wet fingers to his eyes. But they remained as red as before. Well, Kate would just have to see him as he was. He was drying his face when Merriweather returned.

"Your friends are here; they want to see you."

Julian put down the towel. "I'll bet they thought I was dead."

"I think they had feared the worst. They were relieved to hear you were safe. They're just outside." Merriweather indicated the outer door and took a few steps toward it.

Julian followed then hesitated.

"Something wrong?" asked Merriweather, his hand on the latch.

"Just a little unsteady, I'm fine." Was he? He longed to see Kate but worried now about how she felt about him. Did she blame him for Willoughby's death? Nothing he could do about that. Then he remembered Bertie's advice. Did he love her or didn't he? That was the only question and he had known the answer weeks ago. He straightened his shoulders and gave Merriweather a nod.

The doctor opened the door, and there she was.

She wore a white shirt and khaki trouser with a few strands of hair spilling out from beneath her sailor's cap. Her brown eyes were as bright as ever but her smile wavered as she brushed a tear from her cheek. Was that tear for him?

Julian took two quick steps and awkwardly put his arms around her. Then, they moved into a kiss so naturally that Julian had no forethought of it. He was only conscious of her lips, soft and warm on his, her arms pulling him closer until he winced at the sudden pain in his side.

"You're hurt," she said, relaxing her hold on him.

He shook his head, whispering into her ear. "Not anymore, Kate. I dreamed of this moment, of coming back to you of holding you like this."

"I was sick with worry that you might be...that you might not be coming back."

"I was worried about that myself, but here I am." Julian paused and looked into her eyes. "They told me about Mr. Willoughby."

Kate separated from him, the tears rolling down her cheeks as she explained what had happened. "He would have been glad to see that you made it back, Julian. He was worried sick about you – we all were. But he blamed himself for letting you go."

"It was my decision, not his," said Julian, remembering the tough old journalist. "He was good to me Kate. I'll miss him." She nodded and he kissed her again, conscious now of the scab on his lip. He pulled away from her slightly. He wanted to be a comfort to her about the loss of Willoughby just as she'd been a comfort for him when he'd told her about his parents. But he didn't know how to begin.

"You're probably wondering what I'm doing here."

The familiar voice was so unexpected that Julian turned abruptly. He stared at the man, thinking back to the last time he'd seen him in Karmonov's store so long ago. "Parker?"

Parker held up his hand. "I'm with the foreign office. Perhaps I should have told you that from the start but I never expected you to go bouncing off to Istanbul in search of that bastard traitor, Hastings. How did you know to go there?"

Julian looked around the room for any other surprises but saw only Ira whose face was ashen – probably wondering where Noah was. Yes he'd have to explain that, wouldn't he? He turned back to Parker. "Hastings had the Dover shipping schedule in his pocket. I took it from him by mistake along with the journal so I knew where he was going. I would have told you if I'd known you were with the government. Hastings never intended to kill Prince Bertie. He just needed to create enough chaos so their leader Pavel could kidnap the prince then work out a trade for *Resolute*."

"Yes, yes, we were able to figure all that out," said Parker, sticking a thumb under his belt. He took a step closer. "Were you aboard *Resolute* when she took the canal?"

"I was locked below deck during the attack." Julian sat down, feeling suddenly weak. He saw Merriweather about to step in but he waved him back. "I was Pavel's prisoner. And so was Prince Bertie and, so was Noah." He glanced at Ira, then at Kate. "Or so I thought."

"Where is Noah?" asked Ira.

Julian shook his head. "Noah turned out to be a traitor, just like Hastings. He made friends with me only because I knew about the journal." Julian saw the shock in Ira's face; Kate's too. "After Bertie and I escaped from *Resolute*, Noah was with the men who were searching for us."

Julian watched Kate's face go pale, then turn away from him as if holding back her true emotions. Had she cared for him that much? Did she still?

"I thought I knew him," she said quietly. "He must have been in on it from the start; the kidnapping of Prince Bertie I mean."

"We were both wrong about him, Kate," said Julian with genuine regret.

"And what happened to Prince Bertie?" asked Parker.

"He's alive and well. He's here aboard *Inflexible*. I thought you knew."

Parker smacked his hands together. "Well that's heartening news. You should have told us straight out. There isn't anything else you're holding back is there?"

"Only that there's a code in the journal."

"A code? What do you mean?"

"The scribbling in the margins, it's a code. I discovered it when I was doing the translation."

"What? And you're just telling me about it now?"

Julian threw up his hands. "Damn it Parker, I would have trusted you if I'd known you were with the foreign office. You should have told me. But you have code men at the Foreign Office, they should have seen it."

"They lost interest in the book after going through your translation. It wasn't a priority for them. Then we all got distracted by the kidnapping of Prince Bertie."

"The code may tell us where Pavel and his men are hiding. We also think it might be a list of names."

"We?"

"Prince Bertie and I."

"You enlisted the help of the Prince of Wales to decipher a code? How could you have done that? You gave the book back to me in London after you finished with the translation."

"I copied down some of the symbols before giving the book back to you."

Parker's voice took on an accusing edge. "So you planned this whole thing? You've been busy with your own amateurish investigation the whole time?"

By now, Julian was used to that accusation. He just shrugged.

"I think Mr. North has had enough for one night," said Merriweather. "I'll be releasing him in the morning and you'll be able to argue all you like."

Parker turned for the door. "Yes, we'll talk more then," he said on his way out.

Julian's head started to throb again but he'd made up his mind that he wasn't about to let Parker or Beresford or anyone else get under his skin: To hell with them. He had done his best and that was all there was to it.

Kate stayed back after the others had left. She smiled. "I guess I know all your secrets now. Good to have you back, Julian." She gave him a gentle kiss, her hand on his cheek soothing and uplifting. "I'll see you tomorrow."

"Kate, I..."

She walked to the door then turned. "It's all right, Julian. Time for you to rest now."

Merriweather led Julian to his cot and there, for the first time in weeks, Julian laid down under fresh sheets and a clean blanket. Though it was warm in his cabin, he shivered. In a troubled sleep he dreamed of exploding shells that shook the ground beneath him – rocking him with a violence that returned him to the storm-tossed deck of *Whispering Jenny*. He felt his mother's last, desperate embrace and smelled her perfume just before the final roll of the boat. Julian cried out, but still he did not wake, for with him in his dream, there was now a different woman, and another embrace and the sweet scent of jasmine and he was no longer a boy. He spoke her name and she softly spoke his and, in the calm that followed, Julian drifted into a restful, healing sleep.

CHAPTER 24

"I dreamt about you," said Julian, late the next morning, finishing his corn mush and fried pork shavings with a last sip of tea. He sat in the crew's mess hall. He wasn't eating like a king as Bertie had promised but the fare was certainly better than on the road to Alexandria - as was the company.

"I hope it wasn't a nightmare," said Kate.

"No, it wasn't a nightmare."

"You should eat more. You need to get your strength back." She handed him a biscuit.

"So now it's Dr. Wilder?" He took a bite and poured himself another cup.

"That's right. But you can still call me Kate." Her expression warmed. "You've been through a lot, Julian. I can see it in your face. You need to take care of yourself."

They were interrupted by Parker who walked noisily up the aisle to where they sat. "The captain's asked for us in the officer's wardroom," he said to Julian.

Julian sighed and pinched the bridge of his nose. He glanced at Kate who gave him a reassuring nod. "Take the biscuit with you. You'll do fine."

Julian gave her a smile but his heart wasn't in it. He then followed Parker, finishing the biscuit on the way.

"I was too hard on you last night," said Parker as they walked.

"I'm sorry about that but I'm afraid we're in for some trouble with this meeting now. Keep your wits about you and be sure to tell the truth – about everything."

"I don't have anything to lie about," said Julian with only marginal conviction. He took a deep breath and, as they entered the officer's wardroom, all eyes in the room turned in their direction.

Prince Bertie, with a fresh uniform, haircut and combed beard sat on one side of a long conference table along with Fisher, Beresford and a gray haired officer Julian didn't know. In front of Bertie, a half-smoked cigar sent a thread of white smoke up from a silver ashtray. Julian and Parker took seats on the opposite side. Griffin who remained at the door announced the names of all present, the gray-haired officer being Captain Faulks. Curt nods were exchanged as Griffin left, closing the door behind him.

After a long drag on his cigar, Bertie spoke first. "Before we begin, I'd like everyone here to know that the British government and I in particular, owe a debt of gratitude to Mr. North here for rescuing me from the kidnappers. We traveled many days together from Port Said to Alexandria and I must say, even though he is a native born American and a journalist to boot, Her Majesty does not have in all the Empire a more steadfast subject."

Julian was embarrassed at the praise. He cleared his throat, which was a little dry from the biscuit. He wished he'd had some tea to wash it down. "Begging your pardon, my lord, but I was only setting things straight since I was the one who fouled up your original rescue."

Beresford looked up from his papers with the same cold expression from the night before; anger simmering just below the surface. "Yes, I think it's time you explained yourself."

"I'm sorry but it was an honest mistake. At the time I truly thought I was doing the right thing."

"You never should have been there in the first place, North, and you know it," Beresford leaned forward. "The Prince of Wales would have been rescued a month ago except for you. You nearly got him killed, all because of your greed for a big story that you'd stop at nothing to get – is that right?"

Julian faced Beresford's scowl. "No, that is not right."

"Start at the beginning, Mr. North," interjected Fisher, more calmly. "How did you get involved with all of this in the first place?"

Julian told them about the journal and explained the whole improbable story with a few comments from Parker.

When he had finished there was silence in the room until Beresford concluded: "I still think you're nothing but a conniving journalist. I will bring charges against you for this."

Bertie raised his hand abruptly. "I've had enough of this talk, Sir Charles. I've told you what I know of this man and for the time being we'll leave it at that."

Despite Bertie coming to his defense, Julian felt his anger rise. He knew Beresford wasn't one to make idle threats; he might actually go to prison. After all he had been through, to have things end like this was just not fair and he wasn't going to put up with it. He glared across the table. "Lord Beresford, I admit I made a mistake out in the Black Sea but..."

Bertie interrupted before he could go further: "Let's get onto the main issue here," he said taking another drag on his cigar. "It seems we still have a missing warship. What are we going to do about that?"

Beresford folded his arms. "I had a discussion with Mr. Parker this morning. It appears that Mr. North here may be able to offer an insight as to the whereabouts of HMS *Resolute*. Is that correct Mr. North?"

Julian glanced at Parker wondering what exactly he had told Beresford. "Maybe...yes, I think I can."

Beresford's eyes rolled back.

"Tell us what you know," said Faulks.

"As I said, we were held prisoner by this man Pavel - the leader of the anarchists. I was important to him only because of my work with the French journal that I'd been translating. I came to learn that, besides detailing the ideals and the general plans of Pavel's group, the journal also holds other, more detailed information such as where they operate from and, very likely," he hesitated, knowing this might be a stretch, "where HMS *Resolute* is hidden."

"Likely, you say?" asked Faulks.

"All I know for certain is that the journal contains encoded information and Pavel is worried that, with the journal, we may be able to find him."

"It makes sense, gentlemen," offered Bertie. "Mr. North showed me a portion of the code. There is indeed reason to think that it's a list of names and locations: latitude and longitude – probably even some cities and postal addresses."

Faulks scratched his head. "This is dangerous information; why would Pavel be stupid enough to write it down?"

Bertie tapped his ashes. "A large group of men spread out around the world isn't much good to Pavel unless he can somehow communicate with them. He had to have such a list. Besides, he thinks this information is safely locked up within the code."

"Where is the journal now?" Beresford demanded.

Julian turned to Parker who hesitated then reached into his jacket pocket. "I have it right here." He slid it over to Beresford.

Julian was a little shocked that, after all the blood that had been spilled over it and all the trouble it had caused, Parker would be handling the journal so casually.

"The scribbles in the margins are part of the code," said Julian. "If you look closely, you'll see that they are small symbols that repeat, as if they were a kind of alphabet." He pulled out his notes and passed them to Beresford. "I've drawn enlargements of them."

Beresford studied the journal then inspected Julian's tattered notes. He shook his head. "It's like no code I've seen." He handed them to Fisher. "And 'Castlenau,' I don't know the name."

Bertie responded to this: "In my childhood, I knew of a Dmitry Castlenau." He told them about the man's visit to the palace, the man's son, and the unexplained fire.

"So," said Beresford, "this man Dmitry traveled in the highest social circles maybe forty years ago. He should be in the historical records somewhere."

"There's nothing I could find under the Castlenau name," said Parker.

"That, in itself seems suspicious, don't you think?" said Julian.

"Suspicious for what reason?" asked Faulks.

Julian leaned forward, glad for the chance to vocalize the thoughts that had been troubling him for so long. "If Dmitry were a typical elitist, wanting to rub elbows with people of power for his own pleasure and amusement, he would have pursued all the fame and notoriety he could. He would have wanted people to speak his name often and openly. Instead, he chose to remain in the shadows. His royal highness," he gave Bertie a glance, "has only a vague recollection of him, and none of you have heard his name until today. I think Dmitry was a man of power who wanted more power. He didn't associate with people of influence just to make friends - his goal was to forge personal alliances; secret alliances."

"Now, hold on North," said Beresford. "You're a little out of your depth here."

"Alliances to what end?" asked Bertie, ignoring his friend.

"I don't know," said Julian to Bertie, "but, as you and I discussed, you may have a way of finding out."

All eyes turned to Bertie who paused, then explained. "There is a chance that the queen may know more about this Dmitry fellow."

Beresford drew back, his face reddening. "Based on questionable information from this rogue who should be in irons right now, you're going to consult with Queen Victoria?"

Bertie slammed his fist on the table. "Yes, Charlie, I am going to consult with my mother and I kindly ask you again to put a stopper in that damned Irish temper of yours. I have -"

"Hold on, gentlemen," interrupted Faulks, quickly adding to Bertie, "begging your pardon, my lord." Seated at the far end of the table, he had been the last in line to inspect the journal. He had his spectacles on and Julian's notes in his hand. "I may know these symbols."

Julian felt a spark of hope.

Faulks continued studying the page.

"Well, do you or don't you?" asked Bertie.

Julian got up and looked over Faulks' shoulder. He pointed to specific characters. "Because of the way they're grouped, I figure these are numbers, the rest letters."

Faulks shifted his attention from one symbol to the next. Finally, he rubbed his eyes and shook his head. "Sorry, I thought I- They look awfully familiar, but I just can't place them."

Julian then remembered what Ahmet had said. "There was something about the language of Napoleon. Does that mean anything to you?"

"French, you mean," said Beresford, unimpressed. "Of course it's written in French, damn it; of what importance is that?"

But Faulks pondered the words. "The language of Napoleon," he repeated under his breath. He looked at the symbols again. "Napoleon...Napoleon. Yes, you're right; it's the language of Napoleon – his telegraph system. Ha!" He sat back in his chair and slapped his hand down onto the table, a look of triumph on his face. "Ha!"

"What are you talking about?" asked Bertie, as if Faulks had gone mad. "Napoleon never had a telegraph."

At this point, Julian wasn't too sure about Faulks either. He hoped the old captain had a good explanation.

"Oh but he did have a telegraph, my lord." Faulks smiled and took off his spectacles placing them neatly in front of him. "When he was in power, Napoleon erected lines of towers from Paris to Calais, from Paris to Cherbourg and to other cities. The towers were spaced five or six miles apart, each within plain sight of the one before it and the one after it. On the towers they hung a long center beam and, from the ends of that beam, two, shorter, outer beams. The angular position of the beams was set by ropes and pulleys by men at each station. Their configuration corresponded to a specific letter or number. With this system they were able to transmit messages over hundreds of miles in just minutes."

Julian returned to his chair and sat down. He felt a mix of frustration and elation that the code he had struggled with for so long had finally been broken.

But Fisher intervened. "This is a marvelous deduction, Captain Faulks, but it doesn't really solve anything. We may now know the origin of the code, but unless someone here has a codebook on him, we still can't read it."

Julian thought for a moment about the problem. "I think I can take care of that." He blurted this out, not quite thinking it through. He saw that everyone was looking at him again. No turning back now. "I'll need a lot of paper and at least five men – meticulous men, good with numbers, and a telegraph – a real one."

The room went silent again. Bertie leaned forward and snuffed out his cigar. He turned a skeptical eye toward Julian. "Just what do you have in mind, Mr. North?"

Julian explained his idea, formulating some of it as he went along, wondering to himself if it could really work.

Printing House Square, London

Emory North was about to go home for the night when he heard a sound coming from the files in the historical archives. The tall cabinets of varnished oak easily took up half the space on the third floor of Printing House Square. Each shoulder height, they stood row upon row with only a minimum of space in the aisles between.

Had he been imagining things? No, there it was again, the sound of one drawer closing and another opening. He walked silently toward the sound expecting to find nothing more than one of his reporters finishing up some after-hours research.

He passed another aisle and there saw Harry Woodhouse sitting cross-legged on the floor riffling through a file folder. He came up to the young clerk from behind.

"Working late, Mr. Woodhouse?" he asked.

Startled, Harry jumped to his feet then turned to face the managing editor. "Just finishing up, Mr. North, sir."

Julian's uncle took note of the label on the file drawer. "You're looking for information on Napoleon? Why would you do that? This isn't personal business, is it?"

"Not at all. It's something for Julian."

Emory's heart skipped a beat at the mention of Julian's name. He had been distraught with worry since being informed weeks earlier by Willoughby that his nephew had taken on a dangerous assignment and hadn't been heard from. "You know about Julian? Where is he? Is he all right?"

"Well, I suppose he's all right," said Harry brushing aside the hair from his forehead. "He's in Alexandria. He needs help with a code he's been working on." Harry checked one pocket and then another before producing a yellow sheet of paper. "I received this telegram a couple of hours ago." He handed it to Emory who read it quickly:

H. Woodhouse. Extremely Urgent,
Code is from signal towers used in France by Napoleon. Need old French code book to decipher. Check files and send numeral and letter equivalents immediately. J.N. - Alexandria

A wave of relief overtook Emory. Julian was alive – thank God.

"Something wrong, sir?" asked Harry who clearly had no idea that Julian had been in any danger at all.

"What's he talking about - signal towers?"

"I had no idea myself at first. There were some references to Napoleon's signaling system in this file but no codebook." Harry explained what he knew.

"Interesting, but what the devil is Julian doing in Alexandria? He's supposed to be in Istanbul."

"I don't know about that either," said Harry. "He said it was urgent, so here I am."

"Yes, rightly so, and I can help you," said Emory, worried again about Julian. What had he gotten himself into now? "You continue with your search here, I'll check the files under foreign codes." He took a few steps up the aisle then a thought struck him. He turned and put a hand to his chin. "One thing, Mr. Woodhouse; when we find this codebook, how do you propose to transmit the key to these picture symbols using Morse code?"

"Yes, that's going to be a problem, isn't it." Harry pondered the question for a moment then shrugged. "I don't know yet. But I'll think of something."

CHAPTER 25

It was night in Alexandria and Julian struggled to keep his pencil moving. Overhead a gas lamp glowed and across from him Parker slumped in a chair snoring loudly. They were inside the governor's great hall, just down a narrow hallway from Alexandria's only operating telegraph. The stately building had been the seat of government for the past five decades and it stood largely intact atop the highest hill overlooking the beleaguered city.

Starting from the page where he'd left off back in Karmonov's store, Julian had been working for hours carefully drawing out enlarged versions of the Castlenau symbols. He had a dishearteningly thin stack of notes to show for his efforts. His eyes burned and his back ached. In the recesses of his mind he fended off the lingering feeling that this all might be a waste of time. He'd sent his telegram to Harry five hours ago. He should have replied by now. What would he do if Harry failed him?

Hurried footsteps from the hallway startled Julian. Parker stirred.

A marine corporal poked his head into the alcove. "Excuse me; you are Mr. North and Mr. Parker?"

Julian looked up hoping they had heard from Harry. "I'm North."

"The Prince of Wales has asked for you – both of you."

Parker stretched and rubbed the sleep from his eyes. "What could he want at this hour?"

Glad for the diversion, Julian straightened and yawned. He and Parker then followed the corporal to a spacious room on the other side of the great hall.

Bertie sat behind a marble table. He waved them into two chairs. "Progressing with the code, I trust?"

"Yes, we are, my lord," answered Parker.

Julian winced at Parker's 'we'. "Still a long way to go," he added.

"Have you heard from your friend at the *Times* yet?"

"No, I haven't."

Bertie murmured as if reminding Julian of the support he had given him and that he had better come through. He folded his hands. "As you know, we've sent telegrams to the queen as well as to the Foreign Office. We've just heard back." He handed a folded sheet of paper to Parker. "It's from Templeton at the F.O. - you know him, of course."

"I do, my lord," said Parker.

"He's just interviewed the queen, getting her recollections of Dmitry Castlenau and of his boy, Mistral Picard."

At the name, Parker looked up from the page.

"Yes, one and the same," said Bertie to Parker. "Read it aloud." Parker kept his voice low.

Julian listened expectantly to the story of the mysterious pair who had visited Windsor Castle some forty years ago. Templeton's telegram reported the facts: Dmitry and his son had been invited there by Prince Albert, Bertie's father, for a purpose unknown to the queen. They had stayed for one week without incident. There had been many conversations between Albert and Dmitry, most of them in private and the queen had no knowledge as to what was discussed. Then came the fire and with it the queen's conviction that it had been deliberately set by the boy. Her memory was specific and she made mention of the boy's odd green eyes. Templeton quoted her as saying that the boy "had this odd look about him as if he were keeping a terrible secret that would shock you if he told." Parker re-folded the telegram and handed it back to Bertie.

"So, Mr. North, our suspicions were correct. The boy with Dmitry Castlenau was indeed the young Pavel and he was once a personal guest at Windsor Castle. Too bad my father has passed-on; it would be interesting to know why they were there."

"But Pavel wasn't Dmitry's son? And his real name is Mistral

Picard?" asked Julian.

"It appears so," said Bertie.

"That would account for all the money Pavel and his *Will of the People* must have," speculated Parker.

Julian was confused. "What do you mean?"

Bertie explained: "The Picards were one of the wealthiest families in France and remained so after Napoleon's fall even though their numbers had been greatly reduced by the revolution. I suppose you're too young to know about it North; but Mistral Louis Picard, at seven years of age, was the central figure in one of the biggest scandals in Europe back in what - the thirties?" Bertie glanced at Parker who nodded in agreement. "Madam Picard, Mistral's mother, was eight months pregnant when Monsieur Picard beat her to death. Of course, her unborn child died as well. It was subsequently learned that the baby was not Picard's. Only two weeks later, Picard himself died in a duel, killed by Mistral's Russian tutor whose name was never disclosed. All of Paris thought the elder Picard's death was justice well served."

Julian was intrigued. "So, the tutor was Dmitry?"

"Could be," said Parker. "But the only heir to the family fortune was Mistral. And, so far as I know, he was never heard from again - until now."

Julian conjured up the image of Pavel as he had last seen him, and could easily imagine him as a child of such violence. "So Mistral was raised by Dmitry, his father's killer, maybe even his mother's lover. That would make for a complicated childhood."

"Indeed it would," agreed Bertie. "Now this information doesn't help in breaking the code, but it does tell us something about Pavel that could prove important."

"That he's on the hairy edge of sanity," said Julian.

"Well, I think we knew that already," agreed Bertie, "but it also tells us where he gets his money from. What it doesn't give us is the connection between Dmitry Castlenau and Jacques, the author of your journal. Father and son probably but that's something we may never know for certain. At any rate, I thought you should hear what the queen had to say. And perhaps it gave you a brief respite from your work on the code."

They were dismissed by Bertie and, wearily, Julian went back to the journal. He worked through the night, his thoughts now and then returning to the sinister little boy who had grown up to become the dangerous Pavel.

In the morning Fisher provided the help he had promised.

Chairs and makeshift desks were set up in the center of the great hall beneath a high mosaic of swirling golds and blues. On each desk were a few sheets of paper, each filled with lines of symbols that had been transcribed from the journal. But Julian still had not heard from Harry and without the key to the code he had nothing for Fisher's sailors to do. So they just milled around, waiting.

"Here's another one," said Julian, handing Kate the latest sheet of symbols.

She placed it on one of the desks. "You look terrible. Did you get any sleep last night?"

"There was no time. We have to get this all done today. Fisher said he's sailing tonight, with or without the deciphered code. He'll be heading north of the canal to where *Resolute* was last spotted by the ships he'd sent after her. Fisher will have no idea of where to go from there and there's no talking him out of it. I'm not half done here with the code yet and there's been no word from Harry. What the hell's he doing? We should have heard *something* by now."

Kate sat down beside him. "Put your head down, Julian, I'll take over for a while."

"I can't stop. It has to be done and you don't know this code like I do – no one does."

But Kate dug in. "I know it well enough. It's not like you have to be a professor of archeology to see what you're doing." She paused, looking straight into his eyes. "You can't go on like this, Julian. Get some rest."

He let out a long breath, resigned to defeat. He handed her the journal then leaned forward, resting his head on his folded arms. "Just for a few minutes," he mumbled closing his eyes. Almost immediately he fell into a deep sleep.

He awoke some time later to a booming voice. "What the hell is this?" It was Beresford.

Julian kept his head down, feigning sleep as he heard footsteps coming his way. A kick to his feet brought him upright in his chair. "North, you're wasting time," shouted Beresford. "Why aren't these men working? Why aren't *you* working, Goddamn it?"

Julian stirred and wiped his eyes clear. Beresford towered over him. Fisher's men were still scattered around the hall, most sitting on the floor smoking, their backs against the marble columns. Then he saw Kate come marching up to Beresford from behind.

"This man has worked through the night," she said. "He's got to have *some* sleep." She put a few more transcribed pages down on the desks.

"We have exactly ten hours, Miss Wilder. Captain Fisher has laid out his orders and I'll not be second-guessing them. Before we sail, we need to do everything we can to break this code."

"What about Harry?" Julian asked Kate through a yawn. "Have we heard from Harry?"

"Who the blazes is Harry?" asked Beresford.

Julian got up and found himself toe to toe and nearly nose to nose with Beresford. "He's the man I'm counting on to find the code book." He glanced at Kate who shook her head. Nothing from Harry yet – where *was* he? Had he even seen the telegram Julian had sent?

"So, thanks to you," Beresford barked, "all of us are here standing about waiting for some idiot friend of yours."

"Some of us are not just standing about," Kate shot back, bent over the journal again, her pencil busy.

"I'll check with the telegrapher," said Julian.

"I'm going with you." Beresford led the way and spoke to Julian as he walked with great lumbering strides. "The Prince of Wales seems to have a good deal of faith in you. God knows why. You've been nothing but trouble from the start."

"So far, I'd have to agree with you, my lord," said Julian struggling to keep up. He was fully awake now, the sleep had helped.

At the telegrapher's office they found the telegraph key clattering and the uniformed man beside it writing frantically, trying to keep up. Julian held his breath. It had to be Harry's telegram. One glance over the telegrapher's shoulder told him he was right. He gave Beresford a nod. They were about to solve the code that had mystified him for months.

Two pages later the telegraph key stopped its rattling and the operator, sweat dripping from his forehead, leaned back in his chair. He had no sooner put his pencil down than Julian grabbed the telegram and was out the door.

The telegrapher shouted after him. "That's for a Mr. North. You are he I assume?"

"Yes I am," Julian yelled back. Filled with excitement he headed back into the great hall where he caught Kate's eye and with a broad smile raised the sheets of paper over his head. "I've got it," he said, his voice reverberating off the arched walls. Everyone was looking at him – probably wondering 'who's the madman?' But Julian didn't care. He went straight for Kate and gave her a kiss.

Blushing fiercely, she straightened her cap. She whispered: "Julian, there are men here who still think that I'm a man."

"Well, that'll set them straight don't you think?" said Julian, undeterred. He grabbed his chair, sat down and took a breath. Then, he read the first sentences of Harry's telegram:

> *Hello J N*
> *Left beam eight positions one through eight.*
> *Center beam four positions one through four.*
> *Right beam eight positions one through eight.*
> *One is vertical up.*
> *Count is clockwise.*
> *Numbers first.*

The three remaining pages of the message were nearly all numbers.

"What the hell is all that gibberish?" asked Beresford looking over Julian's shoulder.

"Harry's setting it all up," said Julian, sorry he had ever doubted him. "He's telling me the order of things and what it all means."

"Well, I'm glad it makes sense to you. All I see is numbers."

"That's right." Julian took a blank sheet of paper and drew a horizontal line with a shorter vertical line at each end. "Here's the basic structure of the three beams that hung from one of Napoleon's towers. Each of the smaller end beams can be oriented eight ways in increments of forty-five-degrees - the larger center beam, four ways. That makes," Julian did the math quickly, "two hundred and fifty-six different combinations. Harry's using numbers, one through eight for each of the outer beams, one through four for the center beam to indicate the orientation of each beam." Julian pointed to a set of three numbers in Harry's telegram. "Here we have a two, a two and a five, which would look like this." He drew a figure:

"Since he tells us numbers first, and it's the fifth of the series, this symbol must be the number five. Letters, in alphabetical order will be next, possibly followed by symbols representing certain commonly used words."

Beresford nodded without letting on that he was the least impressed. "All right, I see what you're doing now." He glanced around the hall and called everyone to attention. "You men, get in your places now. You have some work to do."

Captain Fisher, who'd just arrived, came over. Beresford explained what was going on.

From Harry's telegram, Julian quickly finished drawing out the key to the code in two columns: the symbols in one, the number or letter equivalents in the other. He drew a large version of it, which he pinned to a board in front of the group, explaining to the men how the code worked.

"Look for numbers first, gentlemen," said Fisher. "Those indicate locations. We can't have any mistakes. Getting this right is critical." He called for a large world map, which he rolled out on the tile floor. As the geographic coordinates or the names of cities were deciphered, Fisher strode around the map using a pointer to identify each spot. A sailor, on hands and knees then marked them with a black X.

As things continued, Parker studied the process. "So each X corresponds to the location of a certain member of *The Will of the People*."

"That's what we think, yes," said Julian. "And the string of symbols following the coordinates in the journal must be the name of the person. Each of them might control a cell of a hundred members – maybe more."

Parker nodded. "With this information, we'll be able to put an end to these anarchists once and for all. No wonder Pavel wanted his journal back so badly."

Kate took a seat. "Julian, tear out a few pages. We can do this together."

He saw the sense of that and grabbed the thin, fragile pages. He tore them off and handed them to Kate, feeling a little like he had just desecrated a Gutenberg Bible.

They worked without stopping, transcribing the symbols from the rest of the journal, feeding them to Fisher's men. By midday, they were two-thirds finished. By late afternoon, they were done. Julian collected the loose pages from the journal and put them back in order, closing the book. He gave it to Parker then had a look at Fisher's map. By now there were hundreds of X's. No country in the world was untouched. Pavel's organization was massive beyond belief.

A ring of men surrounded the map. One of them was Bertie, hands in his pockets. "Excellent work, North."

"Thank you, my lord," said Julian, gratified by the compliment. The prince looked nearly as relieved as Julian to see the progress; his faith in him justified.

"You've got a problem here, though." Bertie pointed to five marks in the Aegean. Of these, four ran in a straight north-south line paralleling the Turkish coast while the fifth lay farther to the west in a completely open expanse of water.

Julian looked closer. "They could be uncharted islands." But he had to admit, something didn't look right.

Kate noticed it too, but her attention was drawn to the western coast of the United States. "What are these marks doing out in the Pacific?" There were at least ten of them, two hundred miles off the coast of California and there was a similar pattern off the coast of Portugal and the western coast of Africa.

Julian's heart sank and his mouth went dry. "Everything's shifted."

An uncomfortable silence fell over the room. Fisher frowned and stepped off the map studying the problem but it was Kate who saw the solution.

"We're off by about two and a half degrees," she said. "That's the difference in longitude between Greenwich and Paris."

Bertie saw immediately what she meant. "They're using Paris as the prime meridian, just as Napoleon did. Very good, Seaman Wilder."

Quietly, Julian breathed a sigh of relief. "Good one Kate."

"That's me, a man of many talents." She gave Julian a wink in a way that immediately derailed every train of thought he had going.

Quickly, Fisher tapped his pointer on the westernmost X in the Aegean. "Reposition this mark," he told the sailor who knelt on the map.

"Here's where it belongs," said Fisher. He tapped a spot one hundred miles off the southwest coast of Turkey. It was the only valid mark in the Aegean. "Here's where your ship is, Faulks, and that's where we're off to." Fisher checked his watch and motioned to the nearest marine.

"Sergeant, get this map rolled up and stow it aboard *Inflexible*. We sail in two hours."

But Bertie had other ideas. "Excuse me, captain, I think it best that I take the map with me to Istanbul. You just worry about getting our ship back. Sir Edward and I will begin tracking down the men on this list."

Fisher immediately saw the sense of that. "Quite right, my lord. We'll see to it." "Where's Parker?" shouted Fisher a moment later, standing beside his desk.

"I'm over here, captain," said Parker, hurrying forward.

"Mr. Parker," said Fisher, "you will go back to Istanbul with the Prince of Wales and you can take the journalists with you." The captain seemed to be relishing the thought of having *Inflexible* rid of outsiders.

"But I can't go back, not yet," Julian blurted out.

Beresford's nostrils flared. "Excuse me, Mr. North?"

"Julian, what are you doing?" whispered Kate.

"I'm going with *Inflexible*" said Julian to Beresford.

"You will go where Captain Fisher tells you to go – Istanbul."

"I'm one of the few who've actually met Pavel and I was the last to see him. I know the journal and I know Castlenau's plans."

Beresford shook his head but Fisher just gave a shrug.

"He's done good work here, Sir Charles," said the captain, "perhaps he could be useful. But I leave it to you."

Beresford stared at Julian. "In my eyes you still haven't redeemed yourself for what happened in the Black Sea. But I find myself agreeing with Fisher – you could be useful." He paused as if dealing with an argument within his own head. "Very well then, you'll come with us, but be Goddamn sure to keep out of the way."

"Thank you, my lord, I will," said Julian, both relieved and apprehensive.

Kate stared at him. "Julian, why are you doing this? Have you got some kind of a death wish?"

"I'll be all right, Kate. I need to finish what I started."

"No, the Royal Navy has to finish this. You don't think they can get along without you?"

Julian knew it wasn't rational but he knew in his heart that he had to go and that if he didn't, he would regret it for the rest of his life. He was done with regrets. "I'm going, Kate."

Kate said nothing.

Fisher put his hands on his hips. "Well, now that Seaman Wilder has given his permission, that question appears settled." He called for Faulks who strode over. "Have all your essential crewmen aboard *Inflexible*. When we retrieve *Resolute*, I want to make sure you have enough men to sail her home."

Faulks gave a crisp salute. "Aye, sir."

The room was bustling with activity but from the opposite wall Julian saw Bertie discretely motioning for him.

269

"Yes, my lord," said Julian hurrying over.

"I'm headed back for Istanbul, and I'm taking our friend Sergeant Rashid with me. The sultan and I have some unfinished business."

"What business is that, my lord?" The words escaped his lips before he realized he had no right to ask such a question of the Prince of Wales. Bertie was no longer his traveling companion.

"It's a private matter," said Bertie, seemingly amused by Julian's overstep. "I'll be using Sergeant Rashid as a translator. I will see to his release."

Julian was glad to hear that Bertie would be looking out for Ahmet and that the sergeant would not be imprisoned for the simple crime of being a Turk.

"There is one thing I need you to do though," continued Bertie. He lowered his voice and explained.

HMS Inflexible

That night Julian stood near the bow and said good bye to Parker and Ira who then walked down the gangway onto the docks. From there they would take a launch to one of the other ships bound for Istanbul. Before joining them, Kate lingered by Julian's side.

There was a chill in the air and she wore her oversized sea coat and had her hair tucked under her hat. Her face was pale. "You don't have to do this, Julian," she said.

"Yes, I do, Kate. You're not going to talk me out of it."

"At least promise me you'll stay out of trouble this time."

"I'll do my best." He looked into her eyes. "Kate, I thought a lot about you when I was gone. I..."

"I was worried for you Julian, we all were - Mr. Willoughby too. I thought I might never see you again and the more I thought about it the more I realized how important you are to me."

The ship's horn blared, making them both jump.

Kate managed a faltering smile. "I know you have your own reasons for doing this, Julian and I won't question them. But I think you're being foolish."

"You're right, I am. I've done a lot of foolish things in the past year, Kate, things that don't make the least sense. I should be back in London working the files for the *Times*. I should have never come to Istanbul, but I did. I should have never met you, but I did."

There were shouts from the dock.

"They're getting ready to cast the lines," said Julian.

Kate kissed him. "I'd better go. Take care of yourself, Julian. I suppose I don't mind you being foolish every now and then; just don't do anything stupid."

"Now there's good advice," said Julian with a laugh. He pulled her close and wrapped his arms around her, his cheek against hers. "You mean more to me than you'll ever know, Kate."

"I'm glad. Be sure to come back and tell me more."

"There's no getting rid of me, Kate. I'll always come back to you."

She lifted her eyes to his. "Good bye, Julian."

Julian watched her go and waved when she looked back from the dock.

A short time later, the last of the marines stepped aboard and the lines were cast. The ship's engines began their deep rumble, reminding Julian of the vibration from the presses back at Printing House Square. Those days seemed a lifetime ago.

CHAPTER 26

The Aegean Sea

By the direct order of Lord Beresford, Julian spent most of the next two days in his cabin - not a prisoner but not exactly a guest. He supposed it was Beresford's way of exacting one more measure of penance from him. It was a price Julian was willing to pay so long as he didn't have to face more serious punishment. He knew Beresford could still press charges if he wanted to.

Julian took the time to shave off his beard. He ate his meals with the crew but was required to sit apart from them thus attracting stares and murmurs of curiosity.

"They all think I'm a criminal," he had said to the guard posted behind him.

"We've been told that's exactly what you are," the sailor replied, keeping his voice low. "And we've been ordered not to speak with you."

"Do I look like a dangerous man?"

"Not to me, but the captain thinks different."

"And the captain's never wrong, is he?"

The man smiled. "Never known him to be."

On the third morning at sea, the engines slowed and the guard abruptly opened Julian's cabin door. "They're calling for you, Mr.

North."

"Who is?"

"Sergeant Maddox."

Julian remembered the gruff marine who had rescued him in Alexandria. Of all the men aboard, Maddox should know that he was no danger to anyone. He pulled his boots on, tucked in his wrinkled white shirt and adjusted his leather suspenders. "Lead on," he said.

In the corridor there was a general commotion with men headed purposefully this way and that. We must have arrived, thought Julian, containing his excitement. HMS *Resolute* and Pavel could be close-by.

On deck he was directed toward a group of marines near the bow; each of them carried a rifle and a kit of supplies at his belt. Some regarded Julian with disdain. The rest ignored him, preoccupied with the dim profile of an island rising up off the starboard quarter. Julian moved closer for a better view.

Measuring maybe five miles across its width and again as long, the island was a featureless dome of yellow limestone rising maybe two hundred feet above the water. As *Inflexible* approached, the dark green vegetation growing high and thick at its westward end became more distinct.

So this was the *X* in the Aegean. As a hiding place for HMS *Resolute*, it looked none too promising. There must be a protective harbor on the other side, Julian thought, but he had a sinking feeling – what if the journal coordinates were wrong?

The wind shifted. To the north, low clouds dotted the horizon. He spotted Maddox looking in that direction.

"Storm's gathering out there," the sergeant was telling another marine. "With these shoals surrounding the island, we don't want to be close to shore when she hits."

Julian took a step toward him. "Hello, sergeant, remember me?"

Maddox turned then gave him a smile. "'Course I do, Mr. American. It'll be a long time before I forget that night. I hear you've gotten yourself into a bit of trouble since then, but I will say you're looking a damn sight better. Hope you're up for this."

Julian was about to ask 'Up for what?' when a whistle sounded and the rail in front of Julian swung out over a rope ladder. He looked down over the side and saw a steam launch bobbing with the waves, black smoke pouring from its stack. A marine at the tiller looked up and gave a ready sign.

"After you," said Maddox.

"You're going out to the island?" asked Julian.

First Officer Briggs stood a few paces behind and answered: "That's right, Mr. North, and you'll be joining us. Right now you're holding us up. We've got provisions for you aboard the launch so move along if you please." Julian looked over the side again.

"Now, North!" boomed Briggs.

He climbed down awkwardly and took a seat in the back of the small boat as the others piled in around him. Over the heads in front of him he stared at the innocent looking island. The man at the tiller handed him a field belt with a filled canteen. He strapped it to his waist.

Briggs was the last to board, taking a seat at the bow. By Julian's count there were eighteen men jammed shoulder to shoulder. They pushed off from *Inflexible* and rode the swells to within a few hundred yards of the island. From there they headed for a sandy stretch of shoreline. One man told a few bawdy jokes and a few others laughed but most of the men were quiet, uncertain about what lay ahead.

The waters grew more choppy, kicking a light spray off the bow. Whitecaps warned where rocks jutted up. Beyond that, the waves grew large and pounded the beach. Only two months ago Julian had nearly drowned in a spot very much like this. At least he was dry and in a boat this time.

The launch entered the shallows and rode the waves in. The engine was shut down and at an order from Briggs, four marines jumped into the water and pulled the boat up onto the sand. Julian climbed out with the rest of the men. A hot wind tore at them. It was nearly noon by Julian's estimation.

"We're going to search this island from fore to aft," said Briggs with the men gathered around him. "Remember, we're here to look for anything unusual - *anything!*"

Julian stood off to one side and could not help forming a grim, disbelieving smile. So intent was Beresford at keeping the loss of *Resolute* secret he hadn't even allowed the crewmen to be told what it was they were looking for. He caught Briggs' eye and silently questioned the wisdom in this strategy but the first officer continued without missing a beat.

"We'll separate into two groups. Each will go around the island in opposite directions, meeting at the halfway point. It's a small island, so it shouldn't take long. If either group finds anything at all suspicious, they will give a signal with a pistol shot." He paused. "Sergeant Maddox, you'll take eight men and advance down the beach that way." He pointed to the east. "The rest will come with me. Have your rifles ready. There may be danger on this island. Make sure you're prepared for anything." Briggs scanned his men. "Any questions?"

"None that you'll answer, sir," muttered the joke-teller, pulling his cap down nearly over his ears.

"That'll be enough, Tanner!" shouted Maddox who turned back to Briggs. "Sorry, sir."

"That man, and Mr. North will come with me in my group, sergeant."

"Aye, sir." Maddox scratched his head at that decision but separated the men accordingly.

As this was going on, Julian scanned the featureless landscape. A few scrawny palms bent in the wind. Parched and brown, they sprouted from jagged cracks in the limestone. He ran his fingers through his hair, then stuffed both hands in his pockets. As a hiding place for Pavel and his men and a twenty-eight gun warship, this place didn't feel right at all.

Briggs moved closer to him, away from the rest of the men. "Is there a problem, North?"

"I may have read the code wrong," admitted Julian. "How could *Resolute* be hidden here?"

"An unlikely spot, I agree, but we're not going to worry about that now. My orders are to search this place until we're sure. It'll take only a few hours. Then we'll move on to the other islands in the area. Even a small error in the coordinates or in our sightings could throw us miles off."

Julian knew this was true and was encouraged by the thought. The sooner they completed their trek around this island the sooner they could move on to one that was more promising.

"And one more thing," continued Briggs, "I want you to know that it was Captain Fisher who insisted that you take part in this expedition. Lord Beresford was dead against it and so was I." Leaving Julian a little unnerved, Briggs walked back to his men. "All right, let's move. Cover every inch."

"Aye sir," said Maddox, heading out with his group.

"Should we leave a guard with the launch, sir?" asked one of the men, obviously looking for easy duty.

"No," said Briggs, "she's staked down and well secured, and we won't be long." He led his group westward with Julian bringing up the rear.

As they walked, the sandy beach quickly rose up to a craggy landscape of yellow-white rocks with jagged edges and treacherous footfalls. The sun blazed overhead and a slackening in the wind caused waves of heat to rise from the hard-baked surface. Julian worked to keep his footing over the steady uphill slope. Every now and then gopher-like animals poked their noses out through the many holes that riddled the limestone. Two hours later they approached the high eastern end of the island.

"We'll round the tip, then stop for a rest," said Briggs. "Ten minutes, no more."

"I haven't seen anything dangerous yet," muttered Tanner after they had stopped.

"Maybe we should kill us a few of these rock rats – they look pretty dangerous."

"At least we'd have us fresh meat for dinner," said another man.

Julian sat down with his back against a boulder and took a long drink. The sea was far below them but he could hear the sound of the breakers announcing that the wind was picking up again - still out of the north. He craned his neck in that direction. The line of clouds was closer, and darker. They would have to be careful not to be caught in the launch when the weather closed in.

Tanner sat with his back up against the same boulder as Julian. "Storm's comin', sir," he said to Briggs.

"Thank you for pointing out what everyone can plainly see."

"That's what I'm here for, sir; to point these things out." He crossed his feet and, closed his eyes. In less than a minute, he was snoring loudly.

When they started out again, Julian decided to walk beside Briggs who now set a stronger pace. Julian wanted to talk with him about the next island they might try since there was obviously no place to hide a warship on this one.

A yell came from behind. It was Tanner.

"What the devil is it now?" asked Briggs.

Tanner stood twenty feet behind the rest of the group. "I don't know, sir. Something's odd here." He indicated the ground just in front of him.

Briggs stalked back, Julian and the others following.

Tanner knelt down for a closer look. "It's this hole in the ground. I saw something coming out of it."

"A rock rat, you mean," said Julian.

"No," said Tanner with the side of his face pressed flat against the ground to look at the hole from the side. He jerked suddenly. "There, did you see that?"

"Bloody hell, Tanner, what do you *think* you saw?" demanded Briggs.

"Smoke," said Tanner still bent over the hole, "There's smoke comin' up from the ground."

At that moment, as if to validate Tanner's judgment, Julian saw a thin stream of black smoke curling up from the hole and, just as quickly, vanish with the wind.

Briggs had seen it too. "What the hell..." He put down his rifle and knelt next to the hole. He took a sniff and jerked back in surprise. "That's the smell of a ship's boiler. There's a coal fire down there."

Hope rose within Julian. He scanned the ground around him then looked out to the sea and marveled. It made sense – there must be a cave. Could *Resolute* be *inside* the island?

"This must be what we're looking for," said a marine. "It doesn't seem dangerous, but it sure as hell doesn't belong here."

Before Briggs could stop him, Tanner picked up a pebble and dropped it down the hole, listening for its landing that came a few seconds later. "That sounded like *metal!* A long ways down too."

"Don't do that again," Briggs admonished, standing up. He looked west down the length of the island. From this vantage point he could see much of the coastline and all the interior of the island. There was no sign of Maddox and the others. "Tanner, run on out there about a half a mile and fire one shot – into the air."

Tanner scratched his head then saw the impatient look on Briggs' face. "Yes, sir - a half mile."

The sky was beginning to darken to the north with occasional flashes of lightning coloring the clouds. Julian looked out to *Inflexible* and saw that she was headed out, away from the island. "Where are they off to?"

"Don't worry, North," said Briggs. "She's just keeping a safe distance from the shoals. No sense being forced aground by the storm when there's plenty of open sea."

Julian remembered the earlier comment from Maddox and saw the logic to the maneuver, but it didn't lessen the feeling of abandonment.

Maddox and his men joined up with them twenty minutes later.

"Looks like we're here till the storm blows over, sergeant," said Briggs. "Gather the men - it's time they learned why we're here."

Maddox looked around, puzzled. "You found something then, sir?"

"Yes, I believe we did."

With the men clustered around him, Briggs told them about

HMS *Resolute*. "I won't go into how or why she was stolen, or who has her," he concluded, "but we're here to get our ship back – or to destroy her to keep her from being misused. At this moment she must be floating in a cavern straight below us. We're probably standing right above her stack."

A thunderclap in the distance and a sudden rush of wind broke the men's silent amazement. Briggs turned to Maddox. "Time to batten things down, sergeant."

"All right," Maddox shouted through the gusts, "find what shelter you can and rig for the storm. Keep your weapons as dry as you can and try to keep on level ground - she's going to be a big one."

Julian went back to his boulder and was joined a moment later by one of the marines - a man with an anchor tattooed on his neck.

"How the devil could the Royal Navy lose a bloody warship?" he said. "You wouldn't know anything about that, would you?"

"Not a thing. I'm as surprised as you that there's a ship down there," said Julian, which was the absolute truth.

The marine spat to the side. "Yeah, well, you know more than you're sayin'."

The sky grew dark. The temperature plummeted. The cool air was a relief at first; then not. Hatless, Julian buried his head into his bent knees and folded his arms as the howling winds converged.

The rain blew sideways, pelting Julian with a stinging cold. He gripped his knees tighter and leaned into the wind. The storm that had sunk *Whispering Jenny* was nothing compared to this. Even without shelter, he was thankful to be on land rather than at sea. He wondered how *Inflexible* was riding it out. He raised his head slightly and looked around but couldn't see a thing – it had turned dark as night.

An hour passed before the wind eased up and the rain fell at a slower but steady pace. The sky brightened just a little. Julian found he had lost all feeling in his neck and in his water soaked extremities but, with an effort, he was able to straighten and stretch his legs. He tested his hands – opening and closing them, trying to get some blood flowing. The half-healed wound in his side began to throb.

Through the rain Julian saw Briggs and Maddox moving from man to man. The men were stirring. "Come on now – on your feet," Maddox ordered, waving them to where Briggs stood on the high ground overlooking the cliff.

Julian stood, then forced his legs to move. It reminded him of his time with Bertie on the road to Alexandria. He realized that he missed his company. The man with the anchor tattoo stood up.

"Quite a storm," said Julian.

The man took off his rain-soaked hat, smacked it against his knees a few times then put it back on. "Seen worse."

They walked to where the men were gathering, Julian's boots sloshing at every step.

"I've made a decision," Briggs shouted over the lessening rain and wind, droplets trickling from his cap. "We're going to break into the cavern. We need shelter and we need our ship back. I mean to get us both."

"Hope he has a good plan," said Tanner to no one in particular.

Julian was skeptical too. Why not just wait out the storm for *Inflexible*'s return? Then he had another thought. He backed away from the group and scanned the still darkened horizon. There was no sign of *Inflexible*. He was stunned. If she had been sunk in the storm then this might be their only chance to recover *Resolute*. It might also be their only chance to escape from the island. Is that what Briggs was thinking?

The first officer was still talking to his men. "The mouth of the cave has to be large. The foliage we saw on the cliff must conceal the opening. All we need to do is to crawl down and find it. It'll be a damn sight better than staying here suffering this water torture." There were some affirmative grunts among the men. "Now, I'll need you, Mr. Tanner, and two others to come with me."

"What? Why me?" groused Tanner in surprise before adding, "sir."

"You were an engineer's mate, correct?"

Tanner nodded, "That was a while back, sir."

"No matter. *Resolute* is down there and we need to get her engines started. That'll be part of our job."

Tanner took on a wary expression. "What's the other part, sir?"

Briggs ignored the question and singled out two others from the ring of men around him. "The four of us will be the first to go down. As soon as we get to the foliage where the going will be easier, the rest of you will follow. When we're at base of the gate we should be able to swim under it and into the cave. We'll board *Resolute* and the four of us will head directly for the engine room to get the boilers fired up. By the smell of it, there should still be some heat left there."

This time it was Maddox with a comment. "The anarchists aren't going to let us just sail her out of there. They'll put up a fight."

"And so will we, sergeant. I'm counting on us surprising them, so it's important that we're all as quiet as possible."

"They might already know we're here, sir. Maybe it's us who'll be surprised."

"That's a chance I'm willing to take, sergeant," said Briggs. "Now, let's get started."

Maddox gave him a skeptical glance, then a salute. "Aye, sir."

Julian walked to the edge of the cliff and looked down. It would be a long fall.

The storm had become a cold, gentle drizzle when Briggs and his advanced group started down. Their progress was slow at first but as they gained confidence they were able to descend at a fairly rapid rate. Tanner was the fastest. Like a monkey shifting from ledge to ledge, he scaled his way down the rocky face and was first to reach the foliage; once there he waited for the others.

Julian kept them all in view. Maybe this would be easier than he thought.

When the last of his team reached the vegetation, Briggs looked up to Maddox, gave him a high-sign, then resumed the decent.

"All right men," said Maddox, "it's our turn." He lined everyone up along the drop-off just as Briggs had. Julian took the center position, aiming to take the same path as Tanner.

The sergeant cautioned them all. "Be sure of your footing before you take each step and when we get down there, keep quiet. There's no telling how many of the anarchists might be about - could be hundreds."

Julian drew in a deep, rain-soaked breath. Then, like the others, he lowered himself to hands and knees and eased himself over the edge. Going from foot holds to hand holds in the rock face, he made what he thought was good progress but after fifty feet, he realized that he was one of the slowest of the group. It was hard work now, the incline steeper. He was breathing hard, struggling to hold onto the wall of wet rock. At this point, climbing back up would be just as perilous as going down. But the rain had nearly stopped and the sky was brightening further. He risked a glance down to where the waves broke white against the coal-black rock. The pattern they formed on the surface of the water defined a deep water channel of comparative calm directly below him. Even so, there wasn't much doubt that a fall from here would be fatal.

"Just move along, Mr. Journalist. Just keep moving along," said the anchor-tattoo man, from a few steps further down.

"I'll make my way sure enough. You just worry about yourself."

"We'd all be sorry to see you splattered over all them rocks down there - wouldn't be anyone to write about us."

"Quiet," ordered Maddox.

"What makes you think I'll be writing about any of this?" asked Julian.

"That's why you're here, isn't it? You're going to make heroes out of us, just like Tennyson and the bloody stupid light brigade. They're all heroes now, but they all died just the same."

Julian was about to ask the man what he knew of Tennyson when his foot slipped out from under him. Julian's heart leaped into his mouth. For one awful moment he swung by a single handhold until he was able to pull himself back up against the rocks. He clung there, unable to move. So this was it. He was going to fall to his death on a barren island that was too small to even have a name.

"There's better footing to your left a few feet," said Maddox from below. "Can you get over there?"

Julian saw a ledge. "I think so."

He crept sideways, remembering Kate's warning not to do anything stupid. How did he keep getting into messes like this? How had Tanner managed to get down the cliff so effortlessly? He inched his way along and reached the ledge just as the wind kicked up again. The sky darkened and rains suddenly fell again in a full downpour.

"Hang on, men!" Maddox shouted. "Don't move – just hang on!"

Julian looked up, horrified. Along the surface of the cliff, a deep groove in the rocks channeled a stream of rushing water directly at him. He was in the middle of a run off. He closed his eyes and held on, thinking of the rocks below. The gush of water hit Julian squarely but he kept his grip. Lightning flashed and a long roll of thunder rumbled directly overhead ending in a loud bang. A fading scream sent a shiver of terror down Julian's spine. One of the marines must have fallen. Julian couldn't look down to see what had happened; he could only hold onto the rock face buffeted by what was now a frigid waterfall. He turned his head so he could breathe. The water flowed around and under him. His fingers were numb. Fear shot through him – he felt his body slipping down.

Suddenly, the waterfall became a torrent that ripped Julian from the face of the cliff. He fell, careening violently off a rock nodule that ripped into his side. Everything around him was a blur. He extended his hands over his head and prayed for something to hold onto. The vegetation on the cliff would be his only chance. He had to be ready to grab onto it. A few more jolts and he was ripping through the foliage.

Then, miraculously, his hands caught on something but it wasn't a vine or branch as he'd expected - it felt like *a rope*. Thank God, he thought with a glimmer of hope.

But the rope only slowed his fall. He tightened his grip, his side burning with pain. His leg glanced off another rock then he lost contact with the cliff and fell free, dangling in midair as if from a spring that bounced him up and then down before coming to a stop.

Julian let out a breath through clenched, shivering teeth. With his arms fully extended over his head, he held tightly onto the rope. He opened his eyes and brought an astonishing scene into focus. Above him stretched a huge dome studded with glassy crystals of milky lavender that faded back into darkness – *he was hanging in the mouth of the cave*. He repositioned his hands on the rope; his arms strained to their limit.

Then, he looked down.

CHAPTER 27

A pool of green water spread beneath Julian, its surface rippled by a hundred streams of water that leaked noisily from cracks in the roof of the cave. To his left, a launch tied to a wooden stake rocked gently. To his right, half in shadow, floated the giant *Resolute*. Julian gasped when he saw her. Shrouded by the cavern, the tall mast, gaping stack and huge guns were completely out of proportion with her surroundings.

Facing the inside of the cave, Julian realized that the rope he clung to was part of a counterbalance that worked the massive double gate which must now be gaping wide open behind him. From the corner of his eye he could see a large boulder suspended by a rope which offset the weight of the gate, allowing it to be easily opened by the efforts of one man. By pure luck, the mechanism had broken Julian's fall and his weight had forced open the entryway.

Below him he saw a line of marines racing for the ship, Maddox leading them, frantically waving them on. They took no notice of Julian and his predicament until they had all run up the gangway onto the ship. Only then did Maddox look up to give Julian a sign first, to keep quiet, then to let go of the rope. Julian looked down. If the water was deep enough to accommodate *Resolute,* it would be deep enough to stop his plunge before he hit bottom. The pain in his side was unbearable. He gave Maddox a nod then, just as he was preparing to let go, he heard a sound from the back of the cave. Maddox and the others heard it too. They took cover as a large man shuffled out of a separate tunnel at the rear of the cavern. He was heading for the gate. It was Boris.

He carried a lamp in one hand and a pistol in the other. The big Russian surveyed the open gate, swore, then walked to the hinge point of the gate. Taking no notice of Julian high above, he put down the lamp and stuck his pistol under his belt. He then reached for the rope and pulled - forcing it tight along its entire length, up to where Julian strained to hold on.

The jerk of the rope sent a sudden, stabbing pain blazing through Julian's ribcage. He lost his grip and fell. He saw Boris look up at him then jump back just as his feet hit the water. The pool was deep and he didn't touch bottom. He surfaced quickly to find that the gates to the cave had slammed closed and, except for Boris's lamp, all was dark.

Deep inside *Resolute*, Briggs felt his way through the darkness down steep metal stairs, heading for the engine room. Behind him one of his men tripped, the stairs ringing. "Quiet," Briggs whispered without slowing. Two decks down, the smell of coal, smoke and mechanics grease told him they were in the right place.

"Tanner, find the fire box. It'll be hot. Use your shirt to open it and you won't get burned."

"Aye, sir," said Tanner.

Briggs could hear the man feeling his way around then stumble. "Follow the heat," he advised.

"Got it," said Tanner finally.

The cast iron door creaked open and the glow of coals smoldering in the firebox lit the room in a dim orange-red light.

"We have heat," said Tanner, "but she'll need some heavy stoking."

"It's a compound engine," Briggs explained, "six pistons, fed by one boiler."

"Aye, sir, I know the type."

Good, thought Briggs, Tanner at least *sounded* confident.

They found a lamp, lit it and the engine room became visible. Steam pipes ran everywhere. Tanner checked them all for heat. He assessed a gauge, thumped it with his fist then opened a valve, causing a short blast of water to sputter out. He closed it. "Water's hot. We should have steam in a few hours."

"We don't have a few hours, Tanner," said Briggs grabbing the lamp. He inspected the pistons and the mechanical linkages that drove the long propeller shaft. It ran nearly a third of the ship's length back through the stern bulkhead. "Everything else looks to be in good shape." He eyed the coal bunkers. "We're low on fuel, but we won't need much to bust out of here. I can give you one hour."

"Can't be done, sir."

"It has to be done," said Briggs. It might be an impossible task but there was no other choice. They might not even have the hour. The anarchists had had only two men posted on the ship and they'd both been easily overpowered before the gates had swung open. Briggs knew there were more of them out there somewhere and they could strike at any moment.

"One hour," he repeated.

"Aye, sir," said Tanner half-heartedly. He handed shovels to the men with him. "Let's get to work, boys."

Briggs headed back up to check on Maddox and his men and on North who he'd last seen dangling from a rope high over the water. He had to admit, the young journalist seemed to lead a charmed life, averting death the way he did. He wondered if his luck was still holding.

Julian hid in the shallow water close to shore watching a lamp coming ever closer. In the darkness, he could hear the footsteps of several men. They held the lamp out over the water's edge. He knew it was only a matter of time until they found him.

"We know you're here." It was Pavel's voice, calling out in English. "Are you hurt? We can help you."

Then the lamp moved quickly and Julian realized they must have seen him. Pavel shouted an order in Russian and two men jumped into the water.

Julian kicked off for deeper water but they were on him too quickly. A pair of strong arms grabbed his shoulders and drew him toward the shore. He struggled but could not break their grip. Other men pulled him from the water.

They propped him up with his back against a boulder. The lamp was held up next to his face. He felt its heat and blinked to ward off the light.

"North?" Pavel asked, incredulous.

Drained of his strength, Julian did not reply. He sat limp and dripping wet. He had gone to a lot of trouble just to end up as Pavel's prisoner again. Then he realized that Pavel may not know about Briggs and his men. Julian thought quickly. He had to give Briggs time to get *Resolute*'s engines going. He had to make Pavel think he was alone.

"How could you be here?" asked Pavel, concern and urgency in his voice. "You escaped at the canal. How did you find us?"

"I didn't escape. I've been aboard the whole time," said Julian.

"You've been in hiding for a month?"

"I stayed in the hold. You have a lot of food there. How else would I have gotten here?"

"And what happened to Albert?"

"The prince is dead. He hit the side of your ship when he jumped off. That's why I decided to stay aboard."

Pavel was silent for a moment. He gave an order and three of his men headed off. "My men will search the ship to be sure. We'd thought the storm had blown open the gates but it was you trying to signal the British ship we'd seen earlier today. Sorry to say, she left hours ago. No one's coming to help you."

Julian was silent.

Pavel nudged Boris and gave a command in Russian after which Boris and the rest of the men walked back to the tunnel. Alone now, Pavel sat down opposite Julian with the lamp between them.

In Pavel's eyes Julian saw not hate or evil, maybe just curiosity – as if he was trying to understand why Julian ever thought he stood a chance against him.

"What will you do with me?" Julian asked.

"Nothing, for the moment. Perhaps I'll take you with us when we sail. You'll witness the history we make."

Julian thought of all the marks on Fisher's map. This madman may indeed have the power to change the world and wouldn't blink an eye at the prospect of thousands dying in the process.

"Still trying to start your war?" Julian asked. "You failed when you killed Alexander, and you failed at the canal. Jacques' plan isn't working too well is it?"

Pavel thumbed the butt of the pistol he carried in a side holster. "What do you know of our plans?"

Julian shifted his weight, pain shooting through his side as he moved. He caught his breath. This was a dangerous game he was playing but at all cost, he had to hold Pavel's attention. "I've read the journal. I know more than you think."

"And what has the journal told you?"

"I know that your real name is Mistral Louis-Picard."

Even in the dim light, Julian could see Pavel flinch. He recovered quickly though and kept his hand on his pistol. "Mistral was just a boy. He died many years ago. I've taken the name Castlenau. I am the son of Dmitry Castlenau."

"It was Dmitry who killed your parents."

"Ah, there you are only half right," said Pavel, showing no emotion. "Dmitry killed my father to protect me. I am the one who killed my mother."

Now it was Julian's turn to flinch. What kind of monster was this?

"My parents were fools Mr. North – *monarchists,* parasites living off other people's misery." He spat out the words. "They deserved to die."

"And you passed judgment on them when you were only ten?"

"I was twelve," said Pavel with a shrug. He rose to his feet and drew his gun, holding it two feet from Julian's head. "Perhaps you deserve to die too."

Julian shrank back, yet forced himself to go on, it was his only chance. "Dmitry killed your father not to protect you but to gain control over you and all your money. It was he, not Jacques Castlenau, who had the grand dream of war and revolution."

"That is a lie," shouted Pavel. "You could not possibly know these things."

"I know that you were the boy who set the fire in Windsor Castle," Julian shot back, "and I know there never was a Jacques Caesar Castlenau." He had come to that conclusion in a flash. Could it be true? "It was Dmitry who wrote the journal. He did it to deceive you into thinking that this cause was some kind of a holy quest, that it was your destiny."

"It *is* my destiny," said Pavel, his voice shaking with anger, "just as it is yours to die by my hand." He cocked the pistol.

Julian began breathing in short quick breaths, panic rising, but he had already made up his mind – he would not go quietly. "It was never your destiny. Dmitry didn't need you. He needed your money to pay for mercenaries to carry out his plan of destruction and anarchy. It was always his quest – never yours."

Pavel shook his head in an almost mechanical way. The strong words had hit home. "You are wrong," he whispered hoarsely, "and Dmitry is dead."

At that moment a metal-on-metal clanking sound came from aboard *Resolute.* It could only have come from Brigg's marines, thought Julian...or from Pavel's men searching the ship.

Pavel jerked to one side, scanning the darkness nervously for the source of the sound. Then he understood at last and turned back to Julian, bristling. "You did come off that British ship. How many of you are there?"

Julian's heart pounded as if trying to break free of his chest. "You should give yourself up."

"I will never do that," said Pavel, his pistol steady. More sounds came from the ship. "You know by now that I will do anything to keep the revolution alive. It is *my* plan now and I won't allow you to stand in my way." Pavel's finger curled around the trigger.

There was nothing more Julian could do. Images of his father and mother flashed through his head. Then he thought of Kate and forced his eyes shut and braced for the bullet that would end his life.

But, in place of a gunshot, Julian heard only a thud.

He opened his eyes warily and saw the pistol drop as Pavel collapsed and fell to the ground in front of him. He stared at the body in disbelief then, just beyond it, spied a familiar pair of deerskin boots.

"Hello, Julian," said Noah, sliding his gun back into its holster.

Julian's throat was completely dry. He tried to swallow. "Is he dead?"

"I don't think so. Can you move?"

Julian slowly regained his senses as Noah grabbed his arm and helped him sit upright.

"What in the world were you thinking of, coming here?" asked Noah. "This has nothing to do with you and you damn well should never have goaded Pavel into trying to kill you. He and these Russians of his have very short fuses."

"They killed Czar Alexander and Whiley too. They're kidnappers, murderers and assassins. How can you count yourself among them?"

Noah glanced at the ship and rushed his words. "I don't condone those things, just as you don't condone all the terrible things done in the name of Great Britain. You are *with* the British because you *are* British. Well, I know you're American but, you know what I mean. I am with these men because I *am* one of them. My grandfather was one of the one hundred who sailed with Jacques Castlenau out of Alexandria. It was the great failing of Castlenau that he had no children to inherit his passion. Over time, men of power and opportunity and money took his name and took over the movement he started. But our ideals have remained true and I believe in them.

"I've known for quite a while about the boy Mistral who became Pavel. But you are wrong about the journal. It's not a fraud. It's what has held us together all these years. It speaks the truth."

"You're blind to the truth. How many innocents will have to die for your noble cause?"

"How many died for the American revolution? Do you question the righteousness of that cause? And what about your Civil War?" Noah stooped to pick up Pavel's gun and the lamp. "You won't question us after we've won and you see the good we accomplish with our power."

"I've seen all I want to see of that."

More sounds came from *Resolute,* this time footsteps could be clearly heard.

"You have to get away from here," said Noah, urgently now. "Go to your friends, wherever they are, but get away from this man. He *will* kill you if he gets another chance, and I won't be able to save you a second time." Noah helped Julian to his feet. "If, by some stroke of good fortune, both of us are alive at the end of the day, I'll explain more, but there's no time now."

"Give up, Noah," said Julian. "Our ship will be coming back for us, you don't stand a chance."

Noah gave him a grim smile. "There are more of us than you know and we have more ships than just this one. You may win here today but in the end, the common man *will* take control of his own fate. I wish things had turned out differently between us - with Kate too. She's yours now, if she wants you. Tell her I said good bye." He turned and headed for the tunnel.

Julian watched the lamplight fade. At his feet he could just make out Pavel's body lying motionless on the ground. It would have been him lying there dead were it not for Noah.

Suddenly, a gunshot rang out, reverberating through the cave. It was followed by another, its flash coming from the ship. Somehow he had to get aboard. He crouched behind the boulder. His side throbbed and he had trouble moving his right leg. He must have hurt it in his fall down the cliff.

There was more firing, this time from the tunnel entrance where Pavel's men were trying to force their way out. Julian could see several bodies lying there. If the Russians were able to break into the cave, all would be lost. The ship would be boarded and Briggs and his men killed. With the next flash of gunfire, Julian glimpsed a cargo netting hanging down *Resolute*'s side. He could use it to climb aboard. He backed away from Pavel's body and edged closer to the water where he eased himself in.

Julian swam through the darkness, pain stabbing him at every stroke. He made it to *Resolute* and felt along her side. The rope of the netting was an inch thick and he had no trouble finding it. A voice came from the ship.

"Is that you, North?" It was Maddox.

"I'm down here," said Julian. They must have been watching for him.

"Climb up, quickly now," said Maddox.

Julian put a foot on the rope and took a step up. His side wrenched with pain and he stopped for a breath. He looked up and saw another face looking down at him. It was Briggs.

"Get your ass on deck, Mr. North, and do it now," said the first officer.

Julian braced himself and took another step up, rested, then took three more. He was nearly to the rail. Breathless, he held his hand up and was grabbed by Maddox who, with the help of another marine, pulled him up the rest of the way.

"We thought we lost you, but kept a lookout posted in case you swam over," said Maddox with a smile. "That was quite a fall you took – got the bloody gates open for us though." He left Julian and went back to his men who were kneeling along the ship's rail on the starboard side, their rifles aimed at the mouth of the tunnel that led further back from the rear of the cavern.

Julian continued to breathe heavily, his back against a capstan, his legs extended on the deck.

"Have you got a gun?" shouted Maddox.

"No."

"You can help with reloading." Maddox handed Julian a spent rifle and a packet of bullets. "Watch out, the barrels'll be hot after we get this little battle going."

"I'm as good a marksman as any man here, sergeant."

"That may be so, but right now you look none to ready to fire a rifle, besides we don't have extra. You just keep watch over here. Yell if you see anything."

Julian loaded the rifle and slid it back to Maddox then felt totally useless.

For a time the only sounds came from the streams of water still falling all around the cave from its crack-riddled roof. The line of marines held their weapons steady, prepared to fire at anything that moved. Julian could feel their tension and his own. He kept his eyes moving, peering over the port-side rail into the darkness, but he saw nothing. He wondered where Noah was and if Pavel had regained consciousness.

The minutes dragged by until Julian saw Briggs running in a low crouch across the deck toward Maddox. They conversed quietly then Briggs left and headed through a hatchway.

Suddenly, Julian remembered something Noah had said: 'We have more ships than just this one.' Did he mean more warships?

He strained up to all fours and made his way to Maddox. "Where's Briggs?"

The sergeant kept his eye on his rifle sights. "He's gone up to the bridge. The engines will be up soon. He's going to try to break us out of here."

Julian rose to one knee, glancing at the hatchway where he'd last seen Briggs. A gunshot made him jump and nearly fall back. It had come from the opposite side of the cave. In the dark cavern, Pavel's men must have been filtering out of the tunnel to take up a broader firing lane. The marines fired off a few shots in response. Their reports resounded through the cave, their flashes like bolts of lightning pierced the darkness.

Julian got to his feet in a crouch and ran as best he could for the hatch. He limped up one stairway, then another before he saw the door to the bridge. Then, he froze. From the shadows inside he saw the muzzle of a gun aimed straight at him.

"Goddamn it, North, I almost shot you," said Briggs, lowering his weapon and walking back to the helm. "What the hell are you doing up here? Get back down to Maddox where you can do some good."

"I'm not doing any good down there."

"So what good did you expect to be up here?"

Julian stepped onto the bridge and steadied himself. He smelled smoke – smoke from the ship's boiler. "I talked with Pavel – and with the American who's with him."

"I don't care if you had a conversation with God himself, I don't have time for you." Briggs checked his watch. "In five minutes I'm giving the signal to start the engines."

"There are other ships," said Julian. "The anarchists have more ships than just *Resolute*."

That got Briggs' attention. "Pavel told you this."

"The American, Noah Sanford told me."

"So maybe they've played this monarch-for-a-warship game before? With other nations?"

Julian shook his head. "I don't know. I just wanted to tell someone in case I didn't make it."

Briggs flashed a smile. "Oh, you'll make it all right. As lucky as you were grabbing onto that rope like you did when you fell down the cliff, you're probably the only one of us who'll get out of here alive."

From the deck below there was more gunfire, and shouting. A man screamed.

"There must be something I can do," said Julian.

Briggs shook his head but then spoke quickly. "There is one thing I suppose you *can* do. I need a lookout when I try to steer us out of here. Fortunately, we don't have to go very far." He shifted the lamp. "I can't see the stern from here at the wheel so you'll need to guide me through the turn." Briggs stepped off the bridge and pointed aft. "The entrance to the cave is there, do you see it?"

Julian spotted an area where a few gaps in the structure of the gate allowed glimmers of daylight in from outside. "Yes, I see it."

"There's a heavy cross beam there, barring the gates closed and, as you see, we're not quite aligned with it. I'll need to steer us through an arc so we hit the beam straight on. If we hit at an angle we may not break through. Once we're out, I'll straighten us so we don't run into the shoals outside the cave. You just have to tell me how far we are from the gates so I know when to make the turn and when to come out of it. Can you do that?"

There was just enough light in the cave for Julian to see the stern. He scanned the distance to the gates and saw the arc that *Resolute* would have to make. "Yes, I can do it," he said, concerned that Briggs was just placating him.

"Good. Remember though, the ship takes time to respond to the wheel, so this will be a tricky proposition. In three minutes I'll give the signal for full reverse. We run the risk of fouling the pistons if the engines are started too soon."

Briggs left and took his position at the helm leaving Julian alone.

The sounds of battle rose up from the deck. "They're charging the ship," Maddox yelled.

Julian couldn't see Briggs from where he stood but he heard him run for the starboard side.

"North!" shouted Briggs.

Julian took two steps back onto the bridge and saw Briggs leaning out the starboard window, firing away. He glanced back at Julian, his face beaded with sweat. "We have to go now." He pointed to the ship's mechanical telegraph that signaled orders down to the engine room. "Pull it all the way to full reverse."

Julian grabbed the lever. It was cold and smooth in his hand. He pulled it down, sliding a marker to the full-reverse position. A bell sounded to indicate the signal.

Briggs kept firing down onto the deck then stepped back to the wheel. "It'll take a few minutes for Tanner to engage the engines. Remember, when we start moving, shout out our heading to the gates – angle and distance."

Julian went back to his lookout post. The smoke was thicker

now but he could still make out the gates. He focused on a particular spot so he wouldn't lose sight of it. As the gun battle at the bow raged on below, he prayed for *Resolute*'s engine to come to life.

CHAPTER 28

Down in the engine room, the long cable and linkage running from the telegraph lever on the bridge had rotated a marker and sounded a bell, relaying the order for full reverse.

"There it is," shouted Tanner to the men still madly shoveling coal and stoking the blaze. "I don't know if we've got any steam but somehow we've got to get this bloody tub the hell out of here!" He kicked at an iron pipe. "I told him we needed more time."

He checked the temperature gauge. It had been creeping up slowly - too slowly. He checked the pressure - higher than he expected. There must have been some residual steam in the boiler. He grabbed the valve he had opened earlier and gave it a half turn. A wet vapor burst out, sputtering and spitting but then it became a steady, dry jet. Tanner closed the valve, surprised. "My God, we've got steam," he said to himself. Then he shouted to the others. "We've got steam!" He raced to another valve, larger than the first, and opened it fully.

"Why ain't it startin' up then?" asked one of the men, his eyes on the black pistons cranks and counterweights of the lifeless engine.

Tanner grabbed an oil mop and slathered one of the bearings. "Just keep shoveling," he said as a jet of steam shot noisily up through a relief port, then stopped. The long rod of the closest piston began to move. It forced its way into a sustained down-stroke, slowly turning a huge flywheel. "That's my baby," coaxed

Tanner. Momentum grew as an upstroke followed. The engine added power with each cycle, each of the six pistons sputtering steam, working in tandem.

"Here we go now," Tanner shouted over the increasing din, grabbing a long iron lever. "Full reverse, aye, captain!" He pulled with all his weight, engaging the gears that connected the propeller shaft through a clutch to the engine. The mechanism shuddered and groaned under the load then, the shaft began to turn.

Julian felt the low rumble course through the ship and his spirits rose.

"They've got 'em going," Briggs shouted from the bridge.

The big ship began to move.

From his vantage, Julian peered over the stern through the dark and the smoke and he could see no sign of the gates now but knew roughly where they should be. He was about to shout his best guess as to their heading when he was nearly knocked off his feet. *Resolute* had suddenly stopped moving. He yelled back to Briggs: "What was that? Did we hit something?" He felt the engine still going, and could hear the propeller thrashing away. The whole ship was shuddering.

"We're hung up on something," said Briggs.

Julian felt the ship pivoting. The deck tilted slightly. Then he turned and saw the problem. "It's at the bow," he yelled. "The cargo netting's snagged on a piling."

"Goddamn it," cursed Briggs. "Get in here. Take the wheel." Julian ran inside and grabbed onto it. He held it steady.

"We'll have to cut through the ropes," said Briggs, "and you'll have to steer us into the gates. Remember – dead on. We have to hit them dead on."

"But..."

"Just do it. You know where we have to go. Just do it!"

Briggs scrambled down the stairs and Julian was alone on the bridge, his bent shape reflected dimly by the dark windows in front of him. He straightened slightly and at that moment the window in front of him was shattered by a bullet that careened into the bulkhead behind him. Julian dropped to a knee. More bullets pinged off the steel wall. He got to his feet but stayed in a low crouch as he regripped the wheel - and waited.

Briggs raced for the bow. His men were fighting in a fury, hand to hand. Beyond them he could see that the main lines had been cast off and that it was only the cargo netting, knotted around a cluster of wooden pilings, that held them to shore. The netting was stretched tight and groaning with tension, the pilings shaking from the pull of *Resolute*. Given enough time, she might break free on her own but there was no time for that. And there was no time to cut through the ropes. There was only one thing he could think to do.

"You, over here," Briggs yelled to one of his marines as he ran to the forward gun turret. The man joined him and they climbed in. Briggs checked the breech. As he hoped, Pavel's men had left the gun loaded. "Get the elevation down," he shouted to the marine, pointing at the cranking mechanism.

The man grabbed the handle and began turning frantically. "You'll bring the whole cave down on us," he yelled.

Briggs knew that that was a distinct possibility. "It's our only chance," he shouted back, working the azimuth gearing. "Just get us down – zero elevation." He squinted through the sights and could just make out the pilings as they came into view. They stood only twenty feet away.

"That's as far as she'll go," said the marine.

"It'll have to do."

Bullets bounced off the outside of the armored turret. The smoke was overpowering. Briggs wiped a sleeve over his eyes. Even if he was successful in breaking *Resolute* free from the pilings, he wouldn't be able to get up to the bridge in time to man the helm. North was on his own. What a fiasco this might end up being: boarding *Resolute* and getting her engine going only to have her bounce off the gate and crash into the opposite side of the cave. At worst it could cost him and his men their lives. At best, it would be the ruin of his mediocre career.

Briggs threw these thoughts out of his head and refocused on the task at hand. He checked the sights one last time. "Here we go," he shouted. He braced himself and engaged the firing mechanism.

Faulks heard the blast two miles away, on the bridge of HMS *Inflexible*. "What the hell was that?" he asked.

They were sailing back to the island at a leisurely pace after the storm had blown itself out an hour ago. The sea had become calm, and the sky was returning to a brilliant blue in the late afternoon.

Faulks picked up his telescope and turned it on the island as Fisher stepped onto the bridge. "Can't imagine what -" Faulks stopped short and adjusted his focus. At the high westward end of the island a cloud of dark smoke was issuing from the cliff. He spoke slowly. "Of all the bloody things! Smoke's coming out of it." He lowered the telescope with a baffled expression. "There's no fire in sight, mind you – the island's just...smoking."

"What color's the smoke?" asked Fisher.

"It's black, why?" He offered the telescope to Fisher.

Fisher didn't bother taking a look. He gave the slightest of smiles and gave his visor a tug. "I'll wager your ship's been found, captain. Helmsman - all ahead full!"

"All ahead full, aye, sir."

"Mr. Griffin, sound general quarters; and get Lord Beresford up here, I think he'll want to see this."

Still confused, Faulks stared out at the island as *Inflexible* picked up speed.

Julian staggered at the deafening boom. The wheel jerked hard to port and he fought to keep it steady. Briggs had managed to break *Resolute* free and she was steaming now in full reverse as if shot from a cannon.

Julian regained his footing then tried to remember the arc Briggs had planned that would guide *Resolute*'s stern directly into the gates. His ears were ringing. The shock of the explosion had totally disoriented him. He felt the ship rumbling beneath him, heading backwards in the dark. He willed himself to think where in the arc they might be. He held course for a three-count, then cut the wheel sharply, praying to God he'd guessed right. He braced for the collision.

The pilings had exploded in a hail of splinters and Briggs was thrown back by *Resolute's* sudden acceleration. He opened the turret's hatch and climbed out into the smoky darkness. His ears rang from the sound of the big gun that echoed through the cavern just as another sound took its place. He looked aft and saw the great stern of HMS *Resolute* plow into the gates. She met the cross-beam just below the stern-rail and hardly slowed, tearing the gate from its mounts and bursting out of the cave with a loud cracking of fractured timber. "We've hit dead on," Briggs muttered, scarcely believing it.

Like a wild boar, the giant warship shouldered her way out of the cave. From the bridge Julian saw a shaft of sunlight pierce through the smoke then flood the darkness. There was a shuddering scream of iron against rock from the starboard side as the remnants of the elevated gangway were torn off.

Still fighting panic, Julian turned the wheel slightly to center the ship. The scrapping sound subsided and he drew a breath; things were happening fast now. The powerful engine pounded away. *Resolute* was still accelerating. The bridge cleared the gates and through the shattered window in front of him Julian saw a deck strewn with tangled rigging and bodies. A last puff of black smoke swirled off the bow and the high cliff loomed overhead as the warship emerged fully from the cave. On deck the marines cheered. Julian stared down at them. My God, we've done it! Finally free under an open sky *Resolute* sped at full reverse directly into a glorious setting sun.

One last metallic scream resounded through the hull. Julian kept his hands on the wheel realizing that the ship was slipping through the narrow lane of shallow coral he had seen from the cliff. He made an adjustment to port and immediately, the sound lessened, then stopped. Satisfied with his performance thus far he stood straight and wiped a hand over his face, his skin greasy with sweat and gritty with coal dust. He breathed in the clean air that streamed in then jumped when Briggs burst onto the bridge, his blackened face beaming with a broad smile.

"You did it, North! You executed that maneuver like a veteran helmsman."

"I might just as well have had my eyes closed. I couldn't see a thing."

"It doesn't matter. You saved us all." He clamped a hand on Julian's shoulder.

Julian managed a hard, dry swallow. "Good idea, firing the gun at the pilings."

Briggs checked the waters behind them. "Looks like we'll be all right," he said at length. "Ease her two points to starboard now and keep her at full reverse, we still need to gain some distance from the island."

Julian complied, and continued to savor the clean air - finally able to release some of the tension that had strained him to the breaking point. He stared at the receding entrance to the cave where black smoke continued to pour out as if from the portals of hell. Julian shuddered at the thought that they had all been trapped inside and could have easily died there.

"What now?" he asked.

"Now, Mr. North, we'll get ourselves turned in the right direction."

The words had just left Briggs' mouth when a loud boom

roared in the distance, followed by the sound of a shell rocketing through the air. Julian's heart jumped into his throat. He dropped to a crouch, his hands still clamped to the wheel.

An explosion threw up a pillar of white water fifty yards off the port side.

"Goddamn it, what's happening?" shouted Julian. "Who's trying to kill us now?"

Briggs pointed to starboard where *Inflexible* was closing on them. "Hell of a welcome for us eh?" he said with a laugh.

"Why are they shooting at us?" demanded Julian, bothered that Briggs could remain so jovial.

"They don't know that it's us and not the anarchists who have control of the ship – that's why. It was just a warning shot," said Briggs. "Full stop if you please, Mr. North."

"Full stop," said Julian, signaling the engine room and taking a long breath. He pried his fingers off the wheel and dried his palms on his shirt.

"It'll take us a while to slow down," said Briggs. "We'll need to convince *Inflexible* that we're not a threat." He began rummaging around. The bridge was a mess. Sea charts were strewn about and stubs of cigars littered the area. He opened a locker. "The signal flags should be here." He shuffled through the stack and pulled two out. "These should do."

Briggs stepped off the bridge and tossed them down to Sergeant Maddox who hoisted them up the aft mast.

Julian watched them unfurl then flutter in the wind. "What do they say?"

The first officer took off his cap and raked his hair back. "Hold fire, HMS *Resolute* reporting for duty."

CHAPTER 29

The next day dawned foggy and still. Captain Faulks and fifty crewmen had transferred over from *Inflexible* the night before and *Resolute* now maintained a position five-hundred yards off the island. At the bow Julian stood beside Briggs who studied the cave entrance with his telescope for any sign of movement.

Things had gone well, thought Julian. The ship was back in British hands. Merriweather had stitched and bandaged his wounds and, though his side still stung with every movement, he had been pronounced fit for duty as if he were part of the crew. But he had slept fitfully and this morning his mind remained clouded with worry over what might have happened to Noah.

"There's a boat coming out," Briggs said. "She's under a white flag."

Julian could just make out the bow of a steam-powered launch emerging from the cave. She glided over the silvery water heading straight for them, her little engine making a rhythmic puffing sound that reminded Julian of *Maracas*. Could Noah be aboard?

"I see we've got visitors on the way," said Captain Faulks walking up from behind. "They want to surrender before we blow up their island."

Briggs handed the telescope to Faulks who waited for the boat to come a little closer before raising it to his eye. "Crammed full," he concluded. "I can see some of the faces – not Pavel's though. Here North, have a look. You know him best, maybe you can spot him."

Julian drew the boat into focus. He shook his head. "I don't see him, but he might be on the other side." He hadn't seen Noah either.

"We'll find him," said Briggs. "I'll get some men together to inspect them as they come aboard. We'll need a makeshift brig."

"Some'll be going to *Inflexible*," said Faulks. He used the toe of his shoe to assay a sticky dark spot on the deck. "Those that remain here will be occupied for the next few days cleaning up the mess they made of my ship."

"They should all be interrogated," said Briggs.

"Do we have anyone aboard who speaks Russian?"

"Not that I know of."

Briggs and Faulks both glanced at Julian who shook his head.

"Well, do the best you can," said Faulks to Briggs. "I personally want to check each man."

"There should be an American with them, if he's still alive." Julian described Noah.

"He's the man who told you about the other ships," said Briggs.

"Yes," said Julian, "his name's Noah Sanford."

"Mr. Briggs told me about your conversation with him – a fellow journalist eh? Let's hope he's still alive, I have a few questions for him and I'll wager that Lord Beresford does too."

Julian knew that, if Noah were alive he faced years of imprisonment. He might even be hanged. "I'd like to remain on deck when the anarchists come aboard if that's all right."

Faulks shrugged. "No harm in it that I can see. As soon as we're done with that, we'll take a party back to the island and explore the cave and tunnel completely. Perhaps we can figure out what Pavel and his men were up to. You'll come with us, North – if you're up for it."

"Yes, sir. I'm up for it," said Julian.

By noon, after three trips from the island, the launch had delivered the last of the surrendering men; some to *Resolute*; some to *Inflexible* - still no Pavel and no Noah. As Sergeant Maddox assembled a line of marines on deck preparing to leave for the island, Julian suppressed a sick feeling in the pit of his stomach knowing he would soon learn Noah's fate.

They set out in three lifeboats. In the first, Maddox and Tanner sat across from Julian and Briggs; Faulks took a position at the bow to direct the boats. Two men worked the oars. As they approached the island, Julian eyed the sheer rock face that had nearly taken his life the day before. From it a tangle of rope hung down over the cavern entrance that yawned before them, black as pitch, still exhaling its sickly, dark smoke. On either side floated the ruins of the massive gates, half submerged, their timbers bobbing with the slight roll of the sea.

"I don't like this one bloody bit," said Tanner as the boat slid beneath the shadow of the entrance.

"For once I agree with you, Tanner," said Maddox, his hand on his pistol. "This place has the feel of evil to it."

The light of day abandoned them and the strokes of the oarsmen slowed. Julian's eyes adjusted to the dark, his lungs to the foul air.

Faulks raised his lantern when they hit the shore. "Light those other lamps," he said, leading his men out of the boats.

"Here's the spot where I last saw Pavel," said Julian, pointing to the boulder he'd sat against.

"This is where the American hit him from behind?" asked Faulks.

"Yes, he knocked him out with the butt of his gun."

"Why would he have done such a thing?"

"He thought Pavel was about to kill me."

"Sounds like he was unsure of whose side he was on," said Briggs.

Julian remembered his last conversation with Noah. At the canal it had been so easy to label him as a despicable traitor who condoned Pavel's ruthless tactics. Now he wasn't so sure.

"Tell me exactly what Sanford told you about the ships," said Faulks.

Julian remembered the words vividly. "He said: 'There are more of us than you know and we have more ships than just this one.' That was all."

Faulks scratched the side of his face. "Worrisome," he said.

"The tunnel's that way," said Briggs, pointing.

The marines from the other boats were already at the tunnel entrance, some dragging the bodies of the dead Russians from where they lay, arranging them in a row. Julian shrank back but then forced himself closer, his boots hardly making a sound against the stone floor of the cave. His stomach tightened.

"There's eighteen of them captain," said Maddox. He and Faulks held their lamps over them.

Julian stepped slowly among the bodies. At the fifth one, his heart fell. He took a step back. "It's Noah. This one is Noah Sanford."

Faulks brought the light closer to the body. "You're sure?"

"Yes," said Julian, forcing himself to study Noah's face. His eyes were closed but his expression was strangely lifelike, as if at any moment the lips might part and he would begin to speak.

"I don't see any wounds," said Faulks, bending low over the body. He put down the lamp and grabbed Noah's shoulder with both hands. He turned him. "There," Faulks said darkly, "he was shot in the back."

Bitterly, Julian realized what must have happened. "Pavel killed him. He shot him from behind. He killed Noah because Noah saved me."

Faulks let the body slump back down. "You can't be sure of that."

"I'm sure," said Julian with conviction born of the remorse and the anger he felt welling up in him. He took a step closer then knelt beside Noah. He reached out and touched Noah's hand, cold, lifeless. "Lower the lamp."

Julian blinked back the moisture from his eyes and fought to control the trembling in his lower lip. He turned the hand and looked close. There, just below the thumb, was the mark he expected to see – an 'H' with a circle around it. "The assassin in Istanbul – Hastings - had a mark just like this one."

"Same as on the cover of the journal," said Faulks who then ordered Maddox to check the hands of the other bodies.

"None of the others has the mark," Maddox reported after his examination.

"And Pavel is not among these men," Faulks added. He turned to Maddox. "Finish your inspection of the tunnel sergeant, but be ready for anything. There could be armed men hiding in the shadows."

Julian walked alone back to the water's edge. He gazed out through the mouth of the cave where the sea sparkled a deep blue that reflected back into the cavern. Noah would be alive were it not for him; and he would be dead were it not for Noah. Why had he taken such a risk? Had he suddenly doubted his cause? Or was it all just chance that had sealed Noah's fate, and with it, his own?

At the root of all of it was the monster, Pavel - Mistral Picard. If he still lived, he could be hiding here on the island somewhere. He had to be stopped. Julian felt his determination rising when a shout came from Briggs.

"Over here," he called out from the dark, farthest reaches of the cave. When Faulks and Julian joined him, Briggs held up his lantern.

Julian turned and looked up. "My God," he whispered, awestruck.

Towering over them stood the emaciated stern-castle of a French man of war, its hulk truncated at the quarterdeck by jagged, weathered planking. The entire structure lay on dry ground, cradled in a makeshift wooden brace that held it straight. The French tricolor hung limp above the gold letters painted on her stern:

Homme Ordinaire

"Ordinary Man," translated Faulks. "There's your explanation for marking on the cover of your book – and for the tattoos.

Julian felt a shiver run through him. "These must be the ruins of their original ship. It's the ship Jacques Castlenau sailed from Alexandria. "

"There are legends here in the Aegean about a ship like this," said Faulks. "She plundered traders and slavers, taking what she could before disappearing."

"This island kept her hidden for decades," said Briggs. "It was only the smoke of *Resolute* that gave her away."

"And the journal," said Julian.

Faulks nodded. "We'll inspect the rest of the cave and the tunnel, then be off. I won't be sorry to leave this cursed place."
As they walked, Julian asked for a favor that elicited a look of understanding then a nod from Faulks.

They made their way through the rear tunnel that opened into a second cave.

"The anarchists lived here like rats!" said Briggs, standing with his hands on his hips, looking at the mess of crates, bedrolls and garbage.

"Still a far sight better than living conditions in most of Russia," said Faulks.

The dripping of water from yesterday's storm could still be heard behind the rustling of Maddox and his men.
"This was their main base of operations," said Briggs, "but I don't believe they intended on spending much more time here."

"Why do you say that?" asked Julian.

"Look over here."

Julian followed Faulks and Briggs to the forward wall of the cave where lumber, nail kegs and supplies were piled high.

"There's a huge amount of building materials and paint here," said Briggs. "I think they meant to box in *Resolute's* guns, give her a new shape, a fresh coat of paint, and pass her off as an innocent trading vessel. She'd move in close to her prey, expose her guns then steal whatever she wanted. Hell, being able to sneak up like that, she'd be capable of sinking any ship at sea or shelling any defenseless port. Nothing could stop her because she would never be found. She'd come back here for supplies and a safe haven, drop off her booty, and sail off again for other targets. They probably have a deal with the Turks for her supply of coal."

"All for the purpose of funding *The Will of the People*," said Faulks.

"That was only part of their plan," said Julian, seeing things more clearly now. "Pavel already had all the money he needed. He intended to use *Resolute* and his other ships to steal more ships. He was going to build a navy – maybe he already has with those other ships of his."

"My God, with the thousands of men they have, they would be more powerful on both land and sea than many nations."

"Pavel needed the help of the Ottomans to steal your ship," said Julian. "In return they helped the Ottomans take the canal to try and reunify their empire. If the Turks had received the assistance they expected back at the canal from Egypt and her allies, the result could very well have been Castlenau's world war; a war in which the only victor would have been Pavel with the strength of his followers - and his navy."

Faulks adjusted his cap. "Alive or dead, Pavel is still on this island. We'll find him and then we'll find his other ships and put a stop to it all."

Just then, Maddox raised a shout from the rear of the cave: "Captain – you'll want to see this. There's a second tunnel."

Julian, Faulks and Briggs hurried over.

"It was hidden behind this crate here," said the sergeant, peering into a narrow opening in the wall. Tanner pushed the crate further out of the way.

"Bring more light," ordered Faulks, waving several marines over, "We'll need to see where it leads."

"I was afraid he'd say that," said Tanner.

In a long single file, six men entered the tunnel – Tanner in the lead with a lantern, Julian the last. They faced a steep uphill grade for the first hundred paces before the tunnel went level then sloped downward. The damp air smelled of salt and mold and, at each step, Julian steadied himself against the uneven, moss-caked walls. Streams of water trickled everywhere, settling in pools that he and the rest of the men splashed through.

"I see light up ahead!" shouted Tanner.

"About time," said Briggs. "We must be clear on the other side of the island by now."

The light trickled in through a stack of small boulders where the tunnel abruptly ended.

Tanner pushed the rocks aside.

The sound of the surf and the light of the sun flooded the tunnel. They climbed out from the face of a low escarpment that jutted up from the sand less than fifty yards from the open sea. Once his eyes adjusted, Julian turned around. The tunnel's opening had been well disguised.

"Follow those tracks there," said Faulks, pointing to a trail of disturbed sand leading to the water then off to the right.

"These are the footsteps of at least two men," said Maddox, leading the way. They came to another, smaller escarpment. Close to the water's edge, a small boat lay half buried under a pile of loose rocks. The trail of footsteps ended there in the wet sand.

Julian ran his fingers through his hair and looked around. This must be how Pavel and Boris intended to make their escape. But their boat was still here. He wandered out into the knee-deep water staying within earshot of the discussion behind him.

"If they didn't take the boat..." The voice of Maddox trailed off.

"So they're still on the island," said Tanner.

Several of the marines cocked their rifles.

"I want a complete search of the area, sergeant," ordered Faulks.

Julian walked back up from the surf. "I don't think we need to do that, captain."

"And why might that be, Mr. North?" asked Maddox.

"They didn't take this boat, because they had a better one."

"They had two boats? How the blazes do you know that?" asked Tanner. "I say we..."

"Tanner, will you kindly bugger off," said Faulks. "You're beginning to get on my nerves."

"Yessir," said Tanner.

Faulks turned back to Julian.

"They were about to take this boat, but then saw our launch," said Julian. He pointed to a bend in the shoreline.

Maddox marched down to the water to see for himself. "He's right sir," Maddox shouted back to Faulks. "We beached her right up there and now she's gone. Two men could have dragged her off - easy."

"The man with Pavel must be Boris, his lieutenant," said Julian. "I didn't see him among the bodies or among the prisoners."

"They could be anywhere by now," said Faulks, looking out to sea. "They've gotten away. Goddamnit to hell!"

A single grave was dug on the island for all, save one of the anarchists who'd died in the fighting.

HMS *Resolute*

In the morning, before a military drum-line, the six marines who had died were given an honorable burial at sea. Captain Faulks spoke over each canvas-wrapped body before it was slipped over the side beneath a British flag. Then, there was a seventh burial.

For Noah there were no drums and there was no flag, and no prayers were read by the captain. His body, wrapped in canvas, lay poised on the burial plank. Only Briggs, Maddox and Faulks remained with Julian along with the two men handling the plank.

"Do you want to say some words?" asked Faulks.

Julian realized how little he knew about Noah. He hesitated for a moment then began. "This man saved my life, and for a short time he was my friend." He placed a hand on the body, feeling Noah's deerskin boots through the canvas. He remembered their times aboard the *Sussex* and their battle over Kate's affections. He wondered what she would say if she were here. He raised his voice over the sound of the wind. "I knew him to be a good man. His cause was noble, but it was a cause not meant for our time. It was a cause born in a revolution that was lost generations ago. Noah himself knew this was so; yet he followed his ancestors and his brothers-in-arms and his heart with honor and courage. Rest now, in peace, Noah Sanford." Julian lowered his head.

The plank was tipped and Noah's body slid down. It hit the water with a splash then slipped silently into the deep. Julian remained standing, staring down at the water long after the ripples had died and long after the others had left.

Later, with *Resolute* still lingering off the island, Julian found Briggs standing next to the bow turret. "If you could spare a few minutes," said Julian, "I need you to act as a witness to what I'm about to do."

Briggs regarded Julian with concern. "And what is it you're about to do?"

"It's for the Prince of Wales."

307

Julian led him through a hatch and down a flight of steel stairs. Walking past a row of cabins, he slowed at one of them but did not stop. "I was imprisoned here," he said, making his way farther down the corridor where only a few weeks earlier he'd been running for his life. The thought gave him a strange sense of separation from those events; as if they'd happened to someone else and not to him.

"Here," said Julian at the door of another cabin. He opened it. "This is where the prince was held." The room looked exactly as he and Bertie had left it – the blankets on the cot neatly tucked in, the chair in which Bertie had sat, still backed out from the desk.

"He was writing just before we made our escape." Julian surveyed the papers strewn across the desktop. Atop them a pen lay next to a dried-up inkwell.

Briggs bent lower, slowly reading one of the pages. "My God, do you know what this is?"

"No. I only know that he wanted these papers destroyed."

"He didn't order you not to read them?"

"He didn't say anything about that, but he wanted a witness to their destruction. You must swear never to speak of them."

"Of course," said Briggs handing over the page he'd just read. Julian studied it, almost hearing Bertie speaking the written words. As he read, he thought of their dangerous run across the Nile delta then placed the sheet of paper back down on the desk.

"He was abdicating his right to the throne of England," said Briggs. "What would drive him to do such a thing? And what changed his mind?"

Julian did not reply at first. Of the many conversations he had had with Bertie, he recalled one in particular that took place on a hill overlooking Alexandria. It was there that Bertie had found his place of calm in the storm of uncontrollable events; a place where simple truths revealed themselves as clearly as the ringing of a ship's bell. Julian smiled to himself. "The prince is a complicated man. He must have had a change of heart."

Julian slid aside the top page, glancing at the others beneath – all drafts of the first, all with the same precise handwriting. He moved the pen and ink out of the way and gathered up all the papers in a stack. "Let's go."

Out on the main deck they headed for the bow, where a clean westerly breeze rippled the Union Jack at its staff and rumpled Julian's hair. There, one by one, Julian held up each sheet of paper and let it be taken by the wind. Each page flew free for a moment before settling atop the waves where Bertie's words dissolved in the water as if they had never been written.

CHAPTER 30

Istanbul

As Julian was laying Noah to rest, Ahmet was dealing with a very different problem. He shifted his weight on the red upholstered leather seat of the embassy carriage then worked a finger inside his starched collar relieving his throat of its tight confines. His pristine white shirt, and English-cut tweed jacket and trousers had been lent to him for this occasion by Sir Edward himself and, except for the collar, everything fit well. Across from him sat the Prince of Wales, silent and brooding in his dark business coat. Outside, a mounted guard of twenty British soldiers galloped, ten leading and ten trailing.

The carriage slowed to a stop. Through the window Ahmet could see the tall gates of the Yildiz Palace. The captain of the guard exchanged words with the officer posted there and Ahmet waited.

Though convinced of the good in what he was about to do, he could not suppress the feeling that he was somehow betraying the patriotic trust he'd had in his country since he was a child. Still, he knew General Ali would have approved, and he had never known a truer Turk than him.

Ahmet felt Bertie's eyes on him as if the prince sensed his conflicted emotions. His gaze held until the carriage began moving again.

"You won't regret what we do here today, Sergeant Rashid, you have my word on that."

Ahmet breathed deeply. "I know you are right, excellency, but it is difficult."

"When we are done here, you will be free to pass judgment and free to do what you like with your future. For saving my life, I owe you at least that much."

The carriage passed through the outer gates of the palace complex and followed the circular drive around. It pulled to a stop beneath a portico at the base of a short staircase of polished marble. At the top of the stairs, dressed in a simple white robe and white headdress, stood Foreign Minister Ismail. This was the man who had plotted the insane mission at the canal. This was the man who was leading the country astray. This was the real traitor, thought Ahmet.

The sultan's royal guard standing behind Ismail snapped to attention. Bertie emerged from the coach brandishing his gold-knobbed cane which he planted beside his right foot. Ahmet followed and took his place beside Bertie, eyes fixed straight ahead.

Ismail gestured in welcome and Bertie walked up the stairs, Ahmet one step behind.

"A pleasure to see you again, your excellency," said Ismail in English. "We were overjoyed to hear that you'd been rescued."

"Is that right?" asked Bertie with a brittle smile. "I would have thought your reaction would be quite different."

"Might I ask the purpose of your visit? We were only informed of it this morning."

"You have my apologies for the short notice, but as you've already been informed, I would like to speak with you in the sultan's presence. I'll reveal my purpose at that time. I've brought my own interpreter."

Ahmet glanced at Ismail registering only indifference from the elder statesman.

Ismail spoke calmly to Bertie: "It is very difficult to arrange a meeting with his royal highness."

"This is not a formal meeting of state," said Bertie. "My business with you and with his majesty is personal, and I caution you - it would not be wise to turn me away."

Ismail regarded the Prince of Wales more closely. "There is no need for threats. We have no fear of you or your empire but we do like to be accommodating when we can. This way, if you please." He motioned to the courtiers behind him.

Trying not to appear too much in awe of his surroundings, Ahmet strode in step with the others as they made their way through the ornate corridors. Half the British guard followed, the rest stayed with the carriage. Eventually the guard was left behind and Bertie and Ahmet followed Ismail into a small chamber ornamented in red and blue tapestries. In the center of the room, seated in a simple chair was the man who could only be Sultan Abdul Hamid II.

He sat perfectly still, his dark eyes staring off at the far wall as if he was the only one in the room – or maybe just the only person in the room who mattered. Ahmet joined Bertie directly in front of the sultan. Ismail stayed a step back from his monarch.

At the introductions, Bertie gave the slightest of bows. Ahmet did the same even though he knew that, in front of the sultan, it was expected that his nose be pressed hard to the floor in supplication.

"I shall get right to the point," said Bertie, addressing the sultan directly with Ahmet translating. "You may deny it all you like, but the facts are: You ordered my abduction. You sided with the anarchist Pavel, and you nearly drew several nations into a war over the canal."

"You do not know this," said Ismail. "You have no proof."

"I do know this, and I do have proof," said Bertie, spreading his legs slightly in a belligerent stance and repositioning his cane with an echoing thud. "I also know why you did what you did."

Ismail glanced at the stone-faced sultan, then turned back to Bertie. "And why is that, your lordship?"

"You were trying to save your empire – the empire of your ancestors, an empire that was lost decades ago."

The sultan showed no emotion but he spoke now in a deep voice, translated by Ahmet. "Why have you come here? What do you want?"

"Reform," said Bertie.

Ahmet wasn't sure he heard the word correctly. He turned to Bertie who gave him a confirming nod. He then squared his shoulders and, feeling as if it were he himself on behalf of all Turks making the demand, he raised his voice and translated the single word: "*Inkilap!*"

"We want you to honor your constitution," continued Bertie, Ahmet keeping up. "We want you to grant real authority to the men within your government who most truly represent the will of your people. We want you to hold fair elections, and we want you to build, not an empire, but an honorable, civilized nation."

Ismail's eyes narrowed. "You cannot tell us what to do."

Bertie raised his voice a notch. "And you, sir, cannot abduct the heir to the throne of Great Britain without consequence. At this moment, the British army is in possession of Alexandria, and the royal navy has blockaded the harbor. We have the power, and because of what you did, we have the right to do the same here. You will reform or we will force you to reform. Five years ago your empire adopted a new and admirable constitution; it is time you govern in accordance with it."

Ismail stepped forward abruptly, his eyes aflame. "We are a sovereign empire. We will not be intimidated."

At this moment, Sultan Abdul Hamid II rose from his chair, his face lined with strain and exhaustion. He shot a withering glance at Ismail then walked quietly out of the room through a veiled archway.

Ismail hesitated, visibly trying to discern if the sultan was just in one of his moods or if he was really giving up the fight to save his empire. He turned to face Bertie. "Your audience is ended," he said in English. He called his guard. "These men will show you out."

"I didn't come here to be put off," roared Bertie.

"As you saw, the sultan is considering your request. We can do no more today."

"It was not a request and we shall be back tomorrow."

"You can do what you like," said Ismail, the calm, diplomatic tone returning to his voice, "and we will do what is right for our people." He took a step closer to Bertie. "Did you think we would submit to you so readily? Our roots go deep in this land which is very different from yours. You should be careful. The seeds of what you call reform may one day bear unexpected fruit."

"We'll take our chances," said Bertie rigidly.

Ahmet followed as the prince turned and strode out of the room back the way they had come. His heart pounded and the word *reform* still rang in his ears as he climbed back into the carriage behind Bertie.

"Well," said Bertie after the carriage door closed, "I suppose that could have gone better."

But Ahmet smiled. "Thank you, your highness. You have given us a place to start. Leave it now to us Turks to do what is best for our country."

Bertie appeared to ponder this statement well after the carriage had left the palace grounds. He finally answered: "History has shown we British to be a nation of meddlers. It is both our strength and our failing and seems tied to our very nature. When we see a problem we step in and fix it, sometimes without thinking, sometimes without anticipating the consequences. I owe you perfect candor in this, Sergeant Rashid: May God give Turks like you the fortitude to save your country from both your sultan and from the likes of us."

Ahmet fixed his eyes on Bertie, remembering the man as he had seen him at the canal and in Alexandria and now at the palace. He spoke evenly. "We could have no better friend in this world than you, your excellency, but we will trust only in Allah and in ourselves to build a better future."

Bertie smiled. "Well said, sergeant. Perhaps you should consider a career in politics."

Ahmet gave a snort, imagining himself being some kind of a statesman. He unfastened his collar button and, through the carriage window, watched the dusty squalor of the outskirts of Istanbul roll by. Politics - what a ridiculous idea.

Four days after leaving Pavel's island, Julian stood on the quarterdeck of HMS *Resolute* as the warship followed HMS *Inflexible* into Istanbul harbor. On the deck below him, marines and sailors in dress uniforms lined the rail. Under a cloudless sky, the two ships maneuvered into position and tied up at the dock where a crowd seemed to be building. An order was shouted and a gangway lowered.

Julian watched an embassy coach pull up, surrounded by a mounted contingent of armed guards. Bertie stepped out and was greeted by a roar from the people gathered there. He acknowledged them with a wave and a winning smile then walked straight for *Resolute*.

From the receiving station at the head of the gangway Briggs glanced up at Julian. "Get down here, North."

Julian hadn't expected to be part of the ceremony and in his khaki shirt, black suspenders and dark brown trousers was ill prepared, but he jumped at the chance. He hurried down and took a position a few paces behind Briggs where he caught the stern eye of Lord Beresford who managed to give him a slight nod as if condoning his presence. Maybe he was finally off the man's black list. Julian took a deep breath, smoothed his hair back and assumed a posture of stiff military attention just as Bertie was piped aboard.

Captain Faulks received the prince first, exchanging salutes and shaking hands.

"Good to have you and your ship back together, Captain Faulks," said Bertie.

"Thank you my lord, it is very good to be back with her."

Bertie greeted Lord Beresford and Briggs in the same way then noticed Julian. He motioned for him to step forward. "We do seem to keep bumping into one another, Mr. North. I trust you gave a good accounting of yourself?"

"I was able to stay out of trouble this time, your excellency."

"Unlike our last encounter?"

"Mr. North proved himself extremely useful, my lord," interjected Briggs.

"High praise coming from a Beresford man," observed Bertie sending a glance to Sir Charles. "Still, I'd expect nothing less of you, Mr. North."

"Thank you, my lord," said Julian, maintaining his formality while reminding himself of all the times he had only dreamed of a moment like this. Less than a year ago he had worried about being stuck with a career as a file clerk and living off his uncle's charity.

Bertie turned back to Faulks. "You'll have to tell me more about how you retrieved your ship, captain. I'll be meeting with Captain Fisher aboard *Inflexible*, if you'd be kind enough to join us? Seeing HMS *Resolute* back in commission, it's clear that you were completely successful."

"Yes, my lord," said Faulks, "we were very fortunate."

It was clear to Julian that the old captain didn't want to be the one to tell him that Pavel had escaped and that he may have a navy of his own that would have to be dealt with.

An hour later, after Bertie had left to board *Inflexible*, Julian walked alone down *Resolute's* gangway. He wore a white panama hat that he'd traded off one of the crew and had a pack slung over his shoulder.

The crowd on the docks had grown. Word of the arrival of the two ships and of Bertie's presence must have spread, thought Julian. He recognized a few of the journalists who were scurrying around for information but saw no sign of Kate.

Then, a shout came down to him. "I say, Mr. North? You are Mr. North?"

Julian looked up to the deck of Inflexible where he recognized the Duke of Sutherland, in his yellow-plumed, black military hat and gold on red shoulder boards, leaning over the rail. "Yes, I am North, my lord," said Julian.

"Do join us if you would," said the duke. "I understand from all accounts that you were the man who opened the gates of the netherworld wherein HMS *Resolute* was kept."

"It was either that or dash myself on the rocks below, my lord."

"Glad you chose the former. There was also something about cutting the telegraph lines back at the canal I think. Not a bad showing for a *Times* man. I doubt we would have gotten the same performance from the *Daily Telegraph*." The duke laughed and waved Julian up.

Julian climbed the gangway and stepped onto the deck, where Fisher, Faulks, Briggs, Beresford, and the duke stood in an arc around the Prince of Wales. He felt like an intruder at a party that was already going strong so he remained on the periphery.

Overhead, signal flags flapped in the breeze. From the main mast flew the Union Jack and, just below it trailed the long triangular pennant of the Prince of Wales. At a lull in their casual discussion, Bertie moved a few steps back.

"A few words to you, gentlemen," said Bertie in a loud voice, getting their attention immediately. The whole ship grew quiet as the Prince of Wales began to speak.

"Thanks to you brave men – except of course for Sutherland over there – the honor of England and her navy has been restored. For that you have my enduring gratitude. You also managed, in the process, to save my life. For that I will remain in your debt until the day I die. Because of the nature of these events, you will unfortunately receive no reward and little notoriety for your role in them. So, my gallant friends, I will honor you now."

Bertie signaled for grog to be brought up for each man in the group. They came in standard, navy-issue tin cups, Julian's being passed back to him without comment by Lord Beresford himself. Of all the headlines he had ever imagined for himself, this far exceeded them all for its unlikelihood. How in the world had he managed to be here among these men?

All around the ship, sailors and marines were gathering to watch.

The Prince of Wales raised his cup in a toast. "Gentlemen, to you and to Englishmen around the world, and to the empire on which the sun never sets, may God save the Queen!"

Julian and the rest of the men lifted their cups. "May God save the Queen," they all answered, draining their cups in unison.

The mix of rum and sweet molasses was warm and calming and Bertie's brief words brought back a recollection of all Julian had been through to arrive at this moment. He wished his parents had been alive to see it. What would they have thought? – their son being toasted by the Prince of Wales. What would Uncle

Emory think? – his renegade nephew finally making himself useful. Silently he raised his cup to them and swallowed the last few drops from his cup. Then, he thought of Kate, suddenly wishing more than anything that she was with him.

The embassy photographer had been standing by and now made his request. "My lords and gentlemen, might I have you in a camera picture?"

With Bertie in the center, they gathered around and raised their cups once again as the photographer, a slight man with a pockmarked face, bent under a black cloth to compose the picture. He directed the man on each end, one of these being Julian, to move first out and then in. Finally, he announced that all was perfect and they had better remain still.

Then, Julian heard a piercing whistle from the docks. It had to be Kate. Just as the powder flashed, he turned to try to catch a glimpse of her. But the crowd was enormous now, pressing along the docks and spilling over into the courtyard. He heard the whistle again and looked back to the photographer and to the others. He spoke haltingly. "Excuse me if you would, my lords, I..."

Bertie answered with jesting seriousness. "What was that, Mr. North? You suddenly have more pressing business? Miss Wilder wouldn't be out there waiting for you, would she?"

"Yes, my lord, I think she is," said Julian.

"Well, stop wasting time," said Bertie with a broad smile and a wave of his hand, "be off with you."

Julian gave an awkward bow and, as he headed down the gangway, he finally spotted her, dressed in blue, just as he had first seen her. She stood a few rows back from the edge of the courtyard with Parker behind her and with someone else – it was Uncle Emory. Had he come all that way for him?

Julian waved his hand high over his head. "Kate, Uncle Emory," he shouted.

Both waved back. Parker saw him too but just stood there, one hand on his walking stick the other in his pocket.

Julian ran past the marine guard and pushed his way through the crowd until he reached Kate. Without a word he wrapped her in his arms and kissed her. Her lips were moist and gentle, then passionate. He pulled her closer, feeling her warmth.

"Welcome back, Julian," she said, breathless when they finally parted.

He smiled. "I took your advice – nothing stupid." He pointed over his shoulder. "We got the ship back."

"Yes, I noticed, though I wasn't quite as worried about that."

Kate held onto both of his hands. "Did you learn what happened to Noah?"

Julian didn't answer right away and he felt her tremble even before he spoke. "Noah's dead, Kate. He believed in Pavel's cause, but he really wasn't one of them. He died saving me."

Kate nodded and looked away for a moment. Then her grip on Julian's hands tightened. "When you and he left that night, I knew one of you would not be coming back. It was just a feeling. Then I worried that you'd both be lost, especially when you left a second time." She gave him a wavering smile. "Noah died saving a good man, Julian."

"Sorry to interrupt," said Parker putting a hand on Julian's shoulder. "What about Pavel? Is he dead? Captured?"

"He escaped. It couldn't be helped. He could be anywhere by now."

"Damn, that man's a danger to us all, how could he have gotten away? The F.O.'s going to be in a tizzy, I'd better see what Beresford wants to do about it." He took a step then stopped. "Good to have you back though." He tapped Julian's shoulder with the knob of his walking stick and headed for *Inflexible*.

Uncle Emory, who'd been waiting patiently, smiled broadly. "Hello, Julian," he said, walking over and locking him in a hug just as he had at Victoria Station. "You're looking a bit beat up but in good spirits I see. I've been following your exploits. You've had yourself quite an adventure – I never knew that translating old books could be so dangerous." The smile left his face. "Really, Julian, you should have trusted me with the truth before you left."

"You would have tried to stop me."

"Damn right, I would have, but I must say everything turned out well. You made a new friend too I see." He threw a glance at Kate.

"She's much more than a friend, Uncle Emory. I'm glad you're here so you could meet her."

"Yes, I got in two days ago so she and I have already had a few conversations. She's a fine woman and a wonderful journalist. I learned about poor Willoughby from a telegram she'd sent from Alexandria – damn shame. We've got some things to straighten out now with the office and all. That's the main reason for my being here – and seeing you of course."

Julian took Kate's hand, suddenly realizing that he would have to make some decisions soon. He had no money and he had no job. Would he try to be a journalist again? Would he go back to London? If he did, would Kate come with him? Whatever he did, he wasn't about to leave her; but what options did that leave for him?

It was with these uncertainties rattling around in his head that he rode in the open carriage beside Kate and across from Uncle Emory, back to the *Times* office. On arriving, he stepped down onto the walkway, helped Kate down, then turned to the office.

The place looked the same as always until he approached the door and saw the bright gold and black words freshly painted on the window:

Near East Offices of the
London Times & New York Times
Managing Editor: Ira Goldsmith
Journalists: K. Wilder & J. North

"Well?" asked Uncle Emory from behind, with Kate beside him. "We hoped you would approve. It'd be a shame to waste such fine lettering, don't you think?"

At that moment, with Julian still in a state of confusion, Ira stepped out of the office, wide-eyed, waving a sheet of paper. "About time you two are back – oh, you too, Emory. I've just received this note from the Turkish Foreign Minister's office. It seems there's going to be an election. Imagine that, an election here in the Ottoman Empire. We've got to put something together for London and New York and we don't have much time."

But Julian was still focused on the lettering on the window. He would be a journalist here in Istanbul working with Kate for both the London and the New York Times to defray the expense. He could only shake his head at how suddenly and how well his future had just come together. He glanced back at Kate who looked hopeful but uncertain.

"What? Is there a problem?" asked Ira, seeing their hesitation.

"No, there's no problem with me," said Julian, smiling.

Kate returned his smile then, as if conscious of Ira's questioning stare, quickly adopted a more business-like expression. "Well, we'd better get started," she said, with a sparkle in her brown eyes. She led the way past Ira into the office where Steven already had the tea ready.

Late that night, after the story had been written, and after a comfortable dinner at Molly's with Kate, Uncle Emory and Ira, Julian sat alone on the edge of his bed, his room lit faintly by the lamp on his desk. He was staring at his sea trunk. It sat on the floor beside the closed door reminding him of all the doubts and fears he'd had on the day he'd packed for the trip to Istanbul. And it reminded him of something else.

He walked to the trunk, raised the lid and thumbed down through a layer of clothes he had yet to unpack. There, tucked into the corner where he knew it would be, was his father's bible. He lifted it out and sat down at his desk, opening to the last entry his father had made in the margins. He read silently:

29 September, 1869 – Julian turned ten today. He is a happy, bright and healthy boy and holds a promising future. Sarah and I hope the best for him. May the Lord protect him and give him guidance in his life.

Julian pictured his father writing those words at his desk late at night before going to bed and he wondered: Had his father had a premonition of the danger ahead that would leave Julian alone and in need of the Lord's protection? Had it been that protection that had seen him through his ordeal with the Castlenau journal?

Or had he just been lucky?

Julian cupped his hands under his chin, the movement causing his medallion to slip out from under his shirt. He held it as it glistened, green in the lamplight and his thoughts, as if steered by an unseen helmsman, turned away from the past. He thought of Kate and of the promise held for them both by the years yet to come.

He straightened in his chair and drew the lamp closer. He picked up a pen and dipped it in the inkwell. Then, Julian turned a page in the bible - his bible now - and he began to write the first of the many entries he'd make in its margins throughout his life.

AUTHOR'S NOTES

For the most part, the fictional action in *The Lost Revolution* is sandwiched between two actual, historical events. The first is the assassination of Czar Alexander II in March of 1881 by a group calling themselves *The People's Will*. The second is the naval bombardment of Alexandria by the British in July of 1882 which proved to be the prelude to their invasion of Egypt. These two events underscore the turbulence of the times and in my mind, help to make the fictional action in this book more believable. In those days, as is still true to some extent today, international adventurism was an accepted tool of foreign policy used by all major nations to gain power, wealth and territory.

As for Napoleon, he did indeed abandon his army in Egypt after a fruitless campaign (except, that is, for the discovery of the Rosetta Stone). Ever the PR genius, he was somehow able to gloss over the failure and return to Paris in a blaze of glory where he ultimately seized total power.

Three historical figures play prominent roles in this novel. The first of these is of course, Queen Victoria's eldest son Bertie:

The image on the left shows him as the Prince of Wales as he would have appeared in 1882. The photo on the right shows him as King Edward the VII. He ruled from 1901 until his death in 1910.

Captain Jacky Fisher is shown here as the youthful captain of HMS *Inflexible*. He would go on to become a leading figure in the Royal Navy and was largely responsible for the design and building of HMS *Dreadnought* in 1906 which is widely considered to be the prototype for all battleships to follow. Fisher died in July of 1920. The epitaph on his tombstone reads: "Fear God and Dreadnought."

Lord Charles Beresford is pictured here as he would have appeared in this book. He earned many honors throughout his long career both as a naval officer and as a prominent political figure. He died in September of 1919.

HMS *Inflexible* is shown here in 1885 with pole masts having replaced the original full sailing rig. Her design included many innovative features in both armor and armament which were later adopted in the design of HMS *Dreadnought*.

A couple of non-fiction books centered on this same era in which you may have an interest are:

Steam, Steel & Shellfire, by various contributing authors and consultants published in North America by Chartwell Books Inc.

And of course the classic, *Dreadnought*, by Robert K. Massie published by Ballantine Books, New York.

Thank you very much for reading *The Lost Revolution*. I hope you enjoyed it. To leave comments and to pick up more background on this book, on me and on my upcoming books please visit www.tomulicny.com – I would love to hear from you.

ABOUT THE AUTHOR

Tom Ulicny lives in the Detroit area. He's the proud father of three daughters and the equally proud grandfather of a seven year old grandson. A retired engineer, he holds two degrees from Wayne State University and, besides writing, enjoys travel, woodworking, and guitar. He now writes full time in the genre of "whatever interests me at the time." *The Lost Revolution*, is his first novel and is available as a paperback on-line and in book stores and as an e-book for the Kindle and other e-readers.

As of this printing date, he's completing a second novel, *The Caruso Collection,* that combines murder, morality and political intrigue with the big-art scene in New York City.

For more on Tom, what he's up to, and links to his books, visit him at www.tomulicny.com .

Made in the USA
Charleston, SC
13 December 2015